BLOOD TIES

BLOOD TIES

THE BONDS ARE PERMANENT

A MAGNOLIA NOVEL

ASHLEY FONTAINNE
LILLIAN HANSEN

RMSW PRESS

Copyright © by Ashley Fontainne 2015

Publisher: RMSW Press, LLC

ISBN-13: 978-0692410578

ISBN-10: 0692410570

Cover and interior design: Ashley Fontainne

Photo credit: Nicholas Raymond www.freestock.ca

 Visit Ashley's website and sign up for her newsletter to receive a free book of your choice here

Follow Ashley on Twitter @AshleyFontainne

For Junior and Ruth

CONTENTS

I

THE DELIVERY

"You ain't your own man, Lucas Hill. Your ass is owned by another. Just his bitch to jump when he snaps those meaty fingers and points," he grumbled. It took all of his concentration to keep his foot steady on the accelerator and the truck hovering at the speed limit. Irritated, he clenched his jaw hard. The sound of his teeth grinding filled up the entire cab. Lucas was still pissed off he was out doing this in the middle of the frigging night. His eyes were bloodshot. Lack of sleep and staring at the dark highway for the last three hours made them feel like he'd poured salt into them.

Swirling another mint around in his mouth, he hoped it hid the smell of the three beers from earlier. He didn't even want to think what would happen if he got pulled over. With his luck, it would be for something like speeding, not waiting the full three seconds at a stop sign, or not using his turn signal before changing lanes. Blinking twice, he made sure to keep the truck in between the white lines. All or any of the minor screw ups would put him in the middle of a shit storm for sure. Lucas had no desire to make headline news like other runners from committing some stupid traffic infraction. Jail time for drug running was stout enough, but he shuddered at the thought of what his sentence would be if some nosy pig poked his face inside the cooler and got the shock of his cop life viewing its contents.

A shiver of panic traveled down his spine, and Lucas gripped the steering wheel of the inconspicuous black Dodge truck with a bit more force. While chewing on the well-worn spot on his bottom lip, he double-checked the side and rearview mirrors. Nope, he was safe. No blue lights behind him and no strange vehicles following either. Normal, sane people who lived normal, sane lives weren't out at three o'clock in the morning. He let go of his crushed lip when the nasty rust taste hit him.

"Damn, another piece of my flesh offered to him. Damn!" he muttered after swallowing the droplets of his own blood.

Lucas didn't fear much in this world, especially not the frigging police or even a stint behind bars. He could handle both with ease. And it wasn't like he sought out trouble; it just seemed to come to him. Like a damned homing pigeon or boomerang—it kept landing right on his lap, no matter how hard he tried to stay on the straight and narrow. His last six-month stint in Lafayette County, Tennessee, had been a walk in the park.

A brawl with the bouncer at *Gigi's Strip-n-Tip* landed him in the slammer after he got too friendly with a damned stripper. What a joke. How were you *not* supposed to touch all that flesh when it was in your face? When it was all said and done, Lucas was convicted of battery after the dust-up with the bouncer. Lucas had some bruises, but the bouncer suffered a broken nose and was missing two front teeth.

Time spent in county lock-ups was a breeze

compared to doing hard time like his old man down in Tucker. The sorry excuse of a father would die behind the concrete walls of the maximum security prison.

Lucas' minor run-ins with the fat, slow, and lazy cops of the Southeast were as easy to handle as banging a virgin. Slip in, slip out, and leave a slight stain of blood behind as a reminder you were there.

He didn't fear the police, the court system, the frigging President of the United States. Not even God himself. There was only one person who set his guts on fire and turned his blood cold. The cold-hearted devil with black eyes and no heart ruled his life—and the lives of others—with an iron fist.

Lucas feared the man enough not to even think his name inside his head, much less speak it out loud. If he made some asinine mistake tonight, and the contents of the cooler resting on the passenger floorboard were discovered, he was a dead man.

No doubt. Dead, dead, *deadski*. Then someone else would be delivering *his* organs in the middle of the night to some sick, rich douchebag with enough cash to pay for new body parts on the black market.

Lucas squinted through the dirty windshield, looking for the blue *Hospital* sign. He'd double checked everything on the frigging truck *but* the windshield washer fluid levels. Who was the dumbshit that prepped the truck for this run? If he found out, introductions would be done properly—with a fist to the face.

"Get a frigging grip, man, this is your twentieth delivery and you've never had a problem." Still, Lucas knew he couldn't let his guard down until the package was in the hands of the buyers.

And the Devil was off his ass.

"What the hell was I thinking getting involved with Ray-Ray? Dumb spoiled little rich prick." The moment he met Ray-Ray in tenth grade, he knew the dude was trouble with a capital *T*. But Ray-Ray had access to the life Lucas wanted—girls, drugs, and hot cars.

Lucas popped another strong mint into his mouth. Sucking in a mouthful of air between his teeth, he let the potent vapor rush to clear his head and focus his driving. His life had been the total opposite of Ray-Rays. His mom struggled to put food on the table and keep the lights on in their small apartment. Clothes came from second-hand stores, and it was a rarity if they fit. Or lasted longer than a few weeks. His piece of shit, no-good father hadn't been around since Lucas was a sperm stain on his mom's panties.

Now here he was stuck in a situation because Ray-Ray had gotten his brains blasted out of his head two days ago by his ex-old-lady's jealous boyfriend.

Right now, Lucas wanted to turn the clock back two years and drink three more Jack-n-Cokes so he would have passed out on Ray-Ray's couch. If he had, he would never have ridden with him to "make a delivery for some quick cash" as Ray-Ray called it.

"Five hundred bucks? For just ridin' shotgun? What you deliverin', Ray-Ray? Gold dust?"

"Nah, man. Just a one-of-a-kind piece for my uncle. That's all you need to know. You just watch our tail, got it?" Ray-Ray had said.

Then Ray-Ray had sealed his fate by telling the Devil about him. Lucas had been the one who noticed something wasn't right about the setup. No sooner had they driven past the designated point, the cops swarmed the parking lot like a horde of ravenous locusts. Ray-Ray and Lucas watched the entire scene from across the street at the Waffle House after they hid the truck in the back parking lot. They tried to act casual when they sat down at the counter and ordered coffee, but their hands shook with fear.

The Devil was impressed with Lucas's skills. So much so, that the job of runner was pulled from Ray-Ray. Lucas was forced to watch as the Devil's enforcer beat Ray-Ray unconscious for including a stranger in the run and the loss of the expensive package. Neither of them said a word of protest when their sentences were handed down. Lucas's street survival instincts lit up like a Christmas tree when he was in the presence of the Devil. After witnessing what the man was capable of doing to his own flesh and blood, Lucas knew better than to question his orders.

And now, at age twenty-five, Lucas was stuck in a job he didn't want with no escape route in sight. He assumed he was hauling drugs. But on his second delivery, Lucas lifted the lid of the cooler.

It wasn't drugs. Inside the slushy mess of ice, was a heart and lungs. He puked for ten minutes. After the shock of that sick vision, he made sure never to open the lid again.

Though Lucas hated shuttling the cold body parts he had grown quite fond of the cash his deliveries put in his pocket. Ten thousand dollars a pop. Unfortunately, his wallet was running on fumes after being behind bars for so many months. When he was released from jail, he went back home and tried to find a legitimate job. He hoped his time away would have given the Devil a good reason to find another runner, but it didn't work. It was the beginning of his third week out of the joint, and he had celebrated his newfound freedom and the lack of contact from the Devil with a few beers while watching a basketball game on television. But his brief taste of freedom ended with a phone call around midnight.

Lucas pulled his head out of the memory. He needed to concentrate on the task at hand. No mistakes. The moon was hidden by a thick blanket of rain clouds. The streetlights were a joke. Why in the hell would someone want to live in this backwoods, redneck city? For Christ's sake, the streetlights were no better than a flashlight with a low battery. He wished the sky would open up and let the rain out, but then he wondered if the frigging wipers worked.

A flashing yellow sign ahead beckoned him to *Fill your tank and your belly!* There was plenty of time to stop and refuel, and he needed to hit the head. Thinking about his boss made the beer and coffee run through him.

Pulling off the main highway, the faint neon green from the old truck's dashboard cast an eerie glow on the white cooler. Once he pulled up to the pump and cut the engine, he yanked off his jacket and tossed it over the cooler.

He reached over and pulled on the black ball cap down low over his forehead. The brown wig attached underneath made his neck itch but he ignored the urge to take it off. Protocol needed to be followed, to the letter, every time. No paper trail was to be left behind. No cell phones, GPS, or anything electronic were to be used during the delivery process. Even the old Dodge he was driving didn't have the fancy tracking equipment of the newer vehicles available. A different disguise was to be used each time and was provided, along with the cash for gas and instructions, under the front seat. The ancient, black rust-bucket was always parked in the same spot each time—at the back end of the funeral home, hidden behind the storage shed under an old tarp. Instructions and cash were taped underneath the seat. The call came in, Lucas went to the truck, and the game began.

Stepping out of the truck and into the

sweltering heat of the Tennessee evening, Lucas shot a final glance over the floorboard to make sure the cooler was well hidden. Satisfied, he pushed the lock down and headed into the store.

Lucas couldn't shake the sensation that Ray-Ray *was* riding with him. Well, at least part of him. After all, it wasn't like Ray-Ray's uncle to let any body part go to waste.

There had been an additional note tonight. A handwritten one that made him cold despite the heat.

Glad you are back. Stop getting into trouble and keep your nose clean. I'm watching you and don't want to hear any more news about my favorite courier locked up behind bars. Because if it happens again, there won't be enough of you left to fill a Ziploc baggie. Got it?

Lucas got it. Loud and clear. As he walked to the counter and paid for his gas, he thought about the line from a movie in his youth. *You ever dance with the devil in the pale moonlight?*

Yes, yes he had. He wanted nothing more than to get off the dance floor and never waltz again. But the Devil owned his dance card. Lucas was so dizzy from all the spinning, he knew he was stuck in the tight embrace of the bloodthirsty leader's arms.

2

A NEW ADVENTURE

"Y ou sure I can't talk you out of this?"

Karina Summers shook a loose strand of black hair from her face and looked up from the empty desk. Her former business partner, Calvin "Cal" Benson, leaned his buff body with casual ease against the doorframe. His dark brown eyes shimmered with a teasing gleam, but Karina swore she saw a small hint of sadness behind them.

The early morning sun streamed through the window and caught the silver streaks in Cal's hair, making him look even more appealing. With his arms crossed over his chest, Cal's enormous biceps bulged, stretching the thin cotton material to its limit. The tattoo of two arms locked at the wrists with silver handcuffs, and the words *Gotcha* in black underneath, seemed to quiver.

"Cal, how many times are you going to ask me the same question?"

"Until I get the answer I want."

Picking up the last box off the top of the desk, she gave him a weak smile. "You're as tenacious as a pit bull. That's what I used to love about you. But remember, my bite is just as strong." Karina watched Cal's tattoo quiver as his muscles tensed.

"Yeah, I know. I have the marks to prove it." A smirk crossed Cal's full lips. "But don't try to change the subject. I can't be swayed by your seductive charms. I'm immune."

Karina used the box like a shield, nudging Cal out of the way. Their hot and heavy romance of seven years ended during her undercover stint nearly two years ago. She ignored the urge to tackle him and shred all that terribly restrictive clothing off his smokin' body. Cal's scent always drove Karina wild.

She learned after their breakup to keep her physical distance and let running their business be the only thing between them. They worked much better as a team on paper rather than between the sheets. "Once bitten, twice shy baby." Karina made it past him and out into the hallway. "Now, be a gentleman and open the door for me? This is my last box."

The sound of Cal's heavy boots reverberated off the hardwood floors as he came up behind her. The energy of his stare sent waves of heat up her back. Karina's mouth went dry. His steps matched her heartbeat in intensity.

"Hmmm. You really do need a break. You just called me a gentleman. That's a first."

"See? Told you," Karina retorted, her smile real this time. "A term I'm sure you're unaccustomed to hearing when said in reference to you."

Karina slipped past his six foot three frame, out the back door and into the bright light. Final goodbyes had already been said to the rest of the gang. Without any sunglasses, the yellow glare of the vibrant sun and the shimmer of heat from the blacktop made her eyes water.

Damn—Cal will think they are for him.

The thought made Karina move at a quicker

pace toward her car. She wasn't about to let Cal think he'd gotten to her. Karina knew this was the right decision for her life. Cal had been shocked when she approached him two weeks prior with the papers to buy out her share of their successful private investigation firm, We've Got Ya! When he asked her why she wanted to sell and she told him, Cal questioned her sanity. After the large payout from their biggest—and longest—investigation yet, Karina needed more than a break. She needed a new direction and a new life.

Karina had enough cash to live off of for at least five years, long enough to figure out what she should do with the rest of her life. At the moment, fresh, smog-free air and a slower pace is what she craved. The life she had been living almost drove her to the brink of insanity. After two years of undercover work and then another year of sitting through the gut-wrenching court trial, Karina couldn't get out of Los Angeles fast enough.

It was a struggle to retrieve her keys out of the front pocket of her jeans. Karina cursed under her breath, regretting her choice of skin tight denim. She should have just thrown on a pair of sweats, left her hair in a messy bun, and came in without a stitch of makeup on. Her last day at work would go down in history. No employee of We've Got Ya! had ever seen Karina *sans* makeup, except Cal. It would give the rest of the remaining staff plenty to gab about for the next few days.

But she didn't. She took extra time while getting ready earlier. Applied just the right amount of eye shadow, liner, powder and gloss in front of the mirror, stopping every few seconds to check out her handiwork. The look was finished with finger-tousled hair and two squirts of *Red* between her breasts. It was Cal's favorite perfume. While driving to the office earlier, Karina felt like he deserved to suffer a bit.

Bastard.

Cal's muscled arm reached past her and opened the passenger door. He was close. Too close. The heat from his body, the smell of cologne and the musk of his personal scent. Cal was playing the same game. Karina bit her lip to keep from biting his. Leaning down, she set the box in the back seat and wished she could just crawl in right behind it and drive away. Instead, Karina stood, snatched the door from Cal's grip, slammed it, and then stuck out her hand. "She's all yours now, Cal. Take good care of her—better than you did me."

"Shut up," Cal growled.

In a flash, Cal pulled Karina to him and devoured her lips with his own. The kiss was long, needy and full of pent up passion. Regret. Sadness. Love. For a few seconds, Karina melted into his strong embrace, reliving their past connection. Swam in the strength of him and the way Cal's body felt wedged up tight against her own. But then the image of catching him doing the same thing with the bottle blonde whore, Misty Pierce, flashed in her mind, ruining the moment.

Coming to her senses, Karina pulled back and slugged her balled-up fist into Cal's mammoth chest. "Be glad I'm leaving the state or I'd make you pay for that," she said with more gusto than she felt. She stayed true to her nature and hid the sadness from her face, preferring to unleash the pain in a rude manner.

Cal responded to her smartass reply with a sly smile and a coy wink.

Bubbling anger rose inside her. Karina was just about to spew her thoughts out when her cell phone rang. "Once again, your ass is spared the kicking it deserves by my mom."

Cal blew her a kiss and she flipped him the universal sign for *Have a Nice Day—asshole.* Karina answered the call at the same time she slid behind the wheel of the Charger. "Hey Mom. I'm leaving the office now. Had to pick up the last box." Cranking up the V-8, a smile appeared when the duel exhaust growled.

"Watch out for the gun-toting rednecks. And if you hear banjo music—run!" Cal yelled from the curb.

"Was that Cal?" her mother asked.

With a flick of her wrist, Karina slammed the car into reverse and tromped the gas. The tires barked and she smiled again. "Of course. Giving me some last minute advice on how to survive living in the South."

"Is that *all* he gave you? No goodbye nookie? No last hurrah in the hay?"

"Mom! Really?"

"Hey, you're the one who insists on sharing all your intimate life details with me. If you don't like hearing those kinds of questions from your mother, then tell your secrets to Ranger."

Heat blistered her cheeks. Karina didn't have a quick comeback for that one. Her mom was right. Karina needed to find a different outlet to vent her emotions. A female friend was out of the question because, well, she didn't have any.

Karina learned a long time ago most females could not be trusted. They feigned friendship, concern and confidentiality—but it was just that–a farce. The second you looked the other way, *wham!* the kidney punch arrived. The most recent jab was delivered by her *former* best friend, Misty Pierce. Their friendship, which began in fifth grade, was over in mere seconds after Karina caught Misty and Cal doing the nasty on his desk.

Bitch.

"I'm on my way to get Ranger from the vet. Then, I'll load up the rest of my bags at the apartment. I should make it to your place around one or so. Okay?"

"Oh, nice topic switch Karina. Guess the answer is no."

Grimacing, Karina drummed her fingers on the stiff leather of the steering wheel waiting for the light to turn green. Though Karina was excited about moving to Arkansas and spending time with Gram and Grampa, the long car ride with her mother to get there made her cringe.

Karina loved her mom with ferocious intensity, and God help anyone who ever tried to hurt LiAnn Marie Tuck. But sometimes, her mom just dug too deep with probing questions. Her mother was only aware of some of the particulars about the relationship with Cal, but not everything.

Once Karina began the undercover investigation assignment for the senior abuse wrongful death case at Jubilee Retirement, she went in so deep, there was no time or the energy left to explain her ugly breakup with Cal to anyone. The plan was to change that during the trip, though it would be hard for Karina to relive the pain. "No switch. Just discussing relevant issues and Cal Benson isn't on that list. So, are you all packed and ready? Was there enough room in the moving van for all our stuff?"

"Yep. Have been since last week. There was enough room, but barely. And I do mean barely. That semi doesn't have enough room in it for a blade of grass. Good thing we both had a moving sale before we started packing. I guarantee you, when we open it, everything will pop out."

"That should make unloading it easy." Karina laughed.

"The movers just left, so I am sitting in an empty house and playing with my cell phone.

Made it to level ninety-two in that candy-smashing game. Had to stop because my eyes started to cross. Now, I'm staring at the blank walls. The new owners will need to repaint. My furniture and decorations hid a lot of flaws."

Karina snorted. "No kidding. I noticed what a horrible housekeeper I am after everything was removed from my place. You should have seen all the dust-bunnies! I didn't even remember that my walls were white instead of dirty eggshell. No refund of my security deposit, that's for sure."

"Well, if you would have hired a cleaning lady to come in while you were gone..."

There was a lot of things I should have done differently while undercover. "I know, I know. But I didn't. Can't cry about it now. So, how was your retirement party last night? Did you get a nice watch?"

"Please. The department stopped that tradition when you were still in diapers. I'm lucky I got a cake and a plaque. I did, however, get one great gift from Crigger."

"Ol' Crig released some cash from his wallet? Wow, Hell froze over and I missed it. Next, you'll tell me pigs are flying in the sky after they shot out of Cal's ass."

This time, her mother was the one who

snorted, followed by a hearty laugh. "Funny girl. Yep, Crig bought two tickets for the Metallica concert in Memphis next month. Front row, baby. And guess who will be sitting next to me?"

Her mom's adorable laughter made Karina smile. She was only a few blocks away from the veterinarian's office, so she ended the call and finished the remainder of the drive in silence.

After today, Karina knew life would never be the same. The next few days would be full of lots of gabbing, slobber and hair from Ranger. There would also be plenty of head-banging music, courtesy of her 60's wild child mother and now retired cop, Sgt. LiAnn Tuck.

It was going to be one of those adventures Karina would tell her children about someday—if she ever had any. With her broken heart still tangled up with Cal's, a one-hundred pound black lab under her feet, and God only knows what type of responsibilities down on the farm with Gram and Grampa, Karina wondered if her uterus would ever house a baby.

At this rate, it sure seemed unlikely.

Liann Tuck sighed inside the empty space of her house. It was strange to sit on the floor and stare at the nothingness. Years of memories packed and boxed away, on the highway and driven by a stranger who couldn't care less about the safety of the contents. She hoped everything arrived in one piece after such a long journey. LiAnn moved over to the window and sat underneath, waiting for her daughter to arrive.

Though Karina tried to hide it, LiAnn knew the move was harder on her daughter than herself. She also knew the breakup with Cal had been very difficult. Her headstrong daughter had never spilled the gory details, but LiAnn would bet her retirement that the collapse of the relationship was because of infidelity. Calvin Benson was a former cop who looked and acted like a Hell's Angel more than a private investigator. She knew the type well, for Karina's father had the same swagger, just with one minor difference. Kirk Summers had been the lead singer and guitarist for the hard rock band *The Hellions*.

LiAnn didn't want to think about her ex. She thought enough about him every single time she looked at her daughter. Except for the fact that

Karina was female, Kirk may have well just cloned his child. No, she wouldn't think about him. The sheltered girl from the 'burbs who fell for the leather-clad, Harley driving guitar player with raven black hair and eyes bluer than the Pacific, didn't exist anymore. LiAnn buried her the second the divorce papers were signed and she left their ramshackle trailer with Karina in tow. Though only nineteen, she had been determined to raise her daughter in a proper environment, away from all the drugs and violence Kirk and his bandmates and managers were immersed in.

And so, she did. LiAnn moved back in with her parents, Junior and Ruth Tuck, to her childhood home in Rowland Heights. The suburbs, which seemed so silly and pathetic when she had been sixteen, took on a whole new dimension when LiAnn returned as a mother with her little bundle of joy. Karina, with her mop of wild, raven hair and eyes the same color as her father's, was the queen of Kingsmill Street and the heartbeat of life for LiAnn and her parents. There was never a worry about her daughter's safety, for the entire close-knit community, full of people generally around the same age as her parents, doted on Karina the minute she arrived.

The three years they spent inside the warm, loving home, allowed LiAnn the chance to move from her position as desk clerk at the City of Azuza police department and on to the sheriff's academy. Within two years after being sworn in as one of Los Angeles' finest, LiAnn purchased the small, two-bedroom house eight blocks away from her parents.

With a sigh of bemusement, LiAnn looked out the window into the bright afternoon sun. It was going to be another gorgeous, sunny California day and here she was inside, stumbling down memory lane. The palm trees towered over the tops of the houses across the street, their tufted branches swayed in gentle harmony with the light breeze. A twinge of regret slithered in LiAnn's belly when she wondered if she would ever see the stunning scenery again. Not that Arkansas wasn't a beautiful state, and it did have those two beloved smiling faces awaiting their arrival, but California would always be home. The sun-drenched beaches and the brilliant sunsets would soon be a thing of the past. She would not, however, miss the traffic, smog and crime.

Especially the crime. God, how much pain and suffering had she seen during the course of her twenty-five year career? Too much, for sure. When retirement arrived, she was more than ready to go.

LiAnn chased the sad thoughts away and concentrated on the move and precious time soon to be spent with her ailing parents. They had moved back to Arkansas almost thirty years ago and she thought her heart would explode from sadness. Her father had been born and raised in Sheridan, a small farming community about forty-five miles south of Little Rock. After he came home from his stint in the Navy during World War II, Junior Tuck fell in love with San Diego and stayed. He let his best friend and childhood buddy, Cecil Pickard, run the farm and planned on staying in Southern California only long enough to rake in some quick cash as a heavy equipment operator. Soon, the explosion of growth required numerous freeways to be built, and Junior Tuck found his own goldmine. The work paid well and the warm, fresh air convinced him to stay.

Well, along with one beautiful, redhead by the name of Ruth Stretch. Once LiAnn's parents met, at least according to the stories they liked to tell, it was love at first sight. Within two years of hitting the shores of San Diego and hanging up his uniform, Junior Tuck married Ruth and moved to Rowland Heights.

Ruth resigned her secretarial position with Reem Aircraft in Los Angeles shortly after she and Junior were married. She took on the duties of both office manager and coordination expert, helping to run the large construction firm. Junior still loved to be on the job site, operating his big Caterpillar road grader even though he had six employees to run the rest of the construction equipment on the other building jobs his firm was responsible to complete. As soon as one freeway was built or a subdivision was completed, he and his team were off to the next job.

It was a demanding and grueling pace and the many years of sitting in the open sun, inhaling diesel fumes and working six or seven days a week culminated in the serious heart attack her father suffered. When the union he belonged to, the Operating Engineers Local 310, learned he had a heart attack while operating his ten ton piece of equipment, they informed him his license to run machinery was null and void. Her dad had been barred from working on any construction job site for liability reasons.

With many hugs and tears, Junior and Ruth

said goodbye to LiAnn and Karina to begin their new life in Sheridan, Arkansas. Pop told her it was the best decision, since the farm was still in decent shape and he knew how to run it. LiAnn and Karina would faithfully visit them in the quaint farming community during her yearly vacations, meeting distant relatives whose names they had only previously heard in conversation or viewed in family photo albums. They had been enthralled with the quiet gentleness, infectious sense of humor and spirit of connection they all seemed to enjoy, especially on lazy Sunday afternoons sharing a sumptuous southern meal assortment of delectable food that tends to encourage one's waistband to suddenly expand to frightening proportions.

After each visit, LiAnn and Karina both knew in their hearts even though they never openly discussed it, that at some point, they would leave the beauty of their southern California homes to care for Ruth and Junior. It would be their privilege to return the loving gift of care and support that they had received during their young years.

The past three years left her and Karina mentally and physically exhausted. They worked nonstop on the investigation and were deeply involved in the heart wrenching details they both unearthed in developing a major crime case that culminated in the death of a vulnerable eighty-seven year old woman. As the criminal investigation unfolded, it was discovered that more victims had been similarly brutalized by neglect that was the hallmark of corporate callousness and greed. Karina's firm had been hired by several family members of victims for a civil suit against the corporation. The investigation was heartbreaking and Karina's undercover stint at several of the facilities up and down the Pacific Coast left her haunted by the memories. LiAnn thought about how Karina's once smiling face had changed. The anguish of all the atrocities hung behind Karina's eyes like a beacon, announcing to the world her anger and sadness at the things she'd witnessed.

LiAnn's phone vibrated, pulling her back to the present. *Now why is Crigger calling?* "Good morning. How's my favorite ex-boss doing on this gorgeous day?"

"Tuck, you always were a burst of sunshine in the morning. I am going to miss that. Everyone else around here is as dull as the bottom of a worn shoe. Sure I can't convince you to stay?"

"I believe we've had this conversation before. My answer has not changed. Besides, I can't stay now. All my stuff is in a van on its way to Arkansas. Can't come to work naked."

Crigger laughed. "Now *that* would definitely be a way to perk up the sour pusses around here."

"Perk up? Don't you mean puke up? I'm sure none of them want to see the naked body of a mature woman. Their lockers weren't full of fifty-five plus year olds—they were plastered with barely legal things parading around in skimpy swatches of material."

"Very funny. Listen, though I enjoy your warped sense of humor, that's not why I called."

"Okay, so why did you?"

Crigger cleared his throat. "Melissa Doster called me this morning. Jubilee filed an appeal, which is no surprise to us, but she wanted me to make sure you and Karina were aware she would be calling you both soon."

LiAnn grimaced but kept her voice light. "Why? She has the case file from each of us, plus the transcripts of our trial testimony in both cases. What else could she need?"

"How many years did you work for us, Tuck? You know how lawyers are—they dig, dig and then dig some more, hoping to unearth some little hidden treasure they missed the first time. But, in this case, I think she really wants to discuss your testimony rather than read about it. Besides, I think she is going to miss the two of you. I mean, from a bystander's point of view, it looked like the three of you got *real* close during the investigation and trial. Who knows? Maybe it's just a ruse to keep in contact with you both."

"Yeah, our bubbly personalities snagged her in our trap. Hmmm, well I don't think there is anything Karina or I could offer up as help. It's not like we hid anything or kept pieces of key evidence. But of course, we are more than willing to be of help. You know how involved we both became in the cases."

Crigger groaned. "Too much. Way too much."

LiAnn's skin prickled at his tone. "How could we not? When I think about the terrible things those bastards did for money...how they ruined so many lives of those sweet seniors, my blood boils."

"Tuck, stop it. That attitude right there is going to put you in an early grave. That temper of yours is going to give you hypertension for sure. You got too close, too wrapped up in it. Never seen you wound so tight inside a case."

LiAnn huffed. "I did not."

"Then tell me why you retired, huh?" Crigger probed.

"You know why," LiAnn whispered.

"Because you got too involved and are all paranoid the same thing might happen to your parents. The second your father called and made noises about the possibility he and your mother might move into an independent living facility, you flipped your lid. Do you think your reaction would have been as swift and strong if you *hadn't* worked the Jubiliee case?"

LiAnn wasn't about to get into another argument with her former boss on the topic of her decision to retire. "Look, Crigger. I appreciate you calling me and your concern. But what's done is done, and the reasons why the decision was made are not relevant at this point. I plan on spending what time my parents have left on this earth near them. Period. End of story."

Crigger sighed. "You always were a hard-headed woman. Okay, I've done my duty and passed along Melissa's message. Have a safe trip, Tuck."

Before she could respond, the line went dead. LiAnn swallowed the lump in her throat and thought about the things Crigger, the only man who'd captured her heart years ago, hadn't said. *I love you too, Crigger,* she whispered to the silent phone.

3

MEMORIES OF THE PAST

Caesar Calvanio secured the heavy briefcase in his wall safe and let out a slight groan. Though he just made another cool two-hundred fifty grand in untraceable cash, he wouldn't let a smile form. His father taught him that business was not something one took lightly and all transactions–the good, the bad, and the ugly–should be treated with respect.

Once his stash was locked away, he made his way over to the enormous solid teak desk, unlocked the side cabinet, and poured a stiff drink. He settled himself in the high back leather chair and stared out the window to the darkened streets below. A few sets of head and tail lights shimmered in the distance, a stark contrast against the backdrop of the ebony night. He sipped his smooth cognac and let himself enjoy the tranquility as his mind wandered inside the murky walls of his past.

He was proud of his bloodline. It was mob royalty, but only on his father's side. The paternal family ties stretched from New York City, Chicago, Miami, and Philadelphia, tracing all the way back to Sicily. He was the bastard son of Carlos Calvanio, born from the womb of his Irish whore mother, who had been one of Carlos' numerous lovers. But the fates intervened and, at the age of three, he went to live with his father and stepmother after the sudden death of his biological mother. Though it was never mentioned (at least not in earshot where he could have heard it), he knew her death had been arranged. His father and stepmother were the parents of four girls, one of which arrived as a surprise when he was fifteen, and there was no male to continue the family's legacy. After the birth of his baby sister, Carmella, his stepmother couldn't bear any more children.

Like the rest of the men in the Calvanio lineage, Caesar was a crafty one. He learned and watched at the feet of the masters, and knew his contribution to the family name would not be gained from the limelight, nor from the typical ways the others had made their fortunes. He watched too many of the old guards go down as technology caught up to the mob and the cops were no longer left scratching their heads with no clue how to stop them. He remembered all the shame and humiliation he felt as he watched some of the more prominent dons being led away in handcuffs, their trials splashed across every news channel after *RICO* arrived on the scene. The glory days were over, the downward spiral started the minute gangs from other parts of the world moved in and the families began expanding their empires during the 80's. That's when, in his opinion, things began to fall apart.

He grimaced at the memory. The drug trade was controlled by lowlife Mexican cartel warlords; the prostitution and sex-trafficking trade owned by the Russians; and the numbers game and shakedowns controlled by the Triads from China and the Yakuza from Japan. This new world of crime left little room for the true gangsters. There was no honor, no loyalty, no tradition or respect. It was simply money, bloodlust and depravity that drove the masses.

His father had been an underboss in the Bonanno family. Carlos Calvanio was part of the clan who ruled over Chicago, Philadelphia and New York City. A time back in the glory days when the Bonanno, Colombo, Gambino, Genovese and Lucchese families ruled their territory with bloody turf wars and shakedowns. The mob had their fingers in a multitude of clean business enterprises to launder their vast profits from loan sharking, illegal narcotics, prostitution and murder for hire, among other things.

He recalled with a slight grin the days he sat on the knees of his *uncles* as a small boy. He had looked forward to their visits as a child, entranced by their stories, clothing and raucous laughter. They held power in their hands and were men of honor. As a teenager, he began actively participating in the wide variety of family business crimes, eager to please the men he worshipped. Even early on, he knew he would have to work twice as hard as the other males to be accepted into the fold, since he was not a full-blooded Italian. He started out small with petty crimes, then graduated to bigger, more violent ones as he aged.

He mastered the art of developing a cold blooded approach to murder and accomplished the task with the precision of a surgeon, carefully planning and strategizing his hits. His stealthy approach as a hitter garnered him the nickname The Cat.

He snuck in, killed with silence and expertise, and slid back out into the night, his prey never seen or heard from again. Even though he was meticulous, he still ended up doing a six year stretch at Attica, one of the toughest Federal prisons in the country.

The rookie mistake he made during a robbery that was to end in murder cost him, but he vowed to learn from it. He swore an oath to himself that he would never again have his freedom taken away by law enforcement. Those six years he spent caged like an animal was when he was introduced into new methods of making money. A new business venture that would keep him under the radar of the police. Though he enjoyed killing some of the low-life thugs he was hired to take out, he wanted more from life.

He owned homes in several states but his favorite place was in Hot Springs, Arkansas.

Though the place had a history that included numerous visits during the turn of the century from mob bosses such as Capone and others, the history was just viewed as a sideshow tourist attraction now. The sleepy, quaint town was the perfect place to slip in and begin to build his new venture. He brought along his much younger wife, Romella, and four trusted confidants to set things up: his cousin Vincenzo Molinero, friend Carmine Del Vecchio, and his half-sister Carmella and her husband, Franco. He set Vincenzo up with a respectable funeral parlor, Franco up with an ambulance company, and Carmella with a homecare business, specializing in offering care services to senior citizens.

Once everyone was in place, he started his business. He recalled his entry into the extremely lucrative real estate business sector of senior housing and a crooked smile crossed his lips. He had attended an association meeting in Chicago of the National Investment Center for Senior Housing & Care Industry on the advice of his lawyer Antonio, who could always be counted on to ferret out greedy businessmen who were not too concerned with following the letter of the law.

The association was made up of owners and

senior executives who attended the yearly meeting to network and absorb the newest laws affecting their industry. It was also the time they directed their lobbyists on how they wanted them to swing governmental issues important to them. But that wasn't what drew him to attend. The biggest reason to be seen at the meeting was to make the important connections with senior housing mid-level executives and owners, other private investors, banking and mortgage connections. He needed to set financing deals in motion to acquire properties or participate in a merger with high net worth partners. He needed a legitimate outlet to launder the massive amount of dirty money his other business ventures generated, and move into new investment options to diversify his vast portfolio.

As he strolled through the various senior housing trade show booths, he waited until his gut, and the physical description Antonio provided, told him he'd found the perfect mark. He'd been there less than two hours when the poke in his belly told him he'd found the one. Caesar stood and chatted with the man whose personal greed oozed out of his pores like some slimy medical condition. The guy was just asking to be taken in. He bragged about the money he'd made over the years, both legally and otherwise. He regaled Caesar with how smart his financial stealth maneuvers were at going undiscovered by state agency regulators, who were brainless sheep feeding at the state trough. The man practically drooled when he mentioned how senior citizens were fat chickens waiting to have their financial feathers plucked.

However, the best part was the obnoxious windbag operated from an office in Hot Springs, Arkansas. And, his company owned a property they were itching to dump. The Magnolia House was a historical landmark in Hot Springs and his new chatty friend, Nick Shonnert, said his company didn't want to deal with the hassle of the upkeep any longer. Nick's company had already poured tons of cash into the place just to get it up to fire code regulations, didn't want to invest any more to completely renovate it to meet Arkansas state regulations for a senior living facility.

Caesar had his eye on the old place for an independent living facility for months and sensed Nick's vulnerability. He sealed the deal when the two of them had dinner later that night. When he dangled the bait that he was interested in purchasing the property, Nick slobbered all over his plate like a rabid dog. They agreed to meet back in Hot Springs in two days to finalize their negotiations for Caesar to buy the place. The hook was set and he knew just how to reel in the hungry fish.

Nick Shonnert wasn't overplaying his considerable wealth. Caesar directed Antonio to dig into his financial holdings. Nick was the Chief Financial and Operating Officer of Happy Days Retirement Living, a conglomerate that owned retirement communities across the U.S. He enjoyed toying with Nick the Prick (as Caesar named him—no one had ever had a more fitting nickname) more than the others. His instincts sensed Nick's envy of the power Caesar wielded during their first meeting and financial discussions. When Caesar became the new owner of The Magnolia House in less than three days, he saw the awe behind the man's beady eyes.

He knew Nick viewed him as a godsend. The fact that he could produce vast sums of immediate cash to consummate expansion of Nick's business interests instead of the long struggle of going through a traditional lending institution route, made Nick's head swim with delight. He counted on Nick's greed to banish caution from his mind and allow him make a very foolish and life threatening decision: he climbed into bed with Caesar Calvanio. Nick's fate was sealed.

Thinking about Nick made his stomach sour, so he poured another glass of Cognac. Nick the Prick had gone from a robust, talkative twerp in his late thirties to an intense, brooding shell of his former self. Back when they first met, Nick was a rotund balding man who was clearly impressed by his fifty-percent ownership in Happy Days Retirement Living, along with being the CFO and COO. After their initial dinner and drinks in Chicago, Nick continued bragging about the multitude of ways his company used to separate senior citizens from their retirement funds. He really did not like the man and it angered him to listen to the outrageous lack of respect Nick had for his elderly clients. Caesar had loved his grandmother Teresa and grandfather Tomaso fiercely, and was heartbroken when they passed away. He decided to terrorize the fat little sleaze ball, which would serve two purposes: personal gratification and a lucrative business deal.

As hardened a man as Caesar was, he still

remembered the solemn promise he made to his grandfather and Godfather, Don Tomaso. His swore an oath that he would not allow another helpless elder to continue to live in agony. The old man's gnarled fingers clutched his during his last few pain-filled minutes on earth, and made him promise. Promise to not let senior people suffer by extending their life just to fill the pockets of greedy corporations.

He watched his grandfather die a slow, agonizing death while his liver and pancreas were devoured by cancer. Though the family sent out feelers across their expansive network, a donor hadn't been found in time. After Don Tomaso died, he decided to forgo the traditional ways his family made their living. It was time for a new resource, a new way to survive and to honor the memory of Don Tomaso. It would consist of seeking out elderly people who were suffering as their days of life were nothing more than one constant gradient of excruciating pain. He would organize the end of their pain, and profit by draining their financial portfolios of his chosen victims as well.

Don Tomaso always said to him, "Get what you want in life right now cause you ain't gonna take it with you."

And that is exactly what he'd been doing for the last twenty years, courtesy of his chance meeting with Nick. He showed Nick that he was nothing more than an inexperienced naive fool when it came to structuring and enforcing creative financial shakedowns.

Cloaked in the darkness of his office, he took another sip of the warm brandy and reached across the desk for a stogie. He took a few puffs then kicked his feet up on his desk, admiring the expensive leather of his shoes. Yeah, he'd taken what he wanted in life and helped ease the pain of those who cried out in agony with each heartbeat. He hoped his grandfather was proud of the man his grandson had become. And, he wondered if Tomaso enjoyed watching him torment Nick the Prick as much as he had enjoyed doling it out. His twisted laughter bounced off the cranberry colored walls in his expansive office. The memories of the night he showed Nick his true colors made him smile.

Once the negotiating process to finance

Happy Days Retirement Living and The Magnolia House was complete, it was time to educate Nick on how a professional Mafia man of honor cemented a relationship with their mark. He let Nick know he was owned...body and soul. Their office meeting was conducted at Nick's Hot Springs, Arkansas, senior property, Green Pastures, after all the employees had left for the day. Settled in front of Nick's fake mahogany desk, he sprang the trap. Grinning like a predatory panther with the deer squarely in his sight, he informed Nick he was now a half owner of Happy Days Retirement Living, as well as all his other properties in seventeen different states.

His first instruction to Nick was to make sure none of the construction of the newest senior property in downtown Little Rock had any problems with delivery of materials and labor. He then informed Nick that twenty thousand dollars per month, in cash, needed to be in his pocket, for protection against any disruption of the work flow.

Nick jumped up from behind his large desk and pointed his finger at him and screamed, "Listen here, you immigrant spaghetti-eater, I'm not about to be taken advantage of like this. You can just forget our financial arrangements. I'm canceling our agreement right now!"

Before Nick could blink twice, Caesar launched himself out of his chair, clasped his strong hands around Nick's bloated throat and slammed him up against the wall. He continued to squeeze Nick's meaty jowls until the pudgy slime ball passed out. He let the body crumple in a heap on the floor, then returned to his seat and lit a cigar. He waited until Nick awoke before he said a word.

"I'm going to cut you some slack, Nicky Boy. This is your first, and last, warning. I'll let your rude behavior slide because I know you don't realize who you're dealing with yet. So, let me explain so we'll be on the same page. I got thirty-six hits. Assassinations is the word you regular civilians understand, all notched on my gutting knife. Underneath this," he said, waving his wrist in the air, the monogrammed gold cuff links glinting off the overhead light, "Armani suit is the body of a killer. Take a gander at this."

Nick never said a word or moved an inch from his spot on the floor. Caesar let the man's terror engulf him as he removed his black jacket and unbuttoned his starched white shirt. Nick's eyes bulged and Caesar wondered if they would burst out of their sockets.

Caesar turned his body so Nick had a full view of his left shoulder. "See these? This one is from a shotgun blast," he said, pointing to the small, black ringed circles ranging in size from nickels to dimes. He turned and raised his right arm. The jagged scars started underneath his armpit and wound around past his hip bone. "And these are from being dragged alongside a Ferrari – the guy I just shot in the head trapped my arm inside. That's a quarter mile of road rash you're looking at." Nick gasped when he saw the angry red and purple mass of tortured flesh and lumpy scars. "And this one that looks like two red railroad tracks is from a knife fight. My friend Carmine stitched me up on his couch without any pain killers—when I was just fourteen years old."

He watched Nick blanch while he put his shirt back on, making sure to flex his rock hard biceps and show off his six-pack. "I'm proud to bear the scars. Shows I'm an invincible made man of respect, and not afraid of anything. Ever heard of an offer that can't be refused?"

"Oh, God, no...please," Nick stuttered.

Caesar didn't let the man utter another word. With one swift punch to the saggy jowls of the wimpy jerk, he shut the man's mouth. He moved to the window and clicked the blinds twice, the signal to Carmine, who was waiting outside in the parking lot. Within minutes, they hefted the disgusting, obese body off the floor and on to phase two of his initiation.

When Nick revived from the vicious assault, he was hanging upside down by his feet suspended from a chain in the ceiling of a cold and dark slaughter house. Nick kept opening his mouth to let out a scream, but failed. Caesar watched as Nick struggled to utter words. Caesar and his life-long friend Carmine laughed at the man's predicament.

"Well, Nicky Boy is awake. Should we tell him where he is since he looks so confused?"

Carmine laughed, shrugging his beefy shoulders. "Up to you, Boss."

With a nod of his head, he directed Carmine to lower Nick onto the concrete floor. He unsnapped the chains from his legs and pushed him roughly into a chair next to a long, concrete slab table. Nick groaned in pain and started to pass out again. Caesar came around from behind the chair and slapped Nick's right cheek.

"Wake up, fat man. It's time you understood

exactly who you're in business with—and why you're lucky enough to still be sucking air."

Caesar clamped his fingers around Nick's jaw. He forced Nick's face to look at the table in front of him, where a multitude of photographs were spread out. Nick tried to jerk his head in the other direction, but Caesar grabbed the back of his neck and forced him to look at each black and white photo which then progressed to colored still shots of a man's tortured and bloodied corpse.

"Nicky Boy, this here is a bunch of photographs I took when a former business partner decided to get cute and threaten to go to the cops. As you can see from this first photo, his throat is cut from ear to ear. The next one shows him hanging by his feet in a meat packing warehouse. Very similar to this place where you are now. We do that to bleed the body out because it's easier to cut up into pieces without all the splashy mess of the liquid flying around. It usually takes about forty-five minutes for the blood to completely leave the body, in case you're curious."

Nick jerked, leaned his head over and vomited all over his bare feet. Caesar and Carmine moved out of the way, as years of experience let them know it would happen.

"This next photo shows him on the concrete slab table which makes hosing off any remaining blood go down the drain with ease. Interesting, isn't it? A human body can be dismembered by cutting at all the joints, just like a chicken or a side of beef."

"Oh, God, please no. Whatever you want—I promise," Nick gurgled, then puked again.

"Awww, we aren't done looking at the pretty pictures yet, Nicky Boy. Don't faint on me now, we're just getting to the good part. This next picture shows how easy arms, legs, and the head pop right off the torso when butchered properly." Nick let out a feeble squeak and fainted. Caesar slapped him again and brought him back to reality. "You back with me now, buddy?"

Nick nodded. "Good, now pay attention to what I'm showing you. This photo shows how we sever the hands from the arms and dip the fingers and head into an acid bath. Throws off the cops and the medical examiner because they can't identify the body. Then we bust the teeth out of the skull with a hammer, and we're ready to bag up each group of body parts in heavy duty plastic bags. Then we can scatter body parts wherever we want."

"Oh, Jesus. Okay, okay. Please, just stop," Nick whined, snot and spittle running down his face. "Anything you say. Just don't hurt my family, okay?"

"Well, I'm not sure you got the full picture yet, Nicky Boy," Caesar purred into the damp, sweaty ear of Nick.

"No, no, I get it," Nick moaned.

"Just in case you're still a bit confused, let me spell it out. Under no circumstances, *ever*, do you want to piss me off. If you think you can cross me, as the expression goes, fugeddaboutit! I can guarantee you that this exact procedure *will* happen to you and *every* member of your family, no question. Am I right Carmine?"

"Yeah Boss, we're the best in the business of making people disappear," Carmine answered in his deep baritone voice.

Caesar and Carmine watched Nick's face contort in agony. Carmine retrieved a trashcan and stuck it between Nick's legs just as he vomited for a third time.

With a weak and quivering voice Nick finally said "Sir, I swear to you I will never cross you.

Just tell me what you want me to do and I will find a way to do so."

"Well, Nicky Boy, I knew you were a smart guy and could see that we can make a huge pile of money together. Now that you understand how our partnership will work, I'm going to outline my ideas to line both our pockets with continual cash flow."

"Okay, okay. You got it. What...what do you want me to do?"

Caesar pulled himself out of the memories from days long since passed. He snubbed out the remainder of his cigar in the crystal ashtray and slung back the last sip of brandy. His bones creaked as he rose from the chair and exited the den. He felt every bit of his seventy-plus years. Making his way up the stairs to the bedroom, he felt a twinge of sadness in his heart at the knowledge Romella wouldn't be there by his side. Even though she'd been gone for over fifteen years, he still felt the pangs of loneliness, though they only seemed to appear when it was time for bed.

Once undressed and under the warm duvet, he looked over at the empty spot where Romella's head full of ebony curls used to rest. God, how he missed her. The one and only good thing he'd ever done in his life was marry the exotic beauty. But, as with all treasure, it came with a high price. Romella was unable to bear children. They tried for years to bring a child into their family, only to be heartbroken with each miscarriage. Six babies lost over the course of their seventeen year marriage, and the loss of the sixth one took Romella with it. Her weakened body and broken spirit never came back from the blood loss and shock of losing another child during her second trimester.

Caesar closed his eyes and waited to slip off into dreams. He hoped tonight he would see Romella in them again, perhaps relive their courtship days. His chest tightened, and he wondered if living with the painful memories was punishment from God for the life he'd led. An earthly version of Hell that grew more painful with each passing day he spent alone. The only comfort was the cold, hard cash he'd acquired over the years.

And as he aged, the money started to lose its appeal. Unfortunately for Caesar, it was all he knew. The only life he understood. So, he kept on, hoping the happiness it had provided him in his youth would magically reappear and warm his stone cold heart again. But, as sleep descended on him, he knew his hands were too stained with blood to ever be clean again.

4

THE TRIP

Karina jumped when her mom asked, "Where are we?"

"Hey, you woke up. About time! We're about fifteen miles from Albuquerque. Why? Do I need to stop sooner?"

LiAnn shifted in her seat, stretching her arms and back from her long nap curled up in the leather seat. Karina winced when she heard the popping of knuckles and neck. The last few hours had been nothing but sweet tranquility. Ranger had sprawled his hulking frame across the entire backseat and went to sleep right before her mom had. For the next several hundred miles, the silence was blissful.

"No, no. I can wait. Did you call ahead and make sure our reservations are still good? It's way past check-in time."

"Yes, Mom. Don't worry. This isn't my first road trip."

"Sorry, can't help it. It's a mother's job to worry. It's one of the side effects of the hormones that rage through your body when pregnant. The baby leaves the womb but the worry is forever embedded. Like some weird, alien life force takes control of your mind. Good grief, it's almost dark. How long have I been out?"

"About five hours. And you said riding in a car for a long time makes you antsy," Karina teased, enjoying the look of irritation on her mom's face.

"No, I said riding in a car for hours makes my bladder turn into the size of a dime. I become antsy when I need to pee and the only place to relieve myself happens to be in some disgusting roadside bathroom—or worse—like out there."

Hot, moist breath draped across Karina's neck, followed by a slick, wet tongue swiped across her cheek. "Ranger seems to be on your schedule, too. He is just much more expressive about his need to urinate." Karina exited the freeway at the rest area sign. "But I can't ask him if he can hold it until we get to the hotel, so let's make a quick stop here."

LiAnn fumbled to find Ranger's leash while Karina pulled into a parking spot by the bathrooms. Before cutting the engine, Karina scanned the facility. Only three other vehicles were there, all semi-trucks. The bathroom area was well lit and there was no trash strewn across the grassy area set aside for pets. The place looked fairly new and meticulously maintained. Still, since they were two women traveling alone, Karina eased her Glock out from under the seat and slid it into the holster behind her back.

LiAnn noticed and commented. "And I thought I was the paranoid one out of the two of us."

"I'm sorry. Aren't you the one who instilled *safety first—no matter what* in my head since I was a kid, or am I talking to my mother's doppelganger?"

"Oh, don't think for a minute I'm not prepared," LiAnn replied, then pulled up her pant leg to reveal the ankle holster with the twenty-two nestled snuggly inside. "I just prefer not to use a hand cannon unless absolutely necessary. You know, my motto is wound them, then cuff them, because interrogating a dead man doesn't get you much information. That little tidbit was one of the first things I learned at the academy."

Karina smirked. "Mine is blast a hole big enough to kill them, then make up your own story. That works much better."

Laughing, they exited the car, Karina struggled to keep Ranger from bounding across the hot pavement before she could shut the door. The late afternoon sun bathed the area in a vibrant orange, tinged with pink and yellow slivers on the edges of the thin clouds. The dry heat radiated off the blacktop and shimmered across the road.

Ranger's nose led him to the only green spot around and he sniffed out all the previous visitors before he found the perfect place to mark as his own. Karina let her mom hit the restroom first and stood outside the entrance with her enormous black dog that looked more like a small bear, and waited for her turn.

Karina looked back west and watched the sun begin its descent. The sky looked like it was on fire and she felt a twinge of sadness knowing she wouldn't get to see it set over the dark blue waters of the Pacific anytime soon.

She rubbed her tired eyes and cleared her throat before her mom walked out and saw her acting like some pathetic, whiny child. She was pushing forty for goodness sake.

"Your turn," LiAnn called, grabbing Ranger's leash. "And believe it or not, it was better than an outhouse."

"Thanks." Karina smiled and slipped off to the restroom. She was surprised at the cleanliness of the place but antsy herself to get to the hotel. She wanted nothing more than a hot shower and a soft bed.

Within ten minutes they were back on the freeway as the sun set behind them and the call of the hotel room beckoned them closer.

Twenty minutes later, they were finally off the road and at the hotel. While Karina unloaded their bags, LiAnn was busy gabbing on the phone.

"Grampa said hey. He's so excited, he went out and bought a whole side of beef today!"

Karina rolled her eyes as she yanked the zipper on her bag, then lifted it off the bed and on to the floor. She liked to think of herself as a vegetarian who, on occasion, strayed. The thought of eating cow every night made her feel sick. "Oh great. Charred flesh every night. My hips will enjoy it as much as my heart."

"With all the work Grampa will have us doing, you'll burn it all off. Oh, and the sweltering heat will do the rest." LiAnn paused and took a look at her disheveled hair in the mirror, then quickly pulled it back into a tight ponytail.

Karina let out a small groan. "Gee, can't wait. I can see it now: my hair will be in a bun all the time and I'll sweat like a whore in..." Her words trail off and she cringed at the bitterness in them. Karina felt like a heel. Her mom didn't deserve to bear the brunt of her anger.

"Karina, stop it. It's not like beef is the only available food. You know how much they both like to cook. They are southern through and through. Eating, a lot, is part of their culture. There will be plenty of other items on the dinner table to pick from. You know that. Grampa's garden is huge, my little part-time vegan. Sheesh!"

Karina's shoulders sagged as she let out a huff of air. "Oh, ignore me. I'm just grumpy from the drive. Glad I didn't pick long distance trucker as a career."

"Hmmm. You sure that's all?" LiAnn's voice was soft yet inquisitive.

Looking away from her mother's probing eyes, Karina grabbed the room key off the dresser and headed to the door. "I need a cold beer, some hot food and a walk with Ranger. Then I'll be back to my cheery self. Promise." Holding the hotel room door open for her mom, Karina gave one last glance at Ranger. His black body was stretched out on her side of the bed, just like at home. The dog pillow she brought along was on the floor, unused as usual.

"I think what you need is a long talk with your Momma. I planned on that in the car but fell asleep. I'm all ears now though."

Karina kept her groan inside this time. There was no escaping the conversation.

An hour later with a full stomach and the three beers relaxing Karina's nerves, they walked Ranger around the block. It was time to unload her mental baggage under the star-filled New Mexico sky. Taking in a heavy gulp of the night air, Karina squared her shoulders. "Remember Misty?"

"Of course. She's been your shadow ever since high school. And, if I recall correctly, worked at We've Got Ya! for a while, right?"

"Yeah, until I fired her ass after I caught her with Cal." Karina gauged her mother's reaction. If she saw any pity or even the slightest hint of sadness, she'd turn into a blubbering mess.

"Oh damn. I was afraid that's what you would say. I wondered if there was more behind your willingness to move besides job burnout."

"It doesn't make sense to me. It's nearly two years and I still hurt..." Karina's voice trailed off.

"Honey, betrayal has always been a bitter pill to swallow. And, if you've held this inside you all this time, why are you surprised it still hurts?"

"I don't know. I'm not, I guess. I'm just sick of the rock in my gut. But, what I'm really tired of..." Karina's words died as a lump of tears pressed against her throat.

"Is still having feelings for Cal?"

Shocked, Karina almost tripped and fell over Ranger. "How did you know?"

"Baby, it's all over your face and in your voice. I just mistook the look. Thought it was making the decision to sell your portion of the business, move to Arkansas, and be so far away from Cal. I mean, I knew you two weren't seeing each other any longer, but, oh, I guess I hoped the split came about while you were undercover. You know, because you were gone so much. Drifted apart. Not because he cheated on you."

Karina huffed and motioned toward the wooden bench up ahead. Once seated, she summoned the courage to continue the conversation. "Well, in the beginning, that is exactly what happened. I mean, I was bouncing from one job to the next all over the state, and Cal had to stay behind and keep the business running. We really couldn't communicate much other than electronically and weren't too sure how long my assignment would last. We agreed to cool things off."

"Whose idea was that?" LiAnn probed.

"Mine, Mom. The more information I found out, and the pain of seeing what those owners were doing to the poor seniors, ate at my insides.

I couldn't sleep at night. My stomach was in a constant knot, and I had trouble eating. It was all I could do to concentrate on the job without putting my Glock in the temple of some of the nastier owners. It drained me, physically and emotionally. At the end of the day, I didn't have anything left over to give to Cal. When we did talk, all we seemed to do was argue, especially about his troubles running the business. I mean, I couldn't help. I was too far away and already had my plate full, and that wasn't fair to him. So, I suggested we take a break and told him he should hire some help. That's when he brought in Misty."

"Let me guess: you thought she was a safe choice, right? Because of your friendship?"

Karina let a cynical laugh escape. "Yeah, silly me, huh? I mean, Misty filled in for us a few times before, so she knew how to handle all the day-to-day stuff that made Cal's head spin. You know, he isn't the type to sit behind a desk in a suit and tie and crunch numbers or shuffle paper. He prefers to crunch people."

LiAnn chuckled softly. "That he does. I've never seen a man who enjoyed cuffing people as much as Calvin Benson."

"Yeah, but only after he manhandled them

first. Cal was a beast on the job. The dormant biker in him emerged and he never stopped until his quarry was in custody. That was just one of the things I loved about him. He never backed down from a challenge. He was always on the front lines, raring to go. He feared no one and nothing."

"Except you," LiAnn whispered.

"Excuse me? What do you mean? The only time Calvin Benson was ever scared of me was the day I yanked Misty out of the office by her dirty blonde hair. When he tried to intervene, I threatened to castrate him. Oh man, did Cal tell you about that or something?"

LiAnn wrapped her arms around Karina's shoulders. "No, honey. I'm not talking about *physically* afraid of you. Don't get me wrong. It's not like you aren't an imposing sight when all fired up, but I meant *emotionally.* Cal feared how being with you made him feel."

"Mom, I love you, but seriously, that's a load of psycho-babble bullshit. Cal had blue-balls and pointed his dick toward the first dirty skank who offered to spread her..."

"Karina Ruby Summers! I didn't raise you to talk like that, and I certainly don't want you letting that mouth of yours spew out that sort of thing around Gram and Grampa! I know you are used to being around foul-mouthed buffoons all day, but I'm not one of them. And Gram and Grampa would keel over if they heard their precious granddaughter sounding like a dock worker."

Karina refused to be tamped down. "Wait just a minute, Mom. You *wanted* me to tell you what was going on, and now that I am, you're going to admonish me for sharing what I'm feeling, or how I felt at the time things happened? That's not fair. Oh, and I seem to recall your mouth can be just as dirty, if not worse. I remember overhearing some of your more *colorful* conversations with Crigger over the years."

LiAnn softened her tone. "I *do* want you to share, sweetheart. And I'm listening. Of course, so is everyone else around here within fifty feet. Your voice does tend to carry when you are on a rampage. I just want you to think about what you're saying before it explodes from your mouth. You know, practice reformatting your thoughts to make them more, um, P.C. And my potty-mouth has waned over the years. A funny little thing called maturity happened."

Karina inhaled a deep controlling breath, lowering her voice. She stared at Ranger's back.

"P.C., huh? Okay, how about this: I decided to sneak away one weekend and surprise Cal. To my shock and horror, I found my former significant other in the arms of my best friend. They were displaying mutual affection for each other at *very* close range. I succumbed to an outburst of anger and escorted said friend out the door in a rough manner. Made sure my significant other was fully aware of my thoughts and feelings at the moment by expressing them verbally. In a moment of weakness, I threatened bodily harm and our relationship terminated seconds later. That was about sixteen months ago, and I am still finding it difficult to let go of some of the *emotional* baggage I still carry from that day. There. How's that for P.C.?"

Finally bringing her wet eyes up to her mother's, Karina expected to see all sorts of emotions. What she didn't expect was to see a huge grin.

Humor danced behind the green orbs and then LiAnn erupted with laughter. "You are my daughter. No doubt. The only difference between us is that, back in my younger days, I wouldn't have just threatened. I would've sliced them off."

For a second, Karina was stunned and unable to form a word. Then she threw her head back and laughed as well, her tears a mixture of sadness, relief and joy. The unleashing of her pent-up emotions she'd suppressed for so long wasn't as difficult as she'd expected.

Minutes later, they were back in their room and preparing for bed. When her head hit the pillow, Karina was out cold.

LiAnn couldn't get comfortable. The hotel mattress was too soft and the sheets felt like sandpaper against her skin. Oh, who was she kidding? Sleep refused to come because her mind was racing with a myriad of thoughts. The worst was the anger she seemed helpless to control.

Stifling a sigh, LiAnn focused on the rhythmic breathing of her daughter. Karina's light snoring made a smile appear. How content the sound of her only child sleeping made her feel.

LiAnn couldn't decide what bothered her the most: the pain her child suffered or how in the world Karina kept what really happened from her. Years of being a detective had made her keenly adept at reading others, so how did she miss such a monumental event in her daughter's life?

Because she is cut from the same cloth you are, LiAnn. A small tear trickled down her face and she swiped it away in a huff of anger. LiAnn didn't realize her daughter had inherited the same ability to hide her pain as she possessed.

LiAnn fluffed the pillow for the third time, then forced her eyes to close. *Yes, this move is just what we both need. A fresh start in a new place, close to our family. The way things should be. Far, far away from the two men who crushed our spirits and left our hearts a pile of mush.*

5

BECOMING A PAWN

Nick Shonnert ran his fingers across his brow and wiped the thin sheen of sweat away. As he did, he felt the creases in his skin and a slight tremble in his fingertips. He wanted to groan but kept his mouth shut. With a nervous glance, he shifted his eyes to his watch and winced at the time. It wasn't even nine yet and the temperature outside was already so stifling that the air conditioner in the building couldn't keep the place cool. Numerous residents had complained about the system to staff members over the last few weeks, pissing and moaning about the lack of basic needs, in comparison to the exorbitant fees they paid to reside on the property. When the daily staff meetings took place, nervous employees would skulk into Nick's office and give their reports of the daily activities at not only Green Pastures, but all of the other properties owned by the company. Normally, he ignored the petty grievances from the old windbags who lived at the sites, but even he couldn't ignore the fact the ancient air conditioning unit at Green Pastures needed an update.

But Nick could have been sitting on a block of ice during a snowstorm in Alaska and he still would be sweating bullets. At precisely nine a.m., his cell phone would ring, and no matter what number was calling him, the person on the other end of the line would be the same. Caesar Calvanio always called the next day after a drop-off and always from a different number. Nick wondered, as he stared at his own cell on his desk, how many disposable phones the old gangster had purchased during the last several years. If Nick had to guess, the answer would be hundreds.

His legs shook, as they did every time before,

during, and after any interaction with Caesar. Nick's thoughts wandered back to the night of terror that shifted the trajectory of his life, and made his world a living Hell. A shudder of fear shot up his back as Nick recalled the soulless eyes inches from his own as Caesar laid out his new business module.

After hours of terror, pain, and witnessing the freak show of all Caesar's numerous battle wounds, Nick could see the tattoo of the leaping black panther with claws extended that spanned between Caesar's shoulder blades. When Caesar flexed his thick back muscles, the imposing image danced with sickening grace. Had Caesar suddenly sprouted a pair of long white fangs and fur, Nick could not have been more terrified.

"You're going to hire some new caregivers for the facility in Hot Springs. Don't worry, we are going to start small, do a test run there first. My associates, Franco and Carmella D'Nucci, just recently started some new businesses in town. One is an elder care agency, and Carmella will provide all the on-site help Green Pastures will need to keep the residents happy and healthy. Our little test run will be on two marks we've already selected. When Carmella's crew gets all the identity and financial stuff gathered up from our two test subjects, she will hand the information over to Franco. Of course, we will already have the information you obtained on our marks, compliments of copies of their files. Oh, and let me give you a little piece of advice here: make sure the information you give us matches what Carmella comes up with. If it don't, then your organs will live on, just not in your body."

"Sure, sure, no problem. I will copy everything in the files you need," Nick choked out, his vocal chords barely able to function any longer.

Caesar's lips formed into a smile, but there was nothing kind or warm behind it. "I like this new attitude of yours, Nick. Don't you, Carmine?"

Carmine nodded his head. "Oh yea, Boss. He's like a little lamb now. Just took a bit of persuading, that's all."

Caesar turned back to Nick. "Now, once Franco gets all the scoop on each person, I call you to set the date when these people are going to have a heart attack or stroke. Your job is to have the managers at each facility trained to call only *one* ambulance service. The other new business venture in town needs some financial support as well. Place is called Lombardo's Ambulance Service. They will send a wagon right over to take the ailing resident to the hospital. Oh, don't look so worried, Nicky! I'm not going to have you do any killing. You aren't made out of the right cloth for that. The caregivers will make sure things look *natural*. The doctor will pronounce them dead and Lombardo's will happily return to pick up the body from the hospital morgue and take them to the funeral home."

Nick felt the rock in his gut lesson a fraction. *At least I won't have to do any killing.*

"Another associate of mine owns a chain of funeral parlors, three of which are right here in Central Arkansas. You ever heard of Slumber Land?"

Nick couldn't find the muscle control to make his throat unlock, so he nodded his head in agreement.

Caesar's smile grew wider as he clapped his cold hand on Nick's shoulder. "Good! See your job responsibilities aren't as difficult as you probably originally thought, huh? You just remember the rules and don't stray from them. Because if you do, the next time we meet here *will* be your last."

Nick thought his heart was going to explode. It was beating so fast and loud, he was finding it difficult to hear all of what Caesar was saying. He had never been so terrified in his entire life. Listening to the two men, who could have easily walked onto the set of *The Godfather* and landed a role, casually talk about murder like they were discussing where to plan their next vacation, made Nick's mind begin to shut down. He finally understood the rest of his life would be controlled by a mafia gangster. There was no way out of the business situation. He wouldn't jeopardize the lives of his family.

Nick began to feel lightheaded. For some odd reason, he thought back to his previous excitement of finding a private investor to quickly further Happy Days Retirement Living's obsessive acquisition of distressed senior housing properties. How foreign the memory of happiness seemed now. He didn't even care about how he was going to explain this new investor to Teri without revealing *why* they must continue the relationship with Caesar Calvanio, especially after he bought The Magnolia House.

That little hurdle seemed like a speck of dust, compared to the mountain his new business partner intended for Nick to climb.

His body and mind were on the verge of collapsing again. Nick didn't make a sound, not even a whimper, when Carmine untied him and helped him stand. Once Nick was able to stand unassisted, Caesar and Carmine walked him to their Lincoln Town Car and placed him in the back seat instead of the trunk this time. Not a word was spoken during the drive until they pulled up to Nick's office. When the car came to a stop and the door unlocked, Caesar turned around from his spot in the front passenger seat and said, "Every Monday morning at nine, on the nose, I will call you. Never, ever miss that call, Nicky. Ever. Oh, and have a great evening with your wife and kids. Tell them their uncle said hello."

After Nick stepped out of the car, he forced himself to walk and not run. Enough cowardice had been shown already, and felt the need to retain some dignity. After all, he'd saved his family from suffering violent, horrible deaths tonight.

Even though he had to trade his soul in exchange for their lives.

Nick jerked when the phone on his desk rang. Glad to be yanked back from the horrid memories, he welcomed the distraction of work. Without looking at the display on the office phone, he snatched the receiver up. "Shonnert."

"Nick, we need to talk."

The sound of the irritated voice of his ex-wife, Teri made his heart race. Their divorce three years ago almost destroyed him. He couldn't blame Teri for packing up the kids and leaving him. Nick knew he hadn't been the greatest husband or father in the world *pre*-Caesar Calvanio, but *post*-Calvanio had turned Nick into a husk of his former self. He couldn't explain the real reasons behind his sudden weight loss, insomnia or quick temper to his family. Poor Teri assumed his sudden change in demeanor meant he was seeing another woman. It cut Nick to the bone when Teri voiced her worries, for he had never, not once in all their twenty years together, broken their vows.

Nick may have been guilty of shady business dealings and had a brash, cocky attitude and lack of concern for the welfare of his employees and residents, but he adored Teri and the kids. For her to immediately assume he was cheating on her, added to the mountainous pile of stress already on his strained shoulders. In the end, he couldn't come up with a plausible explanation for his sudden inability to perform in bed that Teri believed, and she left him.

They didn't speak anymore unless the kids needed something she couldn't provide. Even though her tone was harsh and distant, it still sent shockwaves of grief and remorse through Nick's heart. "Morning, Teri. What...what do we need to talk about?" he responded, trying to hide the pathetic, hopeful tone in his voice. What he wanted to hear was *Nick, let's talk about us. I miss you.* But he knew that would never happen. Once Teri's mind was set, nothing would change it.

"The school called this morning. Said your check for this semester's tuition for Sabrina bounced. The financial aid director also said she tried to contact you all last week, even left several messages, none of which you've returned. If the money isn't in their hands by noon, Sabrina will have to drop out this semester. That's just not acceptable. Period. She only has one more year left, Nick! You should have told me you couldn't afford this semester. I mean, I realize you are probably broke from spending money on your latest play-toy, but that shouldn't stop you from ignoring the financial duties to your children. God knows you've ignored every other duty as a father and husband."

His heart skipped two beats. "I...oh shit, Teri. I didn't know. I swear." He shuffled through the stacks of pink messages on his desk, something he hadn't done in a week. Sure enough, there were four notes to call the U of A financial aid office. "Oh damn, I just found the messages on my desk. I've been really swamped at work. Things are hectic and..."

Teri cut him off before he had a chance to finish his thoughts. "Don't try to concoct some bogus lie, Nick. I learned a long time ago how to read you, and I can hear the bullshit in your voice. Just make it right. Today. I'm not asking you to do anything for me. I'm asking for your child. And her future. Can you do that? Or, do I need to prepare myself to drive to Fayetteville and pick up our daughter, then trash her father the entire way back?"

Before he could say a word, or mention the fact that Sabrina and Shaun had already heard their mother trash their father enough during the last three years, his cell phone buzzed on the desk. Nick's mouth immediately went dry and his heart rate tripled. "I promise, I'll make it right before noon. I've got to go, Teri. Duty calls."

"Is that her name? Duty? Jesus, Nick. I always figured you for a Candy or Tiffany kind of guy," Teri retorted.

Nick swallowed the lump in his throat and slammed the receiver back in its cradle, unwilling to listen to the hatred spewing from the mouth of his ex. He answered his cell. "Good morning, sir. Sorry it took so long for me to pick up. I was..."

"No need to apologize, Nicky Boy, although I do hate waiting. But I won't let your lack of promptness spoil this glorious day. The sky is blue, the sun is shining, and I woke up with a smile on my face after a fitful night's sleep. Cherish each and every day. Embrace every moment alive. That's my motto. The older you get, the more those words ring true. Of course, they also ring true for those who are close to the end of their time here *above* the ground. Know what I mean? Can't help but wonder if last night's package savored his last remaining moments before he went on to the next world. What do you think?"

Goose bumps popped up all over Nick's body. The casual callousness of Caesar's words made him feel sick to his stomach as the acid churned and boiled in his gut. Last night's drop wasn't just the body parts of some random stranger. They had once belonged to Caesar's own flesh and blood, and the man was talking about it like it was just another elderly stranger whose time had *unnaturally* expired. The heartlessness of it all made Nick's head spin and his gut roll into a tight knot. He reached into the side drawer on his desk and snagged an antacid, then popped it into his mouth. Nick was acutely aware from his own personal experience of how cold and soulless Caesar could be, but he'd been nothing more than a business connection to Caesar. Ray-Ray was his *nephew.*

Though he was still unaware of all the particulars surrounding Caesar's decision to end the life of Ray-Ray, it didn't really matter. The deal was done, and not by the hands of Caesar or his freaky goon friend, Carmine. On instinct, Nick looked down at his hands, almost expecting to see residual blood stains from his part in the death of Ray-Ray. For a second, his vision blurred as the sound of the gunshot that ended the boy's life rang inside his mind. Nick remembered the sensation of the cold barrel pressed against his forehead, the overwhelming fear at the choice he was being forced to make. The heat of his urine as it trickled down his legs when his bladder gave out. Nick's choice was to end the life of Ray-Ray or have his own brains splattered on the dirty concrete floor by Carmine.

He actually considered letting Carmine pull the trigger and end his misery. After all, Sabrina and Shaun didn't have much to do with him anymore, and resurrecting a relationship with Teri was completely out of the question, so what did he have to live for anyway? Years of being Caesar's chimp on a tight leash were wearing down on him, the constant fear of being caught by the police and worries that one misstep would cause Caesar to hurt Teri or the kids, made Nick's nerves paper-thin. He had no hope any more. Nick was taking so much medication, his bathroom cabinet rivaled a pharmacy. He had high blood pressure, an ulcer the size of a small baseball, and a wicked case of psoriasis, acid reflux, a weak bladder, and other ailments.

Would it have really been so bad to just let it be over in a boom and flash?

Yet, in the end, he closed his eyes and pulled the trigger as tears streamed down his face. When Caesar whispered in his ear that if Nick failed to perform his assigned duties, he would be the first of many Shonnerts sporting holes in their heads, what choice did he have?

"You're uncharacteristically quiet this morning, Nicky Boy. What's the matter? The heat getting to you? I know the new air conditioning unit hasn't arrived yet. Or is it something else, like your ulcer acting up again?"

Nick crushed his lips together and tried to force his mind to slow down. He had to think and pick out the right words to say, for they could very well be his last. "I'm sorry, sir. Just got off the phone with the ex. Kid problems. Nothing I can't handle, though. So, I assume the package was delivered without any problems, correct?"

There was a long pause and he wondered if he'd chosen the wrong thing to say. Nick winced when he finally heard the old man clear his throat and respond.

"Well, that's good to hear. Always had faith in you and your abilities to handle difficult situations, Nicky Boy. The sacrifices and things we do for our family to keep them healthy and happy, huh? But, enough of that topic. I don't like to get involved with personal issues of my employees. Bad business, you know? And you are correct. Things went as smooth as silk last night, although that is not the reason for my call this morning."

Nick wasn't sure if he should stop shaking or amp the speed up. As per his usual interactions with Caesar, things were always vague and full of innuendos which could be taken in a variety of ways. He stopped trying to second guess years ago what the old bastard meant and simply waited until his *real* instructions were given to him. They would come after the phone conversation, usually in a plain envelope delivered by Carmella, at the end of the day. He shuddered at the thought of coming face to face with the mother of the boy he shot last night. "Understood, sir. I await your instructions on our next project here at Green Pastures."

"Your loyalty hasn't gone unnoticed, Nick. Of course, nothing goes unnoticed by me. I make sure of it. I'll let you go so you can go take care of your personal business. Good day."

Before Nick could respond, the line went dead. The answer to his earlier internal question appeared as he shook like a leaf on a tree during a hurricane. He stared down at the messages from the U of A on his desk for a second, then jumped from his chair and ran to the bathroom. He made it to the toilet with only nanoseconds to spare before he tossed his breakfast, along with some bright red blood, into the commode. As he retched, he wished he would have just let Carmine pull the trigger.

Oh, God, who's next to have their ticket cashed early?

6

WELCOME TO THE SOUTH

"**A**re you really going to try to drive in tonight? I think we should stop and get a room. You've been behind the wheel for over ten hours Karina. That's way too long."

Karina tried to force a weak smile but failed. Her mom was right, for Karina's eyes felt like she'd been inside a sandstorm. It was beyond time to take her contacts out and give her eyes a rest, but she couldn't seem to remove her foot from the pedal. They'd been on the road for hours, but Karina had felt revived and refreshed when they left Albuquerque earlier. After unleashing all her pent up emotions, she had a fitful and dreamless night's sleep. It was a welcome change from the last three years. Plus, the boring landscape of the panhandle of Texas and central Oklahoma made her foot heavier on the gas pedal.

According to the GPS, the leg of this part of the journey was about thirteen hours, so another three didn't seem too difficult. "I'm fine. Now that we've crossed the state line, it seems silly to stop and stay somewhere. The sign back there said it was less than two hundred miles to Sheridan, so let's just push through. Maybe, if you're tired, how about we stop, stretch our legs and grab some food? I need to re-wet these plastic eyeballs."

LiAnn chuckled and fiddled with the empty Styrofoam cup in her hands. "How about we stop at the next rest area and switch places? Take your contacts out and let your eyes rest. Bet they are as red as the taillights. Besides, I want to get behind the wheel of this baby!"

"Can't hide anything from the mighty Sgt. Tuck, even in her retirement or the darkness inside my car! Okay, okay. You win. But, if you get a speeding ticket, don't blame me. The horses under the hood like to run, so you have to hold the reins tight."

With a loud clap of her hands, LiAnn wiggled around in the seat like a little kid. "About time! I've been dying to see what this baby can do. And hey, if we get pulled over, no worries. I'm a retired, well-decorated detective from L.A. Common courtesy from one cop to another is to just give a warning."

Karina's loud snort made Ranger jerk his head up from his perch on the back seat. "Yeah, okay Mom. When it's noted you are from Los Angeles and not Lower Arkansas, we will be lucky if they don't toss us both into the slammer."

"Oh, come on now! It's not going to be like that. Just because we are..."

"Crazy Californian's who've ventured back in time to the old south? Please. I guarantee you if we get pulled over, every inch of my car will be searched *after* they call in for K-9 backup. You *know* they are going to suspect we are running drugs, once they set their eyes on this car. Can you imagine trying to control Ranger with another dog around? Geesh, he would rip my arm off!"

"Well, that's your fault for buying a car that *looks* like we are drug transporters! Seriously! It's black, the windows are tinted so dark people can't see inside, and the tires on this baby look like they should be on a dragster," LiAnn teased.

"Yep, and bought like that for a purpose. Undercover work, remember? I would have been made in a heartbeat had I driven one of those obvious vehicles you cops use. I mean, get real! Those undercover cars *scream* law enforcement. My car never gave me away. Ever. So don't hate on her, especially if you want to drive her." Karina laughed then took the exit.

Karina didn't relish the idea of stopping at a rest area on this particular stretch of freeway. If they were going to get out and do the Chinese fire drill, they needed to be in a well-lit area. The gas station up ahead beckoned with bright, neon lights, and was packed with vehicles. "I'm going to stop here, yank my contacts out and then you can take over. Okay?"

Karina pulled around to the back entrance and joined a line of parked semi-trucks. She fumbled around with Ranger's collar and leash. Her massive, four-legged companion knew when the car stopped moving, it was time to get out. Karina cast a sideways glance at her mom, who was busy tying the laces on her tennis shoes. Her blonde curls tumbled over her head while she hummed some tune Karina couldn't quite place. It sort of sounded like a terrible rendition of "I Can't Drive Fifty-Five."

LiAnn bounced out of the passenger's seat. "Hurry up and walk that beast so I can get us to Sheridan in record time! Look out, Dracula, here I come!"

In the middle of the parking lot, with her huge black dog in tow, Karina's laugh made the people pumping gas stop what they were doing and look in her direction. "Mom, the vehicle's name is *Dragula*, not Dracula. You know, the song by Rob Zombie? Based off of the *Munsters*? Come on now, metal-head, you should know that! After all, you are the one who hooked me on the television show to begin with, and blasted his music in the house for years!"

LiAnn feigned shock. "Oh, excuse me, little missy, for not firing on all cylinders. It's your fault for letting me fall asleep. Again. It takes a while for the cobwebs to disappear. You will get to experience that once you are old as dirt, like me. Now, hurry up with Ranger so I can get behind the wheel of *Dragula*."

Karina just shook her head and let Ranger lead

her to the green grass by the side of the building. As she walked, she swore her mother's humming grew louder. *Please, let her keep humming. If she breaks out into song, I'll jump out of the car.*

"**O**h, I forgot to tell you why Crigger called me the other day."

Karina shifted in the seat, glad for the distraction from the whizzing road. It wasn't like she was afraid of speed. The problem was she wasn't used to being in the passenger seat. She was a control freak. "You mean it was more than just to say goodbye, or try to convince you to change your mind about retirement?"

"Those things were discussed, and might have been the underlying reason he called, but he did actually bring something else up. Something pertaining to us both."

Karina snapped off the blaring radio. "Us both? What could it...oh, no, please tell me it doesn't have anything to do with the Jubilee case?"

The car accelerated just a fraction and was

Karina's answer before her mom ever opened her mouth.

"Melissa called and told Crigger Jubilee filed an appeal. Not too much of surprise. We knew it was a distinct possibility."

Karina groaned and took a healthy swig of water. It didn't help to wash the bitter taste in her mouth. "Yeah, I just really hoped they wouldn't. So, did Melissa call to warn us we might have to come back for court? Jesus, I hope not. If I have to relive all that again..."

LiAnn shifted in the seat. "As of right now, she just wanted to let us know. Not sure why she didn't contact one of us directly, but that doesn't really matter. Crigger said he thinks she will want to verbally go over our testimony, rather than read through the pile of court transcripts. Can't say I blame her, if that is the reason. I mean the paperwork would be ten-feet high!"

Out of all the cases Karina worked on over the years, Jubilee was the only one that still haunted her. She bit her lip to create some pain to focus on, and it made the lump in her throat subside. "Can we shelve this conversation for a later date? Like, when I'm half-drunk off moonshine and tired from working in Grampa's garden all day? You know, so I won't have the mental or physical ability to strap my gun on and go take care of those assholes in the way they truly deserve?"

LiAnn laughed, a deep, hearty rumble she only let out when really amused. "Don't think, for one second, you're the only one who feels that way, sweetheart. I didn't tell you when you were driving, since I figured it would raise your blood pressure, and the speed at which we were traveling."

Karina shot a glance over at the speedometer, which read eighty-five. "Hmmm. Seems to me the trait is hereditary. I believe the sign we just passed a bit ago stated the speed limit on I-40 is seventy. You better slow down..." Before she could finish, the interior of the car turned vibrant blue. The blinking strobes were followed by the loud screech of the siren. "Uh-oh. Too late."

"Oh, stop worrying. I wasn't going *that* much over the limit. It'll just be warning, you watch and see."

Karina turned around in the seat and grabbed Ranger's leash, securing it to his collar in one click. She doubled the thick leather around her hand and cooed to him, hoping her voice would keep him calm. When she turned back around, her mother had maneuvered the car over to the shoulder and shut the engine off.

"Hand me my purse, will you? I need my license and your insurance card."

Karina yanked her mom's bag from the floor, handed it to her, then fumbled around in the console for her registration and insurance papers. Ranger began to growl from the back seat. *This should be interesting.*

When LiAnn rolled the window down, a rush of hot, humid air burst inside, along with a hungry horde of mosquitoes. She swiped at them and said, "Good evening, sir."

"Ma'am. In quite the hurry tonight, aren't ya? Did you miss the sign back there that noted the speed limit here in Arkansas?"

"No sir, I saw it. Just didn't realize I'd gone over the limit, that's all. This is the first time I've ever driven my daughter's car, so I guess I'm not used to the power under the hood."

Karina had to stifle a laugh at the sugary-sweet tone in her mom's voice. *Yikes, she is laying it on thick.* Just as the cop was about to respond, Ranger barked, and all three of them jumped. The cop shined his flashlight in the interior at the same time he took a step back from the driver's window. "Ya got that dog on a leash?"

"Yes sir. Don't worry, he doesn't bite. He is just doing his job." Karina responded, trying not to laugh.

"Quiet him down, now. Ma'am, I need to see your driver's license, registration and insurance."

Karina gripped the leash tighter and stroked Ranger's head with her free hand. He stopped barking but never took his eyes off the man outside the window.

"Sure thing, officer. Here you go." LiAnn passed the requested items through the window. "Listen, sir, we..."

The officer cut her off. "Remain in your vehicle while I run this," he replied with a terse inflection. In a flash, he turned and strode back to his cruiser.

"Of course. I know the drill. I'm a retired cop from..."

"Mom, it doesn't do you any good to talk to someone who isn't listening. Oh, you are *so* getting a ticket. You watch."

LiAnn swatted a mosquito from her cheek. "Want to place a wager on that?"

Karina chuckled, "You're on. Twenty bucks says you get a speeding ticket."

"Done. I say, he comes back here with a smile on his face and a warning to slow down. I'm telling you, professional courtesy. It's in the bag."

When seconds turned into minutes, Karina knew she was twenty dollars richer. If the trooper was going to let her mom off with a warning, he would have already returned. Trooper Bad Attitude was taking too long, which meant only one thing: he was writing up a citation.

Karina saw her mom drumming fingers on the steering wheel, jaw clenched tight. She knew the look. It was irritation and impatience rolled into one. Maybe a smidgen of embarrassment, too.

They heard the car door slam and the heavy steps of the cop's boots on the blacktop. Karina couldn't keep a straight face, so she focused her attention on Ranger.

"I'm citin' you for speedin'. Please sign this and note your court date on the back."

Karina winced, waiting for the explosion. To her surprise, it never came.

"One word of advice, Ms. Tuck. This ain't California. We stick to the rules here in

Arkansas. The speed limit is seventy. Go over it, and you get a ticket. Plain and simple. Mind our rules, and the rest of your visit here in the Natural State will be a pleasant one."

In seconds, the blue lights were gone and the cruiser back on the freeway. Karina watched her mother wait until the cop was gone before starting the engine. The rear tires spit gravel up in the air as she pulled onto the highway.

Karina couldn't stop herself from poking the hornet's nest. "Well, at least he didn't yank us out of the car and tear it apart looking for drugs. Maybe that was his way of saying welcome to the South."

LiAnn scowled. "Not another word, Karina Ruby. Not another word."

7

FAMILY REUNION

It was close to nine p.m. when the GPS announced *You have arrived at your destination.* LiAnn shut the engine off and grabbed her purse. Her previous irritation at the not-so-friendly encounter with a southern law enforcement officer was long gone. She watched Karina scramble out of the car and let Ranger out, then made a beeline for the front door. It opened and LiAnn felt tears form behind her eyes when she saw her aging parents appear on the stoop.

"Lawd a mercy! If you two ain't the salve needed for these old tired eyes!"

In a heartbeat, LiAnn ran up behind her daughter. Ranger jumped around their feet like a puppy as they all embraced in a family hug.

"Y'all sure made good time! Wasn't expectin' ya until tomorra'! What, y'all break the speed limit or somethin'?" Junior Tuck teased.

"Oh...touchy subject, Grampa. Mom gets to pay a visit to Pulaski County's court system in three weeks and drop some cash. What's the fine around here for speeding?" Karina answered.

LiAnn shot Karina a look, but refrained from commenting on the subject. "Pop! Mom! Oh, it's so good to see you both. We just couldn't wait another day. We drove straight through from New Mexico this morning."

"Well, the feelin' is mutual, daughter. Come on in and get yourselves situated. Your ma just made a fresh batch of tea. Let's go sit a spell and get caught up. I want to hear all about your trip, especially the part about the ticket. I'm curious how come you couldn't sweet talk your way out of it."

Within minutes, their luggage situated in their respective rooms and an ice filled glass of tea in their hands, the four of them sat on the back porch and reconnected. To LiAnn, it was Heaven. Her mom insisted they eat and brought two heaping plates of southern delicacies outside. LiAnn and Karina lapped up the food like they were starving. Ranger inspected every inch of the back yard, marking as he went. Once finished, he ate and drank his fill, before curling up in a ball at Karina's feet. Before long, it was close to midnight.

Karina stood up and stretched her weary muscles. "I'm going to take Ranger for a walk then hit the sack. I'm exhausted. And after that lovely meal, I'm sure once my head hits the pillow, I'll be out in seconds. Love you both. See you in the morning."

LiAnn turned her attention back to her parents, and a pang of worry hit her. Though it had only been less than two years since she'd seen them, LiAnn was astonished at how much they'd aged. They were both underweight and sported thinning, stark white hair. LiAnn glanced at her mom's hands and noticed the age spots looked darker, and bigger. The frail skin was pulled tight, the bluish-green hue of her veins more pronounced.

What bothered LiAnn the most was the tremors in her father's gnarled hands. She watched him pick up his glass of tea to bring to his lips, wincing when she saw how much the glass shook. "Pop, maybe we should all call it a night? I don't want you getting overtired. We have plenty of time to catch up tomorrow."

"Not even here a day and already started to crow about my health? You sound just like your ma. I'm fine, just not as robust as I used to be. It's called gettin' long in the tooth, baby girl. Ain't none of us on this earth ever been made to live forever."

Ruth interjected. "Don't you worry 'bout him, darlin'. He's just extra cranky at night. It's 'cause he works himself into exhaustion around here each day. If he'd just hire some help..."

"Ruth, don't start in on that again. This is my land, and I ain't gonna have some strangers trompin' all around it. Period."

LiAnn sensed the tension in the air. The last thing she wanted to do was upset either of them. "Well, you don't need to worry about that now, Pop. Karina and I are here to help. You'll just need to teach us what we need to do. We're fast learners. You point and we'll jump."

"That's right. I'll turn you city girls into country chicks in no time. It's hard work, but rewardin'. First time you taste a meal ya grew with yer own hands, ya ain't never gonna want to eat anythin' else. I guarantee it," Junior replied.

LiAnn smiled and reached over and patted her father's thin shoulder. "I promise, we won't disappoint either of you. Now, it's late and I'm exhausted from the car ride. Let's hit the sack. What time do we need to be up tomorrow?"

"We get up when the rooster does. Don't need no alarm clock 'round here. Rocky crows the same time each mornin'," Ruth said as they all walked inside.

LiAnn followed her mother to the small kitchen and helped put away the food and clear the dishes. She could hear her father in the other room, talking to Karina and cooing to Ranger. The sound of the big dog's tail as it thumped a loud echo on the hardwood floor. The verbal sparring about the best handgun to use between her daughter and father made LiAnn smile.

"Got your room all fixed up. If ya need another blanket, they're in the bathroom closet. Oh, and the truck with your belongin's will be here tomorrow. So, don't you and Karina fret none about workin' around here tomorrow. Y'all be busy unpackin' for a few days, I suspect. Your daddy and I will handle the day-to-day chores until you two get all settled in. Okay?"

LiAnn looked at her mother's face and saw the sternness she recalled from her youth. She also saw the cloudiness from cataracts overshadowing the blue of her eyes. Heavy wrinkles were etched deep into her face, the once-full lips thin and drawn. LiAnn couldn't find the words to respond, so she simply nodded in agreement. She hugged her mom's frail body with a gentle embrace and kissed her cheek, then headed straight to her room.

Once settled under the covers, LiAnn was too wired to sleep. Even though they'd arrived under the cover of darkness, she couldn't help but notice the decrepit state of her parents' farm. The once immaculate front yard, dotted with a vibrant white fence and overflowing with flowers, was gone. Several sections of the fence were either broken or leaning toward the ground, the white paint but a passing memory on the aging wood. The yard needed to be mowed and the lush flowers didn't exist anymore, replaced with nothing but dirt.

The interior of the house wasn't much better, either. Her mother had always kept a spotless house. Now, it was full of old newspapers and a thick sheen of gray dust covered several surfaces. When LiAnn helped put away the dishes, she noticed the ones already in the cupboard weren't entirely clean.

But the thing that bothered LiAnn the most were the fifteen bottles of medications that sat on the dining room table. That was way too much, even for two people.

She made a mental note to ask her mom when their next doctor's appointment was so she could accompany them, and find out just why so much had been prescribed. It wasn't like LiAnn was opposed to taking prescription meds, but the exorbitant amount she saw earlier was simply too much. Once she found out what ailments they both suffered from, she would do some research and hopefully find homeopathic versions.

When her eyelids grew heavy, LiAnn knew without a shadow of a doubt, the decision to move had been the right one.

Ranger was curled up on the floor next to Karina's shoes, his even breathing a sure sign he was out like a light. Karina slid her glasses off and tucked them under her pillow. She tried to find a comfortable position on the worn-out mattress. It took several turns and shifting of the pillows before she gave up and just held still.

She tried to relax but it was no use. It was *that* smell. That same, underlying scent she'd smelled for two years. Death. Age. The mixture of must, decay, and limited body hygiene combined with cheap perfume. No matter how expensive the place, how meticulously maintained by the staff, the scent of the elderly was unmistakable.

When she stepped onto the front porch earlier, the smell slammed into her. It wasn't as strong here as it had been when Karina worked undercover at the assisted living centers, but it was still present. It overrode the smells she recalled from her childhood from the summers spent with her grandparents. The sweet aroma of Gram's freshly baked peach pies. The zest of the lemon-scented cleaner Gram used throughout the house. The rich, musky cherry of

Grampa's pipe. The tangy, tart aroma of the hay from the fields.

Karina's thoughts were interrupted by the chime of her cell phone. Her heart begin to beat faster. It was Cal's message tone. She groaned and wanted to kick herself for not turning the thing to silent. She already had enough jumbled thoughts ruminating around in her head. She didn't need the added stress of communication from Cal. Staring at the phone on the nightstand next to her, Karina waffled back and forth, weighing the pros and cons of seeing what he sent her. Part of her wanted it to say something like *Hey babe, miss you, love you* or something just as equally pathetic and mushy. The other part of her wanted it to be nothing more than *Hey, did you make it okay?* or *How's the weather?* or *Say, what is the password to Quickbooks? I forgot.*

Curiosity won out.

Still driving? Heard there was a big pile up on I-40 near Tulsa. You safe?

On instinct, Karina switched over to the phone's browser and searched out the local news station for Tulsa. She spent ten minutes scouring the site and found no mention of any sort of big traffic accident. Karina let out a small grin. Her instincts had been on the mark. The little white lie was a ruse to contact her. For two minutes, she thought about what to say before she finally responded.

Must have missed the accident. In Sheridan now, all settled in.

In the dark room, she waited for a reply, wondering what Cal was thinking at the moment. Was he contemplating his own response? Did he wonder if Karina had searched out his story? Was he trying to think of some clever comeback, one that had hidden meaning? Or was Karina just fooling herself by thinking he still cared about her?

Seconds ticked by and no response came. Deciding she read way too much into the text, she flipped the phone over to silent, and put it back on its perch beside the bed.

Damn you, Calvin Benson. Damn you.

8

FIRST DAY ON THE FARM

"Rise and shine, sleepyhead. The moving van is here."

The sound of her mom's chirpy morning voice made Karina groan and pull the covers over her head. It couldn't be morning already, for it felt like she'd just fallen asleep. She kept her eyes closed and listened to her mom move around the room. In seconds, the curtains were opened, and bright yellow rays of sunlight illuminated the small space. The vibrant sun weaved its way through the thin comforter and straight through her eyelids. "Mom! Please, close the drapes."

"I will do no such thing. It's after seven, and we've got a lot to do today. First things first, though. Your dog needs to go outside and you need to get dressed, just not in that order. The guys are already unloading my stuff and yours is next. Oh, and two of them are rather yummy looking, so you might want to freshen up first. I mean, talk about rock hard biceps and home-grown buns, goodness! Mmm, mmm."

"Seriously, Mom?" Karina barked from under the covers. "If they're that hot, don't you want them all to yourself?" In a flash, the comforter disappeared as her mom flung it to the floor.

"I said there were *two* of them, and I'm too old to handle more than one at a time. So get up and come help unpack. Chop chop!"

With another groan of protest, Karina left the warm spot on the bed and headed to the bathroom. "You need help, Mom. Serious help. Morning people are certifiable. Look it up on the Internet."

Once dressed and somewhat presentable, Karina made her way into the kitchen and headed straight for the coffee maker. She poured a cup, took a big swig, and winced as the stout brew slid down her throat. The taste of coffee made her nearly gag, but she loved the effect it had on her mood in the mornings. Karina glanced around the small kitchen and smiled. Some things hadn't changed over the years.

Gram was piddling away making a pie and Grampa was seated in his favorite spot, reading the newspaper, his reading glasses perched on the tip of his nose. Her mom sat in the chair to his right, flipping through her handwritten inventory of her belongings, and the television in the corner on the counter chattered away with the local news.

"Morning. Sorry I slept so late. Had a bit of trouble getting to sleep last night." Karina moved over and stood next to Gram, then gave her a quick kiss on her warm cheek. "That smells wonderful. Peach cobbler?"

Ruth beamed. "Yes ma'am. I recall that's your favorite. Plus, if I didn't use up the last of the peaches, they would rot before I had time to can them."

"Oh, can't wait! Next time you decide to bake one, will you let me know? I want to take notes so I can learn how to make one, too."

"Notes? Honey, you don't learn to cook by takin' notes! You just go by instinct and taste," Ruth said, shaking her head at Karina's comment.

"Leave her be, Ruth. Let the girl learn however she sees fit. If that means writin' things down, then that's how it will be."

Karina flashed a warm smile at Grampa, then walked over and placed a kiss on his forehead. "Morning."

"Excuse us, but will one of y'all fine people direct us to where y'all want this?"

All eyes turned to the doorway. Karina nearly choked on a gasp when she saw two men holding her mom's dresser at each end. Her mom had been right on target. Between the thick, honey colored hair, bulging biceps and white t-shirts stretched across their muscled-up backs, these two guys were smoking hot! And they were *twins*. Duplicated hunks with thighs the size of tree trunks and tight, yet small, rounded butts. No wonder her mom insisted she get cleaned up before she walked out of her room. Karina forced her gaping mouth closed.

LiAnn bestowed them a dazzling smile. "Oh, sure thing. That's my dresser. Just set it next to the other boxes in my room."

"Yes ma'am," both hunks said in unison, their voices in perfect harmony together. In a flash, they were gone.

Karina looked over at her mom and mouthed *Oh, my God!* Her mom replied with a silent wink and slight nod of her head. "Guess I better go, um, point them in the right direction for my stuff." Before anyone could say anything, Karina was out of the kitchen and following the two gorgeous physiques down the hall.

Maybe living in the South won't be so bad after all. Sweet Jesus, what do they feed people down here to grow asses that round and firm?

"Hmmph. Guess this means our little gal ain't pinin' over her breakup with her beau any longer," Junior remarked.

LiAnn laughed. "You don't miss a thing, do you?"

"Honey, if I missed *that* raw display of

attraction, it would mean I'm blind *and* deaf. I mean, the girl practically fell all over herself tryin' to follow the backsides of those boys," Junior replied.

LiAnn giggled. "I guarantee you, she isn't thinking about Calvin Benson at the moment. Hopefully, she never will again. Slime ball."

"Do I detect a bit of protective momma bear instinct in your voice?" Ruth asked while sliding the pie into the oven.

"Let's just say, it's a good thing we are here and not in L.A. any longer. On the trip down, Karina finally told me what happened between the two of them. None of it was good. Their breakup wasn't just because of lack of contact, or drifting apart while she was on assignment."

LiAnn watched her mother walk with slow, calculated steps across the hardwood floor, then ease down in the chair next to her. She heard the crackle of the newspaper as her dad closed it.

"Hmmm. Did the wolf sneak in and play with another hen in the chicken coop?" Junior grumbled.

LiAnn sighed, then lowered her voice. "Yes, that's exactly what happened while Karina was on that undercover assignment. And with her closest friend. To make matters worse, Karina caught them together. Really knocked her for a loop. It's one thing to find out you're being cheated on. It's quite another to actually *see* it happen right in front of you. I think she always had it in the back of her mind she would be Mrs. Calvin Benson someday. Made the situation even harder to grapple with."

A shadow of sadness crossed Ruth's face. "Ain't nothin' more painful than being cheated on. Watched my fair share of friends struggle with it durin' my lifetime. Some of them never recovered from it. Took the wind right outta their sails. But, don't you worry none, honey. Karina's in the right place to heal—with her family."

Junior interjected. "I'd say the scab's pretty thick, based on what I just saw. Karina didn't look like a wounded bird to me. You two need to quit worryin' about her. She comes from tough stock. My little spitfire ain't gonna let some mangy mongrel ruin her life. No way. You didn't."

LiAnn swallowed hard and gathered her thoughts before she spoke. "No, I didn't break, but I wasn't ever the same again, either."

Junior's face softened. "I told ya years ago, but you wouldn't listen. Knew the minute I laid my eyes on him he was trouble, just like I did with Karina's father. One may have been a crook and the other a cop, but cheaters come in all types of packages. And they all have the same look behind their eyes. It's called lust."

LiAnn bit her lip before she said something she regretted. The subject of her ugly breakup with Crigger was not a topic she wished to discuss, and certainly not with her parents. Even after all the years, it seemed some strong, negative feelings about Crigger, and Kurt, still lurked about.

She wouldn't stick up for Kurt because she agreed one-hundred percent with her parents on that front. But Crigger? That was a different story. Her parents only knew what she had told them, not the *entire* truth. And the truth was, her relationship with Crigger was way more complicated than *cheater* and *cheatee*. "Well, it's all water under the bridge now. Hopefully, we both learned from our mistakes and won't make the same ones again. I can't speak for my daughter, but I can say that I have no interest in dating. I'm set in my ways now, since I've been single for so long. Besides, with all that needs to be done around here, when would I have time?"

LiAnn stood and went to the counter and

poured another cup of coffee. Her father grumbled something under his breath, but she couldn't make it out. Her attention was focused on the television set and the scrolling headline. Intrigued, LiAnn turned up the volume.

...Shane Simmons was denied bail this morning by Circuit Court Judge Henry Paxton. He was formally charged with first degree murder in the grisly death of Raymond "Ray-Ray" D'Nucci, along with kidnapping, aggravated robbery, and arson. His girlfriend, Renee Clements, was also charged as an accessory in the case. The investigation concluded Ms. Clements helped dispose of the gun and set fire to Mr. D'Nucci's residence, and tried to sell some of Mr. D'Nucci's jewelry at a pawn shop in Little Rock.

His funeral is set for Saturday at three p.m. at St. Michael's Church in Hot Springs....

LiAnn shook her head in disgust as she turned the volume back down. "Guess it doesn't matter where you live, crime never takes a break."

Ruth's brows crushed together with sadness. "Oh, it's been awful. Been all over the news the last few days. An ugly, ugly mess. Course, crime always is. The news report yesterday said the girl used to date the young man, and knew he had money and lots of jewelry. Got her new beau to help her relieve her ex of some of his stuff, then I guess things went bad from there. They robbed him, shot him, cut him up, and torched his place. The report said only some of his burnt body was recovered at the scene. Such a shame. People killin' each other over material things. What's this world comin' to? Ain't they ever heard of workin' for what they want?"

LiAnn queried, "He was dismembered? Oh, wow, that isn't something you hear often. Sounds more like a mob tactic to me. With a last name like D'Nucci, it would make sense. Then again, if it were a mob hit, there would be no corpse left to find. But, judging by the looks of the mugshots, those two surely aren't in the Mafia. I'd say drugs were involved. They both had that zombie-meth look. Can't tell you how many cases our division worked that centered on drugs. Meth is the worst of them. People turn their brains to mush on the stuff, and don't care how they come by cash to buy more. I don't know of one state that isn't suffering because of the white poison."

Ruth fiddled with the kerchief around her neck. "Just last month, there were over five arrests here in Grant County alone. People cookin' that mess out in the woods. One of the labs even blew up and burned over ten acres, less than twenty miles from here. Scary times, indeed."

Junior scowled. He dropped the newspaper from his hands and went to get more coffee. "That's the reason I quit huntin'. Time was when I could traipse around them woods without a care in the world, except keepin' myself quiet and hidden from the critters I was after. Now, you walk up on the wrong place and find yourself in the middle of a war zone."

"Is it really that bad, and that close?" LiAnn said a silent prayer of thanks at her father's decision to stay home and safe.

"Oh yes," Junior replied, then took a heavy swig of coffee. "Why, just last year, ol' Cecil Pickard got shot and almost died. He was settin' up his deer stand, on his *own* property mind you, when two hoodlums attacked him. Beat him up pretty bad, tryin' to scare him into leavin' and never comin' back. But ol' Pick, if ya recall, honey, is stubborn as a mule with its butt stuck in the mud. He let that mouth of his take over. That's when they shot him and left him for dead. It's only by the grace of God he's still pullin' in air. His son got worried when he didn't come back home that night. Went out searchin' for him, found him, and then hauled him to the hospital. Doc said one more hour and it woulda been lights out for good."

A wave of anger hit LiAnn right in the gut. Though it had been years since she'd seen Mr. Pickard, she knew how close her father was to him. The two men grew up together and even joined the Navy on the same day. To say Cecil Pickard was her father's closest friend would have been an understatement. "Poor Cecil! Did the police catch the shooter?"

Junior shook his head. "Nope. Word around town is them boys are connected to some high rankin' muckety-mucks who's keepin' them safe from payin' for their crimes. Don't rightly know if that's true or not, but I ain't takin' no chances. My huntin' days are over."

LiAnn looked out the window into the back yard and out toward the barn. She noticed no cows or horses out back, which was odd. On their last visit, there had been at least ten head of cattle and several horses. "Is that why you don't have livestock anymore, Pop?"

Ruth answered instead. "Nope. I made him sell them last year 'cause it was gettin' to be too much for us to handle alone. Pricey, too. Feed prices have skyrocketed. It's a real shame."

Junior started to say something, but was interrupted by loud barking coming from Karina's room. Karina yelled out, "Uh, can someone please grab Ranger's leash for me? It's either in my car or in the living room!"

LiAnn started to move toward the hallway but Junior stopped her. "I got it, dontcha worry none. Know right where it is. Saw it this mornin' 'fore I went out to feed the chickens. Besides, I want to see if she's droolin' yet. She might need someone to wipe it off her face. Maybe give her a cold wash rag to help cool her off."

With a playful wink, Junior disappeared down the hallway. LiAnn sat back down next to her mother. She could sense she wanted to say something, but seemed a bit nervous to begin. Considering the conversation they were just having, LiAnn figured it must have something to do with Mr. Pickard, so she asked, "How's Mr. Pickard holding up, Mom? Did he fully recover?"

A shadow of sadness made the creases and wrinkles in the frail skin around Ruth's face more pronounced. Ruth snuck a quick glance to ensure they were alone, then lowered her voice. "Oh, he recovered from his injuries to his body, but the one to his heart, no. Never seen a man turn into such a husk of his former self so quickly."

Perplexed, LiAnn cocked her head and replied, "His heart? What do you mean?"

Ruth hesitated, her hands clasped together in a tight knot on the table. "Well, you remember Cecil's wife passed on years ago, right?" LiAnn nodded her head and motioned for her to continue. "After she died, it was just Cecil and his son, Steve. No more kin left in the family. Steve, well, he never married and Cecil was an only child after his baby sis passed on. So, they were all each other had left. When Cecil nearly died, Steve went into a frenzy."

LiAnn tried to bring up fuzzy memories of stories about Cecil and Steve. A random one popped up. Steve was a recovering alcoholic. "Oh no, did Steve start drinking again?"

"Yes. Hard. Three weeks after Cecil was released from the hospital, Steve was killed in an accident. Rolled his truck off Highway 35 after pullin' a bender. It's just a miracle he didn't kill or hurt anyone else."

"How awful!" LiAnn forced her voice to remain quiet, shocked by the news, and the fact neither parent had told her any of this earlier. Then again, her parents were old school to the core.

Conversations about such emotional things *never* happened over the phone or in letters. If the subject matter was a difficult one to broach, or would elicit a painful response, it was not discussed until the parties were face to face.

Ruth leaned in and motioned for LiAnn to do the same. "After that, Cecil just gave up. He quit talkin' to anyone, includin' your daddy. Less than two months after Steve's funeral, Cecil sold all his property and moved to that retirement community in Hot Springs. Told us he couldn't stand bein' around all the things remindin' him of his past. I tell ya, it's been hard on us all. You know he and your daddy are quite close."

LiAnn saw the pain reflected in her mother's cloudy blue eyes. "Is that why Pop started making noises about moving into The Magnolia House? To be closer to Cecil?"

Ruth let out a long sigh while she stared out the window. "Partly. The other part is guilt. The way your daddy sees things, he owes Cecil."

Confused, LiAnn asked, "Owes him? What do you mean?"

Unable to stay seated any longer, Ruth rose and went to the sink, pretending to wash already clean dishes. "The day Cecil went out in the woods, your daddy was supposed to go with him.

He didn't because the truck wouldn't start. He spent most of the day tinkerin' with it before he got it runnin.' Your daddy just can't get past it. Thinks it's somehow his fault his friend got shot. He ain't never said that, but I can see it in his eyes. All those years they watched each other's back durin' the war, keepin' each other alive, out of harm's way, don't seem to matter none. Even after all this time, your daddy still feels it's his job to watch over Cecil."

"Now, that's just crazy! Pop needs to lay the blame right where it belongs, which is on the shoulders of the cowards who shot Cecil. Good grief, Pop could have been shot, too!"

"He don't see it that way. He thinks he coulda talked their way out of the pickle. Maybe could've kept Cecil from spoutin' and sputterin' and they coulda left without blood bein' shed. I told him I thought that was a load of swill, but it's stuck in his craw. Ain't nothin' gonna dislodge it."

LiAnn let out a grunt. "Well, I'll just convince him otherwise. Almost sounds to me like he is suffering from survivor's guilt, or something like it. I mean, I understand how close he is to Cecil, but none of what happened to him Pop could have stopped."

LiAnn didn't get a chance to finish her thoughts. The conversation was interrupted by Karina and Ranger bursting into the kitchen, followed by her father.

"Watch out, rabid dog on a leash. Geesh, I forgot how much he hates strange men!" Karina yelled. In a flash and with a loud bang of the screen door, Karina and Ranger exited the kitchen.

LiAnn exchanged worried glances with her mother, but let their previous topic of discussion disappear.

9

THE DECISION

Caesar hung up from his conversation with Nick, a small smile tugging at the corners of his mouth. Though it had taken several years of grooming, Caesar knew he had Nick right where he wanted him. After he had him commit murder, he knew Nick would never be able to turn on him. How could he? Nick was a member of the club now. The Killer Club.

He stared down at the disposable phone in his hand and almost laughed out loud. Nick had always been a wimpy man. A blowhard afraid of his own shadow. He did have one redeeming quality, and it made controlling his strings so simple, a child could have done it–his family. Nick Shonnert was a morally bankrupt slime-ball on most levels, but his weakness was his wife and kids. Caesar worried a bit when Nick's wife left him, fearing it would be the catalyst that gave Nick the courage to go to the police. Caesar had Carmine put surveillance tails on Nick for the first two years after the divorce, and for a while, it seemed Nick was just like every other divorced man in the world. He'd turned into a sad drunk, a habitual visitor to porn sites on the Internet and a few strip clubs on the seedier side of town. Things changed six weeks ago. Carmine noticed a change in the demeanor of Nick and reported it to Caesar.

When Carmine told him Nick was suffering from numerous physical ailments, and his attitude had changed over to quiet and despondent, Caesar went into action. Decided it was time to solidify the ties with blood, which is exactly what happened the night Nick blew Ray-Ray's brains out.

Caesar leaned back in his chair and lit a cigar. Thoughts of The Prick slipped away, replaced by the events leading up to his nephew's unexpected departure from the world. As the fragrant vapors curled above his head, he thought about the early phone call several days before that sealed Ray-Ray's fate.

Caesar's wonderful dream interactions with Romella, frolicking along the sun-drenched sands in Tahiti, hand-in-hand while the warm water lapped at their bare feet, ended with one shrill screech. The cell phone on the nightstand wouldn't shut up. He groaned and rolled over, sliding on his glasses. His anger spiked when he noticed the clock read five-thirty a.m. Caesar growled with anger because only one caller had the number, and the balls to call him so early.

"What the hell do you want? Better be worth my time. You interrupted a great dream."

Carmine didn't let the nasty response bother him and replied, "Well, if it wasn't for your crazy, drugged up nephew in trouble with the law again, I wouldn't be bothering you."

Irritated, Caesar sat up and flicked the bedside

lamp on. He wished Franco would've shot blanks into Carmella. Their only son was like a bad case of acne: unwanted, impossible to get rid of, and left ugly scars behind. He barked into the phone, "So what's Ray-Ray done now?"

"Fucked-up. Big time. It seems the money we pay him ain't enough to feed his addiction. He decided to try his hand at yet another illegal venture. Thought stealing copper wiring from a construction site for the new hotel on Central Avenue seemed like a grand idea. The idiot actually severed part of his index finger while cutting the wire and then took off running. Left his damn finger behind. When the crews came in the next morning, they knew immediately they'd been robbed. The moron actually went to the emergency room. Told the doc on duty he cut off his finger trying to fix his car. Once he got stitched up, he flipped out and checked himself into a dive motel off Central, and then called me. Guess he figured I would go softer on him than his parents, or you. By the sound of his voice, he was flyin' higher than a kite."

Caesar rubbed his forehead, trying to massage the dull throb behind his eyes. "Jesus, Joseph and Mary!"

Carmine lowered his voice, "Ain't just some

pissant misdemeanor charges this time, Boss. Copper theft is a felony. The cops have his finger and my source tells me a lab technician shoved a Popsicle stick in the bloody stub, rolled it on a fingerprint card, and up popped Ray-Ray's prints. Ray-Ray will be looking at serious prison time. They'll probably charge him with commercial burglary, too. All that means trouble for the whole lot of us. Noses will start sniffing around in places we don't want them to."

Unable to stay still, Caesar threw back the covers and started pacing. His first instinct was to have Carmine tell him where the little panty-stain was hiding, and then pay him a visit. Beat his face into a bloody pulp for being such a worthless piece of trash. A shameful disappointment to not only his mother, but to the entire family. Shove all his teeth down his throat so he could choke on them. The boy had potential in his younger days but ruined his brain with his addiction to heroin. Franco and Carmella had spent untold amounts of money on the boy over the years, sending him to one high-priced rehab clinic after another. He'd come out, all apologetic, ready to "live life straight" then get yanked back into the lifestyle for one stupid reason or another. The most recent cause to run to the needle was his breakup with his on again, off again whore, Renee Clements.

Caesar found himself in the den, his fingers maneuvering the dial on the safe with nimble ease. He could hear Carmine breathing on the other end of the phone, waiting with the patience of a saint for him to respond. On autopilot, Caesar thumbed through his notepad until he found what he didn't realize he was looking for until it slapped him in the face.

"Carmine, come over and have some coffee with me. Now. We need to discuss a few things."

Without a word in response, the line went dead. He knew within ten minutes, Carmine would be at his doorstep. Caesar ambled over to the espresso machine and flicked the switch. A wicked smirk kicked up the corners of his mouth as he stared at his chicken scratch on the yellow-lined paper: *cuore, polmoni, fegato.* He'd just filled all three orders with one body, and solved the pesky problem of his nephew's addiction.

Once the coffee finished brewing, he watched out the window as the first glimpse of sunlight peeked through the trees. The sound of Romella's sweet voice rang through his mind.

"No, Caesar. He's family. Think about how it will destroy Carmella. And Franco. It's wrong. Please,

don't do this. Ray-Ray is the closest you will ever have to a son."

Inside the walls of his mind, Caesar answered the haunting voice of his wife. *Then he should have thought about the extreme consequences to his actions. Blood ties or not, he must atone for his mistakes.*

C aesar's memories were cut short by the chime of the doorbell. He had never been so happy to hear the sound. Reliving the painful interactions in his mind with Romella made his chest feel tight. Heavy. He glanced down at his watch, wondering how long he'd been lost in his thoughts. Another thing about getting older he hated: the loss of time. Age seemed to bring memories of the past to the center of his mind, more often than dealing with the present. He didn't have time for the nonsense. Surprised it was after ten thirty, he made his way to the front door, a terse grin on his face. Carmine would just have to wait for him to finish getting dressed.

With a quick peek through the peephole to

ensure his visitor was who he'd expected, he unlocked the heavy doors and let Carmine inside. Not a word was spoken between the two old friends, but he saw the fleeting glimpse of a question at the casual attire behind the eyes of his most trusted confident. With a slight nod of his head, he motioned for Carmine to follow him upstairs. When they reached the top step, Caesar finally spoke. "Have some fresh coffee while I change. The stuff is amazing. Shoulda' bought one of those single-cup machines ages ago."

Carmine moved over to the sitting area at the front of the expansive bedroom while Caesar tugged off his sleepwear and began to dress. "Mmm, smells wonderful. Hazelnut?"

"Of course. Oh, and make sure to use the fresh cream, not the flavored packets. Makes all the difference in the world." Once dressed, Caesar walked over to the other dresser and slipped on his cuff links. "Sorry I'm running late this morning. Age may bring wisdom, but it also deposits slowness."

From the corner of his eye, he watched Carmine fix and then take a hefty sip of steaming coffee. "Hey, boss. No need to apologize. I'm enjoyin' this hot treat. It *is* fantastic. I'm gonna go get one of these fancy machines after work today. And watch them cracks about age. We ain't but two years apart."

Caesar attached the last cuff link, hiding the pain of the action from his face. Though he hadn't been properly diagnosed because he refused to let some quack poke and prod around, he knew his stiff fingers and swollen joints were from arthritis. Ignoring the drumming, dull pain, he moved over to the mirror to adjust his tie.

The glint of faded gold from his wedding ring in the reflection caused a wave of sadness to settle over him. He'd be forced to remove it soon, before his finger swelled to the point the band cut off his circulation. Even though he'd removed nearly all of the memorabilia of his time with Romella, including photos, her clothes, little gifts she'd given him over the years, Caesar couldn't find it in him to let go of the symbol of their unity. It would be like losing her all over again. His dreams of his beloved wife were more and more frequent now, and the one he had only hours ago was still fresh on his mind. He swallowed hard and forced his hands to stop shaking.

"Boss, you okay this morning? You look tired. Trouble sleeping?"

"Don't ask questions unless you want truthful answers."

Carmine prodded. "When have I ever? I'm serious though. The bags under your eyes are a dead giveaway. You could pack a week's worth of laundry in them. It isn't about our last job, is it?"

Caesar took a deep breath and walked over to the coffee pot. He busied his hands with preparing another cup, ignoring the heavy weight of the question hanging in the air. Carmine didn't push for a reply. He simply sat down in his favorite chair by the window and waited, sipping his drink. If he'd have been anyone else, Caesar would have lit into him for asking such a personal question, poking an unwelcomed nose into his private life. But Carmine had been by his side ever since they were fourteen year old toughs running the mean streets of Brooklyn and then occupying the same cells when sentenced to time in Attica. No other soul, not even beloved Romella, knew him better.

Drink in hand, Caesar turned and joined his friend in the sitting area. He took a long, slow pull of the stout coffee and stared out the window. The view over the expanse of the entire city of Hot Springs was spectacular. His plush surroundings were lovely and inviting, the brotherhood with Carmine strong and comforting. But it wasn't enough. Not any longer.

"I think it is time to change my morning view. Someplace with warm sand, aquamarine water, and sunsets so vivid, they bring tears to the eye." Caesar noticed the enlarged, blue veins on his hands, covered by thinning skin full of ever-growing dark brown spots. The knuckles were red and ugly today. *When did I get so old?*

Carmine's eyebrows lifted in response, but his voice didn't betray his thoughts. "You forgot tanned, toned hot young things in skimpy bikinis. That's always the best part of the beach, at least to me. So, what tropical locale are you thinking for a vacation? Dominica? Bahamas? Oh, what about Tahiti? Those exotic Polynesian beauties with all that thick, black hair..."

Despite his mood, Caesar couldn't help but smile. "You always were a sucker for young ones, eh, my friend?"

Carmine patted his rotund midsection. "Yep. All it takes is a few minutes under the sheets with an eager companion to make a man feel twenty again. You should try it sometime. It might wipe the grimace off your face."

Caesar chortled. "There are more important things in life than ejaculation, Carmine. Besides, I wasn't referring to a vacation. I'm thinking about a more permanent change of scenery. You hit the mark when you mentioned Tahiti. It is the perfect choice for a multitude of reasons."

A wide smile appeared on Carmine's face as he set down his coffee mug. "I must disagree, Boss. It's in man's nature to stay young through pelvic thrusts. Keeps the back limber and skin supple. How do you think I've remained such a stunning portrait of manhood all these years? And, I knew it would be Tahiti because extradition back to the U.S. is not on their law books, and you have a thing for dark haired beauties. But, a permanent move? After all our hard work building our business, you want to leave now? We may be in our seventies, but we aren't ready for the pasture yet. Your treasure chest may be full, but mine still needs some trinkets before I call it quits. This is about Ray-Ray, isn't it?"

Caesar never said a word in response. He wasn't sure what he should say. How could he explain what was really on his mind without sounding like some pathetic, mentally disturbed old fool? He could just imagine the look of confusion, the blank stare that would cross

Carmine's face if he mentioned the dreams of his dead wife had crossed the line into reality. How Caesar saw her, plain as day, in various spots inside the house. At first, she was just an ethereal glow but recently, she not only took on solid form, but started talking to him. Carmine wasn't a deep thinker. He lived fast, quick and for the moment. Carmine enjoyed his role as the muscle in their relationship. He liked to fancy himself as the reincarnation of old-school hit men, enjoying each kill and drooling in anticipation for the next one. When he wasn't using his brawn in service of Caesar, Carmine listened to the voice of his smaller head between his legs.

The man in front of him would never understand Caesar's reasons for wanting to leave not only the business, but the state, no matter how small of words he used to express the eerie thoughts. How could he tell Carmine he sensed his mind was beginning to fracture from either dementia, Alzheimer's, a brain tumor, or worse, and he planned on ending his own life *before* the final crack happened? How could he make Carmine understand, when even he really didn't? What Caesar did know was he couldn't shake the feeling his dead bride had come back to entice him to the other side. How would he start a conversation about how Romella beckoned to him to end his life, take his last breath, in their favorite place in the entire world, and he was struggling to fight the temptation?

Carmine continued. "Boss, if you're worried, don't be. I told you I handled everything. No one will ever tie his death to us. Not even to Nick. The arrests have already been made, and the evidence planted more than damning. I made sure of that. It's a done deal. Lock, stock and barrel. In over fifty years, I've never failed you, and I'm too old to start new traditions."

"If you would cut back on your outrageous spending habits Carmine, maybe your stack of cash would be higher. Paying for expensive female companionship and your predilection for gambling—those are the pastimes of the young. It's time you settle down, find a good woman, and enjoy the spoils of your labor. And no, this isn't about my nephew. Liabilities need to be dealt with quickly, regardless of personal feelings or blood ties. Besides, I trust you. Implicitly. You already know if I didn't, you wouldn't be here."

Confusion spread across Carmine's face. He struggled to understand just what was bothering

Caesar. Finally, a glint of understanding sparked in his eyes. "Hey, you know I was just kidding about what I said earlier. You know, about women? It was spoken in jest, not as a dig against you. To be honest, I respect the unending devotion to Romella, even after all these years. Envy it, actually. You experienced something I only tasted briefly with my lady. I didn't realize until right now how close it is until your anniversary. You're dreaming about your old life with her again, aren't you?"

The small hairs on Caesar's neck and arms stood erect in response to his temper rising. Carmine had just overstepped the invisible lines of their friendship, landing smack-dab in the middle of the source of Caesar's pain. Rather than answer the question, he decided to change the subject, wishing he wouldn't have started the conversation to begin with. "You mentioned a news report. I missed it this morning while I was on my call with The Prick. What's the latest?"

Carmine didn't answer for a few seconds as he studied Caesar's face. He weighed the pros and cons of keeping the discussion alive. His gaze moved to the ring on Caesar's hand. He cleared his throat and went back to business mode.

"Both parties were formally charged and bail denied. The evidence left at both locations is airtight. The rest of, uh, the remains are nothing but a pile of ashes, spread across two counties. No worries, Boss."

Caesar took another sip of coffee while he gathered his thoughts. Though he felt no remorse per se about dispatching his own flesh and blood, he couldn't shake the sense of unease about the whole situation. He wasn't sure what source the edginess stemmed from. Maybe another thing age brought to the table was forced, reflective insights into one's own heart and mind. A peeling back of the thick, dark layers of harshness covering the soul, one piled on top of another from years of cold, calculated acts. Whatever it was, Caesar didn't like it. Not at all. He knew he couldn't control his troubling dreams, but he sure as hell could, and would, control his waking thoughts.

"Good, good. And of course, the recipients of Ray-Ray's generous donations are more than happy. Ecstatic, actually. It is a rarity to be offered younger parts, and they paid handsome prices for the longevity they will bring. I've already packed up your share," Caesar said, nodding his head toward the sleek, black leather briefcase resting on top of his dresser. "It was quite a profitable transaction. Now, where are we on our next donors?"

Caesar watched Carmine stand and walk over to retrieve his share of the spoils. He couldn't help but smile when he heard the crack of Carmine's aged knees as he walked. At least Caesar wasn't the only one out of their duo suffering from a body no longer in its prime.

Carmine let out a low whistle as he thumbed through the stacks of cash. "Now that's what I'm talking about! With this haul, the gaping hole in my treasure chest will be much smaller!"

To bring Carmine out of his money-induced euphoria, Caesar cleared his throat.

"Oh, sorry. Got a little lost basking in the green glow of success. Okay, so as you know, our next marks are going to net us all some serious pocket money. One in particular. He's the perfect target *and* has a clean bill of health. Out of the three, he ain't even on any meds. Only has one lung we can use, but the rest of his parts are pristine."

"Only one lung? There is no worry about whatever disease took the other affecting the healthy one, correct? And, what about family?

You sure no one will come sniffing around after the donors pass?"

Carmine clicked the locks on the suitcase and groaned as he hefted it off the dresser. A few wobbly strides brought him back to his spot in the sitting area next to Caesar. He plopped the briefcase down next to Caesar, grabbed his coffee mug, and took a tentative sip. "The first two you picked, Seth Thomas and Wylie Wilson, are in fair health, considering their ages. The last one, Cecil Pickard, has no diseases at all. A bullet tore up the other lung. Got shot while out hunting on his property nearly two years ago. No one was ever arrested, so my guess is he was shot by his son, who, by the way, is dead. Boy was the only living relative, and from what I discovered, he wasn't worth much. A drunk who tried to stay on the wagon but kept falling off. Old man was worth quite a bit, and I believe junior grew tired of waiting for him to kick the bucket and tried to speed things up. That is just my opinion, of course. Just a few weeks after the old man recovered, kid went on a bender and then got behind the wheel. Died on impact when his truck crashed. Not long after that, the old man sold all his land and moved to The Magnolia. The real estate records indicate he sold the acreage and his home for over ten million. As of right now, our other facilities don't have any great prospects."

Caesar tried, but failed, to stop the smile forming on his lips. "Hmmm. Cecil Pickard has no living relatives, correct? You sure?"

"Yep. Had Franco do a background check on him too, and he found the same as we did–dick. Cecil Pickard was married only once and fathered only one child. His wife died a few years ago, cancer I believe, and like I said, his son died in a car accident. Parents passed over twenty years ago, and he only had one sister, who died when she was fifteen from pneumonia. No cousins, grandchildren or the like. Even the paperwork he filled out when he applied for residency at The Magnolia, lists no living relatives. As you well know, the only visitor to come see him is the old buddy he grew up with, Junior Tuck, who is also listed on his residency paperwork as an emergency contact."

Caesar sipped his coffee and enjoyed the rush of adrenaline. The predator in him enjoyed the hunt. "Yes, I'm well aware. Go on."

"According to what Carmella discovered, it is possible he will need to be dealt with, but we don't know for sure just yet."

"Expound on that, please."

"Carmella hasn't been able to track the location of *all* of the cash from the sale of Cecil's land. Old fucker has it spread out all over and is quite private. Doesn't leave any financial papers, checkbooks, receipts or anything else out in plain view. She's only been able to locate three accounts, totaling a little over two mil. She plans on doing some more snooping tomorrow, when the weekly domino game commences."

"And what part of what you just related ties back to having to deal with Mr. Tuck?" Caesar queried.

"Because the accounts Carmella did find list Junior Tuck as beneficiary upon the death of Pickard. That's why."

Caesar leaned back against the cool confines of the chair, swallowed a sip of tepid coffee and closed his eyes. He could feel Carmine watching him, waiting for a response. His mind rolled around the pros and cons of continuing with Mr. Cecil Pickard as their next target. No family and a clean bill of health were pluses, but a living beneficiary and close friend, one who was a weekly visitor, was a major problem. Something in Caesar's gut told him to hold off.

"Carmine, tell me more about Seth Thomas and Wylie Wilson."

"No family, no beneficiaries, decent health. One had an aortic valve replacement in his heart a few years ago, but has responded to treatment quite well. The other has COPD, but his eyes are almost perfect and his liver is in good shape. Carmella said he brags about never having touched a drop of alcohol his entire life. However, neither of them, even put together, are worth a tenth of Mr. Pickard, but profitable just the same. Why, something eatin' at ya about Pickard?"

Caesar opened his eyes and stood. "I believe some investigating needs to be done into the relationship between the buddies before we continue further with Mr. Pickard. Proceed with another, and make it quick. Pick the one with the best heart. We have a current open order for one that needs to be filled. Soon. Oh, and if you don't stop sticking your nose into my business, I might just use yours."

Carmine roared with laughter as they rose to leave. Both knew Caesar's heart was cold enough to actually live up to what he just said. With his usual comedic flair, Carmine shot back, "You are welcome to my body parts when I go, but you'll have to look elsewhere for a heart. Have to have one before it can be harvested. But I'm all for giving my Johnson to someone else. Preferably, a guy with a short one, so he can enjoy the sensations of having his lover gasp at the sight of it, like it's done for me all these years." Carmine grabbed his crotch and squeezed. "Let this monster live on in another. Live *long* and prosper!"

10

THE MAJESTIC
MAGNOLIA HOUSE

Jimmy Calhoun parked his car in his designated spot by the front door and smiled. He couldn't help it. Every time he looked at the ancient place, so full of history and graceful beauty from times long since passed, Jimmy felt a surge of whimsy in his chest. The Magnolia was a stately stunner for sure. The bronze and gold placard erected in the front lawn announced to all visitors with gilded letters the year the manse was originally erected: 1820.

The mansion had once been the heart and center of Hot Springs, built on a small rise that overlooked the entire city. The original owner spent six years of his life overseeing the construction of the sprawling estate, in hopes of making his young bride less homesick for her native Germany. No expense was spared as the mixture of architectural design meshed together. Germanic influences were infused with the opulent styles of French and Mediterranean. From the wood to the brick, to the Romanesque inspired backyard, complete with three porticos and a small vineyard, to the highly-polished maple, cherry and oak floors. The original structure had forty bedrooms, twenty bathrooms, a ballroom, three formal dining rooms, a library, smoking den, and a kitchen bigger than Jimmy's entire house. Chester McFarland completed his dream and built a one-of-a-kind spread, which covered over seventy-five acres, and made his young wife happy. Then, he died three weeks after moving from a head injury, sustained in a horseback riding accident. His widow lived the remainder of her life inside the walls, childless, her only companions the staff who stayed on.

With no heir to the property upon her death, ownership of The Magnolia passed through many hands over the years. The final individual owner, Shelby Sasafia, sunk his last remaining bit of savings he'd accumulated during his life, just to keep the place from falling apart. When he died, penniless and alone in the mid-80's, The Magnolia went up for sale. The once stately manner had fallen on hard times. The wood was old, warped, and in need of serious attention. The mortar between the bricks cracked, crumbled and fell out in chunks. The enormous, three story winding staircase, built entirely from teak, sported gaping holes in the steps, and so many spindles were missing that from a distance, the staircase looked like a mouth with numerous teeth knocked out after losing an epic battle with the local bully. The vineyard was overrun with weeds, no sign of the once vibrant vines. The massive stables, once full of over fifty horses, had collapsed in on itself.

The plumbing and electrical had been updated in the 60's, and Shelby Sasafia tried to continue the trend in the 80's, but died before he could completely renovate all twenty bathrooms. The entire place needed not only a major overhaul, but an owner who had deep cash reserves to not only bring the place up to par, but keep it that way.

The city of Hot Springs had hoped that someone would swoop in and buy the eyesore, restoring it to its former glory. But, the history of the place hung on like a deer tick embedded deep under the skin of a hound dog. Between the deaths that occurred there, some of the less-than-stellar owners of the past, down to the rumors of the place being haunted, ruined any chances of someone willing to take on the challenge. No one wanted to invest the cash to restore it, or say they were the proud owner of a former house of ill repute, gambling den, speakeasy, failed restaurant, and home for unwed mothers that just *may* or *may not* be inhabited by the ghosts of the past.

With no buyers, and a city unwilling to step up to the plate and take control, nor able to demolish the place for fear of public outcry (which had happened twice when the subject came before the board members of the city) the once beautiful piece of history sat in stony silence, each day rotting and dying a bit more than the one before.

Jimmy stepped out of his cool car into the humid afternoon air. He stopped and stared and the elegant, restored concrete stairway leading up to the front of the building. The newest additions to the property were a sloping walkway big enough for wheelchair access and a covered parking lot for over one hundred vehicles. He was more than thankful someone *did* step up to the plate and buy the crumbling property. With a sad smile, he recalled all the times he and his wife dined inside the walls, back when the place had been converted into a restaurant. Now, almost fifteen years after the original purchase by a corporation that specialized in independent living retirement communities, The Magnolia finally was living up to her name once again. It sparkled and shined in every nook and cranny, and housed thirty seniors who had the resources to afford the exorbitant monthly fees. When Jimmy first retired, he gave serious consideration to selling his own home and moving in, since he didn't relish the idea of spending his golden years knocking around inside his house all alone. Instead, he satisfied his needs by being a volunteer.

On Tuesdays and Thursdays, Jimmy arrived

and held painting classes for any and all seniors who desired to learn. On Saturdays, Jimmy sat in what once was the ballroom and read to those who wished to hear classics from their younger years.

Jimmy picked up his pace and trudged up the walkway to the massive, double-front doors. He was greeted by cool air and the delicious smell of lunch. As he crossed the front foyer, he veered right and followed the sounds of chatter from residents in one of the formal dining areas. Winding his way through the tables, Jimmy said hello to each table full of residents until he made his way over to the long serving line. In seconds, his plate was packed full of broiled chicken with mushroom sauce, green beans smothered in onions, two piping hot butter rolls and cornbread dressing.

"Hey, yo, Jimmy! Over here. We saved a seat just for ya!"

Jimmy turned to the sound of the brittle voice of Wylie Wilson. Sure enough, the old man sat a few tables away, along with another resident, Seth Thomas. The two men were active participants in Jimmy's painting class (though neither of them could draw a circle, much less paint) and always sat in the front row on

Saturdays when Jimmy narrated the classics. He wasn't too fond of Seth. Never could get a solid read on the man. Seth was too quiet. Seth was a former librarian who looked at him with squinty, watery blue eyes in what Jimmy could only conclude was disdain. Though Seth never commented or corrected Jimmy when he made an occasional pronunciation error, Jimmy sensed the subtle undertone of superiority.

Wylie Wilson, on the other hand, was Jimmy's favorite resident. At eighty-seven, he barely reached five-foot-six with his cowboy boots on. Wylie had a pair of bowed legs a steer could run through without touching either knee. He was bald, save for a small thatch of snow white hair that sat right on the top of his head. Even when he was still, it waved like a wheat field in motion. His cheeks and nose were bright red, due to fifty-plus years of his devotion to drinking Jack Daniels straight. Wylie possessed a rowdy sense of humor and was always the first one to think of a practical joke to play on an unsuspecting victim.

Wylie's son, Weston, brought him to live at The Magnolia four years ago, right before Jimmy became a volunteer. According to the yarns

Wylie liked to engross anyone in earshot with, his son forced him to sell his home and move from Magnet Cove, since Wylie continued to get into trouble with local law enforcement. Wylie just couldn't understand why they objected to him driving his 1973 Cadillac Coupe de Ville on the town sidewalks as he was trying to locate various stores he wanted to visit. After Wylie's fines hit the thousand dollar mark from mashing a few parking meters on Main Street flat, and the State of Arkansas pulled his drivers' license, Weston grew tired of his father's shenanigans. At first, he had Wylie move in with him so, according to Wylie, he could *keep an eye on him*, but that decision proved to be a fiasco. Weston made the mistake of showing his father how to use the computer, and one day while Weston was at work, Wylie stumbled on a website full of tons of practical jokes. Being the prankster he was, Wylie decided to try some of them out. All at the local Walmart.

After three months of trying out all the funny ideas, Wylie was escorted from Walmart by his embarrassed son, after hearing an earful about his father's exploits from the manager. The manager informed Weston his father had set all the alarm clocks in housewares to go off at five minute intervals. Once, he walked up to an employee in the pet supplies department and told her in a very official tone "*Code 3 in housewares. Get on it right away.*" He went to the customer service desk and tried to reserve a bag of chips. He set up a tent in the camping department and told the children of other shoppers they could come into the tent if they would bring pillows and blankets from the bedding department. The final straw happened when over the clerk's objections, he entered the women's wear dressing room and closed the door. A few minutes later he hollered "*Hey, where is the toilet paper kept in here?*" which caused the clerk to launch into an anxiety attack and scream for help.

Less than a week later, Wylie was living at The Magnolia and his son didn't visit him for six straight months. They had finally made peace with each other after a full year, then Weston passed away from a heart attack. Three years ago, Wylie underwent surgery to replace his aortic valve, and the recovery process knocked some of the wind out of the old man's sails for nearly eighteen months. But during the last three months, Wylie got some of his former spunk back and started playing harmless jokes on some of the residents.

Jimmy changed directions and sat down at the table. He gave a curt nod to Seth and a hearty smile to Wylie. "Good afternoon, gentlemen. Thanks for the seat. Lunch looks and smells delicious."

Wylie shoved in a mouthful of chicken drenched in gravy, chomped loudly for a few seconds, and then wiped the dribble from his chin. "I tell ya, Jimmy. The Magnolia got some of the finest cooks around town! They keep feeding me like this and I'll be as big as a house by Christmas. I surely will."

Out of the corner of his eye, Jimmy watched Seth take a tentative bite of green beans, a frown of worry across his brow. "Keep shovelin' it in like that, Wylie, and you will have to have another go under the knife. I can hear your arteries hardenin' from over here. You need to stick with greens and beans. More roughage. Keeps things flowin' just right."

Wylie waved his fork in the air with a dismissive flick. "I ain't gonna spend my remainin' years on this planet festerin' and worryin' about how I live. What fun is there in that? It's not like anythin' I do at this point will change the fact that I'm gonna die. We *all* are, Seth. Between the two of us, who do you think will have the most regrets? I'll give ya a hint—it ain't gonna be me."

Seth huffed. "I have no regrets. And I plan on livin' on way past one hundred. Why, I've got the liver of a teenager and the eyes of a jungle cat! And that's because..."

"*I ain't never touched a drop of the devil's brew,*" Wylie said, mimicking the mantra Seth had repeated so many times, even Jimmy had lost count. "Yes, we *know*, Seth. And all your borin', I mean, *careful* livin', still stuck you with no good lungs and heart. *They* are already over the one-hundred mark."

Jimmy watched the interaction between the two friends and sensed things were about to get ugly, so he intervened. "You boys coming to painting class today? I brought some new brushes and colors. Thought we could work on the flower stills from last week. Not a cloud in the sky today, so the bright sunlight will fill up the art room with perfect light."

Just as Seth and Wylie were about to answer, he watched their expressions change as they stared behind him. Jimmy felt a warm hand on his back. Before he could turn around, Carmella

D'Nucci poked her head over his shoulder and grabbed Seth's glass of tea before it toppled off the table top.

"Afternoon, gentlemen. Glad to see you all eat so healthy. Mr. Thomas, Mr. Wilson, how are you all feeling today?" Jimmy scooted his plate over as Carmella wrangled herself into the seat next to him and propped her elbows on the table. She gave him a bright smile and said, "Mr. Calhoun. I see you are getting fueled up for class today. What's on the paint palette today?"

Wylie let out a low whistle. "Ms. Carmella, if I were just twenty years younger, I'd make a play for you. I surely would. You're just about the prettiest gal I've seen in years, except for my Irma, God rest her soul."

"Wylie! What a thing to say. Mind your manners," Seth grumbled.

Wylie shot back. "Get your jockey's out of their twist, Seth. Ms. Carmella knows I'm only joshin' her. Besides, the gal needs a laugh, after all she's been through. Gotta say, I'm surprised to see ya here today, Ms. Carmella. We all figured you'd be out for a while, considerin' everythin'. Laughter is always the best medicine, ain't that right, Ms. Carmella?"

The look of amusement mixed with pain

glinted in Carmella's deep brown eyes. Tears shimmered behind them, and she blinked them back before they spilled out. Jimmy was surprised to see her back at work so soon after the murder of her son, Ray-Ray. She shot a quick look at Jimmy. He could tell she was hiding her pain from her charges. She winked at him. "Oh, now Seth. Don't let ol' Wylie get your goat. I appreciate his humor. Honestly, if one more person asks me how I'm doing, I'll explode. I'm taking things minute by minute. Wylie, your playful spark is definitely back, which I'm thrilled to see. Now, if I could just get you to transfer some of that energy into keeping your apartment clean, I wouldn't have to spend so much time there. Although, right now, anything to keep my mind off...well, it's just a welcome distraction."

Wylie roared with laughter. "Honey, I don't clean my apartment because that's women's work. Never cleared one dust bunny or washed a load of laundry when my Irma was alive, and I'm too old to start new traditions. Besides, that's all part and parcel of the monthly fees I pay, am I right? I mean, come on! What kind of fool would I be if I didn't have a fine young thing like you around, keepin' my livin' quarters straight?

I may be old, but I ain't stupid. And, I'm more than willin' to keep you distracted as long as you need! But, I promise to behave and show proper respect at your son's service. Saturday, right?"

Jimmy nearly choked on his mouthful of food. Carmella let loose a tinkling giggle and smiled. Seth turned three shades of red from embarrassment. Once Carmella finished laughing, she lowered her voice and motioned to her left with a slight nod of her head. "Yes, Saturday at three. Now, enough about me. Either of you make any headway with Mr. Pickard?"

Wylie answered. "Nah, he still keeps us all at arm's length. Tried to get him to play a game of checkers yesterday, but he acted like he couldn't hear me, which I know he can. He just don't seem to have adjusted to bein' here yet. Old coot just wanders around here like an ol' zombie, never smilin' or talkin' to anyone, except when his friend comes by. Even then, he don't say much. His buddy does most of the yappin'. Ol' Pickard mostly listens."

Seth nodded in agreement. "We asked him if he'd like to join us for lunch today, and he didn't even have the courtesy to respond. Just kept on shufflin' over to his favorite spot, sat down, and stared out the window. Haven't even seen him take a bite from his plate. His food is probably cold by now."

Carmella bristled and got up from the chair. She leaned over and gave Wylie's shoulders a warm squeeze. "Well, boys, it's been fun, but I guess I best go check on him. Can't have my charges not eating, least not on my watch. You stay out of trouble, Wylie. Keep an eye on him, Seth. Good seeing you again, Mr. Calhoun. And Wylie? Thanks for making me smile today."

In a few quick strides, Carmella was across the room, talking to Mr. Pickard. The three men watched her sashay away, the thin scrubs revealing a firm, round rump. Under his breath, Wylie mumbled, "Lawd-a-mercy, can't those twenty years disappear?" and then went back to the business of eating.

Jimmy watched Carmella try to have a conversation with Mr. Pickard. Even from across the room, he could tell it was one-sided. He took one last, small nibble of his lunch, washed it down with a long gulp of water, and stood. "I'm off to set up for class. Thanks for the company, gentlemen. Don't be late."

"Say, Jimmy, when we gonna get us a real live model as a muss?" Wylie asked.

"It's *muse*, you ignorant redneck," Seth corrected.

Jimmy wondered how in the world the two men ever became friends. Seth wielded his perceived intellect like a sword, and Wylie was just an old, retired blue collar worker, who happened to luck into a trade that made him quite wealthy–land excavation. The years of being outside, under the burning rays of the unforgiving sun, had turned the man's skin to a crisp, wrinkled brown. Wylie almost looked like an overcooked Thanksgiving turkey. The sun's rays also seemed to burn away the sections of his brain where tact and manners resided.

Wylie ignored the jab and continued. "I'm sorta tired of lookin' at borin' fruit. Hey, I know! You should call the college and ask if an art student wants to make her some quick cash as a *muse*. I'd surely pay good money to stare at a young, naked honey a few hours each week. With that kind of inspiration, I might just become the next Donatello."

"You mean Michelangelo. Donatello was a sculptor, you old fool. Your debauchery and ignorance have no bounds, do they? Makin' googly-eyes with a woman young enough to be your daughter, on the heels of losin' her only son, then turnin' right around and askin' to paint a naked woman! Why am I friends with you?" Seth moaned.

"Well, whichever! Stop interruptin' me, Seth! That's just plain bad manners. And you call *me* the ignorant redneck! Besides, it don't rightly matter none which *ello* I meant. Art is art, right? God didn't make any finer piece of work on earth than a naked woman. I told you, Seth. I will have *no* regrets when I leave this world. You stick with me because secretly, you don't want any either. You're just too proper to admit it."

The conversation between the two old men ignited into a verbal disaster zone. Jimmy walked away, shaking his head at the geezers. In all the years he'd known them, he had never witnessed civility last for more than an hour. He gave a quick glance over to where Mr. Pickard sat and noticed Carmella was nowhere in sight. Mr. Pickard's friend had joined him, along with two other women. Jimmy recognized one as the wife of the friend, but the other was a new face. A lovely, fresh face. He paused and stared at the tanned beauty. Long, blonde hair with wisps of gray framed her cherubic face, cascading down past her slender shoulders. Bright, green eyes sparkled and a wide smile graced her face.

Mesmerized, Jimmy watched as she leaned down and gave Mr. Pickard a warm embrace, and then sat down next to him.

He immediately saw the familial resemblance and knew the woman was at least related to Cecil's friend, Mr. Tuck. Daughter, probably, guessing by her age. Jimmy's old ticker doubled its pace, and a surge of excitement moved in his stomach. The happy flip-flop he hadn't felt in years spread through him. A mixture of emotions tumbled inside him. Jimmy fought the sense of guilt at the lustful thoughts running amok in his mind, ones he hadn't experienced since his wife was alive. It wasn't like he didn't take time to admire the opposite sex on occasion. After all, he did teach art. Though he was supposed to go upstairs and prepare for painting class, something about the woman drew him to her, so he made his way across the room to introduce himself, a stupid grin plastered on his face.

11

MENDING BROKEN
FENCES

Karina wiped a bead of sweat from her forehead, immediately regretting the action. The dampness on her skin was replaced by a streak of white paint from her dirty fingers. The urge to sneeze, again, welled up inside her. She buried her swollen nose in the crook of her arm, unwilling to let another one escape.

Under her breath, Karina cursed her body's response to the Arkansas air. The minute she stepped outside and cranked up the mower, her nose rebelled. Violently. So did her eyes. Her contacts didn't stand a chance at the constant outpouring of tears. Karina was forced to take them out and wear her glasses while she worked outside.

The restoration of parts of the dilapidated fence and mowing down the high grass in the front yard had been her project for the past hour. Karina needed the physical release after the voicemail she'd listened to earlier. It was a good thing her phone had been on silent and she missed the live call. Her mother's fears about Gram and Grampa hearing her dock-worker mouth in full, foul swing, would have come to fruition.

The second she heard the familiar voice of Misty, softly begging for forgiveness, whining for a chance to talk, lamenting the fact that Karina moved away without a chance to hammer things out, her anger skyrocketed. Went right through the stratosphere. It was not the way she wanted her morning to start off. What she really wanted to do was load her gun, traipse off into the woods, find a sturdy tree, tack up a picture of Misty, and blow it to Hell. While screaming the lyrics to her favorite metal song about hating someone at the top of her lungs. Good, old fashioned, blow-shit-to-smithereens therapy.

Instead, Karina begged off going with the rest of the family to visit Grampa's friend, Cecil Pickard. Smashing nails with a hammer would help rid her of the rage, and keep her out of trouble. Plus, she just wasn't ready to walk into any type of senior center, even an independent living one like The Magnolia. It would just bring back too many unwanted memories.

If Karina saw any hint of mistreatment or shoddy care, she wasn't entirely sure she would be able to stop herself from storming into the office of the owners. She didn't want her grandparents to see her fly into a rage, so, Karina decided not to go. With a promise made for next week, she told her disappointed Grampa he'd have a surprise waiting when he returned.

Sneeze averted, Karina scanned the yard and, despite the heat, bug bites, and filth, smiled. She'd made decent progress and was quite proud of her handiwork, even though she'd probably lost ten pounds from sweating. Another two or three from all the damned vampire-like bugs feasting on her blood. To her right, she saw the broken sections of the fence on the ground and her smile disappeared. They'd require more than just a coat of paint, or hammer and nails. A trip to the local lawn and garden store would be necessary, so she could buy some wood to replace the bug-infested pieces. Plus, she needed to buy more paint. The lone gallon of white exterior was almost empty, and Grampa didn't have anymore, at least she didn't find any in the barn or garage earlier.

Looking down at her clothes, which probably held about a quarter of the gallon, and then at her watch, she groaned. Gram said they would be out for about three hours, and Karina wanted to finish the job before they returned. Show them how handy the city girl was in the country. What a cosmic joke. If they could see her now, with more paint on her clothes than on the fence, her left thumb swollen and bleeding after smacking it twice with the hammer, she'd never live it down.

There was no way she'd get in her car covered in white paint, grass flecks, and sweat. She would have to go change out of her soaked t-shirt and jean shorts. Put on a pair of shoes without the strange, greenish sheen from freshly mowed grass.

Idiot. She ruined a perfectly good pair of running shoes. Karina made a mental note to buy a pair of work boots while out. A final glance around the yard made her heart clench. So much needed to be done to restore the place to at least how she remembered it. The barn needed to be torn down and rebuilt. Trying to salvage it would be a waste of time.

Grampa once told her when she was around ten that *his* grandfather was just a little tyke when it was originally built. Karina did a quick mental calculation. It meant the structure was nearly two-hundred years old. If the wood had ever sported a color, she couldn't tell. The roof sagged, the front doors didn't close, and the smells inside were awful.

Karina had run in and then right back out, when she was scrounging for paint supplies earlier. Thoughts of snakes, spiders, and bats, or the roof collapsing, filled her mind, and she had to fight the urge to say fuck it and pick another project to work on.

A light breeze rustled through the oak trees, bending the tips of the tall grass in the uncared for field. Grampa's tractor sat in the middle of the field, the overgrown grass touching the tops of the tires. The once vibrant green and yellow machine she used to love riding shotgun on when Grampa worked, had a strange, orange tint to it. Rust. Tons of it. Karina wondered how long it had been sitting in the same spot.

Karina closed her eyes and took a deep, cleansing breath. The sweet scents of wild honeysuckle and magnolia blooms soothed her sore nasal passages. Her mind recognized the aroma and the smell immediately showered her mind with visions of childhood. The odors may have been the same, but the sounds around her sure weren't. No mooing cows in the pasture. No soft whinnies from Firestorm or the other horses. The only sound leftover from her memories was the clucking of the chickens, and even that wasn't very loud. Karina counted only ten on her way to the barn earlier. For some reason, maybe just the distorted recollections of her younger mind, she seemed to recall at least a hundred or so pecking around in the yard. Everything had changed. A deep sense of sadness made her chest feel heavy.

Karina shook her head to rid herself of the trip down memory lane, and her current foul mood. She felt out of sorts. Off. Not in sync. It wasn't just from the heat or allergies, or the voicemail from Misty. Though her previous job wasn't exactly a daily repetition of the one before, it felt strange not having a one to go to. For a moment,

Karina wondered if the feeling, the sense of imbalance, was what retirees went through once they said goodbye to their work life. With no set schedule, no concrete plans for the day, the feeling of being lost in a dark forest sort of crept in.

No, she wasn't going to let all this emotional bullshit get to her. There were other, important things to focus on. Projects like mending the fence, taking care of things Gram and Grampa couldn't any longer, were exactly the reasons the decision to move were made.

Once the place was up to par, all sparkly and shiny, she'd work in tandem with her mom, and convince Gram and Grampa they could take care of a few head of cattle. Maybe a horse or two. Riding the trail down to the creek had always been one of her favorite things to do when she was little, and it hit Karina hard when she realized that wouldn't happen again anytime soon.

While back in L.A., Karina had pictured herself in jeans, cowboy hat, and boots, riding atop her favorite horse, Firestorm, as she corralled a cow from the pasture. Of course, she knew Firestorm had passed last year, but the desire to feel that free again never left her. She'd assumed, mistakenly, Grampa would have bought a new horse. It never occurred to her the barn would be empty when they arrived.

Karina swished the last bit of paint on the brush on the same piece she'd been painting for over ten minutes. The hard labor was supposed to force her to concentrate on the mundane tasks, rather than thinking about her aging grandparents, her pathetic excuse for a friend, or the life she would never live with Cal.

All this mushy, sentimental crap made Karina want to vomit. No, it made her want to shoot or punch something. Or someone. Hard. Rolling around in the mental dumpster filled with reeking emotions wasn't like her.

She was a tough chick, quick tempered and not one to let things get to her. Years on the job had turned her heart to stone. It was a necessary safety valve. Dealing with lowlife criminals on a daily basis would drive a person bat-shit crazy if emotions were allowed to remain at the surface.

But everything changed after she went undercover in the Jubilee senior abuse case. Years of tracking down bail jumpers, catching people on video for one crime or another, working undercover to determine if a boyfriend/ husband was a cheater, hadn't prepared

Karina mentally for what awaited to shock her sense of compassion in the senior housing industry.

Everyone, including the toughest hardheads, had a soft spot. An Achilles heel. Cal's was his love of animals. God help the hapless soul who harmed a furry creature in the presence of Calvin Benson. He was always bringing a fluff ball of some sort home to take care of until he found it a good home. A malnourished cat. Sick hamster. Starving puppies. When he brought home Ranger, a wormy, half-starved bedraggled knot of fur, Karina didn't give the creature twenty-four hours to live. But, Ranger proved her wrong, and to her and Cal's surprise, bonded with her instead of him.

Her mom's cause was abused women. The only time Sgt. LiAnn Tuck had ever been reprimanded at work and given "forced vacation days" happened when accidental bumps and bruises showed up on a few of the men arrested for beating the shit out of their wives.

Karina's was the elderly, and the reason she never became a cop, as planned. Six weeks before she was to head to the academy, she nearly beat a man to death after witnessing him roll a homeless old man–all caught on video by a surveillance camera across the street.

Hopes of following in the footsteps of her mother ended, and pushed Karina in the path of Calvin Benson. She met him while attending the court-ordered anger management classes that kept her out of jail. After listening to each other's stories, they became an item, and eventually, business partners. Cal's temper got him kicked off the force, but his burning desire to catch the dregs of society hadn't diminished. Neither had Karina's. So, they combined their skills and started We've Got Ya!

Karina adored the elderly, and watching them in pain or being neglected struck a nerve. A very sensitive and volatile one. Maybe it was because she was so close to her own grandparents. Or maybe it was because she could sense the loneliness so many of them wore like an accessory. No more children to raise, no more work to attend to, and loss of mental and physical strength as the end drew closer. The sensation of feeling useless, no longer needed, a burden on their families. Heartache at being forced to watch loved ones pass on. Bodies that no longer functioned as they had in their prime, forcing them to rely on others to help them complete the daily tasks of living. The look of life sparking in their eyes when the doors would open, the hope of one of their loved ones coming for a visit, shining like a beacon on their faces. Then, the shattered torment of realizing the visitor was for someone else, and another day would pass. Alone. The vulnerability of the aged as technology overtook the world, leaving them lost and confused. Diminished mental acuity made them easy targets for criminals. And the senior housing sector of the world, at least the ones she'd worked undercover at, took full advantage of their trapped quarry. The more emotional upheavals Karina witnessed, the more her shields cracked, until they crumpled to the ground.

While undercover, the emotions Karina had to keep in check daily, began to wear on her nerves. All her strength was concentrated on keeping her mouth shut as she witnessed so many unspeakable things. It was completely against her character, and fighting the urge to kick the shit out of several staff members at various locations, took a toll on her mental state. Prior to the assignment, Karina never really took stock of her life. At least not from an emotional viewpoint. Things just...were. She owned a successful business, lived in a nice apartment right by the beach, drove a great car, a gorgeous hunk of man to keep her warm at night, and a family who loved her. That was enough. But, as she tried to sleep at night in the unfamiliar places while undercover, her mental walls began to crack from the stress. She found herself thinking about her future. One she wanted to include Calvin Benson as her other half.

A life she had secretly hoped to lead with him. His touch. His smell. The way his hooded eyes looked at her when his passion was in full swing. Umm, the sensation of his strong hands as they moved over her body, poking, prodding, stroking. The sound of his deep, throaty laughter when something amused him. The way he whispered "I love you" in her ear, or mumbled her name at the peak of ecstasy when in bed.

No, no, no! Shrugging her shoulders, Karina brushed the feelings off her, like they were unwelcome pests. There were too many things that needed to be done around the farm, and no time to ruminate about her old life. After all, what did she have to complain about, really? She had a bank account full of enough cash to last her at least five years while she figured out what her next career move would be. Dragula was paid for, she was healthy (except for her newly discovered allergies) and she was surrounded by a loving family. Karina Ruby Summers didn't need a man to make her life whole, or so her mind told her. She wasn't some whiny, clingy heroine who needed validation from a man! Karina was a modern woman, raised by *another* modern woman, and took no shit from anyone. Cal ruined everything they had together, and she was not about to waste any more of her time pining for him. No second chances. Period.

Where did the woman with the quick tongue and temper go? The one who got into trouble several times during her youth, especially when her teenage years hit. What happened to the girl who was suspended from school after giving a very loud and expletive-filled opinion to a smarmy math teacher named Mr. Jolly, after a *very* embarrassing stint standing in front of the class, trying to solve a difficult equation?

Oh, yeah, she got old. And sentimental.

The ache inside Karina's heart wasn't listening to her catty mind. Neither her internal baby alarm. The incessant buzzing late at night, the warning her eggs were close to drying up, was about to drive her looney. It was the oddest thing. When she had been with Cal, who never, *ever*, wanted children, no bells rang in her head. But, that had changed the minute their relationship ended.

Karina thought about it for a moment while she stared out across the overgrown hayfield. Did she really want a child? Or was the craving for one just her mind's way of transferring her painful emotions about Cal to something else? On instinct, Karina's hand moved across her taut, slender belly. No. Her longing for a child had just been sitting on the backburner because she secretly hoped once she and Cal married, he would change his mind about children.

Stop it, girl. Just...stop it. She put the brush back inside the empty can, wiped a straggler tear away, and started toward the front porch. In a fit of anger, she spun back around and kicked the empty paint can halfway across the yard, sending the brush in one direction, the metal container in another. Satisfied with herself, she continued to the porch. Swiping at the mosquitoes buzzing around her damp face, she cursed her skin's aversion to bug spray. If she was going to live in such humid state, full of insects big enough to hitch a ride on, she needed to find some sort of repellent that wouldn't turn her skin into blotches of itchy, red patches.

Before she made it to the first step, Ranger jerked his head up from his spot under the swing and growled, followed by a loud bark. Karina followed his gaze out to the driveway, squinting under the sun's vibrant rays.

A lone pickup truck rumbled up the road, and parked next to her car. When the cloud of dust settled, the door opened. Taking the steps two at a time, she grabbed Ranger by his collar before he took off to greet the intruder with a wet nose to the crotch. When she glanced back up, Karina was surprised to see who came for a visit.

"Ranger, inside!" The big dog hesitated, determined to stand guard. "Ranger! *Geh rein!*" Karina opened the front door and he scooted inside, his low growl reverberating through him. "*So ist brav, Ranger. Bleib,*" she cooed, and then shut the door. Her beloved dog was stubborn when it came to strangers, but he always listened when Karina gave him commands in German.

"Afternoon, Ms. Karina. Looks like you've been busy today. Gotta ask, did you just talk to your dog in another language?"

On instinct, her fingers flew to her disheveled

hair. Karina grimaced, knowing she just added some new white streaks to it. The images of her head looking like a skunk sped by. "Aren't you the observant one? Yes, it was German and, I lost my fight with the paint. So, what brings you by, um, Bryce, isn't it?"

"Wrong brother. I'm Bo," he drawled.

Karina's tongue went dry. She was a sucker for the sexy dialect, especially coming from the mouth of the young stud in front of her. "Oh, sorry. Huh, I bet that's never happened before. Okay, so, Bo, what brings you by? Did you leave something here the other day? I know it isn't about the invoice. We already paid for the move."

"No, ma'am. My visit today ain't got nothin' to do with unloadin' your belongin's."

Karina watched a sexy smile appear on his full lips. Wisps of his blond hair poked out from under his Stetson, curling up around his ears. His white shirt looked three sizes too small, and about ready to bust apart from the strain of his ripped muscles underneath it. Bo turned and reached inside his truck to grab something. Though she tried not to stare, Karina couldn't take her eyes off his perfectly shaped ass, clad in stone-washed denim. *Yeow, but it's hot down South.*

While his back was to her, Karina tried, but failed to smooth out the wrinkles in her damp, cotton shirt. Heat jutted up from her chest to her face when she remembered she wasn't wearing a bra. Karina was commando – without makeup, a nose brighter than Rudolph's, and eyes swollen and puffy. She was sort of surprised the boy didn't grimace when he walked up.

"Uh, I was just about to leave. Need to get some more paint. What..." her words trailed off when Bo turned back around. He held a gallon of white, exterior enamel at the end of his strong fingers.

"Couldn't help but overhear you talkin' to your grandpa about paintin' the fence the other day. Thought you might need some help. You don't exactly look like the type who's ever painted one before. Actually, you look more like you should be on the cover of a magazine or somethin'. Or, in one of those commercials on TV about comin' for a visit to California."

Karina bristled. "Nice enough, and though I appreciate the thought, and the fake compliment, I don't need any help. I am perfectly capable of fixing things on my own. And, as I mentioned, I was just about to leave.

Got some other things besides paint I need to buy. So, thank you for the gift, but..."

Without a word, Bo ignored her protests and sauntered to the back of his truck, hefting a stack of fence spindles from the bed. As he walked back toward Karina, his grin was even wider. "Gotcha covered, ma'am."

Karina recognized the glow of interest on his face, immediately feeling her cheeks burn. The man, no, the *boy*, didn't come to just show some southern hospitality to a new resident. The kid was *interested* in her, which she found amusing and annoying at the same time. He couldn't be more than twenty-three. Way, way too young for her. Karina wasn't quite ready to add the title of cougar to her long list of others just yet. Bo was barely above jailbait age. She started to protest, to spit out something rude and negative that would send the boy packing, but Karina's entire body froze when he stopped less than two feet in front of her.

His bright, blue eyes swept over her with such intensity, she could almost feel the heat of their caresses. Karina's pulse quickened. Bo tossed the wood to his right, set the paint can down, and took his hat off. In one swift, probably well-practiced move, his t-shirt disappeared. Karina had to bite her lip to keep from gasping at the sight of his toned, tanned physique.

Holy. Shit. I'm in sooo much trouble. He's the one who should be on a cover. Playgirl, to be exact. The boy is so gorgeous, he could sell cigarettes to the Surgeon General.

His smoldering stare lingered on her breasts before moving to her swollen thumb. "I see the hammer won the last battle," Bo said, bending down to scoop up the tool to Karina's right. He slid his hat back on and moved closer, clasping her uninjured hand with his rough, calloused fingers. "Let me show y'all how to play with country toys without gettin' hurt. Easy enough. Just follow my lead. I promise, I'm a good teacher. Had *lots* of practice over the years."

Karina should have told him to go home and play with toys more age appropriate, like a *Tonka* set. Should have mentioned she had a black belt in Jujitsu, and could take his lofty ego down a few pegs with only one or two swift moves. Given him an earful about this being the twenty-first century, and to leave behind his ancient social misconceptions about women. Or, maybe Karina should have challenged him to take his gun out of his truck, which she had no doubts he had, and see which one of them was a better shot. Wipe the confident smirk, the southern boy swagger, away from his beautiful face after she schooled him at target shooting. Let him damn well know she wasn't some airheaded beach bunny whose only interests in life centered on shopping and achieving the perfect tan.

Instead, Karina let his charms snake right through her and attach themselves to her hidden libido. He was so close, she could smell his cologne, and the faint scent of cinnamon on his breath. The strength in his fingers sent chills up her spine, the image of them touching every part of her slammed into her mind. She tried to clear her head and think of some smartass retort, but came up with shit. *If he can wield this much power over me with most of his clothes on...oh, boy. Things just got really interesting.*

Thoughts of what's-his-name disappeared with just one, thousand-watt grin from the hunk in front of her. With a coy smirk, she took her hand out of his, flicked the tip of his Stetson and replied, "Bo, you just opened up a can I'm not entirely sure you can handle."

Bo's laughter was rich, deep and throaty. He scooped up the paint can and motioned for Karina to lead the way. As they walked toward the fence, he replied, "There ain't nothin' I can't handle," and then began to hum the song *California Girls*.

I'm in such trouble.

12

DEEP INSIDE THE INDUSTRY

Nick Shonnert sat in his car and waited in silence in the long line at the bank. He grimaced after looking at the clock on the dashboard–11:30. There were six cars ahead of him, and they hadn't moved in over five minutes. He glanced back toward the front door and saw just as many people standing inside as he did outside, mostly elderly. It dawned on Nick what day it was—retiree payday from the good ol' U.S. Government. Great. Freaking great.

Though it was well over one-hundred degrees outside, the interior of his Lexus finally cooled down enough his ass didn't feel like it was on fire. But that really didn't matter to Nick at the moment. Not only did he have personal business to attend to, but he couldn't stand being on property at Green Pastures any second longer, terrified of a visit from Carmella. While he waited for his turn in line to get the cash for Sabrina's tuition, Nick let his freaked-out mind wander to just *how* he wound up in such a screwed-up nightmare.

Nick had never been proficient in athletics due to his myopic eyesight and lack of body coordination, though he surely had the desire to be the next big-name ball player. After his father died of cancer when he was just four-years old, his mother remarried a burly contractor, William Olsen. Their stepfather/stepson relationship was rocky at best, and Nick never felt the need to bestow a title to the gruff man that in any way tied to a parental figure. Nick always called him simply Olsen.

Olsen tried to teach him the joys of hunting, fishing and football. When each of those activities failed, Olsen took a different tactic. He tried to get Nick interested in construction. It was "in a man's nature to build" was Olsen's favorite saying. Nick still had a small scar on his knee from a fun-filled day at a construction site, after Olsen drug him to work. At seven, Nick was still terrified of heights, and when Olsen insisted he climb up the ladder behind him to work on the roof of a house, the day ended on a sour note. Nick fell after only making it up four rungs on the ladder. He lost his balance and landed on hot blacktop. Olsen grumbled and whined the entire drive to the hospital, and only took Nick because a co-worker insisted the gash needed stitches.

All Olsen's attempts to turn Nick into a "manly-man" were to no avail. Nick was never considered more than a puny wimp, gifted only with an unusual affinity for mathematics. He knew it was Olsen's view of him, for it had been one of his favorite go-to expressions when drunk.

During the first few years of marriage, Nick

watched Olsen struggle to provide for his new family. Nick's mother, Marjorie, did her best to keep a clean house, extend the life of their clothes with countless patches, and fix meals they could eat without choking on. When Nick complained about his outfits or the bland meals, his mother reminded him once his stepfather finished night school, things would improve. She told Nick so many times he lost count about how he should be proud of the fact his stepfather was going to school for free, courtesy of the GI Bill he earned while serving in the Second World War. A big smile would appear on his mother's face as she gabbed about how wonderful life would be, once her husband finally obtained his contractor's license.

When Olsen did get his license, he lucked into a primo job: construction superintendent for John Flynt, owner of B & I Construction. According to a conversation Nick overheard his mother having one day with his grandmother, John Flynt had a reputation as a stern businessman with a quick temper. He was the kind of man who would sell his own house if the right price was offered. Nick's mother balked at first when Olsen took the job, since her new husband was cut from the exact same cloth. She worried the two, strong-willed men would butt heads. It didn't take too long for her worries to disappear.

Olsen kept telling his little family he just *knew* Flynt wanted him to take over the business when he was ready to retire. Said he felt like the old man was grooming him, since both of Flynt's two young daughters were "air-headed dimwits." Olsen had a habit of crashing at night in front of the television, usually with a beer in his hand, after a long day working with his hands. Nick's mom would gush and coo, telling Nick they would never eat like paupers again. And soon, very soon, their clothes would come from fine department stores, not the local Goodwill.

Sure enough, everything changed the night when Olsen stumbled home, drunker than ever. Olsen rolled around on the couch, a big, stupid grin on his face, and told his embarrassed wife and shocked stepson about his crazy evening.

"Me, Flynt and Darryl Johns, you know, Flynt's accountant, stopped by like we always do for a few shots of Jack Daniels at The Red Dog Saloon. Darryl and Flynt were busy yappin', so I didn't pay much attention, until I saw this crazy look on Flynt's face. It was like he was sucked in to the words Darryl was sayin'. So, I perked my own ears up. The topic on the table was gettin' into a ground floor business venture created by the U.S. government. Darryl called it affordable housing for senior citizens. Said it was somethin' different than the standard nursin' home."

While fixing him a stout cup of coffee, Marjorie asked, "I don't understand. What does that have to do with Flynt's construction business? Or you, for that matter?"

Olsen laughed and nearly fell out of the chair. He pulled a small notepad from his pocket. "Woman, I ain't done with my story yet. I was so confused at first myself, I took notes. Let's see, oh, yeah, Darryl said..."

Nick had gone to bed, rather than listening to Olsen drone on. But as things changed in the Olsen household and the money poured in, Nick decided to investigate this new business venture his stepfather was immersed in. He spent hours researching in the school library. He discovered in 1965, the government started Medicare and Medicaid. The U.S. Department of Aging had created a division called Operation Medicare Alert, which employed teams of older Americans to inform isolated elders about the new financial benefits available to them.

In 1969, President Richard Nixon's

administration began the Supplemental Security Income program, which was geared to augment a senior's finances when they reached the age of sixty-five. Senior men and women had a financial windfall to add to their savings to assist them to live more comfortably as they aged. When one added in the military benefits provided to soldiers and their spouses or widows, those additional funds enhanced their financial portfolio in their retirement years.

The more Nick studied, the more excited he became. As a numbers freak, he could see the potential for making a killing. He understood why Flynt's business was booming. Their business concept of providing housing for seniors who were no longer able to physically maintain the interior and exterior of their homes was pure genius. Retirement communities, rental housing complexes designed for older adults who were generally able to care for themselves, were beginning to sprout up all over America, and Flynt wanted to get in on the ground floor. The communities provided three meals per day, housekeeping services, activities and socialization opportunities. If a senior needed additional assistance, they could enlist help from a home care agency, at an additional cost.

Even as a teenager, Nick drooled about the revenue generated by senior communities. Everything from developing the home care services business from top to bottom, all *a la carte*, so the resident did not need to relocate to a nursing home, was a cash cow. He was fascinated by the statistics of projected need by senior citizens for such an alternative living option. Offering those services, as well as financial projections of owning the land and constructing the property oneself, would be a business goldmine.

For everyone associated with B & I Construction, it was like winning the lottery.

Olsen was in charge of all the construction aspects at first, since he really didn't understand all the intricate details. When Nick approached Olsen and told him he'd like to help, at first Olsen laughed, reminding him of the ladder fiasco. However, when Nick sat down with him and showed him all his mathematical calculations, things changed. That moment at the kitchen table changed the relationship dynamic between stepfather and stepson. Olsen was impressed by the crafty ways Nick found to make even more money, and smiled. He'd slapped Nick's back with a hardy wallop, and said, "The country keeps producing people over sixty-five faster and faster each year! It's an unending supply of cash walking onto our properties!"

For the remainder of Nick's childhood, thankfully, he didn't see much of his stepfather. The man was constantly traveling, overseeing the construction of new communities. Olsen was consumed with making money. He spent nearly two years straight in Oregon, which nearly caused Nick's mom to go out of her mind. When Olsen did fly home for a weekend or call during the week, Nick overheard their conversations. Olsen would remind Marjorie that Flynt owned a number of pieces of undeveloped land throughout the State of Oregon, and they were working hard to follow all the building criteria and licensing regulations required. If they didn't dot every *I* and cross all their *T's*, all the hard work would be for nothing. Marjorie's worries ended when Olsen started sending large sums of money home.

When home, Olsen strutted around like a proud peacock, bragging about the fact there wasn't another developer in Oregon considering taking on such a new and untried business venture. What he was working on was groundbreaking, and once the kinks and bugs were worked out in Oregon, could easily be repeated anywhere.

While Nick was in college, things almost blew up when John Flynt found out he was dying. Years of inhaling unfiltered cigarettes and dust from his construction job sites had taken their toll on his body. The first three communities in Oregon were up and running, and four more were in development in Arkansas and three in Texas. But Flynt's failing health wouldn't allow him to travel any longer, and the medication he was on screwed up his mental state. He sold the properties in Oregon to Jubilee Retirement for a shitload of cash. At the age of fifty-nine, John Flynt handed the keys to his construction company over to William Olsen, and gave him fifty-percent ownership in the company he formed to run the properties, Happy Days Retirement, Inc.

From 1980 to 1999, when they constructed their 100th retirement property in the U.S., business didn't just boom, it ka-boomed. Nick graduated college with a degree in finance in the mid-80s, so Olsen brought him on board as

COO. Nick's financial maneuvering pushed the business ethics to the red line, but took Happy Days Retirement, Inc., to the level of a multi-billion dollar institution.

However, Nick considered himself woefully under-appreciated and compensated. Plus, he couldn't stand the way his stepfather treated him around the other employees. After all, the cash rolled in by the truckloads because of *his* financial finagling, not Olsen's. One day at work, a new plan formed. The other fifty-percent of the company was owned by Teri Flynt. Her sister had died in a car accident several years before, leaving the shy, introverted woman with long, brown hair and a bland face, and not much in the brain department, in charge of half of the company. Teri Flynt never balked or questioned the decisions made by Olsen or Nick. She only came to the office once a month to pick up her check.

The light bulb went off when Nick caught her looking at him in a way she never had before. When it dawned on him Teri was attracted to him, Nick pounced. It was the ultimate career move. He'd wine and dine the woman until she agreed to marry him, and when Olsen died, they would own one-hundred percent of the company. Though hatched through deceit and for a completely different reason, while Nick courted and wooed Teri, he surprised himself when he fell in love with her. It took two years, but when they finally walked down the aisle, Nick was the happiest man on earth.

His life changed, for a while, when Olsen died. For a few years, Nick enjoyed being the big man at Happy Days. Teri stayed home with the kids, and he had the freedom to run the company as he deemed fit. Of course, it didn't last long, all because of one, ill-fated trip to Illinois.

Oh, if I could just go back to one moment in time and not make that trip to Chicago...

Things went from horrible to downright unlivable not long after. Being in bed with a mobster was never something Nick could have foreseen. Nick had just been blind and greedy, drooling like a Pavlov dog at the staggering amounts of money Caesar Calvanio had access to—all from "private" investors who wouldn't care about the shady, underhanded dealings conducted by Happy Days. Before he could really grasp what was happening, Caesar Calvanio swooped in and devoured Nick's soul. In one bite.

On top of the nightmare of knowing his ass

was owned by a mobster, business was starting to falter. Not because of the side body parts sector. That arena was booming. When headlines across the nation screamed about a California jury awarding close to twenty-five million dollars to a family of an eighty-seven year old woman abuse victim, things changed. The civil suit followed on the heels of the criminal case, where the owners of Jubilee Retirement were convicted of manslaughter. Jubilee spent millions on a slew of top-notch lawyers on both cases, but it didn't matter. Soon after the verdict, TV stations started showing interviews with family members and former employees of Jubilee with sickening rapidity over every news outlet coast to coast.

The horrifying details of how a lady resident was cruelly neglected by the staff at the senior property outraged listeners. Photos of the large numerous bed sores covering the senior lady's buttocks and back were leaked to the press by one caregiver, who had begged the managers to transport the woman to the hospital. Her request fell on deaf ears and, during her tear-stained interview on *Current State!* she cried, "They actually told me to mind my own damn business. My manager said the company couldn't afford the loss of revenue if she moves out."

Jurors were interviewed by reporters, stating they were shocked and deeply angered by the testimony brought out at trial. They bemoaned the systemic understaffing and a lack of care training. They mentioned how it seemed Jubilee's retention policies were designed to keep heads in the beds, putting profits above the care of their residents. Another juror, a retired teacher, said she, and other jurors, were stunned to learn in the punitive phase of the trial that Jubilee hadn't paid any federal income taxes in three years, despite balance sheets that showed annual revenues climbing to $1.25 billion, profits reaching $116 million and a stock market valuation soaring to $1.34 billion.

Calls for immediate government investigation and new rules governing the senior industry were trumpeted by politicians seeking re-election, as well as senior advocacy groups. These same groups had been warning the states for years of these types of egregious care failures in the larger companies, some who owned hundreds of senior communities. Jubilee's financially aggressive property acquisitions, which totaled in the hundreds of millions of dollars, were spotlighted by the family's attorneys as proof the company was more interested in expanding their empire than providing proper care services to their residents.

Nick rubbed his grumbling stomach at the memory. He read online two weeks ago Jubilee's attorneys filed appeal. The case was a business nightmare of epic proportions for Nick's business. Happy Days Retirement's financials suffered as many of the adult children of his communities immediately relocated their loved ones, and the fall in monthly revenue made his ulcer twitch with painful spasms.

A car horn from behind him brought him out of his funk. Nick pulled forward and struggled to find his voice to request a wire transfer from the impatient teller. Irritated, she informed him he would need to come inside. He groaned.

This day just can't get any worse.

13

LEARNING FROM PAST MISTAKES

"I can't believe you did so much today, sweetie! I wish you woulda told me you planned on bein' outside, though. You've got so many bug bites, it looks like you've got the pox! Next time you are gonna work outside, I'll give you my secret weapon against those nasty bugs: Skin-so-Soft. Works like a charm, keeps your skin smooth, and smells good. Now, hold still while I put this poultice on you."

LiAnn stifled a laugh watching grandmother slather granddaughter's neck, shoulders and arms with the white concoction. It looked like cocaine paste. The look of embarrassment on Karina's face was hysterical.

When the first dollop was applied, Karina wiggled her nose in disgust. "Ugh, that reeks Gram. What's in this magic potion of yours? Skunk oil?"

Ruth smiled as she continued to cover Karina's neck. "Never you mind child. I've gotta teach you to cook before I start sharin' my medical potions with you. Just hold still. In a few minutes, the smell will disappear, and you'll be thankin' me once the itchin' stops."

"Let me see your thumb, honey," Junior interrupted.

With a sheepish look on her face, Karina held up her swollen thumb. She shot LiAnn a look that screamed "help me." LiAnn turned her face away and busied herself with setting the table for dinner before she burst out laughing.

"Ouch!" Karina yelled, jerking her hand back. "I'm...it's okay Grampa. Nothing is broken, I promise. Just split my thumbnail. It'll grow back. I'll just wrap it up and make sure to baby it for a few days."

Junior patted Karina's shoulder. "Honey, I appreciate everythin' you did today and am pleasantly surprised by all the hard work you put in. But I can't bask in the excitement for too long, knowin' you injured yourself in the process. You ain't used to farm work, so let's talk about the best way to tackle the next project *before* you start, okay?"

LiAnn saw red seep into her daughter's cheeks, so she intervened. "You missed an interesting visit today at The Magnolia. The place is simply spectacular. It was like walking back in time. When we toured the gardens, I almost expected to see ladies in long gowns holding umbrellas over their heads as they sipped tea. Don't see architecture like it anymore. There is a three-story staircase made of teak that is breathtaking. Oh, and get this: they even have art lessons every Tuesday and Thursday of each week. Free of charge to non-residents, as long as you bring your own supplies. And the man teaching the class has years of art experience. I know how much you love to paint, so you need to come with us next Tuesday. Did you leave out your painting stuff, or is it in storage?"

Karina faked a smile as she left the table.

"Really? Now there's a first. An art room with a teacher who knows what he's doing? This I've got to see. And yes, my art box is in storage. Got to make a trip there this weekend. I think I left some of Ranger's toys in one of the boxes, too. If I don't retrieve it, he will eat all of our shoes before the end of the week."

Junior let out a snort. "Oh, don't let your ma get you all riled up about it. Yeah, it's a nice place and the room has perfect lightin' to paint by, but that ain't the reason your ma wants to go back. It surely ain't."

"Really?" Karina arched an inquisitive brow. "Oh, do tell, Grampa. I'm tired of being the topic of conversation for my lack of outdoor skills."

"Pop!" LiAnn wrinkled her nose "Seriously? What are you talking about?"

A huge grin spread across Junior's face, followed by a coy wink at Karina. "First day out in public and your ma done found her a suitor. One who's quite enamored with her, too. I believe I overheard lunch plans for next week bein' made before we left."

"Junior, enough!" Ruth exclaimed.

Karina laughed. "Oh, Gram, not even *close* to enough! Mom has a date? Already? Must be the blonde hair and those huge boo..."

LiAnn cut Karina's words off before she finished. "All right, Karina Ruby, that is enough! Pop, I don't have a date with Jimmy! He will just be joining us at lunch on Tuesday with Cecil, and he offered to have Karina and I attend his painting class. That's it! Suitor. Pft!"

"Jimmy? On a first name basis after just one day? I'd say he's a suitor for sure," Karina joked, and then laughed out loud. "Does this Jimmy have a last name, or should I just start calling him Daddy?"

LiAnn slammed the last plate on the table, indicating the topic of discussion needed to be dropped.

Enjoying the banter, Junior said, "Now sugar, don't ya go gettin' all excited about rilin' your ma up about her new love life. That would be like the pot callin' the kettle black."

A red stain spread across Karina's face. "I knew it! I knew it was a set up. It was *your* idea for Bo to come by today, wasn't it? Oh, why didn't you warn me ahead of time? I could have at least put on a bra!"

Junior grinned. He leaned back in his chair, folded his arms over his chest, and then gave his best impression of innocent, puppy dog eyes. "I set up nothin' that wasn't already in motion, sugar. I just answered a few questions posed by an interested party, that's all. No harm, no foul. The boy was already hot on your tail, er, I mean, *trail*. And judgin' by your reaction, I think you sort of like the chase. Besides, he stuck around today, right? Even after seein' ya at your worst? That's a mighty good sign, in my opinion."

Ruth stomped her foot on the floor. "That's enough, all of you! Supper is ready, so Karina, take your dog outside and let's sit down to a nice meal and keep the conversation civil, shall we? Lordy, you three are just too much sometimes! And Junior, we are so havin' us a talk this evenin'. We surely are. That nose of yours needs to stop pokin' around in their lives! They are grown womenfolk, for goodness sake!"

All three of them stared at Ruth, who stood in the middle of the kitchen with a stern look on her face, hands firmly planted on slender hips. Ruth was the sensible one, and not a fan of practical jokes or raunchy talk. Especially during a meal. They all knew she was serious, and not to be trifled with once her mind was made up.

The foot stomp was a warning beacon. LiAnn had seen it so many times during her youth. Karina gave LiAnn a wicked smirk and then whistled for Ranger. In seconds, the big dog was by her side. Karina used her hips to push the screen door open and Ranger bounded outside. Karina followed, and over her shoulder she yelled, "This conversation will be continued later. No way am I letting this go! A suitor. What a riot."

Karina fidgeted in the rocker, trying to find a comfortable position that didn't make her numerous bug bites start itching again. Though she appreciated the effort, once Gram and Grampa retired for the night, she had made a beeline for the shower. She couldn't wait any longer to wash off the smelly mess Gram slathered over her earlier.

As long as she didn't touch the raised red bumps, she would be fine. Once comfortable, Karina took a long pull from her beer and smiled, grateful for the screened-in porch. The last thing she needed was more holes poked in her skin from the freaking little bloodsuckers.

The humid air hung like a heavy, wet drape around her bare shoulders. Karina wondered how long it would take her to acclimate to the drastic change from living in Cali. The cold beer helped keep her hand cool and brain pleasantly fuzzy. It had been a really long day, physically and mentally.

"Want some company, or are you consumed with thoughts about something else? Maybe a certain hunky twin named Bo?"

Karina looked up to find her mom standing in the doorway. Ranger's tail thumped at her feet, followed by a low whine. "Only if you bring another beer. I'm out."

LiAnn smiled and showed off the pair of beer bottles in her hand. She passed one over to Karina, and then eased down in the chair across from her. Ranger yawned, stretched, and then walked across the floor and nudged her leg for a pat on the head.

The five beers Karina already downed loosened her tongue. She blurted out, "Mom, how did you get over what happened between you and Crigger? Or, have you? I mean, oh, well, you know. Like the song says, how do you mend a broken heart?"

Even in the darkness, Karina saw her mother flinch at the question. Part of her felt a twinge of guilt for asking, but the other, bigger part, sensed they both needed to dump out all their old relationship baggage. If new men were in their future, they wouldn't stand a chance of having a normal, healthy connection with another if their minds were still filled with ghosts of the past. It was high time they worked through their collective angst and got on with life.

LiAnn bristled. "Wow. Nice and direct. Little trick you learned from Cal?"

Karina ignored the dig. "You, actually. Remember, I've seen you in action when interviewing someone. No gentle tugs at the bandage. You just rip it right off and get to the heart of the wound. Figured I'd do the same. It's something I've wanted to ask you for years, just never got around to it. Seems like the appropriate time just popped up. I mean, we came here to take care of Gram and Grampa, but I think we both are ready to restart our lives. Right? If there was any hope for our past relationships to be salvaged, one, or both of us, would have stayed in Cali. Am I wrong?" For a few minutes, the sounds of the night and Ranger's breathing were the only things Karina heard.

Finally, LiAnn let out a deep, long sigh. "You

sure you really want to know? I don't think you're going to like it."

"Hey, I already dumped out my sack of shit about Cal on you on the way down here. What happened between you two can't be any worse. I must say, even though it hurt, I do feel better. Besides, you'll feel better once you let it out, because then you can let it go. I think." Karina gestured with the beer bottle. "Oh, I don't know. One minute I hate Cal. The next minute I hate myself for still thinking about him. Guess I must be on the road to recovery, because today with Bo, was the first time in years the pain of our breakup disappeared. For a while. Probably because the boy's incredible six-pack mesmerized me. Sent me into a tizzy is a better description. Ignited a bit of interest in someone else, which is something I haven't felt in a long time, even though it was brief. How's that for some psycho-babble bullshit?"

LiAnn let out a bitter laugh. "On target. So, go on."

"If what Grampa said earlier is true, and there *is* a new suitor on the horizon for you, and maybe for me as well, then the past needs to be dealt with. You have pined over Crigger, and what he did to you, long enough. And I have done the same with Cal. The only way to start fresh is to spit it out, stomp all over it until nothing remains, and start walking toward the future. Agree?"

LiAnn responded after a long sip of beer. "My, my, alcohol makes you quite poetic. Demanding, too."

Softening her voice, Karina leaned forward. "Concerned would be a better word, Mom. You two split up years ago. I was what, eighteen? Nineteen? And you haven't dated anyone since, unless you've been hiding that from me." Karina searched her mother's face for a reaction. None came. "So, I'm right. No one since Crigger. Why, Mom? I know his infidelity hurt you but, was there something else, too? I mean, do I need to go load my gun right now and head back to L.A.? Is that why you never told me what all went down between the two of you? Were you afraid I'd end up in jail or something?"

"If your plan is to make the guilty party pay for our breakup by pointing a gun in their face, you wouldn't need to head back to L.A. The guilty party is right in front of you."

"What...what are you saying, Mom? Crigger cheated on you!"

"I thought my response was quite obvious. Crigger didn't break my heart. I broke his."

"I...I don't understand?"

"We were in a precarious situation. He was my boss. We did a decent job of hiding our relationship from the rest of the department, but if we got married, well, obviously, we couldn't hide that."

Karina interrupted. "True, but one or both of you could have just switched departments."

"Yes, that was discussed. Numerous times. In fact, the night he proposed, he told me he had already put in for a transfer to Vice."

"He *proposed?* As in, asked you to marry him, gave you a ring while down on one knee?" Karina sputtered, eyes bulging from shock. "You never told me *that!*"

"I never told you because I didn't accept. When I said no, our romantic relationship ended. Not because of infidelity. Crigger didn't start his relationship with Caroline until *after* I declined his marriage proposal. And, since they married less than six months later, and everyone assumed it meant he'd been unfaithful, I didn't correct that assumption. It seemed, I don't know, easier to let that be the case, rather than face what the truth really was. For that, I am sorry."

Momentarily at a loss for words, Karina sipped her beer. Crigger *proposed?* And her mother said no? "Good thing I'm sitting down, because you just knocked me for a loop. So, if he wasn't cheating on you with Caroline, why didn't you marry him? Why...did you change your mind, Mom? I *know* you loved him. Saw it in your face, even when he wasn't around! Did you find out something shady about his past?"

LiAnn let out a small snort of derision. "No, honey. No man has ever had a cleaner background than Andrew Crigger. Believe me, I checked."

Karina set down her drink and stood, her steps a tad wobbly as she walked across the floor. Kneeling down, she wiped away the single tear on her mom's cheek. "Why, Mom? Why did you turn him down?"

It took LiAnn several seconds to answer. When she did, her voice cracked with pain. "Because of you, Karina. I turned him down because of you."

Shocked, Karina lost her balance and fell back on her rump. Ranger scooted closer, his wet nose sniffing her to make sure his master was fine. Without really thinking, Karina let her hand pat the dog's giant head, shushing him. "Me? What do you mean, Mom? I wasn't *that* much of a difficult teenager, was I?" Bright green eyes full of fresh tears stared down at her, the look of sadness and regret making Karina's heart pound with grief.

"I...I couldn't risk making the wrong choice again. I screwed up royally the first time with your dad. Figured my man radar was skewed, so I wasn't about to do it again. After the fiasco when you finally met Kurt, all the pain I watched you struggle with...there was no way I'd risk subjecting you to that a second time. I worried constantly about bringing a new man into your life. What if you got attached to him, and then we divorced? I wasn't about to add any more emotional man-baggage on your back. I already loaded it up plenty by choosing wrong the first time."

The words took a while to absorb through Karina's alcohol-soaked mind. The topic of her father was a subject rarely discussed. Karina had only met him once, when she was thirteen. Up until she hit puberty, Karina had no real interest in learning anything about the man whose last name she carried. It wasn't until the first father/daughter dance at school was announced that the nudge to discover her paternal roots began. She'd asked her mom about him, and she remembered the day they went for a long drive up the Pacific Coast Highway, her mother answering all her questions. How they met. What was he like? Why did they divorce? How come he never tried to contact her? When Karina prodded and insisted upon meeting him, she had to wait for six months, since Kurt Summers was still in prison for armed robbery. His music career had tanked, and he turned to a life of crime to feed his addictions.

The one and only meeting had been horrific. Kurt Summers was a hardened criminal. The last ten years spent in and out of jail and drug rehab had turned the man into a jaded, hateful soul. Even though she'd been young, Karina sensed the ugliness in him. She had envisioned a sweet encounter, full of hugs, kisses and promises to be a part of her life. Wanted to hear things like, "Oh, daughter, I've missed you" or "So glad to be a part of your life now" or even "I know I've made mistakes in the past, but for you, I will work on not repeating them."

Stupid, childish dreams of connecting with the father Karina grew up without, who secretly loved her. Instead, the leather-clad, tatted-up biker looked at her with lust, like Karina was a potential date, rather than his offspring. The brief reunion ended with Karina in tears and her mother almost arrested after pulling her gun on Kurt as his hand reached out to cop a feel of his own child's ass. A shudder of disgust slithered up Karina's spine at the awful memory.

She pulled herself back to the present and found her mother staring out across the yard. A thin, silvery ray of moonlight glinted off the tears on her cheeks. Karina's own welled up in her eyes. She had buried the dreadful day deep down inside, refusing to think about the human trash who contributed half of her DNA. Obviously, her mother had not. The worry was embedded so deep for her daughter's safety, she refused to let herself be happy. The sadness of it all, the unbelievable sacrifice made to ensure her only child's safety and happiness, made Karina feel a myriad of emotions. Her fingers shook as she reached out and touched her mom's hand. "Oh, Mom. I...I don't even know what to say, other than I'm so sorry. And, I love you. So much."

The chirps of the katydids and crickets, along with Ranger's gentle whines, faded as they clung to each other on the dark porch. Soon, both of their backs were soaked with tears of regret for what had been, what could have been, and what never would be.

LiAnn whispered into Karina's shoulder, "See, I said you wouldn't like it."

Karina pulled away and looked at her mom. "Well, at least I no longer feel the need to grab my gun and shoot someone, other than myself for being such a rude, gigantic asshole for opening up a bag of awful memories."

A fragile smiled creased the corners of LiAnn's face. "Honey, if all the assholes of the world got shot, there would only be a handful of people leftover."

Ranger tried his best to lick away the tears from Karina's face. She brushed his slobber off her cheek and got up. A twinge of anger made her grit her teeth. Her mother had thrown away an entire lifetime of happiness because of her overprotective nature. All because of some low-life thug. It wasn't fair. Wasn't right. Years gone that could never be reclaimed. A complete, total waste of time and worry. Two hearts broken for nothing. All because of *her*. No way would Karina let that trend continue. Period.

Karina paused at the screen door. "Mom?"

Moist eyes and a tear-stained face looked her way. "Yes, sweetie?"

"Stop. Just stop. I'm not a little girl anymore. Stop trying to protect me from the world, because honestly, you can't. You taught me to be strong, remember? I *am* strong. *You* are strong. Jesus, stronger than even I thought you were. You sacrificed way too much for me. Way too much, and honestly, I don't want to be your reason for ending up all alone in this world. I don't need to be coddled, or for you to spend one more second of your life worrying about me, or how I will react to things. Period. Crigger has been a widower for what, two years now? If things are beyond repair with Crigger, which my guess would be yes, since you two didn't reconnect after his wife passed, then *move on to someone else.* Find someone who makes you happy, like maybe this Jimmy guy. Haven't seen you blush in *years,* like you did when his name was mentioned. And, if it isn't him, and he turns out to be just a fun pastime, as I suspect Bo will be for me, then so be it. But please, promise me you won't walk away from love again because of me. I can't stand the thought."

LiAnn's jaw set with determination. With a

slight nod of agreement, she rose from the chair. "Only on one condition, darling daughter."

A wary smile pulled at Karina's lips. "Anything, except don't ask me to give up my gun."

"Ha! No, the condition is *you* take your own advice and do the same. Fuck Cal Benson."

"Deal," Karina replied, opening the door. They left the porch and walked arm and arm down the hall toward their respective rooms. "Ha, you said fuck. Guess that maturity thing doesn't work all the time, huh?" Karina grinned. "Tomorrow, I want to hear all about Jimmy."

"And I want to hear all about Bo. But fair warning–if you tell me his last name is Duke, I will *never* let you live it down."

Karina stifled a giggle. "Now *that* would be classic, right? Don't worry, his last name is Barton."

LiAnn brushed her lips on Karina's cheek. "Oh, thank goodness. Get some rest, sweetie. See you in the morning. Love you."

"Love you, too, Mom. Nite."

14

THE END OF RAY-RAY

Caesar ignored the sting of the painful memories of Romella's funeral, which hit him like a freight train as he walked up the concrete steps of the church. The same church where the last goodbyes were said to his wife years ago. When Franco and Carmella started making arrangements for Ray-Ray's service, and mentioned they wanted it to be held at St. Michael's, Caesar wanted to protest. Wanted to tell them no way, because he wasn't sure he could handle sitting in the same sanctuary. But, he couldn't. It wouldn't be right to deny his grieving sister and her husband anything during their mourning. After all, Caesar was the one who put them inside every parent's worst nightmare.

Once inside, the haunting sounds of organ music hit him, along with the overwhelming scent of gardenias, Carmella's favorite flower. Every conceivable spot they could fit was covered with the fragrant flowers. He scanned the seats, which only held a few mourners, mostly the elderly patients Carmella cared for, until he saw Franco's bald head. As he walked down the aisle, Caesar saw a few other faces he recognized, but didn't acknowledge them. The one face he assumed wouldn't be in the crowd, wasn't. Nick the Prick didn't have the guts to show up. It was a good thing, too. The sniveling fool was at least smart enough to realize he wouldn't be able to cope with the emotions.

For a split second, Caesar wondered how, if any, interactions between Carmella and Nick had gone during the last few days. He'd lay a cool million down on the bet that Nick had kept his distance from Carmella. As Caesar walked in solemn silence, he wondered if he'd truly made the right decision to involve Nick. At the time, it seemed the perfect way to not only solidify the relationship, but also to ensure Nick would never, ever, consider crossing him. Pull him out of his divorce-funk and back to the tasks at hand. After all, though it could be accomplished, running his business ventures might prove to be difficult without Nick as the middle-man. Caesar wasn't sure if he had it in him to train another stooge.

Caesar was in no mood to be pleasant or talkative. He paused at the pew where Carmella, Franco and Carmine sat, winced as his knees cracked from kneeling down, and absentmindedly gestured the sign of the cross. When finished, Caesar slid in next to his family. Carmella reached over and gave him a stiff hug, and the always stoic Franco simply nodded his head.

None of them said a word to each other as they waited. Everything surrounding the murder of Ray-Ray that needed to be discussed, already had been. The day his death was announced by a somber police detective, Caesar played the dutiful uncle and had Carmine drive him over to their house, sitting and listening while watching them scream and cry. Once the outbursts were over, Caesar offered to take justice out of the hands of the legal system and arrange for the killers to die slow, painful deaths. Franco was all for the idea, but Carmella balked, which had actually surprised him. Out of the pair, Carmella was the hard one, a tough-as-nails broad if ever one had walked the earth. After all, they grew up under the strong heel of the same father. There were no warm fuzzies inside the walls of the Calvanio manse. Only harsh, painful lessons about life, honor, and loyalty. Carmella didn't even shed a tear when her three sisters died on the same day in a car accident. Nor did she show any outward emotion when her mother and father passed not long after. The one and only time Caesar had seen Carmella cry, up until she heard the news about her son, was at the funeral for their grandfather.

So, Caesar had been shocked when Carmella said no to the hit. Instead, she wanted the killers to experience the humiliation of arrest, a very public trial, their dirty laundry broadcast to the entire world. Watch them squirm in front of the judge, knowing they would spend the rest of their lives living like caged animals. Smile with satisfaction at their distraught family members when their sentences were handed down. Of course, after Carmella's valiant little speech, she went back to her spiteful broad roots. Said if the justice system failed to hand out a guilty verdict, she wanted her son's killers brought to her so she could dispatch them.

Within minutes, the service began. As the priest conducted the somber ritual, Caesar fought hard to control his own emotions. The shiny, black casket at the end of the aisle, draped in an enormous spray of gardenias and roses, started to blur, finally disappearing. It was replaced by the ornate, white casket he'd picked out for Romella, and next to it, sat the tiny, pink casket that housed their final, unborn child.

Caesar couldn't stop his hands from shaking, even after clasping them together so tightly, his knuckles throbbed from the pressure. Though he'd grown accustomed to seeing the ghostly figure of his wife appear during the day, almost craved the interaction just so he could see her face, pretend Romella was still alive, it was quite another to be faced with her casket. It was a cold, slap in his grizzled face that she was, in fact, dead. A heaviness of regret and sadness slammed into Caesar's chest.

"You don't deserve to be here, Caesar. Neither does Carmine."

Caesar had to force his body not to jump at

the sound of Romella's gravelly voice. It sounded muffled, distant. All wrong. It wasn't the same sweet, tinkling voice from his dreams. The one his ears yearned to hear from the glorious lips of the woman he'd loved. It was raw, raspy, and full of accusatory anger. Caesar couldn't control the shudder of fear tingling through him when it dawned on him Romella's voice was coming from inside the casket less than twenty feet in front of him. Blood filled his mouth as Caesar clamped down hard on his inner, bottom lip, to keep his groan of agony inside.

Inside his mind, he answered his wife. *"Romella, please. You don't understand. I had to. Ray-Ray's actions put all of us at risk. I had to stick to the code to keep us safe."*

The casket lid made a strange sound as it opened. The creak of the metal drowned out the organ music, and set his nerves on fire. In petrified horror, Caesar watched it pop up, pushed by the bony, gnarled fingers of Romella. The enormous diamond engagement ring he gave her the night he proposed glinted under the cathedral's lights. In seconds, her corpse exited the slender tube, the flowing dress Casear had picked out for her to be buried in, no longer white. It was stained with a mishmash of drab colors, and hung in tatters around her rotting body. Romella's once magnificent mane of black hair was in knots, held together by putrid flesh. When she opened her mouth to speak again, her jawbone creaked. Plumes of yellowish, thick liquid spewed out of her mouth, flowing down the bones in her face, landing on the filthy dress. The stench of her crossed the distance between the two of them in seconds. Caesar felt lightheaded and nearly passed out. Romella's corpse moved over to the small casket of their daughter.

"Do not try to condone your actions by blaming another, darling husband. I know that is your specialty. After all, you blamed me for years for not being able to provide you a child. Remember? Even after the doctors told us to quit trying, that my body just couldn't handle bearing children, you pushed on. Because it was what you wanted. To hell with anyone else's wants or needs. It's always been about you. Always. Nothing and no one stands in the way of The Cat. And drop your facade of mobster, you old fool. You ran like a frightened kitten when you left Attica, and climbed into bed with that worthless Jap. You don't live up to the oath you took. The one you swore to uphold. Family. Please. Just because you brought a few

relatives with you to help run your pathetic schemes, doesn't make you a Godfather. Believe me, your precious grandfather is beyond livid about your decisions. Thinks you are weak. A pussy. One who should never have been brought into the family. He had quite a lot of things to say to your father about that bad decision when he arrived. Lit into him for allowing you to carry his name. You have shamed the Calvanio name, even in eternity."

Unable to stop them, warm tears leaked out from Caesar's eyes as he watched the rotting corpse of his wife float down the aisle toward him. Her outstretched arms held the mummified remains of their last child out to him. He cringed at the sight, closing his eyes. Caesar was overwhelmed with emotions by the hateful words coming from his beloved wife. Never, in all their previous interactions, had she spoken to him with anything but love, kindness. Though Caesar knew he was experiencing yet another break in reality, it pained him beyond belief to listen to Romella's accusations.

"Lies, Romella. All lies. I do honor my oath, and my family, every day! We left a dying industry and created a new legacy. One that has provided not only a comfortable living, but has benefited others. Nothing has gone to waste. I've made sure of that.

These people, they were at death's door anyway! I kept them from suffering a slow, agonizing death. They couldn't take their wealth with them, so what's the harm in what I've done? You are wrong. Don Tomaso would be pleased with what I am doing. I know it. Doesn't matter who my partner is, or whether he is part of the Family or not. Business is business. And please, don't be angry with me. You know it's not true. You wanted children, too. You said you did. You wanted to keep trying. I...never blamed you! I love you, Romella. I miss you every day. You know that! Haven't been with another since you left me."

The garbled cackle from Romella surrounded Caesar, filling his heart and mind with sadness and regret.

"You can lie to yourself all you desire, darling husband. But not to me. Though my eyes have rotted away, I still see. I know everything. You are losing your marbles, husband. One brain cell at a time. You realize that, right? All those blows to the head, first from your extended family, and then from your cellmates. Your brain is turning into mush. If it weren't for Carmine, you wouldn't have survived your stint in prison. Or, don't you remember that? Remember how much you owe him, your fucking life, and the awful ways you've

repaid him? Oh, and our bed hasn't always been empty. You may not have remarried, but you certainly haven't been faithful. A little trick I'm sure you learned from your whoredog father. Holes to fuck don't count as cheating if no emotions are involved, right? Isn't that what he taught you? I believe those were the exact words he said to your slut of a mother, right before he killed her. I know you remember that night—even though you were young. You were cowering in your room. Heard it all."

The memory of the night he'd all but forgotten roared up from the deepest recesses of his mind. The images made his head swim, releasing the pent-up, childish fears he'd fought for decades to hide. Caesar couldn't take much more of her taunting. *"Romella, please. Why are you doing this to me?"*

"Are you begging, Caesar? Asking for mercy for your evil ways? Pleading for the pain to end? Ha, it won't do you any good. Reaping what you've sown, that's what is happening to you. Oh, you are such a hypocrite! Even Carmine thinks you are some sort of saint for remaining faithful to me. Ha, the joke's on him. How do you think he'd feel if he knew you screwed the only woman he ever actually had feelings for behind his back? For years? That

you were the one who set up her car accident so she wouldn't break off their relationship by telling Carmine that she'd not only been boinking his best friend, but she carried his child? That her heart, lungs, liver and eyes lived on in others, and your own nephew had been the one who killed her? Bet he wouldn't be your lap dog anymore, would he? Do you really think your precious Don is proud of that? Do you believe he would approve? Oh, and your pathetic decision to involve more outsiders into the folds of your so-called family–bad idea. Nick Shonnert and Lucas Hill should never have been brought in. Period. You broke the first rule of family bonds, Caesar. If he were alive, do you think Don Tomaso would have agreed with those choices? Trust me, the answer is a resounding no. He can't wait for your arrival, which by the way, will be soon. Actually, none of us can wait. You know, all the people you've fucked over during your wretched life? The ones you sacrificed for one pathetic reason or another? Do you think your cohorts Franco and Carmella, will be able to forgive you for what you've done? The answer is not just no, but Hell no. You sit there, all pious and full of feigned concern by their sides, knowing full well what you did. One day, it will all come to light, right before your end. We all are waiting. Waiting for our turn with you down here. Ray-Ray, your father, and the rest of your family have enjoyed exchanging notes about you, and have a lot planned for when you get here. We all do. You have a lot to answer for, darling husband, and not just from me. The Piper is coming soon, and the price is hefty. Very hefty."

"No!" Caesar wailed out loud. With his eyes still closed, he reached forward and grabbed the thick wood of the pew in front of him. When he felt a warm hand touch his back, his eyes flew open, expecting to see Romella's ruined face inches from his own. Instead, it was Carmella's.

"I know, I know. I miss him too, Caesar. He loved you as much as you loved him. He was such a good boy. Such a good boy," she choked out, wiping the tears from her face with her other hand. "But we will get through this. Ray-Ray's death will not go unpunished. We all will make sure of it. The Calvanio clan takes care of things. Always."

Caesar raised his head and looked at the end of the aisle. Sure enough, the black casket that housed the remains of his nephew was back, the pallbearers in place, ready to carry him from the sanctuary. His eyes swept the expanse of the church, but no sign of his dead bride and baby remained. A shudder of disgust made his mouth and body tremble. Caesar swallowed hard, put his arm around his sister, and nodded in agreement. The entire Calvanio/D'Nucci clan watched with somber eyes and silent mouths as the casket was carried out to the waiting hearse. They followed behind it, out into the bright, summer sun.

Carmella and Franco left Caesar's side to shake hands and greet the few people in attendance at the front door. Caesar shoved his shaking hands deep inside the pockets of his pants, casting one last, wary glance to the sanctuary. His thoughts about the dreamed interactions with Romella were interrupted by Carmine.

"These things ain't never easy, especially when it's family. I need a drink, and pardon me for saying, but it looks like you do, too. Shall we?"

Caesar took a deep, cleansing breath, shaking the visions from the morbid encounter from his head. He was starting to slip more and more, and the breaks in reality were arriving faster, and lasting longer, than before. The past interactions with his wife had never, ever been so vivid, or disturbing. Caesar would need more than a drink, he would need an entire bottle, to rid himself of what just happened. With a nod of agreement, he turned and said his goodbyes to Franco and Carmella. In seconds, he and Carmine were walking to their vehicles, on their way to their favorite bar, The Regency, for what Caesar knew would be an epic drunk.

Less than ten minutes later, a solemn Caesar and Carmine walked inside the dimly lit bar, the smell of stale cigarette smoke and body odor coating them like a blanket. As they walked to the back of the bar toward their favorite spot, Carmine gave a slight nod to the bartender, who quickly prepared their standard drinks. For a Saturday, the place was unusually quiet. Only a few lonely souls were interspersed throughout the place, sipping on their drinks in silence. The pool room was empty, and the jukebox was quiet. Once at their designated spot, Caesar and Carmine slid into the cool faux leather seats and watched Billy deftly balance the full tray of brandy and whiskey to their table. When Caesar noticed a familiar face at the end of the bar, his face betrayed his internal thoughts.

Carmine recognized the look of annoyance and followed Caesar's gaze. "Oh, shit. Not expecting to see him today. Hope he didn't notice us when we walked in."

Caesar slid out a crisp, one-hundred dollar bill from the folds of his pockets and handed it to Billy, after he set the tray down in the middle of the table. Billy gave him a small grin, turned, and walked back to his spot behind the massive wooden bar. Once out of earshot, Caesar replied, "We couldn't get that lucky. Damn. He's sloshed. Hope he hasn't been running his mouth."

Neither men looked up when the hesitant footsteps drew closer. They both smelled the stench of booze on Nick Shonnert while he was still ten feet from their booth. "Sorry I missed the funeral. Hope Carmella and Franco forgive me, but I just..."

Nick's voice trailed off as he lowered his body in the seat next to Carmine. Caesar ground his teeth in disgust, wishing he could just grab the heavy bottle of brandy and slam it upside the Prick's bald head. He'd never seen the man intoxicated before, and was used to Nick scurrying around like a petrified mouse when around him. Seemed the alcohol gave the bastard some balls. Instead of wrapping his hands around the prick's neck, Caesar kept his hands otherwise engaged by pouring himself a double. He tossed the drink down his throat with one huge gulp. As the liquid burned down his esophagus, Caesar began to mentally plan out the death of Nick the Prick Shonnert.

15

BREAKING OUT OF PRISON

Lucas Hill was a nervous wreck. He stood in the middle of his small, dirty kitchen, and stared at the pair of Dockers and the dress shirt hanging on the back of the dining chair. Last night, when he put them there, he'd made up his mind he would attend the funeral of his one-time friend, Ray-Ray D'Nucci. But that was when he'd been half-drunk and safe inside the walls of his apartment. Between the blaring sun streaming through the kitchen window and the stout cup of coffee in his hand, Lucas waffled on his decision. When drunk, he'd cowered in his room and reminisced about the early years with Ray-Ray. How much fun they'd had together when young bucks. All the women they'd bagged, the numerous times they took Ray-Ray's Corvette out and smoked any and all competitors who dared to challenge the crazy Italian to a race. Sneaking into the expansive liquor cabinet late at night at Ray-Ray's parents estate, the parental units completely oblivious to the two boys outside in the pool, laughing and stumbling around, trashed on overpriced hooch.

The truth was, Lucas missed his friend, and all the gorgeous girls who would drop their wet panties when around the young stud. For some reason, southern girls drooled over Ray-Ray, with his dark curls, naturally tanned skin, and of course, his money and willingness to throw it around like it was confetti. Ray-Ray had been a chick-magnet for sure, and the magnetism was so strong, sometimes the fallout landed on Lucas's dick. Honeys weren't attracted to him, unless he waved a fistful of cash at them first. Lucas missed *those* times, certainly not the horrible nightmare he'd been living in the last few years.

Once sober, the warm memories of a life long-since passed, departed. Cold, hard reality slapped Lucas awake earlier, along with a throbbing headache and a queasy stomach. He didn't want to go to the stupid funeral. Seriously, what was left to bury? Lucas wasn't quite there, but was close to being happy the drugged-out fool was dead. Ray-Ray loved to party in his teens, but when he discovered heroin, he turned into a strung-out junkie. The habit started not long after he'd gotten his ass stomped to Hell and back by his own uncle and his freakish goon. In a way, Lucas did feel sort of sorry for Ray-Ray. Sort of. After all, his own flesh and blood nearly beat him to death, and used him as a courier of harvested body parts. How could Ray-Ray *not* have turned into a raging addict? Even Lucas teetered close to the edge sometimes. So far, he'd been lucky his nerves were calmed by bud and booze, and a good piece of ass. Unfortunately, the later hadn't occurred in months. Lucas needed to remedy that–soon. His hand was only capable of so much, and his balls ached to be emptied.

The queasiness in his gut doubled while he

pondered whether to say screw it and go for a ride, or get dressed and attend. If he didn't go, how would he explain his absence to his boss? From the beginning, the Devil had given him a long list of strict instructions to stick to, including never to been seen together out in public. Hot Springs was a fairly small town, and if, by chance, Lucas happened to bump into his boss out in public, no eye contact was to be made. No acknowledgement at all. He had been told by Carmine to "turn tail and leave" and make sure to remain calm. He'd followed the instructions to the letter, but Lucas was torn about whether he should today or not.

Lucas's job as a courier was done without personal contact from his boss, and he was beyond thrilled that was the case. Being near the man in person made his guts burn and his blood pressure spike. The phone call to alert him to a new mission always arrived from a random number, with the caller (Carmine, he figured) asking if he could talk to Rachel. Lucas always gave the same answer, "You have the wrong number." Then, he would get dressed, head to the funeral parlor, uncover the truck, grab the note that contained directions to his destination, and be done. Lucas never even had physical contact with the person who he delivered the organs to. He would simply drive to the location, arrive at exactly the appointed time, do a loop through the parking lot, and then go to the nearest gas station and wait. Watch for a car to pull up, blink its lights twice, and then Lucas would exit the truck, put the cooler in the truck bed, go inside and buy a bottle of water (with cash, of course), and when he returned to the truck, a suitcase full of cash sat where the cooler had been. He would drive back to the funeral parlor and leave the suitcase under the front seat, go home, and a few days later, find a plain manila envelope full of cash in his mailbox. The old gangster was beyond obsessive when it came to keeping his identity hidden and his old bag of bones out of prison, and by default, it had kept Lucas safe as well.

Was the cold-hearted devil even going to attend? Lucas took a sip of coffee as he walked over to the cabinet. He grabbed two aspirin and chewed them up, followed by another long swig of coffee. Who was he kidding? Of course the old geezer would attend the funeral of his nephew. But, would the old mobster even notice if Lucas wasn't there? Again, who was he kidding? The man didn't miss a *thing*, and Lucas had the strange sensation the old schooler would be offended if one of his *associates,* (as he enjoyed calling Lucas on occasion) didn't pay his respects.

Decision made, Lucas swiped his fingers through his damp hair. He hadn't even left yet and was already sweating bullets. If he was going to do this, he would have to settle his nerves down. The thought of being inside a church, plus near his boss, made his stomach flip. The two aspirin burned in his gut as they competed for attention with the strong coffee. Lucas set his mug on the counter and headed to the bedroom to find his stash. A few seconds later, the sweet smell of weed hung in the stagnant air. It took two full bowls to stop his hands from shaking and his sweat glands to ease up. Satisfied he could maintain during the service, Lucas took a quick shower to wash away the skunk smell.

As the hot jet spray beat down on him, Lucas wished he was still in jail. At least it would be a legitimate excuse for missing the funeral. He laughed out loud inside the empty bathroom at the realization that in a sick, perverted way, he was imprisoned. And Lucas would never, ever be paroled until the old warden was dead.

Or he was.

Thirty minutes later, Lucas rolled up on his Harley. He parked across the street from the gaudy, over-the-top concrete monstrosity known as St. Michael's, and shut the rumbling engine off. He kept his sunglasses on, using them as a shield so he could scan the area without *looking* like he was a nervous cat walking through a kennel full of rabid dogs. A few people walked up the stairs and went inside, most of them so old, they would break in half if they fell down. The knot in his stomach tightened when he saw the devil's henchman, Carmine, stroll up the stairs, wearing a suit that screamed Mafia. From the gaudy material, the slick-backed hair, the black shades and matching leather shoes, it was almost comical. The most ironic part, at least to Lucas, was he figured people would walk by the bastard and think *"Wow, he could play a mobster for sure!"* not even considering he actually was one. After all, the era of the Mafia was over.

Yeah, right.

Lucas slowed his gait down, waiting for the

arrival of his boss/nemesis. A few more people trickled in and went inside the massive doors, but not the one he was looking for. His stomach tightened. Was Caesar already inside? He hoped not, because Lucas had no intention of making a lap around the casket, just so he'd been seen paying his respects.

He realized the weed was wearing off faster than he'd anticipated. As Lucas opened the doors and stepped inside, the hairs on his neck bristled. The music made his skin crawl. Organ music reminded him of every horror movie he'd ever watched. It always seemed to peak when some big-busted, nearly naked broad was about to get chopped up into little pieces by the crazed killer. Lucas licked his dry lips, slid off his shades, and slipped into the pew closest to the door.

No one paid him any attention, which was fantastic. To his surprise, not many people came to say goodbye to Ray-Ray. Then again, how many friends could Ray-Ray have had left? Though they hadn't spoken much during the last several years, Ray-Ray's descent into addiction wiped away most of his former life, and friends. Lucas scanned the crowd one last time, wondering if Tiffany Birtress or her sister Tana had showed up. Though improper, Lucas smiled a bit at the memory of the sisters, and the night he lost his virginity to Tana, while Ray-Ray defiled Tiffany in another room. Tiffany was the one groupie who really had feelings for Ray-Ray. Lucas's smile disappeared when he remembered the ugly shouting match after Tiffany caught him in mid-pump with Tana. He was wasting his time looking for either of them in the church. If anything, they might show up to the gravesite and spit on the dirt.

Lucas let out a quiet sigh. He shouldn't have thought about Tana. Best piece of ass he'd ever had, and like he did with everything else he touched, Ray-Ray ruined it. Plus, it didn't help thinking about pussy again. It had been way too long since he'd had some, other than the whore Lucas picked up at a bar the second night he'd been released from jail. They both had been too trashed to really perform. He needed a nice, wet snatch to release some of his anger into.

The hairs on the back of his neck popped up, the sensation of cold fear made his jaw tighten. Lucas didn't need to look for the cause of his panic, for he knew exactly what it was. Keeping his eyes in his lap, he saw Caesar Calvanio walking down the aisle. Lucas stared a hole through his khakis, unwilling to raise his eyes to see if the old fucker saw him. He didn't need to. His burning gut told him enough.

Within minutes, the service started. Instead of listening to the drone of the dude up front in the long dress and fancy hat, Lucas concentrated on keeping his legs from bouncing. Not only was this his first funeral, but it was also the first time he'd ever been inside a church of any denomination. He almost expected to burst into flames when he walked in. When his mother died, cash was tight, so her final sendoff had been nothing but a simple service at the cemetery. So, he was surprised when he felt a lump of tears in his throat. They certainly weren't from sadness over Ray-Ray's passing. As Lucas swallowed hard and ground his teeth, he realized they stemmed from missing his mother, who he rarely thought about much anymore, and the loss of the person Lucas *could* have been.

All the mental, emotional bullshit disappeared from his mind with one ear-splitting cry. Lucas's mouth gaped open when he heard the devil wail from his spot next to Mrs. D'Nucci. The man either missed his calling as an A-list actor, giving the performance of a lifetime as a grieving relative of the dearly departed, or he was truly upset about Ray-Ray's death. Never, in all the years Lucas had known the cold-hearted bastard, had he *ever* seen the man display any emotion other than anger. Normally, Caesar Calvanio was a man of few words, and when he did speak, the carefully chosen words cut like hot daggers into the flesh. It unnerved Lucas for some strange reason. Though unsure exactly why, all he knew for sure was the urge to leave overwhelmed him.

Caesar's head was down while Mrs. D'Nucci patted his back. Lucas scanned the crowd and noticed most of the mourners were watching the spectacle, so Lucas used the distraction to escape the church without being seen. It took less than ten strides from his spot on the pew until he was outside in the bright sun, away from the disturbing sounds from inside.

The high from the weed long gone, Lucas picked up his pace. His nerves were on fire, and since he couldn't risk lighting up in the middle of downtown Hot Springs, he decided to cool the flames inside him with a cold beer. The Regency was less than two blocks away. Though not one of his regular haunts, he didn't care. Lucas needed a drink. Several, actually. He cut across Central Avenue, and as he entered the dimly-lit place, he felt a sense of relief. It was off-season, so the regulars to the track who normally swarmed downtown after the horse races were gone.

"Sure is a hot one today, eh?" the scrawny bartender asked. "Whatcha drinkin'?"

"Hotter than the flames of Hell, dude. Tequila, with a beer chaser." In a flash, his drinks were in front of him. The tequila burned as it slid down his throat, but Lucas welcomed the distraction. He took a long pull from his beer, belched, and asked, "Menu?"

"Here ya go. Kitchen is closed at the moment. Our cook is off today. I can fix anythin' that don't require heat, though. I make a mean sandwich."

Lucas scanned his options and then handed back the sticky menu. "Tuna on wheat please. Extra mayo. And hit me again."

For the next twenty minutes, Lucas enjoyed the meal, drinks, and the buzz. The bartender left him alone, busying himself with the other two customers. Lucas figured he caught his drift he wasn't much up to chatting. The booze was running through him, so Lucas got up and made his way to the head. When he reached the bathroom, he stumbled a bit on the slick floor.

His stomach grumbled, and he realized he didn't just need to take a piss. He made to the stall just in time.

Minutes later, Lucas splashed cold water on his face and stared at his reflection. Christ, he looked like a walking corpse. He needed to lay off the booze and weed, maybe start working out again. Eat healthier.

Yeah, like those things are the reason you look the way you do.

He jerked the bathroom door open and started to walk down the hallway. He'd have one more drink. No tequila, just a nice, cold beer, and then head home. Maybe after a short nap, clean up and go to Little Rock. Hit the bar scene and find some strange. Lucas smiled at the thought, a woody only seconds away, but the second his grin and hard-on appeared, the sound his ears heard made him freeze in his tracks. Cocking his head, Lucas listened, hoping he was wrong.

He wasn't. The voices coming from the other side of the wall, less than ten feet from him, he'd recognize anywhere. The Devil and his trained goon, Carmine.

Shit!

Panic tore through him, making Lucas's guts rumble, and his dick nothing more than a flaccid noodle. Did they follow him to the bar? Was he about to be ambushed, punished for being at the funeral? For leaving before the service was over? Maybe they planned on giving him a lesson in person for being gone for six months. It didn't really matter what the reason was. Hell, knowing the two blood-thirsty monsters like he did, they didn't need one. Blood pounded in his ears and sweat pooled under his armpits. Lucas touched his back pocket, relieved his wallet and keys were there, and not on the bar. The discovery made his racing heart slow a fraction.

While holding his breath, he forced himself to calm down. If they had followed him, and planned on beating him to a bloody pulp, or worse, they missed the perfect opportunity when he was on the can. Footsteps approached, and then Lucas saw the bartender carrying a large tray of booze, heading, he assumed, for their table. Then, more steps, as the drunk he saw earlier sitting in the corner of the bar wobbled their way. Lucas bit his lip, and made his decision.

He was getting the hell out of Dodge.

With slow, quiet steps, he backed down the hallway. When he reached the exit door, Lucas bit down on his lip harder, because the damned thing was padlocked. He couldn't believe it. Who in their right mind would put a lock to keep customers *in*? How many safety codes did that violate? Lucas almost laughed, because the only safety violation he was concerned about was his own.

Not going to die today. No way.

He veered to his right and slunk into the bathroom. There was a dirty window above the stalls. It would be a tight fit, but he could do it. Lucas had no choice. The thought of walking out the front door, risking being seen by either of them, made the bile travel up his throat. Once inside the stall, he shut the door and grabbed the ledge, hoisting his body up. He tugged at the latch, freed it, but the window wouldn't budge. The building was old, and countless layers of paint sealed the window shut. Anger rising, he balanced his weight on his stomach, using both hands to work the window. No luck.

Sweating profusely, Lucas slid back down and stood on the rim of the toilet. He took off his shirt, balled it around his fist, and started to hoist himself back up to the window. When he heard heavy footsteps from the hall, followed by the slurred voice of a male, Lucas stopped. His blood ran cold when Carmine barked, "Nicky, let me help you to the john. Looks like you're gonna puke any minute."

On instinct, Lucas crouched down, his feet balancing on the edge of the slick, white rim. He held his breath, thankful he'd worn his new tennis shoes rather than his boots, or he would have already lost his footing. He tried not to jerk when the bathroom door opened. The sounds coming from the other side of the stall made goose bumps pop up all over his clammy skin.

Like a quiet church mouse, Lucas never flinched, barely breathed, as he listened to the short conversation between the two men.

"Please...I'm sorry. I didn't mean to offend Caesar, I just...oh..."

"You are just drunk and acting like a pussy. A big, fat, slimy twat. You know, in all my years, I ain't never seen such a huge pussy. Ever. And a stupid one, too. Did you really think you could just come over to our table and sit down for a chat? We aren't *friends*, dumbass."

Lucas cringed at the harsh words of Carmine. His mouth was full of spit, but he refused to swallow it, fearing any noise would give his presence away. Lucas could hear the other guy sniveling and sniffing snot back up his nose, his words so slurred they didn't make any sense.

Footsteps approached, the shadow of feet appearing under the stall door. Lucas thought his heart would stop beating when he heard the slap of palms hitting the floor. He knew what was happening before the drunk spoke.

"What...what are you doing, Carmine?"

"I'm making sure we ain't disturbed while we have ourselves a little chat. You know, so I can make sure you understand what rules you broke today, and make sure it doesn't happen again. Lucky for you, it's just the two of us. Now, let's talk. Well, I'll talk. You'll just listen. Maybe saying some silent prayers that we's in a public place. It's all that's saved me from ruining that chubby face of yours."

Lucas sat perched on the toilet like he was just an extension of the porcelain. For the first five minutes of the one-sided conversation, he kept expecting blood to spill all over the floor, so he really didn't listen too much of what was said. But, when Ray-Ray's name was mentioned, along with some other juicy details, Lucas's ears perked up.

"Now, I'm gonna call you a cab and pour you into it. You're gonna go home, sleep this off, and get your shit together. No more screw ups, or drunk in public episodes. Wanna get trashed, do it at home. No more whining like a little baby. Maybe while you are home, you can search for your balls. You open that mouth of yours again like you did today around us, you won't be only dead, but you and your family will be in so many pieces, it'd make a hundred-thousand piece crossword puzzle easier to put together. Got it?"

"Yes, I got it. Please, please just leave my family out of it. Please," the other man whined.

Within seconds, the bathroom door opened and the men left. Lucas could hear Carmine on his cell, calling a cab. He wasted no time. With his shirt still balled up around his fist, Lucas hoisted himself back on the ledge, punched his hand through the window, and climbed out. The shards of sharp glass dug into his thighs and back, but he didn't care. Dropping to the ground, he slipped his shirt back on while he trotted down the alley toward the front of the bar. Lucas stopped and waited, watching for the cab. The wait wasn't long, and soon, he watched the drunken, frightened looking man climb in the backseat. Lucas gave a quick scan of the front, and seeing no one, took off running toward the parking lot where his bike was parked. He was breathing heavy when he jumped onto the hot leather seat, fired up the engine, and raced down

Central. Taxicabs were a rarity in Hot Springs, so it only took a few seconds for him to spot the bright yellow car about half-a-mile ahead.

Lucas hung back, following from a safe distance. Dueling emotions battled for control. One side told him to turn around, go home, and forget what he'd just seen and heard. The other part told him he just might be onto something. He didn't know anything about the man he was following, other than his name was Nick, he was connected to Caesar and Carmine, and Ray-Ray. The more Lucas thought about it, the stronger the warm sensation in his stomach became. The sensation was something he hadn't felt in years, and almost didn't recognize. He couldn't shake the feeling that whatever the man knew, however he was involved with the old mafia fucker, might be enough ammunition for Lucas to use to extract himself from under Caesar's control. How he would accomplish it was something he'd deal with in the future. First, Lucas needed to find out all the information.

As he followed, the orangey, red sun just beginning to start its descent over Lake Hamilton, Lucas wondered if he was on the road to salvation or the path to Hell.

Only one way to find out.

*L*ucas watched from his perch on top of his idling hog. Even a block away, he could see the drunk stumble from the backseat of the taxi, wobbling as he tried to keep himself steady before he executed a classic face plant. If the guy had been some random Joe, he would have laughed at the sight. Even though Lucas didn't know the dude, he knew enough.

The guy had ties to the Devil, and other than Ray-Ray and the goonish henchman, Lucas had never met anyone who did.

He was about to change that.

A few rays of orange light from the disappearing sun blazed across the sky. It would be dark in less than an hour. Lucas waited until the man entered his house before engaging the gears. He swung the bike hard to the right, executing the perfect U-turn, careful not to speed. Drawing unwanted attention was not what he needed. The neighborhood the dude lived in was what his mother would have called "upscale" and Lucas figured not many of the rich neighbors drove hogs around.

There was no way he was just going to pull up, park his bike in dude's driveway, and then ring the doorbell. While following the taxi earlier, Lucas made sure to remember every turn and which street he was on. Thankfully, the dude lived only six blocks from Bikes-n-Mikes, a "family-friendly" biker bar catering to the rich wannabes with kids in tow. A great place for the mom and pop to slug down a brew while their kids played on the Karaoke machine.

Lucas pulled into the parking lot. The place was packed, and no one would notice yet another hog parked outside. He shut the engine down, pocketed his keys, and headed back the way he came. Though less than a mile away, Lucas walked at a slow pace. By the time he found himself standing at the edge of dude's driveway, the sun was long gone, his shirt soaked with sweat. With a quick glance around the street, Lucas realized no one was outside, so he slipped around the yard, easily hopping the fence. His heart thundered in his chest. Though he didn't live on the good side of the law, Lucas had never stalked anyone. Or broken into their house. He was walking a thin line, and he knew it. If he got caught before he obtained the information he needed, Lucas was a dead man.

The only light on was from the back porch, so he crouched low and watched his footing, careful to keep on the soft grass. As Lucas neared the edge of the side of the house, he could hear the drunk mumbling. Lucas froze, listening to see if the dude was chatting on the phone or just gabbing to himself. It didn't take long for him to figure out his quarry was talking to no one. Lucas stood, pulled his switchblade from his pocket, steadied his nerves, and sprinted from his spot.

"Don't move or say a word. Got it?"

A set of red, bloodshot eyes looked up at him. Lucas expected to see fear behind them. He was surprised when he didn't. The man simply stared at him with a haunted, eerie gaze. He did as Lucas ordered. His right hand stopped in midair, the glass full of booze inches from his lips.

Lucas motioned with the knife toward the house. "Anyone else here?" The man gave a brief shake of his head. "Get up and go inside. You'll take me on a guided tour first. No offense, but I take no one's word as the truth. Gotta see with my own eyes. If it's like you say, we'll come back out here and have us a chat."

The man complied and stood, setting his drink on the small bench beside him. Before the old drunk could blink, Lucas looped his arm around his neck, and stuck the tip of the blade to his temple. "You lead. Pull any tricks, and I'll slit your throat. We're gonna make a circle, room by room. Turn the lights on in each one, then off when we leave. Slow and steady."

Though the man didn't speak, Lucas sensed his fear. The man's body trembled as they entered the house. In under two minutes, they were back at their original starting point in the kitchen. Lucas couldn't help but compare the situation to so many of the cop drama shows he loved to watch. While they moved through the empty house, he made sure to take in everything around him. Satisfied they were alone, Lucas loosened his grip on the captive's neck. Securing the house was the first hurdle cleared, and Lucas let out a small rush of air, not realizing he'd been holding it the entire time. Before he let go of the man's neck, he asked, "Got any beer?"

The man nodded yes, motioning his head toward the fridge. "Good. I need one." He let go and stepped over to the door that led outside. "Grab some, and let's have us that chat now."

Lucas backed out onto the deck and leaned against the wooden railing. The man shuffled out the door, handed the can of cold beer to

Lucas, and just stood still. Lucas noticed silent tears were running down his face, but he didn't look sad, scared or worried. For a full minute, Lucas stared at him, trying to pinpoint the expression. When it dawned on him it was relief, Lucas took his first swig of beer. He'd already played the role of bad cop, so it was time to bring out the good one.

"Sit. Let's talk. Name's Lucas. Yours?"

The man sank into the chair he'd been sitting in before, never taking his eyes off Lucas. When he spoke, his voice was raspy. Quiet. "He sent you here to kill me and didn't even tell you my name?"

Taken aback, Lucas almost spit out his mouthful of beer. "Dude, no one sent me. I came here all on my own. I'm not here to kill you. Actually," he replied, pausing to take another sip of beer, "I am here to help you. And me. After what I saw today, I believe we have a common enemy. I call him the Devil. You know him as Caesar Calvanio."

The reaction was immediate. What little color the booze brought to the surface of the man's cheeks disappeared. The relief behind his weary eyes was gone, replaced by fear. Lucas noticed tremors in Nick's hands. He would need to dig deeper into his bag of television cop interview tricks to get the suspect to open up.

"I'll tell you what I know, and what I miss, you fill in the blanks, okay Nick?"

"Why did you ask me what my name was if you already knew? And, if you aren't here to kill me, then why did you come?"

Unwilling to tell him everything just yet, Lucas lied. "Noticed your nametag on the kitchen table. Nick Shonnert, Manager of Green Pastures. That's an old folk's home off Central, ain't it?"

Nick's brows furrowed together. "Yeah, so?"

"So, here's my first real question, Nick. How does a guy who manages an old farts home have connections to a mobster like Caesar Calvanio?"

"I...I don't know what you're talking about. I don't know anyone by that name."

Lucas took another swig of beer, then reached into his pocket and pulled out a cigarette. Once lit, he leaned back further on the railing. "Your face tells a different story, Nick. You should see your eyes. They say just the opposite of your words."

"What is all this? Why do you care who I do, or don't, know?"

For dramatic effect, Lucas took a long, slow

drag off his cig, letting the question linger in the air until the smoke he'd exhaled disappeared. "Because Ray-Ray D'Nucci was once my best friend, and I want to know why you killed him."

The haughtiness from seconds ago, vanished. Nick Shonnert deflated like a popped balloon. He sank back into his chair, his shaking hands immediately covering his face. "Oh, God, you are here to kill me. Just...get it over with. I can't live like this any longer. Can't...deal with what he made me do. Please, make it fast."

Lucas saw it then. The remorse, the overwhelming sense of being caught in the sticky web of Caesar Calvanio. He knew what that was like. When inside Nick's house, Lucas saw the family pictures. The sound of the man pleading for his family to be spared inside the walls of the bathroom earlier, hit him again. Nick Shonnert was another pawn, just like Lucas was. Someone to whip into submission. Lucas was brought into the family fold and never questioned his role, after witnessing just how cruel and vicious the Devil could be. This man, he had a family. People to protect. Lucas would bet his life that the broken man in front of him had been blackmailed to kill Ray-Ray. He didn't have the killer vibe. For a second, Lucas empathized with him. Understood being trapped, willing to gnaw off anything to get away.

He snuffed out his smoke and walked across the deck. Lucas sat down in the chair next to Nick, keeping his voice even and slow. "Nick, I didn't come here to hurt you. Or harass you. As I said earlier, we are in the same sinking ship. Caesar Calvanio has kept me under his thumb for years now. I want a way out. My guess, from your responses, is you do, too. I think, between the two of us, we can figure out a way to jump ship and swim to shore. So, no more games. I'll tell you how I got roped into being the body parts delivery boy, and you tell me everything you know about Caesar. Deal?"

A spark of hope ignited behind Nick's eyes, but only for a brief second. Dejection replaced it as his head shook from side to side. "No, no. I can't. We can't. He'll kill my family."

The second Lucas heard the words, his original plans changed. No matter what information he learned from Nick, even if Nick had pictures, videos, fucking hand-written instructions penned by the Devil himself, it wouldn't matter. They couldn't go to the police. If either of them rolled on Caesar, the price on their heads would be so high, every hit man in America would come after them. Even in jail, or whisked away into the witness protection program, wouldn't insure their safety.

For the first time since the nightmare of being Caesar Calvanio's mule, Lucas didn't push aside his anger. He embraced it. Used it as the tool needed to dig out of his own grave, and to put the Devil in his. He leaned forward, his face inches from the reeking mess of the broken man in front of him. "Not if we kill him first."

Nick's eyes bulged, his mouth hung open like an out-of-breath trout. "Don't...even say such things out loud! For all I know, my house is bugged!"

Lucas rose, pulling out another smoke from his pocket. He wished it was bud instead of tobacco. "Let's continue this conversation over there," he said, pointing to the edge of the darkened yard.

Nick remained glued to his chair. The man was beyond scared. He was petrified. Lucas thought about bringing out the bad cop again, but something in his gut told him it wasn't the right approach. Instead of forcing the old drunk from his seat, Lucas knelt down and whispered in his ear, "I'm guessing you know where he lives, which is something I don't. I'm also guessing that the body parts hidden inside the coolers of ice he forces me to transport, originally were old fuckers from Green Pastures. Well, except for my most recent delivery. I believe I took Ray-Ray for his final ride."

Nick didn't answer, and he didn't have to. Lucas could tell from the stunned look on his face that he'd hit the mark. Lucas waited, giving the idea a chance to soak through the booze. For a minute, he worried Nick was going to pass out. The scent of fear rolled off him in waves, making Lucas hold his breath. Finally, with an almost imperceptible nod of his head, Nick acknowledged Lucas was on target.

With a grin a mile wide, Lucas held his hand out to Nick. A strange expression crossed Nick's face as he accepted the help. He grabbed Lucas's hand and stood, wobbling a bit. Lucas let him lead the way across the soft grass. After about twenty yards, Nick turned to face Lucas. The fear behind his eyes was gone. Hope beamed across his brow.

"What do you need from me?"

Lucas smiled. "Tell me everything, from the moment you met him. Leave nothing out. Then, I'll do the same."

Lucas watched Nick stare into the cloudless night. His shoulders stiffened as he took in a huge gulp of the humid night air. "Caesar won't be our only problem. There are others. Ones just as cold and callous. If we do this..."

"When, not if. I'm well aware he won't be our only target. Keep talking."

16

UNDER THE SPELL OF
THE MAGNOLIA

"This place is simply breathtaking." LiAnn smiled, her head bouncing from one direction to the next, taking in the scenery around them. Along with her parents, they stood at the grand front entrance to The Magnolia House. Even though this was her second visit, the place was beyond stunning.

Junior tugged on his daughter's arm. "Come on, darlin'. We'll be late for lunch with Cecil if we keep standin' around here, watchin' you drool," he drawled, holding the front door open.

The minute she walked inside the grand foyer, her grin increased. LiAnn wished Karina would have joined them, instead of staying back at the farm to work on the knee-high grass in the fields with Bo. She knew a major part of Karina's decision to stay home centered on exploring the potential of a new relationship with Bo, but she also sensed other reasons for Karina's unwillingness to visit The Magnolia. Karina simply wasn't ready to deal with the memories that were sure to flood her mind upon entering a senior living facility.

LiAnn tried to tell her the place was different, nothing at all like the previous places Karina had seen, but it was no use. Until Karina was mentally ready, LiAnn could talk until she was hoarse about the delicious aromas of food, the intoxicating mixture of roses, gardenias and jasmine, the heavy dollop of lemon-scented floor polish, and it wouldn't matter. Karina would come when she was ready.

LiAnn's eyes feasted on the opulent decor, the graceful staircase glistening as sunlight streamed through the numerous windows. The ornate decorations, from expensive oil paintings on the cranberry-colored walls, to the delicate vases full of fresh cut flowers on every available space, were beyond impeccable.

She leaned over and whispered in her mother's ear. "Okay, so if *this* type of retirement home is available when I'm ready, sign me up. No wonder you and Pop thought about moving here! Talk about living like a king and queen. Yikes, I bet the monthly rental fees are ridiculous!"

"It ain't cheap, that's for sure," Ruth replied. "A one-room apartment is over five-thousand dollars a month."

"Holy shi..I mean, yikes, that is steep," LiAnn replied, careful to keep her voice low as they entered the dining area. She gave a quick scan of the large room, impressed by the layout and the over-the-top decor. There were about twenty, round tables that could seat about six people each, strategically interspersed so enough room was between them for easy movement of the elderly residents. Not one was vacant. Groups of diners with snow white hair and wrinkled skin sat, gabbing and smiling as they ate lunch.

"Ah, there's Cecil. Come on, let's get our plates and get situated. I'm ready to whip his butt at dominoes this week. He killed me last time. I gotta get some of my money and pride back," Junior said, followed by a wink.

Lunch was served on fine china, with crystal goblets full of sparkling water at the end of the lunch line. While in the serving line, LiAnn scanned the dining room for Jimmy. When she didn't see him, a fleeting sense of sadness hit her. She realized she'd actually been looking forward to seeing him. LiAnn listened with only one ear as her parents greeted other seniors while they made their way over to sit with Cecil.

"I was beginnin' to think y'all stood me up!" Cecil said, rising to his feet to pull out LiAnn's chair. He gave her a bear hug, which she returned, after setting her plate on the table. "My, my, Ruth. You sure got some good genes. This here gal gets prettier and prettier each time I see her. A real blonde bombshell."

LiAnn watched her mother blush from the compliment, planting a light kiss on Cecil's cheek before she sat down.

"Good to see you again, Mr. Pickard! You look happy and healthy. Must be from all this fine living here! Wow, what a place, huh?" LiAnn replied, as all of them sat back down at the table.

"Yep, it sure is. Ain't no other facility within three hundred miles that can hold a candle to the grand old broad. Though I ain't too fond of the management or staff, they sure know how to revive a dyin' place."

For the next twenty minutes, the conversation around the table was filled with laughter and recollections about the past. LiAnn smiled and nodded at what she thought were appropriate times, but her mind was focused elsewhere. After the conversation with Karina, LiAnn brushed away her worries and fears, and prodded her mind to stop second-guessing everything and think with her heart, not her screwed-up head.

Though she wasn't entirely sure Jimmy would be the one to bring her out of her decades long relationship funk, LiAnn sort of hoped he would be. He was a good ten years older, at least she suspected he was, but still quite attractive.

She forced a smirk away, thinking about the thick, salt-n-pepper hair on Jimmy's head, almost positive it was a hairpiece. It was too perfect not to be, and LiAnn found it amusing a man his age still worried about his appearance. Jimmy had a quick, easy smile, and beautiful brown eyes that still held the glow of youth. He seemed well-educated and knowledgeable on quite a variety of subjects. He wasn't bulky or brutish, which was the normal kind of man who caught LiAnn's attention, though he was well built. In his youth, Jimmy Calhoun probably set tongues wagging and heads turning. The look on his face when he spoke about art made the years vanish from his face. LiAnn found that fascinating, for some odd reason.

"LiAnn, did you hear me?"

"Oh, no. Sorry, Mom. Was lost in the room. What did you say?"

"I asked if you're gonna eat, or just sit there gawkin' like a lost goat. Or, lookin' for one," Ruth prodded.

"Ooops. Can't help it. This place is just amazing. And I've seen lots of historic places in Cali. Even Hearst Castle. It's just so beautiful." She twisted around in her seat and pointed to the floor-to-ceiling stained glass windows, depicting a young woman on an enormous horse. "I mean, I can't stop staring!" LiAnn hoped she sold the act, since she didn't want any of them to know what she'd really been thinking about.

"Good afternoon, Mr. Pickard. I see you have guests again today. My, my, but your friend list just keep growing! Soon, we'll have to get you a bigger table."

LiAnn turned back around at the sound of the somewhat familiar voice. It was attached to the woman she met last week, who'd introduced herself as the head of healthcare. Carmen or Carmella something-or-other.

She stood next to Cecil, her claw-like hand perched on his right shoulder, her long, red nails shimmering under the overhead lights. Her eyes were dark chocolate brown, her skin a tawny bronze. Full, red lips slathered with entirely too much gloss parted, revealing a set of perfect, pearly whites. A head full of jet black hair framed her face, ending just above her shoulder blades. The cut was made to soften her features, but it was woefully inadequate.

Though her smile and mannerisms screamed kindness, there was a harshness to her features. But, the thing that struck LiAnn the oddest about her was the way the woman looked her. It almost made LiAnn feel like she was naked.

Cecil commented first. "Afternoon, Carmella. You remember Junior and Ruth Tuck? And their daughter, LiAnn? They came to have lunch with me, then check out Jimmy's paintin' class. Well, LiAnn did. You know I can't draw nothin' but a wobbly circle, and even that ain't pretty. I stick to playin' dominoes."

"Mr. and Mrs. Tuck, good to see you again. What wonderful friends you are to Cecil. Bringing your entire family here to enjoy his company. He just lights up like a Christmas tree when you all are here. Does my heart good to see you smile, Mr. Pickard."

LiAnn watched Carmella smile as she patted Cecil's back, her dark eyes sweeping over the table. They lingered a bit too long on LiAnn, and she found herself returning the harsh gaze. A strange look crossed the woman's face, almost like fear, but passed as quickly as it arrived.

Did she imagine it? LiAnn shot a glance over to her mother, raising one eyebrow. Her suspicions were confirmed when Ruth returned the gesture. *She noticed, too.*

"Nice to see you again, Ms..., oh, forgive me, I've forgotten your last name," LiAnn answered, hoping her words sounded truer to the ears of others than they did her own.

"You too, and its D'Nucci. Carmella D'Nucci. Now, I must apologize for eavesdropping, but I couldn't help but overhear how much you appreciate our little slice of Heaven here at The Magnolia. Looks like you are about finished with lunch, so would you like an official tour of the place?"

LiAnn shook her head. "Thank you, but Cecil already gave a grand tour on my visit last week. I plan on spending my afternoon learning how to paint. I little bird told me Jimmy Calhoun is quite the teacher." LiAnn noticed a look of concern, and maybe a hint of sadness, flicker behind Carmella's eyes.

Carmella scanned the room, glanced at her watch, then back over to LiAnn. "How fun, and yes, we count Jimmy as quite a prize here at The Magnolia. No other senior facility has an art teacher, much less one as renowned as Jimmy. Class may start a tad late, though."

"Oh, why is that?" LiAnn queried.

"Jimmy is running late. But, he's here now, upstairs in the art room. He had a bunch of supplies with him, since he plans on starting a new piece today."

A new face appeared next to Carmella, and LiAnn saw a look of playfulness in his face.

"Well, thank goodness, 'cause I'm tired of starin' at fruit! What I'm hopin' is, that this here beauty will be our *muse* for the day. Darlin', I could stare at you all day and never blink once, even if ya remain fully clothed!"

"Mr. Wilson! You are just too much, you know that? What a way to make a first impression on

Mr. Pickard's guests. Ms. Tuck, allow me to introduce you to Mr. Wylie Wilson, The Magnolia's unofficial prankster, and mouth of the south, which sometimes erupts."

LiAnn laughed, along with her father, but her mother looked beyond irritated, and Cecil blanched from embarrassment. LiAnn immediately liked the old man. Though he was a bit rough around the edges, she sensed his kind nature. It radiated from him. The man was just one of those who enjoyed making people smile, and the world needed more like him. LiAnn stood and extended her hand toward the man. "Why, Mr. Wilson, you do have a way with words. I'm afraid, though, I'm only here to have lunch with a family friend and attend class as a student, not the model."

"Dadgum, today just ain't my day! Well, how about this? Would ya be willin' to make an old man happy by sittin' next to him in class? Give him some braggin' rights to the rest of the old farts around here by bein' seen next to such a beauty? I heard ya was an ex-cop, and boy howdy, that made my blood pound! I promise, I won't bite, unless ya want me to." Wylie winked.

"Oh, you are bad, aren't you? I might have to

get my handcuffs out to keep you in line," LiAnn teased, returning the conspiratorial wink.

Wylie beamed from ear to ear, and then turned and spoke to Cecil. "Cecil, no wonder you sit around here like a bump on a log when they ain't here! You're dreamin' about this here goddess, ain't ya? You've been hidin' her from us all this time, ya old miser! Oh, and darlin', you can cuff me anytime ya wish. It will be somethin' else I can cross off my bucket list: handcuffed and at the mercy of a gorgeous female cop."

Cecil shook his head in mock disgust, his cheeks actually turning pink. "Manners, Wylie. Manners! No wonder Seth gets so irked at you. Does that mouth of yours come with a filter?"

"I'm warning you, Mr. Wilson. I like to play rough. And it wouldn't count anyway. I'm retired," LiAnn said with a smirk. The entire table laughed, and she patted the seat next to her for the old man to join them. Out of the corner of her eye, LiAnn noticed Carmella never moved from her position behind Cecil. She also noticed the smile on the woman's face was faker than the acrylic nails on her fingertips. Her eyes focused on LiAnn again, and this time, LiAnn recognized the look.

Hate.

Carmella cleared her throat and said, "Well, it seems you all have a full table, so I guess it's time for me to finish my rounds. Mr. Wilson, you behave around these ladies, especially since one is a cop! You surely don't need any more run-ins with the law. It was a pleasure to see you all again. Hope you enjoy class with Jimmy, and come back for a visit real soon."

Before any of them could say a word, Carmella turned and was gone. She wound her way through the maze of tables and out to the foyer. The second she left, LiAnn felt the atmosphere change.

Wylie lowered his voice and said, "I still can't believe she's back at work so soon. Then again, keepin' the mind and body engaged will help her not think about her grief. Goodness, what a strong woman that one is."

"What do you mean, Mr. Wilson?" LiAnn asked, intrigued by the statement.

Wylie continued. "Her son's funeral was this past Saturday. Never seen a mother so, I don't know the right word, stoic? I surely don't know how she keeps a smile on her face. After I lost my boy, it took me months to come out of my grieven' hole. The only time I saw her show much emotion durin' the service was when someone sittin' by her started to lose it."

The lightbulb went off in LiAnna's head. "D'Nucci! She is the mother of the boy who was dismembered and burned, the one I heard about on the news, right?"

Ruth gasped, her hand flying to her mouth. "Oh, my, I never put the names together! How could we have missed that, Junior? We've been here three times since his death, and never paid our respects to the woman! She must think we are rude. Cecil, why didn't you tell us?"

Cecil stuttered, "I...honestly, I didn't know. I don't watch TV, you know that Ms. Ruth. And, she never said nothin' to me about it, and I don't talk much to..."

Wylie interrupted, "You don't talk to anyone, really. Actually, Seth and I wondered if you even could talk. Seth thought you might have had a stroke or somethin'. We've been tryin' for months now to bring you outta your shell."

Cecil bristled. "I keep to myself because I like it that way, Mr. Wilson. If I got somethin' to say, I say it. Just haven't been in the mood recently. You only came over here because two lovely ladies are at my table. So, stop tryin' to rile me, or make me feel guilty for not chattin' sooner. The door swings both ways, ya know."

LiAnn felt guilty at her previous assumption about Carmella. No wonder the woman cast off such a negative vibe! Her only child murdered in such a gruesome, horrible way. A shiver of disgust slithered up her back. If she ever lost Karina, she would die of a broken heart.

She thought about what Mr. Wilson said about the woman being stoic. Hell, Carmella was beyond stoic. She was a hardened piece of marble. Back at work only days after burying her child? That wouldn't be the case for her if Karina died, or, God forbid, had been murdered. There would be two caskets at the front of the church: Karina and hers.

LiAnn couldn't stand to think about such things, so she stood, extended her arm toward Mr. Wilson, and asked, "I'm ready to start making your friends drool, Mr. Wilson. Shall we head up to the art room and learn how to create a masterpiece?"

"Darlin', I was born ready," Wylie gushed.

"You two behave, now. Junior, I'm off to quiltin' class with Betty. Cecil, try not to drain all the cash in his pocket today, will you?" Ruth admonished.

Junior glowered at his wife, but Cecil grinned from ear to ear. Mr. Wilson tugged on LiAnn's arm, leading the way to the elevator.

Two hours and one ruined shirt later, LiAnn stared at the horrid collage of colors on the canvas in front of her. Though the shades were lovely, her rendition of an open Bible on top of a wooden table, nestled next to an old, blue jug filled with pink and yellow daisies, was nowhere near the real thing.

Her artwork looked like she painted it with her toes. Blindfolded. Karina certainly didn't get her artistic abilities from her. She glanced up and saw Jimmy was making his way toward her, stopping briefly at the side of each senior in the class, chatting with them about their creations.

Embarrassment flushed her cheeks. The thought of letting someone see her colorful monstrosity was bad, but LiAnn would be beyond mortified if an artist like Jimmy took a peek. His beautiful work graced the walls, from the subtle colors of a late afternoon spring day, to the vibrant splashes of reds and oranges of the sun setting over the shimmering blue waters of the ocean. The man was beyond talented. He was gifted.

Jimmy was chatting up Mr. Wilson, gushing over his color choices and brush strokes. The other participants were gathering up their supplies, gabbing about each other's artistic talents as they left the room. One of the other men, *what was his name? Seth?* walked over to Mr. Wilson, and with just one negative comment about Mr. Wilson's painting, the two men started arguing. Loudly.

LiAnn had to bite her lip to keep from laughing. Jimmy moved between the two men, admonishing them for acting so rude in front of a guest, and both men got up and left, grumbling insults at each other under their breath. Apparently, Mr. Wilson's crush on her was short-lived, for he left the room without even one glance back.

Thankfully, instead of coming over to inspect her work, Jimmy remained in his spot by Mr. Wilson's empty easel. He smiled, big and wide, his eyes gleaming with humor. "So, I sense a bit of nervousness on your part. You aren't quite ready for a critique on your work, are you?"

"Oh, perceptive. No, I'm not. I mean, you just ate lunch not too long ago, right? Wouldn't want to make you sick. It's kind of a disaster. No, not kind of," LiAnn answered, glancing back to the hot mess she'd created. "It *is* a disaster. I need remedial art class lessons. You know, start out with finger-painting or something."

Jimmy laughed. LiAnn sensed he was genuinely amused by her embarrassment. His tone switched once his laughter subsided. In a husky voice, he almost purred, "Ms. Tuck, the beauty of a piece of art isn't created by the hands of the artist. It is generated from the eyes of the viewer. And, from my position, I've seen nothing but a breathtaking canvas, created by the hands of the gods."

No one had *ever* spoken to her like that before. Ever. LiAnn felt her heart skip a beat and blood rush to her face. *Wow, he's good. Move over, Casanova.*

His beautiful brown eyes lost the sparkle of humor, filling with the heaviness of attraction. While holding her gaze, Jimmy wiped his stained fingers on a towel in slow, calculated moves. Seductive. Sensual. Like his fingers were exploring her body, rather than wiping away the streaks of acrylic. The sensation was overwhelming, and something LiAnn hadn't experienced in *years.*

It took a few seconds to control her vocal chords. She swallowed hard and retrieved her purse from the floor. Unaccustomed to such raw displays of sexuality, LiAnn felt a bit unnerved, and completely out of her comfort zone. "What an appraisal on something you haven't yet seen, Mr. Calhoun. Do you...do you mind if I leave it here and come back to work on it again next week?" *Oh, great comeback, LiAnn. Your flirting skills are rusty. No, they flat out suck.*

Ignoring her words, Jimmy strode over and stopped when he was but a mere foot from LiAnn. He'd way overstepped the personal space bounds. She smelled his spicy cologne, mixed with a faint aroma of paint fumes.

With a slight nod of his head toward the easel, Jimmy reached out and took LiAnn's hands in his, using the towel to wipe the smudges of paint from her fingers. His hands were strong and gentle at the same time while he worked the cloth in slow, rhythmic circles. Jimmy's burning gaze never left her face.

"I would be inconsolable if you didn't return next week, ma'am. Your beauty inspires me to do great things. Ones I haven't thought about, or done, in years."

His magnetism and old-school charm was strong. It wasn't like LiAnn was a stranger to being flirted with, especially in her youth. But the times before had all been rather raunchy, explicit. The brazen would-be suitors not shy about saying what they wanted to do with her full breasts and plump lips, among other things.

The obnoxious men had been put in their place with a few, sharp barbs hurled from her mouth, along with the threat of bodily harm if they didn't leave before LiAnn lost her temper.

Jimmy was different. Though the heat radiating from him was intense, and full of just as much animal attraction as others had exuded, it was subtle. Intriguing. Downright sexy as hell, and something that knocked her senses off kilter.

She saw the want, the need, the burning desire behind his hooded eyes. A pang of worry shot up her spine, wondering if hers reflected the same. His beautiful eyes also held a hint of sadness, no, loneliness. Her mother mentioned on the drive over that Mr. Calhoun was a widower, and several of the single lady residents of The Magnolia had tried to sink their claws into

Jimmy when he first started volunteering. According to her mother, Jimmy never showed any interest in anyone, which left a trail of broken dreams for a last chance at a budding romance throughout the community.

Her internal questions about whether Jimmy felt the spark between them last week had just been answered. They spoke volumes about what he was thinking. Her heartbeat went into overdrive as he continued to manipulate her hands in his own. It left her almost dizzy with emotions she didn't know she possessed any longer. She surprised herself when she responded, her own voice low, husky. "I'm not one for leaving others disappointed, Mr. Calhoun. Guess this means I will be a full-time student of yours until I learn to master creating a piece of art. So, I will see you next week."

Jimmy brought LiAnn right hand to millimeters from his lips. His warm breath caressed her skin, sending a shiver of anticipation racing through her body. LiAnn expected him to gallantly kiss her palm. Instead, Jimmy's voice was low, throaty, barely above a whisper. "Oh, I don't believe waiting until next week will do at all. I was thinking about dinner. Tomorrow. I know the perfect, quaint Italian restaurant not far from here. Then I can take you on the scenic tour of Hot Springs. It is a place full of hidden mysteries. I hope it's not too bold of me to assume you like Italian food? It is, after all, the choice of gourmet chefs around the world for sensuality in and on the tongue."

What am I getting myself into? No, no second guessing. You've spent your entire life doing that, and look where it got you. Alone. Take a chance, you fool. No more fear.

"Not at all. I love Italian food. Always have. Shall we meet around seven?"

17

ADVENTURES IN THE WOODS

"So, you sure you can get this hunk of junk running? Looks to me like it's a waste of time. Maybe I should just call someone to come haul it off and then go buy a new one?"

Karina watched with amusement while Bo worked on the rusty tractor. His feet were surrounded by a myriad of tools while he messed with the motor. Sweat glistened off his tanned back, which was minus a shirt–again. It seemed the boy had an aversion to T-shirts. Streaks of grease covered his hands, and there was a big smudge spread across his forehead where he'd swiped away a mosquito on his face minutes before. His thick, honey-colored hair started to curl around the edges of his neck and forehead. Dear God, but the scenery was fun to watch. At least his second visit to the farm she knew about ahead of time, and she was more presentable. A touch of makeup, hair pulled back into a sleek pony, and a bra to corral the girls.

Bo produced a lazy grin. "Girl, you've got to learn to slow down some. This ain't L.A. Southern folk take things slow and easy. Don't get your panties in a twist. I'll get it fixed. Got plenty of time to get her up and goin' before the sun sets."

Karina took a sip of tea and stared out across the fields. Acres and acres of overgrown grass and weeds awaited the dull blades of the old tractor. Though it was beyond entertaining to watch Bo work and trade barbs with him, they needed to get a move on. It would take hours to mow the acreage.

The second the thought crossed her mind, the engine sputtered, coughed out a plume of black smoke, and roared to life. Karina watched as Bo straightened from his bent-over perch under the hood, slammed it shut, and shot her a wink. It was so sexy, it made her knees actually wobble.

In a flash, Bo scooped up the tools, threw them back into the toolbox, and then climbed up and sat behind the wheel. He held out his hand and, feeling like a kid again, Karina grabbed it and climbed up next to him. A smirk of satisfaction crossed his lips as he slid on his hat and engaged the gears. Karina never said a word, she just leaned back, slipped off her new cowboy boots, stuck her bare feet on the dash, and let memories of her younger days flood her mind.

One hour and two sweaty bodies later, the tractor sputtered and died. Karina glanced around, grateful at the amount of land mowed before it conked out. She expected Bo to start fiddling around with the controls, maybe grab the toolbox and open the hood, but instead, he jumped down and held out his arms for her to follow. Karina shot him a grin, turned, and exited the machine on the other side.

"Well, guess we got the last bit of juice the old girl had in her," Karina teased, patting the hot hood with her hand. "Time to put her out to pasture. Oh, wait, she's already there."

Bo sidled up to Karina, his own grin full of all sorts of underlying tones. Pure, raw sexual availability was the dominant one. "City girl. I've got a lot to teach y'all, don't I?"

Karina swiped at a mosquito buzzing around her arm. She'd slathered herself in Gram's idea of bug repellent, Skin-so-Soft, and to her surprise, didn't have one bite on her yet. The little bloodsuckers swarmed, but didn't land. "I don't think I need to be a country girl to figure out our ride just croaked."

Bo eyed her up and down, lingering on her damp T-shirt. "Honey, it ain't dead. Just thirsty. Like me."

Karina was thoughtful for a moment, then grinned. "Ah, no gas?"

Bo smiled sweetly as he took off toward the tree line. Over his shoulder, he yelled, "Yes ma'am. She's outta juice, and so am I. Come on, race y'all to the creek. Loser has to skinny-dip."

Karina forgot all about the bugs, the empty gas tank, or the fact Bo seemed to know his way quite well around her grandfather's farm. Her sense of competition, the need to always win, ignited her legs. Bo was fast, but she was faster. Years of running track in high school, combined with long legs and hatred of losing, made the dry, freshly cut hay kick up behind her.

In a few seconds, she surpassed him, her arms and legs pumping at full speed. Karina knew the way to the creek from visiting it numerous times in her youth, and the shortcuts. Once they hit the woods, they zigzagged through the dense brush. She could hear him behind her, maybe about five feet away. Spurred on by her frenzy to best him, Karina refused to look back.

She jumped over a downed tree, veering sharply to her right. If she remembered correctly, about ten yards up ahead was a big boulder jutting out over the edge of the creek. Sure enough, when Karina reached it first, she cast a quick glance behind her to see how close Bo was. He lagged only a few steps, so she turned back around and jumped. The cold water was a welcome reprieve from the intense heat, and she gasped in delight before her body went under.

When Karina surfaced, she expected to see Bo

right beside her, frolicking in the refreshing water. He wasn't. He stood at the edge of the boulder, his hands on his knees, breath coming in gasps. Sweat poured off him, but instead of looking defeated, he had the air of satisfaction gleaming on his face.

"What's the matter, country boy? Didn't think the city girl could beat you, huh?"

"Girl, I let you win. Because really, I'm the winner here."

Karina swam to the bank. She stood and shook the water from her hair. "Please. I may be older than you, but I am definitely faster. And how are you the winner? I believe the bet was loser has to skinny dip, right? Now see, to me, that puts me in the winner category, not you."

Bo didn't answer. His actions answered for him. Before Karina could blink, he shed his cowboy boots, tossing them to the ground below the boulder. He grabbed something from his pocket and in a flash, jeans and underwear crumpled in a pile around his feet. Karina held in her gasp of delight as she drank in every bit of his stunning body. She didn't have much time to drool over the visual because Bo jumped off the rock, executing the perfect cannonball before he disappeared under the dark water.

Karina knew the attraction between the two of them was strong. While they worked on the fence the week prior after his surprise visit, every time she glanced in his direction, she'd find him already staring at her. And not just a stare of interest.

It was full of raw, unabashed hunger. She recognized the look. It was the kind that said, "Yeah, I want to do you sideways" not "Gee, I think you're interesting, let's get to know each other and maybe go on a date."

Karina didn't have time to ponder over just what in the hell she was doing, or thinking. All rational thoughts, vanished as Bo surfaced. With a few strokes, Bo swam away from the deeper water and toward Karina. About ten feet away, he stood, the muddy water dancing just below his hip bones. Rivulets of water streamed down his torso, making small trails through his blond chest hair. In seconds, he stood next to Karina in all his glory.

Karina pulled her bulging eyes away from his rock hard abs, noticing what he held in his hand. The pack of condoms were crushed tight in his palm. *He sure is confident in his seduction skills! Hmm, wonder if he was ever a Boy Scout?*

"Seein' you in a wet T-shirt was my plan all

along, so see, I couldn't lose no matter what. Gotta tell ya, I'd place a week's worth of pay on your gals winnin' *any* wet T-shirt contest they was entered in. Like I said before, you need to be on a calendar. Naked."

"You know, if you wanted to see me naked, you could have just asked," Karina whispered, her words tangling up in her throat. *Jesus, he does want me, and boy, do I want him! Oh, what the Hell!*

Bo moved closer, his lips millimeters from Karina's. Her breath was warm and smelled of cinnamon and sweet tea. After reaching up and stroking her cheek, moving a section of her dripping hair away, Bo murmured into Karina's ear, "Okay. I want to see you naked *and* on top of me."

She almost came right then. Karina hadn't been with anyone in over two years, and Bo's animal attraction, his sensual touch, whipped her into a frenzy. Desire slammed into her mind, obliterating everything else. She didn't care about the fact she was out in the middle of the woods. Or on her family's property. Or someone might be watching and walk up on them.

All she cared about was letting Bo's full erection inside her. Her fingers couldn't move fast enough to get rid of her clothes. Bo let out a small laugh as she tried to wriggle out of her wet shorts, which was a difficult task.

He knelt down in the water, cupping his hands around her quivering butt. She buried her fingers in the mound of damp hair on his head and groaned, grinding her hips forward. With one hard yank, the shorts disappeared.

As well as his warm, wet tongue inside her.

Hallelujah, I'm in Heaven.

The sun had started its descent in the west, casting shades of orange, red, and pink across the sky. The reflection off the water was breathtaking, but it paled in comparison to what Karina was snuggled up against. The last several hours drained them both. Bo was an amazing lover. Karina climaxed so many times, she lost count. His fingers were just as magical as his mouth, but when he entered her the first time, she came after just two strokes.

Between the warmth of the late afternoon sun and all the places Bo's hands caressed, Karina's skin tingled with delight. The hot sex underneath the cloudless sky, the sense of risk of being caught and the joy of exploring Bo's tantalizing body, left Karina breathless, and a tad embarrassed. No, a *lot* embarrassed. She gave a sideways glance to the pile of used condoms and held in a snicker.

He'd been prepared, full of himself and the knowledge she would succumb to his advances. Their bodies had melded together with ease, and she was surprised at his skills for such a young buck. The creatures of the forest sure had a show put on for them as Bo explored every inch of her body. Thinking about his magical tongue sent another shiver of desire race through her. Rather than giving into the temptation, she decided it was time to learn more about the man who made her scream out "Oh, God!" at the top of her lungs several times.

"So, Bo, now that we've established the fact we are attracted to each other, I want to know more about you. I mean, I'm acquainted with what your mouth and body can do, so tell me about who's in here," Karina asked, pressing her hand against his chest.

"Ain't too much to tell, darlin'. I'm twenty-nine, have a twin named Bryce, and grew up here in Sheridan. Love to hunt, fish, and every now and then, get all redneck and go muddin' in my truck. Guess I'm just a typical southern boy, right?"

Karina couldn't help but smile at Bo's assessment of himself. Honest. To the point, no frills attached or bravado spewed out. Hearing he was older than she originally thought made Karina feel somewhat better. Their age difference wasn't enough to push the relationship into cougar territory.

Of course, she didn't even know if this was the *start* of a relationship, or just a good old fashion one-night stand sort of thing. Either way, she was curious about him. Karina propped herself up on her elbow, marveling at his gorgeous features kissed by the rays of the sun. "Good start. Okay, so here it is, the middle of the day and you are here with me instead of at a job somewhere. Other than moving furniture, what else do you do?"

A teasing gleam appeared behind Bo's eyes as his hand moved across the swell of Karina's hip. "Well recently, I noticed I'm pretty good at makin' your eyes roll backward."

The throbbing in her sore crotch intensified as Bo's strong fingers traced a circle across

Karina's bare skin. She shook off the urge to mount him again, determined to find out more about him. With her luck, he was married and had a handful of children running around. "Oh, no doubt about that, but I mean, you know, do you have a job? Did you go to college? Are you married? Kids? Most importantly, why were you hell-bent on seducing an older woman? Oh, and by the way, if you tell me you're married, I'm going to kick your ass. Believe me when I say, I am more than capable."

Bo's touch increased in intensity as his hand moved to the small of Karina's back and then around to her front. He slid in between her thighs and rubbed her mound. A lazy grin spread across his swollen lips. "Here is the long and short of Bo Barton. I ain't married and haven't sired any offspring. My dad owns a ton of farmland, and my family ain't hurtin' for money. My brother and I do side work durin' the off-season to keep busy. Bryce and I both have degrees in farm management and will take over the place when our dad passes on."

Karina moaned softly as Bo's fingers slid inside her. She closed her eyes and went limp as his sweaty body shifted and he moved on top of her once again. His hips ground into her, his warm lips grazing her check then up to her ear.

"As far as you're concerned, I've wanted you since I first laid eyes on you. Age don't matter to me none. You're a fine filly, and I just knew you'd be a wild ride. That's the short part about Bo. Here's the longer version."

Karina gasped as Bo entered her, thoughts about anything else vanished as they rocked in heated harmony on the soft grass.

"I wonder how many neighbors heard me scream out your name?" Karina teased, her fingers toying with the golden curls on Bo's chest.

"There ain't no one out here this time of year. Too hot. Now, if it was huntin' season, my answer would be different. And we woulda had us an audience. Boy, they woulda been happy with the view. I know I am. You are somethin' else, Karina. Like I said, knew it the first time I saw you."

Karina swatted at a mosquito on Bo's abs,

irritated the little bloodsuckers were back. She glanced over at the water, wincing at the cloud of them hovering above the surface. Any second, they would descend upon their naked bodies and feast.

Though she didn't want to break the tranquil moment, she gave Bo's belly a light pat and stood. Once on her feet, Karina kept in the groan of pain she wanted to release inside. The pounding between her legs was intense. God, she would be walking funny for *days.* "I believe our clothes are dry now. Come on, let's go. I need to get back to the house before my mother sends out a search party. She's sort of overprotective like that, so fair warning."

"I don't know what kind of man y'alls used to in California, but I ain't the kind to worry about. I'm as gentle as a kitten with a heart of gold. At least that's what my mama says."

Karina couldn't help but laugh as she pulled her shorts on. "It's too early to tell about your heart, but you're certainly gentle. At times. Honestly, I preferred the rougher, lion-like moments."

Suddenly, Bo was right beside Karina. He held out his hand, a warm, genuine smile on his face. Bo's other hand reached down and cupped

Karina's right breast, giving it a light squeeze. "Yes, I reckon' from your screams, ya did." He lifted Karina's chin up to meet his gaze. "Rest assured, darlin', I ain't a liar, and I was raised right. I know how to treat a lady, though sometimes I get the steps out of order. I think the first one was I was supposed to do was ask ya out on a date. It's your fault I got mixed up, comin' out here lookin' all sexy as hell in those shorts and t-shirt. I've had a hard-on for ya since the day I was movin' your furniture. So, Karina Summers, I would like to take ya out for beer, bootscootin' and barbeque. What do ya say?"

Karina's mind filled with hundreds of reasons to say no. She pushed them all away, refusing to let the past control her life any longer. "Only on one condition."

Bo cocked his head to the side, grinning as they walked through the woods. "Which is?"

"You teach me how to two-step, and don't laugh at me while I learn. Fair?"

Bo gave Karina's hand a quick squeeze. "Deal. I done told ya, I'd make country gal outta ya yet. Now, come on, let's go gas up our ride. I've gotta head home and eat. I worked up quite an appetite. Plus, it's your turn to spill. I wanna know all about the woman who likes to scream out my name when I'm inside her, and why she thinks she can kick my ass."

18

TIME TO REBUILD

Karina smiled watching Ranger bound around the backyard, chasing fireflies like a carefree puppy. The moon was almost full, and the silvery light illuminated the freshly mowed pasture. As Ranger performed his jumps, the moonlight made his coat look gray, like a ghost. She tipped back the beer and took a long swig. The sounds of the katydids were so loud, it was like she stood in the middle of a nest of the creatures. It was a welcome relief to the annoying sounds of the city. Karina took a deep breath, drinking in the pungent air.

Ranger needed to quit playing around and finish his business so she could go back inside, but she couldn't bring herself to scold him. He was just too cute. She needed to help clean up the dishes from yet another artery-hardening meal fixed by Gram. Thankfully, the table had also been full of fresh vegetables, so Karina had loaded her plate up with tomatoes, green beans, spinach and banana peppers, leaving little room for anything else.

It was almost sunset when they chugged up on the tractor, and everyone else was already back. After exchanging pleasantries with Grampa, Bo left, promising to return the next day to finish, then pick her up at seven for "a night out on the town." Once he was gone, Karina walked into the house and straight to the bathroom. She ran out of hot water twice while soaking her pleasantly sore body.

When Karina caught herself humming, something she *never* did, it dawned on her she was happy. Content with life, like a hundred-pound weight had been lifted off her back. Her old life in Cali had finally been put to bed. What happened, happened. It was over, and way beyond time to move on.

Karina's gaze wandered over to the edge of the woods, immediately bringing back the earlier events of her afternoon with Bo. Though unsure of where her life was heading at the moment, or how the budding relationship with Bo would progress, or end, she didn't care. Hell, all the worry might be for nothing. Bo got what he wanted, which was an afternoon of screwing a willing participant. The chase was over, the prize won, and it was among the realm of possibilities Bo would just move on.

Karina would take things day by day. If it turned out her and Bo ended up being only friends with benefits, great. She really couldn't see a scenario where they ended up anything more, which was okay. After all, they didn't have a whole lot in common, other than mind-blowing sex. If they remained an item, would she be able to keep up with his demanding libido when she was older? Doubtful. Hell, he'd worn her out earlier, and she wasn't even in her forties yet.

How would she react when someone assumed she was his older sister, or even his mother? Oh, she knew. They'd get a swift punch in the gut, or an earful from her dirty mouth. *Stop it, girl. Just...go with the flow. Walk in, eyes open, with no expectations. You came here to build a new life. So, build it!*

Karina heard footsteps behind her. Expecting her mom, who had been uncharacteristically quiet during dinner, all geared up and ready to dig into the reason behind Karina's glowing face and ridiculous grin. She was surprised to hear the voice of her grandfather instead.

"So, I see you and Bo got the tractor goin', and quite a bit mowed down. Looks good," Junior said.

Karina tried not to wince at the knowing look behind Grampa's cloudy eyes. He reached down and patted Ranger's head after lighting his pipe. He blew out a plume of smoke, and Karina's cheeks flushed with heat.

She wondered just how much he knew about her afternoon activities. A sense of paranoia hit her as she considered someone Grampa knew might have been out in the woods, watching the entire spectacle. Maybe made a phone call, requesting the X-rated wilderness adventures of his kin stop.

"Plan on finishing it up tomorrow. We, uh, ran

out of gas. Bo said he would bring by extra when he comes back."

"Ran out of gas, huh? Now that surprises me. Ol' Bo's worked on his family's farm his whole life. He shoulda been better prepared."

Oh, he was prepared, that's for sure.

The knowing glint was behind Grampa's eyes again, so Karina changed the subject before dying from embarrassment. He stood there, in his favorite attire of overalls and a straw hat, grinning like the Cheshire Cat. "You aren't supposed to be smoking, you know. The doctor said..."

With a look of irritation, Junior waved his hand to shush Karina. "Don't go gettin' all bossy with me, girl. I know what the doc said, and I don't care. I ain't gonna live out the rest of my years like a timid mouse, afraid of doin' anythin' that might make my time shorter. People live, people die. That's the way of the world. I could go live like a monk for the rest of my life. It ain't gonna stop the inevitable. It's hard enough knowin' I can't do the things I used to because my body won't listen to my brain. I mean, look what I've become. An old man who can't even do for himself. The day before y'all arrived, I tried to mow. Couldn't stand lookin' at the shape the ol' place was in. Didn't want you or your ma workin' yourselves to the bone. But the heat got to me before I even made it out to the tractor. Though your gram and I do appreciate y'all comin' down here to help us, and all the work you're doin', it's, I don't know. Humiliatin' is the best word, I guess."

Karina moved closer and put her arm around her grandfather's frail shoulders. "Grampa, there is nothing to feel humiliated about. We love you both and *wanted* to make this change, this move. You didn't ask, we offered."

Junior let out a sigh. "I know. And believe me, Gram and I are so happy to have y'all here. I mean, this place," Junior raised a shaky hand, pointing toward the hay fields, "is our legacy to you both. Eight generations of our family has owned all this, and we'll leave it all to you and your ma. Does my heart good to see ya both takin' good care of it. Your ma's got the house all shiny and clean, and lordy, all the work you've put in outside? Means a lot. A lot. But, it still sticks in my craw sometimes that I can't do it anymore."

Karina was at a loss as to what to say. How would she feel if in his shoes? The mind solid, but the body weak? She shuddered and hugged him tight. "Never mind that kind of talk. It's what families are for, right?" She pulled back and whistled for Ranger. "Listen, Grampa, if it's okay, I would like to talk to you about the barn. I know it's been around for generations, but that's the problem. It's in poor shape, as I'm sure you know. When Bo and I were inside it earlier, looking for gas, he agreed with my assessment. It's unstable, and needs to be completely torn down and rebuilt from the ground up. Bo offered to bring his brother and a few friends to help construct it, when the time comes."

A shadow of sadness creased his brow as Junior focused his gaze on the crumbling building. "I know, sugar. I know. It's just really hard to let go of things in the past. Part of gettin' on up there in age, I guess. Old folks like me need to eyeball items to keep our younger days fresh in our heads. Had me some great times inside the four walls over the years. My pa taught me everythin' I needed to know about bein' a man inside it."

Karina winced when she noticed tears shimmered behind his eyes, immediately feeling like an ass for broaching the sensitive subject matter. Suddenly, she watched his soulful eyes become playful.

"Okay, so your gram don't know this, so just between the two of us little birds, but my first taste of bein' a man happened in the hayloft with Marci Sue Davenport. Mercy, the girl was a beauty. Gave me a right proper sendoff before I left for the war. Right proper."

Blinking twice in shock, Karina burst out laughing, tears streaming down her face. "Grampa, you are too much! As the kids say nowadays, that was too much information! I...uh...wow. Believe me, I won't say a *word* to anyone. I would prefer to never think of it again."

"Whatsa matter, girl? Were you under some strange impression my only romp in the hay was with..."

Tears ran from Karina's eyes. Her sides hurt from laughing so hard. She caught her breath and held up a hand in protest. "Please! No more. I get it. I don't want to, but I do."

"Hey, if it weren't for that ol' gal breakin' my heart with a Dear John letter while I was overseas, I woulda never met my Ruth. Even sadness has its reasons."

"You're right, as always. Though you could have simply said that last part without the other." Karina smiled and took a sip of beer. "So, back to the *original* topic at hand. The construction, or reconstruction I should say, of the barn."

In a flash, Junior's tone shifted. "I know it needs to come down before it collapses on its own, but I can't do it. I don't want to be here when it happens."

Karina wiped away the wetness from her cheeks, thankful to be back on topic. "Believe me, Grampa, I understand. It's a part of my life, too. I remember following you around inside, watching you tinker with the tractor, build things, telling me stories about our family. But the memories are here," Karina pointed to her head, then his, "not encased in the old wood. It won't matter if the structure is new or not, they will still remain inside us."

Junior tapped out the spent tobacco and cast a woeful glance toward the barn. He nodded his head once in solemn agreement. "You're right, sugar. It is a danger in the condition it's in, and it would be a cryin' shame to continue to watch it die a slow, agonizin' death. Tell you what: you and your new squeeze take care of it, just let me know when you plan on startin'. I'll use it as an excuse to take your gram to Branson for a few days. She's been beggin' me to take her for years, and all them contests she keeps entering ain't come through, so now is a good time. I...don't want to watch it come down."

Karina whistled for Ranger again, and turned to walk back toward the house with her grandfather. "That sounds like a plan. Want me to help set up the trip? I can book everything online. You just let me know when you want to go."

"Let me talk to Gram first. Gotta check with the boss before I go makin' plans. Guess I better get on it, since harvest season is comin' up soon, and I know Bo will be busy."

"Sure. Oh, and Grampa? Bo and I are nothing more than friends at the moment."

Junior stopped in mid-stride, eyeballing Karina with a look of bemusement. "Friends, huh? I ain't never seen two friends beamin' from ear to ear after spendin' the day in the hot sun mowin' before, that's for sure."

"Grampa..."

"Honey, I ain't judgin'. I've known that boy since he was knee high to a grasshopper. Comes from good stock, and he ain't never been nothin' but polite and respectful to me and your gram. Hard worker, that one is. You could do worse, that's for sure. From what I heard, you have."

Thankfully, Karina was spared having to respond by the appearance of her mother at the back door.

"There you both are! Karina, come help with the kitchen, please. And Dad, Cecil called. He wants you to call him back. He sounded sort of upset."

19

FIRST STEPS

Karina took off her glasses and rubbed her burning eyes. The past hour had been spent staring at the laptop, searching out hotels, the best route to get there, and things to do in Branson. Though she enjoyed the research, even though it was for the simple reason of helping out her grandparents, rather than cyber-stalking a criminal, it was familiar. Karina wouldn't admit it to her family, but she missed the hunt, as she always called her investigations. Digging, probing, searching for little tidbits to combine together, forming a complete workup of her quarry.

The research concluded Branson was a little over a two-hundred mile drive from Sheridan. It would make for a long car ride for her grandparents, and one Karina didn't want them to make on their own. Mom would need to go with them.

When the cell phone buzzed, Karina glanced down, and her anger rose fast when she recognized the number. She hadn't heard a peep from Cal since the night of her arrival. "Figures he would contact me after the glorious afternoon I had." Karina squared her shoulders. There was no way she was going to ruin the remainder of the evening by reading his text "Screw you, Cal," she flicked the button, powering down the phone.

She rose and stretched, disturbing Ranger, who had been asleep at her feet. Bending down, she patted his blocky head, cooing gibberish to him. Both turned their heads at the sound of a soft tap on the bedroom door.

"Karina? You still up?"

Instead of answering, Karina walked to the door and opened it, ushering her mom inside.

"Hey, you're up late. What's wrong, Goldilocks? Bed too soft? Too hard?"

"Funny, I could say the same thing to you. Looks like you've been cruising the virtual highways too long. Your eyes are as red as my shirt."

"They've been that way ever since we cut all the hay. At least I didn't get all stuffy and start sneezing again. I just look like I've smoked a blunt. Or several." Karina laughed, plopping down on the chair in front of the small desk. "Talked to Grampa earlier about tearing down and rebuilding the barn. He gave his blessing but doesn't want to be here when we do it. He mentioned taking Gram to Branson, so I've been looking for a nice hotel for them to stay at. You know Gram; she's so cheap, she'll want to stay at a roadside dive or something. Pack a cooler full of food to eat while there, instead of eating at a nice restaurant. Not going to happen. I want them to be in an upscale, fancy and *safe* place. My treat, of course. And for you to drive them. No way do they need to make the trip through the mountains on those windy roads. Grampa's vision isn't what it used to be. Gram gave her blessing, so I'm looking at setting things up for next weekend."

LiAnn grinned. "Oh, sounds like fun! I've heard there are some great shows there, and lots to do. I don't mind driving, but not in their car. It's too small, and Pop's truck is a rattle-trap. And Mom isn't cheap. She's frugal. Big difference, you know."

"Frugal. Cheap. The word chosen doesn't erase the fact Gram keeps a tight grip on her wallet. And don't worry, Mom. You can drive *Dragula*. Just remember to watch your speed. The cops around here already got your number." Karina winked. "Or you could just buy your own car and take them in it. Maybe a big SUV with a gas tank the size of a small boat. How you've made it all these years without your own vehicle is beyond me."

"I didn't need one in L.A. I could go anywhere I needed to with public transportation, plus I had my unit for work. And you as backup. I preferred to save my money, rather than spend it on a hot rod."

Karina shrugged her shoulders. "What can I say? I like to live on the edge. Can't take possessions with you when you die, right? If I could, I would have saved up and bought a Lamborghini. Tooling around in the clouds in that baby truly would be Heaven."

Curious about Karina's earlier remark, LiAnn asked, "So, you said *we* earlier. I assume you plan on using the handsome Bo Barton to rebuild the barn? You sure the work will get done? You know, in between bouts of playtime?"

"Was I that obvious?"

LiAnn sat on the edge of the bed. "Honey, the heat between you two could be picked up on a thermometer. Besides, not much hay was cut in comparison to time spent in the fields. Oh, and the biggest clue? The fact that your shirt was on backward when you arrived back."

Karina shook her head. Her mom didn't miss a thing, especially not something as obvious as clothing thrown on backward in a hurry. With a few taps on the keyboard, she logged off and joined her mom on the bed. "Bo's just teaching me how to be a laid-back Southerner, that's all. He's all about taking things slow and easy."

LiAnn stifled a giggle. "Wow, you must be tired if you're giving me the G-rated version."

"Aren't you the one who said I needed to be more PC on the way down here?" Karina retorted. She cocked her head and stared at the messy, blonde curls piled high on her mom's head. Though pushing hard on sixty's door, the woman was still gorgeous, especially when humor danced across her face. "Besides, after my conversation with Grampa earlier, I decided it was high time to tell my steamy love life to Ranger like you suggested. Boy, did he ever get an earful. Good thing he can't understand a word I said, or he'd think I'm a slut."

Rather than rising to the baited statement, LiAnn cleared her throat and changed the subject. "Speaking of slow and easy, there's a reason I'm up so late. I wanted to talk to you about my wardrobe."

Amused by the sudden topic switch, Karina replied, "Why, did you finally get tired of looking at starched white shirts and khakis? And exactly how does slow and easy tie into your closet of boring duds?"

"You know, your mouth is...oh, never mind. I'm too tired to jump into a verbal sparring match tonight. Yes, I'm sick of looking at my old clothes, and need your fashion sense to help me pick out something to wear tomorrow night."

"What's going on tomorrow...oh, wait! Jimmy asked you out, didn't he?" Karina gushed. *What an idiot I am, assuming the bemused look on Mom's face was because of my interactions with a man, not vice-versa.*

"Yep. Right after painting class. I think he just

felt sorry for me, since my artwork was horrendous. Whatever the reason, we are going to dinner in Hot Springs tomorrow. Some fancy Italian place, so I want to dress up a bit. I realized when rummaging around earlier, I don't even own a pair of heels!"

Karina jumped off the bed and motioned for her mom to do the same. "Okay, time for bed then. I planned on working on the hay fields again tomorrow, but that's shot to hell now. I'll just call Bo and tell him he has the day off. I'm taking you shopping. There isn't a thing in your closet that could even be considered appropriate attire for a first date."

LiAnn followed, but stopped when she reached the door. "Sounds like a plan to me. Oh, and one other thing, well, two actually, I want to talk to you about before we hit the sack."

Karina smirked, "I told you already, I'm only doing the PC version of my life now."

"No, it's not about your afternoon romp with Bo. Just one look at your face tells me all I need to know. You're positively beaming."

"Okay, so what is it then?"

"First, you need to come with us on Thursday to The Magnolia. I'm telling you, Karina, it isn't anything like what you've got stuck in your head.

Never seen any senior living place like it before. Ever. I think, once you visit and see what *real* retirement living is like, it will help the bad memories from Jubilee disappear."

Karina swallowed and forced herself not to hang her head in shame. She hated the fact she was disappointing her family by not going, but she just wasn't ready. "And the second item?"

"I want to introduce you to Jimmy. As I mentioned before, my man radar is skewed. Want to make sure he passes your sharp eye before I even think about jumping into a relationship. So, Thursday, will you come with us? Jimmy needs to see that at least someone in our family has artistic talent."

Despite her misgivings about stepping foot in a senior living environment, Karina couldn't say no to the pleading face of her mother. "Okay, okay. Stop twisting my arm. But wait...I'll meet him tomorrow, right? Isn't he coming to pick you up for your big date?"

"No. I'm...not sure where all this is heading, so I'm not quite ready for that. If things go sour during our dinner, I want an escape route. A way to leave. So, I'm taking Mom's car."

"You always think ahead, don't you, Mom?"

"No other way to live, darling daughter."

"Now, off to bed so we can hit the stores early tomorrow."

"Fair enough. Goodnight, sweetheart. Love you."

Karina responded with a light kiss on her mom's warm cheek. Once alone, she grabbed her cell, flicked it on, and sent a text to Bo.

"*Taking mom shopping tmr. You have the day off from work. Ha ha. Grampa said next weekend is fine about the barn. Guess we need to get some material. See you at seven.*"

Karina crawled under the cool sheets and turned out the bedside lamp. She didn't have to wait long for a response.

"*OK. Got 2 go buy more skins anyway C U 2mr wear something easy to take off.*"

Karina chuckled inside the walls of the bedroom. *No doubt.*

She put the phone on the table next to the bed, but curiosity overrode the sense of irritation. She picked it back up, and with a few clicks, pulled up the text message from Cal. "*We need to talk. Call me ASAP.*"

A heavy stone of sadness and guilt slammed into her gut. Why now? Why not discuss things back when it first happened? He didn't want to discuss his infidelity. Cal was more interested in keeping their business running. Suddenly, every assignment he went on was out of town. The chance to hash things out never happened because Cal Benson didn't want to talk about it. Expected Karina to just lump the whole debacle into the crapper, flush it away, and go on with their relationship. Pretend it never happened. A "momentary lapse in judgment" is what he'd called it.

My ass.

Instead of responding, Karina deleted the message. There was a time in her life when Calvin Benson ruled every thought.

Not anymore.

"I recommend you try Feinmart first. Reasonable prices and good quality clothin'. If you can't find anythin', then try Today's Woman. It's only a few blocks away from Feinmart," Ruth offered while fixing a cup of coffee.

"Thanks for the suggestions, Gram. Those places are in Hot Springs, right?" Karina asked, her fingers flying across the screen of her phone.

LiAnn watched in amusement. Her daughter was more than fond of her electronic device. Karina was addicted.

Ruth nodded. "Both are easy to get to. You just take the Bypass…"

"Got it, right here, Gram. See? Technology is fantastic. When it works."

"Technology. Please. What if the directions ain't right and you end up on the wrong side of town?" Ruth replied, a hint of worry in her voice.

Karina laughed. "Well, that has happened before, just not to me. Sorry, I didn't mean to cut you off, Gram. I'm a bit excited to finally take Mom shopping. Time to get her some clothes to show off all her assets. Sure you don't want to come with us?"

Ruth smiled and took a sip of coffee. "My days of traipsin' around stores are over. My knees just don't enjoy it anymore. You two have a good time."

LiAnn took a long drink of the cold, lemon-infused water. She was parched. Four hours and six stores later, Karina finally gave her approval on several items, including a pair of the sexiest black heels LiAnn had ever seen. The trunk was full of bags, and LiAnn was a hot mess from trying on clothes, tromping from one store to another, the stifling heat slapping her in the face each time they walked outside. Her stomach grumbled in anticipation of lunch.

The smirk on Karina's face, the look of bemusement and satisfaction from a successful day of shopping, brought a smile to LiAnn's. Karina looked more relaxed, calmer, and most importantly, less haunted, than she had in a long time. Even the worry lines on her face weren't as pronounced. In a word, Karina was radiant.

When they walked into the restaurant, the waiter practically tripped over his tongue as it rolled out of his drooling mouth. Karina was oblivious to the way men, and some women, looked at her. She always had been. But LiAnn never missed the gaping mouths and bulging eyes as people watched her child enter a room.

Lunch arrived, delivered by the hands of the enamored waiter, who fawned over Karina like she was the Queen of England. It was hysterical. He finally slunk away after assurances from Karina that no, she didn't need any more water, or salsa, or chips, napkins, etc. LiAnn kept her laughter inside by filling her mouth with a hefty bite of burrito.

"This has been so much fun! Dressing you, helping you pick out clothes, it's like playing with a life-sized Barbie. Just one with bigger boobs," Karina teased, in between mouthfuls of her vegetarian taco. "You need to wear the black dress with those killer heels. Minimal jewelry. Hair loose and down your back. I guarantee your date will melt, and it won't be just from the God-awful heat."

LiAnn almost choked on her chip. "Karina!"

"Sorry Mom, but it's the truth! I think you've forgotten how stunning you are after all these years of hiding your assets under boring white cotton and khaki slacks. So, spill. I want to know more about Jimmy."

LiAnn wiped her lips and shrugged. "Not much to tell, really. In his seventies, I think. Just a guess though. He is a widower, not sure about kids. Didn't mention any, and you know, if you have them, you talk about them. He's a retired teacher who happens to be a fantastic painter. Oh, you will love his work. Wait until you see it. He's a gentleman, full of old school charm. That's really all I know at this point."

Karina's eyes lit up with amusement. "He must be quite the charmer if you agreed to go on a date with him so soon. So, just dinner? Then what? Movie? Bowling? A private painting class with your body as the canvas?"

LiAnn rolled her eyes. "Just dinner. I'm taking things slow, unlike you."

Karina immediately blushed but didn't respond. Instead, she just smiled and shoved a huge forkful of food into her mouth.

LiAnn finished tousling her hair, grimacing at the reflection in the mirror. She stared at the black heels sitting on the edge of the bed, waiting for her to slide them on. Cramming her feet inside them, and then trying to walk, was going to be a joke. A huff of irritated air left her lungs.

She shouldn't have let Karina talk her into buying them. How sexy would falling flat on her face inside the restaurant be? Instead of putting them on, she turned back to the mirror and fiddled with her earrings. Karina was right about the little black dress. It hugged all her curves in all the right places, and the black material hid her flaws quite well. LiAnn reached down and grabbed the red lipstick tube on the desk, wincing when she noticed her hands shook. She forced them to stop so she could touch up her lips without looking like the Joker.

Breathe, woman! It's just dinner.

A loud knock at the door made LiAnn jump, causing her to drop the tube onto the floor. Bending down to retrieve it, she yelled, "Come on in."

The door opened and Karina sauntered inside. LiAnn gasped. Her beautiful child was wearing a pair of jeans so tight, sitting down would be impossible without cutting her in half. The new pair of dark brown calfskin cowboy boots gleamed. Karina topped off her date attire with a low cut, white halter shirt completely open in the back, tied around her neck, the straps flowing in loose waves down her back. Her raven black hair pulled back, exposing her long, graceful neck. It hung down in soft curls behind her. Karina looked beyond stunning.

"You actually plan on dancing in that? How? Can you even breathe? Aren't you afraid something will pop out while bustin' a move?"

Karina laughed as she twirled around, showing off the entire look. "Uh, you've seen my date. He's a hunk. A *young* hunk. I wanted to make sure his eyes stayed on me tonight. I'm going to be competing with twenty-something's shaking their groove things, remember?"

LiAnn shook her head. "Oh, you won't have to worry. All eyes will be on you tonight. Poor Bo might be forced to fight other wolves off."

"Good, then that means I accomplished what I set out to do!" Karina replied, beaming. "But enough about me. Look at you! Holy Hotness, Batman! Maybe *you* should change. Don't want your first date to be at the hospital. You know, because old Jimmy had a heart attack after you walk in, looking like dessert in a black dress. Oh, put the shoes on! I want to see the full package before I leave for my date."

LiAnn's cheeks inflamed as she waved off Karina's compliment with a shaky hand. She turned and stared at the heels of torture and grimaced. "Okay, okay, give me a minute to work up my nerve. I'm afraid I'll fall over."

"You won't," Karina replied, moving across the floor. She yanked the shoes off the bed and held them out to LiAnn. With reluctance, LiAnn took them and flopped down on the edge of the mattress. LiAnn stifled a groan of irritation as she crammed her toes inside. She reached out her hand to Karina to help stand.

"Yeow, Mom. You're as tall as I am now! Oh yeah, Jimmy will have a heart attack for sure. But, just in case his ticker is strong, I brought you a present."

LiAnn blanched when she looked down at what Karina held in her other hand. "Seriously?"

Karina grinned wickedly at her. In a flash, she yanked LiAnn's purse from the bed and slid the pack of condoms inside. "Yes, seriously. Always be prepared, right? Don't want a baby brother or sister at this stage in my life. I like being the only child."

"Menopause took care of that problem years ago..."

"Duh, Mom. Like I don't remember all the times you froze me out of the house. However, there are other things–uglier, nasty things besides children–you need protection from. Best to be prepared."

"Sure you can spare them? I mean, won't *you* need them tonight?" LiAnn shot back, eager to take a dig at Karina.

"Believe me, Bo is beyond prepared. Probably has a case of them in his truck."

Before LiAnn could say anything, Ranger started barking. From the living room, her father yelled, "Bo's here. Karina, where's Ranger's leash?"

In a flash, Karina swiped an air kiss near her mom's ear. "Have a good time, Mom. I know I will."

20

FIRST DATE JITTERS

LiAnn sat inside the car, frayed nerves keeping her fingers from opening the door. She watched people walk in and out of the front entrance, wondering why she was having such difficulty breathing. Glancing at her watch and noticing it was seven on the dot, LiAnn's heart rate spiked. Jimmy had arrived ten minutes prior and was probably sipping a cold drink, wondering if she stood him up or not, or was just being fashionably late. LiAnn was doing neither, only trying to corral her nerves to a manageable level.

She took a deep breath, grabbed her purse, yanked out the pack of condoms, and stared at them. Her daughter, ever the prankster. What kind of child gives her mother a package of condoms?

A lovable, crazy one.

Clutching the package in her hand, LiAnn opened the door and stepped out into the brick-oven heat. After locking the car, she concentrated on taking small steps so she didn't fall as she walked to the entrance. LiAnn looked around, thankful no one was outside and deposited the gift from her child in the garbage by the front door. Once inside, LiAnn's nerves settled a bit as the rush of cold air slammed into her.

"Good evening. Welcome to Bella's Place. Party of one?"

"I'm..uh, no. Meeting someone. Jimmy Calhoun?"

The waiter's broad smile was faker than the faux decor of an Italian villa. "Ah, Mr. Calhoun! He is in the back at his favorite table. This way please."

She followed, trying to concentrate on the

ambiance rather than her nerves. They wound their way through the intimate tables until they reached the back of the restaurant. LiAnn was surprised how few people were seated. She wondered if the food was any good or not. Jimmy spotted them, smiled, stood and pulled out her chair. The waiter disappeared, and LiAnn's throat went dry. Jimmy's eyes took in every inch of her, the look reflecting back from them was more than approval.

"Good evening. Pardon me for gawking, but you're simply gorgeous. A true beauty, you are."

"Thank you," LiAnn replied, trying not to stutter. Jimmy looked great himself. Dressed to perfection in a soft gray suit, topped off with a vibrant blue tie and silver cufflinks with sapphires in the middle of each one. "You clean up nice, too. This is a different look. No paint spatter."

Jimmy smiled, warm and inviting. It almost irked LiAnn, because he didn't seem nervous at all, and she was a mess on the inside. She tried to cut herself some slack. After all, it had been over fifteen years since she'd been on a date, so of course she was nervous.

Jimmy's eyes never left LiAnn's as he reached out and took her hand. He brought it up to his lips, just as he'd done in the art room, only this time he did plant a delicate kiss on it. "I hope it's not too bold of me, but I ordered for us already. I didn't wish to be interrupted by pesky questions from the staff. Roasted chicken with mushroom cream sauce and Ecco Domini Pinot Grigio. Tiramisu for dessert. Asked them to bring dinner to the table at precisely eight o'clock. It will give us time to get better acquainted before we dine."

LiAnn stiffened. Unaccustomed to not only someone taking complete and total control, or having enough interest to plan ahead, anticipating every want or need, words escaped her. Jimmy took her silence as disapproval. He let go of her hand, a wounded look flashed across his face.

LiAnn found her voice. "Oh, no, I'm just...sorry. I'm nervous. Not used to someone fawning over me. Though nice, it's kind of odd. Remember, I'm a SoCal girl, used to doing things for myself. I forget I'm in the South now, where manners, grace, and charm still flourish. The dinner choice sounds wonderful. Thank you."

Jimmy settled back in his seat, a look of relief on his face. She needed to relax, and the only way she knew how was to allow the brash, cocky cop to take over. Treat the evening as a fact-gathering mission. Learn more about the man seated next to her from an investigative standpoint, rather than a personal one. The second the decision was made, LiAnn's tight muscles relaxed.

"I'm relieved to know I'm not the only one who's nervous. You should have seen me getting ready earlier. Increased perspiration caused me to change shirts twice."

"You certainly hide your worries well, Jimmy. I would never have guessed you were anything but calm."

Jimmy smiled then cleared his throat several times. "How about we start this evening off by examining a few items, shall we? Should help ease both our minds, I believe."

Intrigued, LiAnn nodded in agreement.

"Good. Okay, first things first. We aren't naive, young things searching for a life partner. Starting on our journey, wondering where it will take us. We aren't doe-eyed individuals eager to find the *one* to start and raise a family with. We've been down that path already. Lived our lives to the fullest. At this stage, we've both experienced, at least once, great love. Am I on target so far?"

LiAnn couldn't help but smile. Brash honesty.

She liked the openness but wasn't too fond of the veiled remarks about their ages. She wasn't even sixty yet. "General vicinity, I believe."

Jimmy took a deep breath then continued. "I loved my wife. Her death haunts me every day, even after all these years. I made peace a long time ago and learned how to live in a strange, new world without her. Never sought out new companionship. The need, the *want*, was never there. I fulfilled my loneliness, the emptiness inside, by volunteering at The Magnolia. Teaching art, reading, sharing creativity with others, allowed me to be happy. No, not happy. Content. I settled for contentment. But after meeting you, and the feelings you brought to the surface, ones I thought were lost forever, I don't want to be content anymore. I want to live, laugh, enjoy life again. With someone who makes my heart skip a beat before it beats for the last time. I believe that someone is you."

Unsure what the appropriate response should be, LiAnn took a sip of water. She wished the wine was available. What Jimmy just said to her made her own heart flutter, but not in a good way. His words were probably the sweetest, most genuine compliment she'd ever received. Bar none. It should have made her giddy with excitement or swoon as she clutched her chest in one of those movie "Awwww" moments. Instead of feeling all sentimental and gooey, the prevailing emotion in LiAnn's head was awkwardness.

While preparing for the date earlier, her mind spun with all sort of scenarios about how the evening might turn out. One scene even included the evening ending at Jimmy's house after dinner. After all, LiAnn was attracted to him, and it had been a *really* long time since she'd been with anyone. A *really* long time. So long, in fact, she worried dust bunnies would fly out of her crotch if things turned amorous. LiAnn had been prepared for the Lothario/ Casanova version, one ready to seduce and charm her into the sack. Surface level attraction, plain and simple, was what LiAnn assumed tonight would be all about. What Jimmy delivered seemed like a marriage proposal of sorts, and it made her uncomfortable.

"Jimmy, I think you went beyond an examination and just performed a full dissection. I appreciate your honesty, so I will reciprocate. I'm just here to have a nice dinner with a man I find incredibly artistic and charming. Am I attracted to you? Yes, but your charm isn't the only reason I decided to join you tonight. My daughter insisted I put my past behind me and move on, and I am finally ready to do so but plan on taking things slow. Snail-paced slow. My father would call it courting. What you just said does not fall into the category of slow. At all. Maybe it's me, being overly cautious. But honestly, what you said made me wonder if you think we both have one foot in the grave already. I don't view myself, or you, that way at all."

"I didn't mean for it...wow, guess my dating skills are rusty. Haven't been on one in a *very* long time. I was just trying to express my thoughts, which it seems, I failed at. Miserably. Allow me to try again?"

Despite the strange situation, LiAnn couldn't help but smile. At least Jimmy was trying to be honest even if it was a bit overbearing. "Of course."

Jimmy graced LiAnn with a sheepish grin as he cleared his throat. "What I meant to express was you intrigue me, LiAnn Tuck. Not just because of your beauty, or the fact you are a retired policewoman, which, by the way, is a first for me. I've never known one personally before. I enjoy your company and would like to get to know you better. I'm not looking for anything but pleasurable companionship. If that means a good friend only, fine. If it develops beyond that, even better. I have no expectations on my end. I was trying to say I wasn't looking for a replacement mate, or someone to have children with. There, better?"

"Much. That's how I feel. To the letter."

"Good! Now the air is cleared, so let's simply talk. Get to know each other. After all, isn't that why we're here?"

LiAnn relaxed her stiff shoulders, nodding in agreement. "Yes, it is, and the best way I know how to accomplish that is to ask questions. I'll go first. You haven't mentioned anything about children. Do you have any?"

A look of sadness swam behind his dark brown eyes. He didn't need to respond because LiAnn could tell his answer would be no.

"Afraid not. My wife and I never got around to it. We were both busy with our careers, kept thinking we would one day, but the day came too late. By the time we were ready, financially and emotionally, her body wasn't."

A twinge of sadness poked in LiAnn's chest. No wonder the man was so lonely! The thought of no Karina in her life made LiAnn's heart ache. "I'm so sorry. That must have been difficult."

"It was, but we learned to deal with it. Filled the void with charity work, lots of vacations and our friends. So, what about you? I've heard you mention your daughter, but any other children?"

"No, Karina is my only child. It seems to be a trend in my family. I was an only child, and so are both of my parents."

"Mr. and Mrs. Tuck are fine, fine people. The ladies of The Magnolia love your mother's quilting class. Ever since Mr. Pickard moved in, your father hasn't let a week go by without coming to visit at least twice. They seem to have quite a bond."

"Yes, they sure do. They grew up together. Mr. Pickard even ran Pop's farm for years while he lived in Los Angeles. They are more like brothers, rather than just friends."

"Such bonds are a rarity in the world today. I have my share of friends, but no one I would consider myself extremely close to. You?"

LiAnn let out a small laugh. "Nope. My daughter is my best friend. Oh, that sounds sort of strange saying it out loud, but it's the truth. I had her so young, I was still somewhat of a child myself. We act more like sisters than mother and daughter. Plus, the hours I worked didn't really allow me much time to socialize."

Jimmy smiled, motioning for the waiter with a slight flick of his hand. In seconds, the man returned with a bottle of wine. Once their glasses were full and the waiter gone, Jimmy held up his glass. LiAnn did the same. "A toast to the bonds of family. May they never break."

They clinked glasses and each took a drink. The wine was crisp and refreshing, just what LiAnn needed. "How long have you been a volunteer at The Magnolia?"

"Coming up on four years. Once I retired, I had to find something to occupy my time with. Keep the mind fresh, the fingers nimble. Help release the creativity and zest for youth in others. However, I'm considering giving up my Saturday reading visits. My vision isn't what it used to be, and recently, I've been suffering from severe headaches afterward. I think the strain of trying to see is too much. I suggested to the staff they purchase audio books to play instead."

"Though I hate to hear about your vision issues, I'm glad it hasn't seemed to affect your painting. You are very gifted. Unlike me. Now, my daughter is a different story. Karina's paintings are beautiful. Her artistic capabilities came from her father. I believe I have talked her into coming to your next class tomorrow, so you will get to see for yourself."

Jimmy beamed. "Lovely! I can't wait to meet her."

LiAnn paused, taking another drink of wine. Her over-inquisitive mind was in full gear. "Why the Magnolia?" Jimmy gave her a questioning glance. "I mean, why did you decide to volunteer there instead of teach art at a college, or start your own home studio?"

"Ah, I see what you mean now. Well, quite simple, really. The head of nursing is the mother of a former student of mine. She asked if I would consider it. I jumped at the chance because I've been fascinated with The Magnolia ever since I can remember. The place is not only beautiful and historic, but full of treasured memories for me."

"Do you mean Carmella D'Nucci?"

Shocked, Jimmy replied, "Yes. Do you know her?"

"Well, not really. I've met her twice while visiting Mr. Pickard. Plus, I heard about what happened to her son. Such a tragedy. Was he, I mean, you know, the one...?"

"Yes. Oh, it's so sad. Ray-Ray had such a

creative eye. Watercolors were his favorite. He was gifted with raw talent, it just needed to be fine-tuned. Unfortunately, he succumbed to the trappings of a creative mind, ones numerous other artists have fallen victim to. Addiction and insanity. It seems substance abuse and mental issues appear more often in creative minds rather than the minds of analytical thinkers. Don't worry, though. I seemed to have missed those two problems."

"That's good to know. Although if you were insane, would you know it?" LiAnn quipped.

Jimmy laughed. "You know, I probably wouldn't. Guess you will have to decide if I'm sane on your own."

LiAnn shifted gears. "You know, when I first met Mrs. D'Nucci, her vibe rubbed me the wrong way. She looked at me not only like she knew me, but hated me. Of course, once I found out about her son's murder, I reneged on my previous assumptions about her demeanor. The woman sure is strong. I would be beyond consolable if something happened to Karina. Work would be the last thing on my mind. I would shrivel up and die."

"Though I'm sure some of her unpleasant vibes, as you called it, stemmed from Ray-Ray's death, I imagine the majority was from competition. Carmella D'Nucci is a beautiful woman, one used to all the attention in a room on her. When you walked in, I'm sure that changed."

The waiter appeared with their dinner before LiAnn had a chance to respond. The food looked and smelled divine, so their conversation died down while they ate. During the silence, it gave LiAnn time to roll around their previous discussions, and soak up her perceptions about the date so far.

Jimmy was pleasant enough, and though she couldn't quite pinpoint exactly why, LiAnn's previous attraction to him had waned. There was a neediness in Jimmy she hadn't noticed before, and it sent her internal alarm bells off. After her third bite of chicken, LiAnn made up her mind. The only relationship between the two of them would be as friends.

The remainder of the evening was spent swapping stories of their lives. LiAnn glossed over things, telling only the minimum in answer to Jimmy's rapid-fire questions. By the time nine o'clock rolled around, she was ready to call it a night.

Alone.

The dust bunnies between her legs were safe for the time being. When LiAnn told Jimmy she enjoyed the evening but needed to go home and check on her parents, the look on his face was unmistakable. He was disappointed and didn't say much as they walked out to her car. They stopped at the driver's side and Jimmy watched with sad eyes while LiAnn unlocked the door. He reached past LiAnn and opened the door, but never moved. The needy man was gone, replaced by the charming Casanova.

"Thank you for joining me for dinner, LiAnn. As I said at the beginning of the evening, you're an intriguing woman. I hope to see you again, soon."

Jimmy was close, his face inches away from LiAnn's. The want, the need, the heavy lust he exhibited the day he asked her out, was back. In full force. Wine, garlic, chicken, and tiramisu lingered on his breath, his musky aftershave unable to override the aromas. Desire danced behind his hooded eyes. Jimmy leaned closer, his lips parted, and LiAnn was trapped by his smoldering stare. His hold on her broke right before his mouth ascended from the shrill chirp of LiAnn's cell phone.

Crigger's ringtone. Figures.

In a flash, she was inside the car. LiAnn forced an apologetic smile as she grabbed the door handle. "I'm sorry, but I'm just not ready for anything other than friendship, Jimmy. Thank you for a lovely dinner. I'll see you in painting class tomorrow."

The car turned over on the first try. She backed out of the spot and peeked in the rear view mirror. A twinge of guilt slithered around in LiAnn's stomach. Jimmy hadn't moved. She was glad it was dark so she couldn't make out the look on his face.

LiAnn drove for a few blocks before pulling into a gas station by the freeway. It was time to fuel up before heading back, plus she wanted to check her cell. She kicked off her heels and threw them on the passenger floorboard. No way would she ever put them on again. Her feet ached. Barefooted, LiAnn stepped out of the car and refueled the tank. Once finished, she slid back inside, grateful for the air conditioner, and scrolled through her cell.

Two missed calls, both from Crigger. She shook her head and laughed out loud, the irony of his timing hysterical. The voicemail indicator blinked, so she pushed the button to listen.

"LiAnn, its Andrew. I...need to talk to you. Call

me the minute you listen to this message. I don't care what time it is."

Stunned, LiAnn stared at the screen. The only time Crigger used her first name was before, during, and after sex, or in the midst of a heated, personal argument. LiAnn hadn't heard him say her name since the night he proposed, which was years ago. Tears welled up in her eyes, and LiAnn couldn't stop her finger from pressing "play" again. Crigger's voice brought a rush of emotions to the surface. It dawned on her why she didn't, couldn't, connect with Jimmy Calhoun.

Because LiAnn was still deeply, desperately, unequivocally, in love with Andrew Crigger.

Taking a deep breath, LiAnn wiped her eyes. She scrounged around in her purse for the headset. Once the annoying thing was situated in her ear, LiAnn pulled out of the gas station. Traffic was light, and in less than a minute, she was on the freeway. She hit redial on her phone, sweat pouring from her palms. Crigger picked up on the second ring.

"Hey, thanks for calling me back. Do you have a minute? We need to talk."

Yes, Crigger. Yes we do. The hair on LiAnn's arms bristled, followed by a chill of worry up her spine. Something was wrong. She sensed it in his voice. Instead of giving in to her emotions, the way the sound of his voice made her head and heart swoon, LiAnn forced her voice to remain light and airy. "Hey to you too, Crig. What's up? Not out catching bad guys tonight?"

There was a long pause before Crigger replied, "Melissa Doster...she, um, was in an accident."

Crigger's words were like a punch in the gut. LiAnn gripped the steering wheel with more force, pushing aside her emotions. Cop mode roared back. "From the tone of your voice, she didn't survive."

Crigger cleared his throat. "No, I'm afraid she didn't. I'm sorry, LiAnn. I know how close you two were. It just happened less than an hour ago. Hasn't even hit the news yet. I wanted you to hear it from me, rather than the media. Her...passing will affect a lot of things."

"Yes, it will. And, thanks for telling me. So, what happened? Car accident? When is the funeral?" Silence. "Crigger...are you still there?"

"Yes. She wrecked her car on I-5 on her way home from work. There, uh, won't be a funeral. Only a graveside service."

LiAnn's heart sank. No funeral after a car accident usually meant a mangled body, one a mortician couldn't fix. A wave of sadness pounded in her chest. Poor Melissa. A tough-as-nails woman, driven to make the owners of Jubilee accountable for what their greedy schemes had done to seniors. Married for less than four months. A warm tear slid down LiAnn's cheek when she thought about the loved ones left behind to continue on without Melissa.

Lost in memories, LiAnn forgot she was on the phone with Crigger. She jerked when he cleared his throat.

"LiAnn?"

Blinking back her tears, LiAnn replied, "Sorry. Just...trying to digest it all. Will you let me know when and where the memorial will be so we can send flowers?"

"Of course. Listen, I need to go, but, uh, if you need to talk or anything, you know, about Melissa or whatever, call me on my cell. Starting Monday, I'll be on vacation. Okay?"

His voice, the tone, was quiet. Sweet. Hesitant. She knew the offer wasn't just because of Melissa's passing. Another tear wandered down her face. He still loved her, and God, she never stopped loving him. LiAnn forced her voice to remain steady. "Sure thing. I've got your number, Crigger."

As usual, Crigger hung up without saying goodbye. LiAnn bit her lip and let out a long sigh. In the dark confines of the car, she whispered a prayer. Comfort for the grieving family of Melissa Doster and silent thanks for her blessings.

21

PLANNING THE END

Caesar dropped the pen on the desk, biting his lower lip to keep from groaning out loud. The joints of his knuckle sent shockwaves of pain up his arm. Glancing up at the grandfather clock in the corner of the bedroom, Caesar was shocked to discover he'd been at his desk for a little over four hours. It was almost three o'clock in the morning. He rubbed his hands together, hoping to massage the pain away instead of taking more aspirin.

He tried not to let anger overtake his mind.

Dealing with an aging body was one thing. As time marched on, it was expected to move slower, lose muscle tone, gain wrinkles, become winded by activities. Have joints the size of golf balls, thinning hair, or bowel trouble. Though annoying, those issues he could handle. However, the loss of the mind, the inability to rely on a once sharp memory, losing time, seeing things, infuriated him.

The detailed notes on the desk in front of him was the first time in his entire life Caesar had ever written down his plans. Ever. Up until a few hours ago, only vague notes were kept on open orders, written in Italian, but if anyone ever found them, no one would ever suspect they pertained to anything shady. Random scribbles about hearts, lungs, livers, eyes and sometimes a pancreas or two, would appear as a strange shopping list of a man who enjoyed eating things most people would turn their nose at. Orders came in the form of chess moves from another former Attica buddy, Master Noriaki Yamashita, delivered to a fake email account created years ago.

For the last few months, Caesar had waffled back and forth about retiring. At first, he was stubborn, refusing to accept the fact his mind was slipping. But after the sickening experience at Ray-Ray's funeral, Caesar had no choice but to face reality. When clear-headed, he knew his mind was playing tricks on him. It was releasing his own inner angst for the life he led, for some of the things said by the apparition of Romella, only Caesar knew. The horrible things he'd done to not only strangers, but people he cared about. His breaks in reality were arriving faster, and lasting longer, than even a few weeks prior.

It was time to get out, leave the business to others. Walk away from it all before he became trapped inside the halls of his twisted mind. The thought of others watching him break down, turning into a demented, driveling old fool, made him sick to his stomach. Caesar Calvanio would not spend the rest of his life being cared for. Pitied. Reliant upon others to wipe his ass, feed him, wash him. No way. He would go out with one last, big score, and slink off into the sunset, and fade away like blips of dreams. Take what little remaining moments of sanity he had left and spend them surrounded by the beauty of the islands, hoping and praying for the sweet appearance of Romella before he pulled the trigger.

Caesar looked back down and studied the

notes he'd written earlier. Instructions for Carmella, Franco, Vincenzo and Carmine. The role each of them would play, who would take over, and who wouldn't survive the final plans. He stood and walked over to the nightstand to grab his cell. It took a few seconds for his stiff fingers to punch in Carmine's number.

"What's up, Boss?" Carmine grumbled, sleep still heavy in his voice.

"Need you to bring the others to my house for dinner after work tomorrow. Be here at six. Don't be late."

"Sure thing. Everybody?"

"Yes. It's time. Oh, and I have some things I need to attend to on my own, so you won't need to come by for our regular visit. See you at dinner."

Caesar didn't give Carmine a chance to respond. He hung up the phone, gathered his notes, slid them under the pillow, and climbed into bed. Caesar needed to rest before he made his big announcement.

He was exhausted but fearful of sleep. After the horrific encounter with Romella while awake, he was terrified of what would happen when his subconscious was in control. What Caesar craved was the warm, sensuous interactions from before. Like frolicking on the sun-drenched beaches of Tahiti with Romella, her raven hair full and shimmering under the sun as they made love at the water's edge. Or just her presence at the edge of his bed, silently watching over him, her eyes beaming with love.

But the putrid, rotting version of her corpse is what came to mind when Caesar closed his eyes. The vile, truthful words she said to him started to replay. So, instead of thinking about his long-dead wife and her spot-on accusations, Caesar let his mind wander to his younger days. A time when his body *and* mind were at their peak, and he entered the life that would define him.

Caesar thought about his lifelong friend, Carmine Del Vecchio. Pictured him lounging in the bunk below with not one ounce of flab and a head full of black hair. Buff. Brawny. Tough as any street thug ever was, were, or would be. How Carmine had protected him for the first two years they shared a cell in Attica. Though Caesar wasn't some puny punk and was more than capable of handling two or three men at a time, a group of them was another thing. The second the steel doors slammed shut, Caesar Calvanio, son and grandson of Carlos and Tomaso Calvanio, was a marked man.

Carmine watched Caesar's back and his intimidating physique and brash attitude kept Caesar safe until he was released after time served. Less than two days without his buff bodyguard, Caesar was nearly beaten to death. He tried, but couldn't really remember much about the day. Brief flashes of him standing, wet and cold in the shower bay, trying to wash away the grit and grime, the always present funk, of prison life. When Caesar shut the water off and turned around to grab his towel, he found himself staring at six men. He recognized them all. They were members of the El Rhukn gang.

Alone, without Carmine's protection and the guards out of earshot, the thugs descended upon him. To enhance their cred and reputation in the prison by going after the son of a famous mobster, they attacked Caesar without mercy.

Caesar tried to withstand the blows, swinging wildly at anything moving, but it didn't matter. There were too many. Pain tore through his right side. With one hand covering his face and the other trying to stop the bleeding from the shank wound to his side, Caesar tried to regain his composure. Though he managed to land a few solid punches, he was outmatched. His body collapsed on the cold tile, blood oozing from his face and side. Everything blurred, but just before he passed out, Caesar heard the voices of the guards. When he awoke, Caesar was inside a hospital room at Bellevue General, a thick, heavy bandage around his head and side.

Splashes of images of interactions with his father whizzed by. The discussion in the hospital room about Caesar's brain injury and subsequent emergency surgery. Four broken ribs, a shattered nose, a skull fracture. It was hard to understand his father's words from the continuous internal buzzing in his ears. Conversations held in the dead of night, his father relating how he took care of things. How he'd orchestrated a meeting with the warden of Attica, Benjamin Tadesco, to ensure Caesar's safety for the remainder of his time behind bars.

The look of satisfaction on his father's aged face as he spoke about the threats to kill the warden's wife and children if one hair on Caesar's head got mussed. How he explained in vivid detail to the petrified warden that his son's well-being in prison would be directly tied to the longevity of the man's family. The empty, cold smile as he told Caesar all about his new cellmate and protector, Master Noriaki Yamashita. The shame in his father's voice as he told Caesar he was weak, his reputation shot to hell. He would never be able to command others once out of prison, for the news of his beating would tarnish him for the remainder of his life. The cold, calculated look as his father informed Caesar he would need to lay low, perhaps disappear for a few years out of the country, once his time was served.

Time zoomed forward and Caesar found himself back inside his cell, staring at the slender, tattooed Asian. The images switched again, hovering around the late night conversations inside the dark cell as Caesar learned about his dangerous companion. Noriaki Yamashita was part of a Japanese Yakuza crime family, one with great influence that operated freely from major U.S. cities.

In a low whisper, Caesar was told to address the man as *Master* Yamashita. Just one look at the head-to-toe ceremonial tattoos of dragons, demons and daggers was enough to make Caesar comply with the request. Though the man was smaller than Caesar, the air about him made Caesar take note. Plus, Caesar was still recovering from his injuries, and didn't want to add any more.

More images flashed by of the rigorous training Master Yamashita forced him to study in the wee hours of the morning. Caesar's lanky body transformed quickly from the painful training. The final conversation inside the walls of their cell the night before his release, came next.

"Listen well, Calvanio-san, my dedicated student. These words will provide the edge needed to assure you survive and prevail in the battles of life. The greatest power for a man is to develop a warrior mind. The ability to embrace *mushin no shin* – the mind without a mind. Just as a mirror reflects objects without clinging to the images, the warrior mind is to flow free from one object to the next without impediment.

"All warriors have elite physical skills. It is those who master the mental side of the game who triumph over their adversaries. A skilled warrior is dangerous. A motivated warrior who applies dedication, extreme mental discipline, and determination, is deadly. The epitome of courage is indifference to death. The warrior must be ready to die at all times."

Caesar's memories shifted again, bringing him to the moment he walked out of the prison and went back home. Even his family was hard pressed to recognize him. He possessed the strapping physique of an Alpha male, but his biggest strength was the mental toughness provided by the deprivation lessons from his mentor. Master Yamashita had skillfully succeeded in establishing the Yakuza mindset in Caesar as automatically as taking a breath.

After his release from prison, Caesar went back to his old life. His father used him, once again, as a bagman to collect on past due debts and a hitter, along with Carmine. Though successful, it wasn't the life he wished to lead. Caesar was demoralized that he was no longer a captain of his crew but merely a street soldier without rank. While his grandfather slowly died from the cancer eating his body away, Caesar would lay in bed and remember the conversations with Master Yamashita. The offer on the table to come anytime to Asia and learn further about the ways of the Yakuza. How their *family* differed from his. How the Yakuza way was superior because they didn't rely on the ties of familial blood to make up their groups. Family members couldn't always be relied upon to remain loyal. Loyalty wasn't a birthright, it was a permanent bond, solidified with sacrifice and blood.

Caesar left the states after Don Tomaso died. Packed a few belongings and slipped out of the country. Told his father he wanted to explore other family business ventures. Spent almost eight years in Japan under the strict eye and tutelage of Master Yamashita's second-in-command, Akitaka Saito. His time in Asia opened Caesar's eyes to a whole new world of generating massive amounts of wealth, and a completely different way of thinking. After being introduced to the Yamashita family's predominant source of revenue, body parts bought and sold on the black market, Caesar traveled all over Asia, honing his new craft.

Although he enjoyed Japan, and the beautiful, exotic women, as the years passed, the pull to return to the states nagged him. Caesar had his share of relationships, but it wasn't until the most beautiful woman he'd ever seen appeared in his life. Romella romped and played in the azure waters of the Pacific as Caesar walked along the beach. She was on a student visa, studying Japanese at Tokyo International University. Caesar was determined to make the young beauty his wife, and didn't give up until he did.

Caesar knew Master Yamashita was savvy enough to recognize the Calvanios pined for the states. Through messages conveyed through Saito-san, Yamashita told Caesar he should consider expanding their business venture to the United States. Weeks were spent hammering out the details, searching for the perfect location to begin. Caesar was the one who aggressively campaigned for the location to be in Arkansas. Master Yamashita gave his blessing on Hot Springs as Caesar's business headquarters. So, Caesar bid his friend and *sensi* farewell and returned to New York, his much younger bride in tow.

He'd been back for less than a year when tragedy struck the Calvanio family. His three older sisters died in a car accident on their way back from Jersey, and their deaths sent Caesar's stepmother into a depression so deep, she never recovered. Even Carmella couldn't reach her. Victoria Calvanio downed a handful of Valium a few weeks later, hell-bent on joining her daughters on the other side. Grief-stricken, his father Carlos dove head first into the bottle. One night, not long after the death of Victoria, Carlos Calvanio stumbled down the back streets of New York, so drunk he passed out in an alleyway. A gang of young thugs thought he was homeless and decided to roll him. Carlos fought back and shot two of them, before the others unloaded their clips into him. Carlos Calvanio bled out on the dirty, black pavement of New York before the ambulance arrived.

After his father's funeral, Caesar had a long talk with Romella, Carmella, Franco, Carmine, and Vincenzo. Explained how the family was vulnerable, and it was time for a change. Romella was pregnant at the time, and retired early to bed. Once she was asleep and out of earshot, Caesar laid out his true plans to the remainder of his family, and within four weeks, they all moved to Hot Springs.

Those were the days, the ones Caesar craved to relive. Warrior strong in body and mind. Possessing those memories with vivid clarity, rather than the current ones haunting him, calmed Caesar. His eyelids grew heavy, along with his heart, when the vision of the day he met Romella took over.

Soon, my love. Soon, we'll be together. Forever.

22

THE INVESTIGATION

"I still can't believe she's gone. I should have called her!"

LiAnn tossed the last bit of chicken feed onto the ground and stared at Karina's distraught face. LiAnn convinced Karina to come outside after breakfast, away from the ears of her parents, and break the news about Melissa. While they worked in tandem, LiAnn listened to Karina prattle on about her adventures the night before with Bo, and then gave only minimal answers about her date with Jimmy. At first,

Karina didn't seem to notice her responses were clipped, since Karina was a bit hung over and amped up about her night on the town. Once the coffee kicked in, Karina asked her what was wrong, so LiAnn dropped the bomb.

Walking over to the spot where Karina stood, dumbstruck, LiAnn put her arm around her neck. "That was my first reaction, too. I feel awful. Yet another reminder life can be over in the blink of an eye, so cherish every second. Right?"

Karina nodded in agreement, wiping a tear from her face. "I'll take care of sending flowers from us. Oh, wow, this sure puts a damper on things. Her poor family. Oh, and her husband! They just got married! I wonder what's going to happen with the Jubilee case. Did Crigger say?"

"No, he didn't, but I imagine the deputy P.A. who assisted Melissa, Cheddy Singleton, will take over."

Karina rolled her eyes. "Ugh. Cheddy is an idiot! Never could figure out how he passed the bar. Seriously, he couldn't find a hole in his pants even if his hands were on it!"

"Don't worry, honey. The case is solid no matter who is sitting in the prosecuting attorney's chair."

Karina furrowed her brows, a look of confusion

on her face. "What time did Crigger say the accident happened?"

"Around five o'clock Pacific. Why?"

"Hmm, well, I was just trying to figure out if the cryptic text Cal sent me had anything to do with Melissa's accident, but the time frames don't match up."

Grateful for a topic change, LiAnn asked, "Cal contacted you? What did he say, er, type?"

"He sent me two texts the night before, asking me to call him. Plus, I had a voicemail from him last night. Had my phone on silent while I was out with Bo. Cal sounded concerned. Guess I should call him though I really don't want to. Can't imagine what he wants to discuss. It's a little late to gab about us. Oh, I know, maybe he and Misty are getting married and he wants to know if I'll attend the wedding."

LiAnn pulled Karina toward the house. "Why don't you order flowers for Melissa and then take a nice, long shower before you contact Cal? Wash the beer fuzzies away before you call him back, okay? Don't want to start the conversation out on the wrong foot, right?"

"Good idea. Somehow, I don't think I'm going to enjoy hearing his voice. Just a hunch." Karina smiled.

They walked in silence to the back porch. Once inside the house, LiAnn headed straight to the coffee pot and refilled their mugs. She handed Karina a cup as her father walked into the kitchen. He looked upset and in a flash, LiAnn was by his side. "Pop? Are you feeling okay?"

Junior waved his daughter away as he poured himself a cup of coffee. "I'm fine, quit worryin'."

Karina piped up, "You don't *look* fine, Grampa. What's wrong?"

Junior sank down in the chair at the table and frowned. "Oh, I just got off the horn with Cecil. He said somethin' is wrong but wouldn't tell me over the phone. Asked to come over here for lunch, instead of us goin' to see him. Plus, he specifically asked all of us to be here. That's the first time he's ever asked to come over since he's been at The Magnolia, so I'm worried he's got bad news to share. Hope it ain't his health."

LiAnn and Karina exchanged knowing glances. At Cecil's age, whatever he had to share probably was health related. "I'm sure it's nothing to worry about, Pop. Maybe he just needed to get away from Wylie's mouth. It sure can run amok sometimes. We'll be glad to have lunch with him."

Junior let a feeble smile appear on his face.

"Yeah, could be. The man is annoyin', that's for sure."

"Did I hear you right, Junior? We're havin' company for lunch? Mercy, I better start cookin'!" Ruth exclaimed.

"I'll help, Gram," Karina offered.

Ruth made a beeline for the pots and pans. "Ain't you workin' in the hayfields today, sweetie? Or did your late night with Bo wear him out?"

Karina's face turned three shades of burgundy and LiAnn couldn't help but laugh. Karina shot her a look of irritation, so LiAnn responded back with a wink. "It seems to me an afternoon spent sweating under the sun would be of great help. You know, it will remove the last traces of alcohol from your system."

"Really, Mom? Oh, let's change topics, shall we? We want to hear all about *your* date last night with the charming Jimmy Calhoun. Gee, he will be so disappointed you won't be attending his painting class today. Or, will he? Gosh, and I was looking forward to calling him Daddy."

Before LiAnn could snap back, Ruth interrupted. "Enough! Honestly, you two are a mess sometimes. LiAnn, you help me with lunch and Karina, it sounds like your help just arrived," she said, pointing out the window, "So you best get out and help him finish the mowin' before noon. Make sure to invite Bo to lunch as well. If he's gonna date my granddaughter, then I need to get to know him better."

"Gram, we aren't dating..."

Ruth waved Karina's words away like pesky mosquitoes. "Call it what you like, girl. I may be old, but I surely ain't dumb. That boy's a suitor for sure."

"Yes, ma'am." Karina sighed. Without another word, she slunk out the back door, Ranger right behind her.

"Whew! It sure is a hot one today, I tell ya!"

"Come on in, Mr. Pickard. Good to see you. Lunch is ready. Pop's in the kitchen, along with everyone else."

LiAnn held the door open and watched Cecil Pickard shuffle through the doorway. He smiled at her, but she could tell it was forced. He took off his cowboy hat and LiAnn saw his fingers shake while he held it. *He's really nervous. Oh, no, please don't let this be bad news.*

Cecil followed her down the hall to the kitchen. Karina sat at one end of the table, alone. Bo left before lunch to pick up samples of paint for the barn. LiAnn assumed the boy wasn't quite ready to be grilled by her family. Cecil sat down in the chair next Junior, exchanging pleasantries. LiAnn helped her mom set out the fried chicken and all the trimmings.

"Sorry to be so vague on the phone, Junior, but what I got to say, I didn't want nobody to hear. Thanks for lettin' me come by."

"No thanks needed my friend. So, spill. You've got us all riled up, wonderin' what in tarnation is wrong. Whatever it is, we're here for ya."

With a sheepish grin, Cecil looked around at everyone at the table. He took in a long, slow breath then huffed it back out, his cheeks puffing up. "I know that, Junior. You always have been, and I appreciate it, I surely do. That's why I'm here–y'all are good people. Trustworthy. Okay, I...ain't exactly sure where to begin. Guess I'd like to say first off, my body may be old–I may creak a tad when I walk–but my mind is still sharp. I don't forget things, especially when it comes to money. I know how much I got, which banks I have accounts at, and do all my transactions in person." Cecil paused while he gathered the remainder of his thoughts.

Ruth interjected. "Cecil, take ya a few bites. Get some protein in your belly before you pass plum out. You're as white as a ghost!"

"Okay," Cecil took a hefty bite from the chicken leg, followed by two forkfuls of green beans.

The rest of them nibbled at their plates, waiting for Cecil to continue his story. LiAnn had a feeling she knew what was coming next, and the thought made her angry. *Someone at The Magnolia is stealing from him.*

"Last Thursday, I went to the banks like I do *every* Thursday mornin', you know, to draw out some cash, check on things. Since I have all this money now and not much else to occupy my time with, I take weekly visits to stay on top of it all. Everythin' was fine until I pulled up at First State Southern. Realized when I parked I left my wallet in my apartment. I drove back to The Magnolia to get it. The elevator was full, so I took the stairs up to my floor. My room is at the end of the hall on the second floor, and Carmella was closin' the door to my apartment. I remember thinkin' I was losin' my mind. I mean,

I forgot my wallet and figured I left the door open, too, and Carmella was nice enough to close if for me."

Karina immediately piped up. "Who's Carmella?"

LiAnn answered, "She's the head of healthcare at The Magnolia. The one who kept throwing strange looks my direction. Her son, Ray-Ray, was murdered, remember me telling you?"

"Oh yes, right! Uh, she works there? That's not good at all. Mr. Pickard, did it look like she was just passing by and closed the door, or was she actually exiting the room?"

"It looked like she walkin' out, but I wouldn't bet my life on it," Cecil answered.

"I don't know about the rules here, but in other states, that's a definite no-no. The staff at independent living facilities are not allowed to go into the living areas of a resident without their permission or presence, except in a life-threatening emergency. Somehow, I don't think you leaving your door open falls under the category of emergency, and I assume you've never given her permission to enter your premises, right?"

Cecil shook his head no.

LiAnn's instincts lit up. "Did you say anything to her, Mr. Pickard?"

"Ms. LiAnn, at first I just stood there, unsure what to do. She saw me and put a huge, fake grin on her face, ramblin' on for me to be more careful about shuttin' my door and lockin' it. Kinda like she was scoldin' me. I mumbled my thanks and went inside and retrieved my billfold. I looked around. Nothin' seemed out of place. No cash was missin' from my wallet, and I don't use credit cards. I even poked around all the hidin' places I keep my bank statements, but nothin' seemed wrong, so I brushed it off and went about the rest of my day."

"I'm confused, Cecil. You already told me this last week on the phone. Don't you remember?" Junior asked.

"Junior, I ain't done with my story, and yes, I remember. Told you my mind ain't old, just my body. That was just the warm up. This here's the main course. Today's Thursday, which means I go to the banks. When I got to First State Southern, the bank manager, Mary Rutherford, called me into her office. Asked me if I tried to set up online access to my account within the last week. I didn't rightly know what that meant until she explained it to me. You know me, Junior, I ain't never owned a computer and wouldn't even be able to turn the dang thing on if I did. Shoot, like I said, I don't even use any type of plastic! If I want money, I go to the bank and draw it out, or on occasion, write a check. That's it. So, when I told her no, she said someone did try to set one up with them. They didn't get somethin' right and the system denied it."

"Ahh, now I see why you are all in a tizzy. You think someone nabbed one of your bank statements?" Junior said.

"Yep, sure do, Junior. It just makes me sick. This money is more of a curse than a blessin'."

Hearing the heavy emotion in Cecil's voice, LiAnn asked softly, "You think its Carmella, don't you? Is that why you didn't want to discuss this on the phone with Pop? Are you afraid she might overhear you?"

Cecil swallowed hard, a look of deep sadness creased his brow. "Though I hate to say it, and I surely wish I was wrong, my gut tells me yes. She...oh, I don't know. Somethin' behind her eyes just ain't right. There's a fakeness to her, if that makes sense. And it ain't just because she is a dead ringer for Morticia Adams, either."

"Does The Magnolia have cameras, maybe in the hallways?" Karina asked, her voice tight.

"I don't know, never paid any attention," Cecil answered.

"Yes, I noticed a few when we toured the place. They're quite old, though. Not sure if they were for show or they actually work. Are you thinking what I'm thinking?" LiAnn posed the loaded question to Karina.

In a flash, Karina was on her feet. "Great minds think alike, Mom. I'm going to see if my bag of stuff from We've Got Ya! still has the surveillance cameras in it. I think I left out one of everything, you know, for old time's sake." Before anyone could respond, Karina was gone.

"What's she talkin' about, and what do you have in mind?" Cecil asked.

"My guess would be she wants to put up a camera in your apartment to see if she can catch the thief red-handed," LiAnn answered, hiding the grin she wanted to let out when she heard Karina squeal with delight from her room. "Even a high-priced lawyer can't dispute the evidence if their client is on tape, clear as day, committing a crime."

Karina's footsteps thundered down the hall. She slowed her gait when she entered the kitchen, holding the spying equipment out like a trophy. "Mr. Pickard, this bank manager…"

"Mary Rutherford's her name. Sweet woman."

"Okay, Ms. Rutherford. Did she happen to mention whether they filed some sort of report about the attempted online activity with any authority?"

Cecil looked confused for a moment, his thin skin furrowing around his eyes as he tried to remember. "Yes, she did. But I can't rightly recall all of what she said. Somethin' about trackin' virtual addresses and such."

Karina's voice was low and soothing. She knelt down next to Cecil and said, "What that means is, they are trying to locate the specific computer used to access their website. All computers have their own address, kind of like a VIN number on a car. Did she say they know where the IP address originated from?"

Cecil furrowed his brow as he tried to remember. "She might have, but I really can't remember. I was so upset, all I could think about was comin' here to talk to y'all."

Karina reached out and put her hand on Cecil's arm. "Mr. Pickard, would you mind if we went back to visit with her? I would like to ask her a few questions, see what the status of things are.

Get a better handle on what happened, and what they are doing about it."

"I was sort of hopin' you'd offer. That's why I decided to come over. Junior told me all about you and your mom, what you went through in California on that case. How can I go wrong with an ex-cop and a private detective in my corner?"

Karina smiled. "Would you mind if I set up a camera in your apartment, too? The feed will connect to no one but me, and I promise to keep an eye out. I will fix it so it starts recording when it detects motion, and when it starts recording, the video will come straight to my phone."

"Do you really think you need to go that far, Karina?" Ruth queried.

"Yes, Gram. I do."

LiAnn cleared her throat. "Mr. Pickard, we should also make a stop by all the locations you have accounts at, and inform them what happened at First State Southern. Make sure they are aware so in case someone tries to open an online account, they'll flag it."

"Yes, great idea, Mom. But I'm thinking we should throw out some bait so we can catch the bad guy, or gal, quicker. Mr. Pickard, what are you doing next weekend?" Karina asked.

Surprised, Cecil stuttered, "Not anythin' in

particular, other than listenin' to Jimmy finish reading the end of *The Count of Monte Cristo*. It's his last day to read to all of us. Why?"

Karina let a wicked smirk appear. "How would you like to go to Branson for four days, all expenses paid? Mom's driving Gram and Grampa. You need to go, too. And make sure you make it known around The Magnolia, especially around this Carmella chick, you'll be gone."

"I, uh..."

Junior responded first. "Cecil, that's a fine idea. We haven't been on a vacation together in years. You and I can fish while the girls shop. You just let my gals do their thing. They'll figure out what's goin' on, and who's stealin' from ya. Dontcha worry none."

"Junior's right, Cecil, and we won't take no for an answer. LiAnn and Karina will make sure you, and your money, are safe," Ruth offered.

"Ms. Ruth, y'all is just too sweet. Junior, as I've always said, y'alls a lucky man. You've been blessed with a fine family. Okay, I'm in! So, what's the next step?"

"We all finish eatin' our lunch before anyone does anythin', then y'all can start your plannin'," Ruth instructed.

All of them mumbled agreement at Ruth's

stern words. Karina returned to her seat and shoveled her food so fast, LiAnn worried she might choke. LiAnn could see the excitement, the spinning wheels, behind Karina's blue eyes. Her own adrenaline had kicked in, the anticipation of solving a puzzle made LiAnn's skin tingle.

23

DIGGING DEEPER

Karina parked Cecil's car in his spot at The Magnolia. She hit the speaker button on her mom's cell and called her own. "Mom, you all set with my phone? Parked and ready?"

"Just pulled into the gas station across the street. Ready to get the show on the road."

"Awesome!" Karina turned to Cecil and asked, "Okay, you know your role and what to say if asked any questions, correct?"

Cecil responded, "Yep. When inside my apartment, and if we run into someone who wants to poke their nose into my business, we act like you're my great-niece, Vivian, visitin' from California."

"Great. Okay, Mom, we're going in." Karina looked at Cecil. "You ready?" He nodded and they exited the car. She made sure to keep her steps slow to match Cecil's. Karina groaned inwardly at the temperature. It had to be over one hundred degrees, and the humidity was so high, it was like standing in a steam bath. She pulled her hair away from her neck and jerked it into messy bun.

Cecil chuckled. "Ain't got used to the heat yet, huh?"

"Nope. Doubt I ever will. How in the world are you not sweating? I think I've lost ten pounds in the last few weeks just from loss of fluids."

Cecil shrugged his shoulders. "Years of pourin' sweat dried up my glands, I guess. So, if we run into Carmella, or anyone else, do we just keep goin', or do we stop and I introduce you?"

"We don't want people thinking anything is amiss. Just act natural, and follow my lead. You're in good hands now."

"You know, you amaze me. You've got all this fancy-dancy spy equipment, a gun, and yet are as beautiful as any woman I've ever met. For the life of me, the only reason I figure you're still single is because you intimidate men. Hell, I know you and you scare me."

Karina laughed. "It's going to take a strong man to corral me, that's for sure."

"Ain't that the truth? I mean, you got the information you needed from Ms. Rutherford in two shakes of a lamb's tail. Poor woman's still probably scratchin' her head. All that fast, California talk left her discombobulated. Probably will have the same effect on Carmella, if'n we run into her. Southerners don't talk that fast, in case you haven't noticed."

Karina smirked. "Oh, I've noticed. Everything, including speaking, moves slow here. Like investigating a computer crime. I can't believe the bank isn't right on top of things. Ridiculous. But, I got all I needed from her, and I promise you, my former partner will have an answer for me," she glanced at her watch, "in about an hour."

Cecil shook his head in disbelief. "Way over my head. I hope I'm wrong about Carmella. There are other staff members, you know, the cleanin' crews, cooks and such. From what I know, Carmella has been at The Magnolia for years, so why would she start a life of crime now?"

"Money does strange things to people, Mr. Pickard. Once they get a taste for it, like an addict, they want more, and will do whatever necessary to feed their habit. You wouldn't believe some of the things I witnessed people do when I was undercover. So, I have a quick question before we start: why Vivian?"

Cecil's eyes, which had been full of worry and stress for the past several hours, lit up. "Vivian Leigh is my favorite actress. Oh, when she wore those beautiful gowns in *Gone with the Wind*, I thought my eyes would pop outta my head. She was the epitome of beauty, grace, and strength. You remind me of her."

"Wow, what a compliment! You're so sweet, Mr. Pickard. I do love that movie, except for the ending."

"Why?"

Karina flashed Cecil a wicked grin. "Don't tell my mom I said this because she would flip if she heard me, but Scarlett should have told Rhett to shove it up his ass and slammed the door in his face. Now *that* would have been classic!"

They both laughed as they drew closer to the front entrance. Sweat pooled under Karina's armpits and dribbled down her back. By the time they made it up the steps, her shirt was soaked. It wasn't just from the overbearing heat, either. Her adrenaline was amped up, along with a twinge of worry spreading through her chest. Karina was about to step foot in a place that would bring back disturbing memories. Pushing aside her own mental crap, Karina followed Mr. Pickard inside as he held the door open.

Once inside, a cold rush of air slapped her in the face and made goose bumps pop up all over her arms. Karina gave a quick scan of the place, noting the beautiful decor. Her mom was right on target: the place was gorgeous. Breathtaking, actually.

To her surprise, the young woman at the front desk didn't even acknowledge either of them as they walked by. She was too busy reading a textbook of some sorts. Her lack of concern for the safety of the elderly residents irked the shit out of Karina. Granted, she had walked in with a resident, but no sign-in sheet? Was the receptionist so lazy she couldn't even raise her eyes to see who just walked in or even open her mouth to say good afternoon? *What the hell happened to Southern hospitality?*

On top of the lackadaisical doofus at the front

desk, Karina quickly noticed the cameras in the lobby and front sitting room weren't functioning. They were throwbacks to at least the early 90s, the big, bulky kind that flashed red when activated. They weren't blinking. When they reached the stairs, Karina's mouth twisted into a grimace, for the damn camera wasn't even plugged in. *So much for security footage. The flip side is my worries about listening devices just took a nosedive.*

No one was in the front sitting area, nor on the stairs as they walked in silence to the second floor. The scent of fresh gardenias was strong, mixed with the aroma of whatever food had been served at lunch. The odor was even worse on the stairs. It wasn't like she didn't enjoy the smell of fresh flowers, but too much of anything was beyond annoying. So far, other than the pretty decorations, her assessment of the place was dim. The old adage about judging a book by its cover had never been more on target.

She glanced over at Cecil, who seemed quite nervous. His hands trembled while he fumbled with his key to unlock his door. After three unsuccessful attempts, Karina put a reassuring hand on his shoulder. "Want me to try?"

"Sure. Guess it's a good thing I was just a grunt

in the military. Never woulda made it as a spy. Too jittery."

With a flick of her wrist, Karina unlocked the door. Cecil stood aside and let her go in first then closed the door with a bit too much force behind him. "Why don't you have a seat while I check out your fancy digs, Uncle Cecil?" She followed her statement with a slight wink. To her surprise, Cecil winked back.

"Sure thing, Viv, right after I fix us a glass of cold, iced tea. It's hotter than a June bug in a fryin' pan today."

For the next few minutes, they traded idle chitchat while Karina walked the living room, kitchen, dining area and front bathroom. She made sure to stop at places with full access to the living area, pretending to admire knickknacks, pictures or décor, but didn't see any evidence of a hidden camera. A bug would be impossible to find without sweeper equipment, so she had instructed Cecil to continue the uncle/niece charade while she poked around.

There was one picture on the desk of Cecil's small family. It sat inside a dark black picture frame, one full of scrolling swirls around the metal edges. It was the perfect hiding spot.

"What a great picture of all of you,"

Karina gushed, picking up the frame. "Oh, yikes. Uncle Cecil, you need to talk to your cleaning lady. She sure isn't doing a very good job of keeping things dusted! Do you have any Windex and a soft cloth? Maybe in the bathroom?"

It took a few seconds for Karina's game to sink in, but finally Cecil responded, "Uh, yeah. Think there might be some in my bathroom. Under the sink."

Karina excused herself and went into the master bedroom. Shutting the door behind her, she made a beeline for the most obvious areas to hide a camera or a microphone. Nothing. Same with the bathroom. While inside the restroom with the door shut, she pulled her mom's phone from her back pocket and set it on the sink, turning on the small camera and powering up the mini microphone. Then, Karina waved at the screen. It only took four seconds for a text reply.

"Got it!"

Karina gave a thumb's up and secured the camera and bug to the frame. Once back in the living room, she tossed her purse on the couch and sat down on the chair in front of Cecil's massive wooden desk. It had the perfect view of the entire living area, all except the bedroom. "There, all clean." The cell vibrated once in her pocket and she yanked it out. The text read: *"Perfect location. Can see and hear everything."*

She crossed the room to where Cecil sat on the couch. Bending down to hug his neck, Karina whispered, "All set. Remember, act normal. We'll see and hear everything." After letting go, she rose and said, "Thanks for a great day out on the town, Uncle Cecil. I've got to run, so I'll call you later, okay?"

Cecil followed her to the front door. Right as his hand touched the knob, someone knocked. They exchanged glances, Cecil's full of panic. Karina looked out the peephole and responded with a dazzling smile. "Hot Springs is full of all sorts of adventures, Uncle Cecil!" She jerked the door open and purposefully bumped into the visitor. "Oh, sorry! Didn't see you standing there! Almost knocked you on your ass! Now that would be an odd way to make an introduction, huh?"

Karina's ramblings gave her enough time to size up the woman standing in the doorway. Even without the annoying name tag, Karina knew she was Carmella D'Nucci. The black hair, sharp features and air of authority left no doubt. Internally, Karina laughed at the look of shock on the woman's face. Karina upped her rate of speech into high gear.

"Uncle Cecil, now I know why you moved into The Magnolia! Talk about sexy nurses! Hi, I'm Vivian Pickard, Cecil's great-niece." She squinted at the nametag, moving her head closer to Carmella's shocked face. "Carmella D'Nucci. Oh, Italian, huh?" Karina playfully swatted Cecil's shoulder. "Uncle Cecil, you always did have a thing for Italy, eh? So, nice to meet you, Ms. D'Nucci. You keep an eye out on my uncle here. He's quite a handful sometimes! Now, I'm coming back to town next weekend, so how about lunch?"

"Mr. Pickard, are you okay? I heard a loud noise like your door slamming or something. I came to check on you," Carmella interjected.

Karina moved closer to Cecil and squeezed his hand. "Oh, sorry about that. I didn't mean to shut it so hard when we arrived. Guess I don't know my own strength. Hope I didn't disturb any of the other residents." Karina turned her focus back to Cecil. "So, how about lunch next Saturday? Got to get my calendar synced ahead of time, or I won't remember a thing. You game?"

"Love to, sweetie, but I can't. Going to

Branson for the weekend with the Tucks and their lovely daughter. Plan on catchin' me some fish!"

"Oh, sounds like fun. Okay then," Karina planted a loud kiss on Cecil's soft, wrinkled cheek, "then I guess I will see you in a few months on my next trip to Memphis. Love you."

Though not looking directly at Carmella, Karina could feel the intense heat from Carmella's gaze through her peripheral vision. The color had vanished from Carmella's cheeks and she did look remarkably like Morticia Adams! The woman looked freaked out. No, beyond freaked out. Carmella D'Nucci looked like she was about to vomit.

"Why, Mr. Pickard, you are full of surprises, that's for sure. First your lunch table is overflowing with new guests, and now a visit from your niece. And here I thought you didn't have any family left." Carmella arched a thin black eyebrow in concern.

The tone of Carmella's voice sent waves of anger up Karina's spine. Even if she wasn't the prime suspect in stealing from Cecil, Karina still wouldn't have liked her. The way the woman stared at her with her big, brown eyes, like

Karina was a walking corpse or something, was hysterical.

Deciding to make the bitch even more uncomfortable, Karina touched her forearm. "Ma'am, are you okay? As Uncle Cecil here might say, you sort of look green around the gills, like you've seen a ghost or something. Should we call *you* a nurse? Do you need to sit down?" The woman actually shook Karina's arm away, like it burned her. Hatred replaced the fear in Carmella's brown eyes. Though it lasted only a split second, it was unmistakable.

"Oh, sorry, didn't mean to stare. It's just, well, first of all, I don't think I've ever heard anyone talk so fast in my whole life. Still trying to process all of what you said. And, I can't help but do a double-take. You are the spitting image of...a friend of mine who passed years ago. I mean, it's sort of eerie. You could be her twin. So, pardon me for staring, and interrupting your visit. Mr. Pickard, if you need anything, please let me know. It was nice to meet you, Ms. Vivian."

Karina waved goodbye, not even trying to hide her confident smirk. In five quick, long strides, the oh-so-freaked out Carmella D'Nucci was gone.

Cecil whispered, "Well, that was..."

"Beyond odd. She didn't just look guilty, but scared out of her mind. You buy that crap about me resembling a dead friend?"

Cecil shook his head. "Nope. You really got her riled up, I tell ya. Think she'll lay low for a while?"

Karina patted his hand. "For a few days, yes. But I guarantee you, if she truly is the culprit, she won't be able to resist an empty apartment while you're gone next weekend. I'd bet my car on it, and I love *Dragula*."

"Let me walk you out."

Karina waved Cecil off. "No need. I know my way. Remember, if you need us, call the house. Simply ask for Vivian, and we'll know something is wrong. Okay?"

"Sure. And, thank you. For everythin'."

Karina smiled warmly at her grampa's closest friend. "Not a problem. Glad to be of help."

24

THE PERILS OF COFFEE

LiAnn sat inside the car, the air conditioner on full blast. She watched the small screen as Cecil walked back inside his apartment. He shut and locked the door then stood still inside, a confused look on his face. Cecil scanned the living room, letting his gaze rest on the desk. His arm trembled as he gave a brief, awkward wave. LiAnn didn't like seeing him look so out of sorts and frail, so she exited the video program.

A few seconds later, Karina appeared at the

front entrance. She jogged across the street and jumped into the car.

"Holy crap it's hot outside," Karina whined, adjusting the vent to blast her face. "Can't wait for winter."

They swapped phones, and LiAnn commented as she maneuvered the car out of the parking lot, "Maybe you should have just walked over here instead of running, huh?"

"Funny, Mom."

"Listen, you need to call Cal. He called three times and sent two texts while you were inside with Cecil. I almost answered on the third call but figured it would be best for me not to speak with him. Might say something I'd regret later."

Karina fiddled with her phone, tapping and scrolling through the screens. "Good thinking. Oh, yes! He got the information on the IP address. Wait, don't leave yet. I need to call him back and probably take notes. Will you pull back to a parking spot? Say, why didn't you tell me that Carmella chick looked like the little sister of Morticia Adams? I thought Cecil was just exaggerating. I mean, wow, scary. Apparently I made her freak. Said I looked like one of her dead friends. Gross."

"She does look like she belongs in a long black dress, cutting off the tops of roses with shears. I just failed to mention it before because I didn't pay too much attention to her in our previous interactions. And yes, I heard the conversation with Ms. Fake Fingernails. Lucky you."

"Yeah, no kidding."

LiAnn put the car in park. "Hey, before you call Cal, tell me, how did your earlier conversation with him go? Was he shocked to hear from you?"

Karina chuckled while rummaging for paper and pen in her purse. "I never actually spoke to him. I just sent him a text, asking him to check out the IP address."

"Wait, didn't you call him earlier, before Cecil arrived?"

"Nope. Bo arrived early, so I went out to help him mow."

"Oh, then this conversation should be interesting."

Karina produced a devious smile. "Don't worry, Mom. I'll put him on speaker so you can listen, too. If Cal knows you're listening, he won't dare say anything I don't want to hear."

"Good thinking. Such a smart girl."

Cal picked up on the second ring. "About damn time, Karina! I've been trying to..."

"Hey, Cal. Sorry. Mom and I have been busy learning how to be farmers, and now we're helping out a family friend who someone is trying to steal from. Just finished putting a camera and bug in his apartment, so we can catch and hear the perp on video. That's why I needed a run down on the IP address. Someone tried to open an online banking account, not long after the vic spotted an employee leaving his place. So, tell us, what did you find out?"

There was a long pause, followed by a heavy sigh. "Hey, Sgt. Tuck. How are you?"

Karina winked and LiAnn returned it. "Fine, Cal. So, what's the verdict? I'm hoping it's not an overseas IP because that will just complicate matters."

"Oh, it's not. Don't worry. You've got yourselves someone local. Came from an internet cafe in Hot Springs. Name of the place is The Coffee Mug and it's on Central."

"Fantastic! Thanks, Cal. Should be easy to find. We'll head right over there."

"Karina, wait. Listen, I need to tell you something else before you go," Cal said, his voice louder, more insistent. "So don't go off playing good cop, bad cop, until I do, okay?"

Karina sensed the worry in Cal's voice and

responded, "I don't like the sound of that. What is it?"

"I've been trying to connect with you for several days now to tell you..."

Karina interrupted, "Sorry. As I said, we've been busy."

Cal snapped, "Karina! Be quiet and just listen."

"Calvin Benson, I know you didn't just *tell* me to be quiet..."

LiAnn heard the anger roar to life in Karina's voice, and it set her nerves on fire. "Enough, both of you. Cal, what is it?" Karina opened her mouth to protest, but LiAnn motioned for her to be still.

"You know I keep a close watch on who comes to visit the website, keeping track of all IP addresses and such."

"Yes, yes, I know. You always were afraid of hackers," Karina interrupted.

"Karina, seriously. Listen. Three days ago, someone visited from an Arkansas IP address. Searched all over the site and clicked on all the links pertaining to you. I mean, they didn't visit *any* other part of the site unless it had something to do with you."

Stunned, Karina slumped back in her seat.

"What in the world? By the way, I thought you were going to update it, and remove me, you know, since I'm not your partner anymore?"

"Give it a rest, Karina, will you? I've been busy. At first, I thought maybe you'd attracted some cyber-stalker, you know, someone who decided to check you out. Or maybe you applied for a job or something down there, and an HR company was researching your credentials. But that's not it."

Worry crept into Karina's voice. "So, what is it then?"

"After you sent me the text earlier with the IP address you wanted me to investigate, I didn't need to do much research. Took me a few minutes but I recognized it. It's the same one."

"What the hell?" Karina shouted. Her anger filled the car. "Well, that certainly does change things. Big time. There is no way it can be a coincidence. Period."

LiAnn's stomach lurched with the same queasy feeling she used to get when on a case. Her daughter was right: there was no way it was a coincidence. She'd bet her retirement that the black-headed bitch Carmella was behind it, but for what reason? Why in the world was she interested, especially enough to cyber-snoop, in

Karina? Up until a half hour ago, Carmella didn't know Karina existed.

"Mom? Mom! Hello?" Karina snapped her fingers, bringing her mom out of a funk. "Let's go. I want to get to The Coffee Mug so we can play good cop, bad cop. Oh, and this time, in the mood I'm in, I get to be the bad cop. I don't have the acting skills to play nice today. I'm beyond pissed. I'm the *investigator,* not the *investigatee.*"

LiAnn didn't say a word in response. She backed out of the parking lot and shot out, tires squalling. Karina punched in the address and the droning voice of the GPS system gave them directions.

First thing LiAnn noticed when they walked inside The Coffee Mug was there were no cameras. Dandy. The place was small, with seating for maybe twenty people. There were only six computer terminals, and they looked at least five years old, if not older.

The place wasn't anything like the ones LiAnn had been to on the West Coast, other than the fact it was a coffeehouse. A young man, in his early twenties, leaned against the counter, tapping his fingers away on his phone. He didn't even look up when they walked in. LiAnn exchanged glances with Karina and gave her a knowing wink, pulling out her billfold. Karina did the same. They both walked up to the counter. LiAnn peered at the name tag on the kid's shirt.

"Good afternoon, Carl. I'm Detective LiAnn Tuck, and this is my partner, Detective Summers." They both flipped their wallets open, showing their old badges for only a split second. "We're here to investigate a possible cyber-stalking crime, and need to take a look at your security footage from last week."

It took a few seconds, but finally Carl pulled his eyes away from his phone. "Can't help you. We don't have video surveillance. Owner says we can't afford it, which I sure can't understand, given how busy we always are."

His crass attitude didn't bother LiAnn, for she was used to it. Her daughter was another story. Before Karina exploded, LiAnn tried again. "Since there seems to be a lull in the crowd, it looks like you have a moment to chat." Carl shrugged his shoulders with indifference. "So, no cameras, huh? How about a log for guests to sign? Got one of those?"

Carl scrunched his face, his light blue eyes shifting between the two of them. Suspicion danced behind them. "Got a warrant?"

"Not yet. Trying to do things the easy, civil way first. Give you and this fine establishment a chance to show no collusion was involved in the crime. You know, be able to tell the press when we arrest the criminal that the folks over at The Coffee Mug cooperated fully with the investigation. Because when businesses don't, it usually means they are involved in the illegal activity."

"Look, lady, I ain't got nothing to do with what people do when they come in here to get online. I don't ask, don't pry, and don't look. Made the mistake of peeking when I first started working here, and got an eyeful of some sick porn site I still have nightmares over."

LiAnn leaned her elbows on the counter and gave Carl a huge grin. "Now see, cooperation and honesty. That's all we're looking for. So, a log? You have one?" Carl nodded. "Good. If you'll just let us take a look at it, I promise we'll be out of here in two minutes. Let you get back to work. Okay?"

Carl huffed and reached under the counter, producing a small spiral binder. "Fine."

Karina moved to peek over LiAnn's shoulder. LiAnn flipped the pages back to the week prior, surprised at the amount of people who'd come to use the free Wi-Fi. When she turned the page to three days ago, LiAnn had to bite her lip to keep her thoughts inside her head. From the corner of her eye, LiAnn saw Karina stiffen.

"Carl, got a copier in the back?" Karina asked, her voice low, sinister. LiAnn recognized the tone. Her daughter was close to full meltdown. When Karina was mad, she yelled. When the volcano was about to explode, she barely whispered.

"Yeah, first door on the left past the bathroom."

Without a word, Karina took the binder and stomped down the hall. LiAnn heard the copier fire up. In seconds, Karina was back, her face flushed crimson, a few droplets of sweat on her brow. She tossed the log on the counter.

"Thank you for your cooperation, Carl. We've got what we needed. Just one more question and one favor, and then we'll be out of your hair, okay?" LiAnn asked.

"What's that?" Carl replied. Nervousness crept into his voice.

"Noticed from the sign-in sheet, you usually are the one working on Mondays and Tuesdays."

"Yeah, so?"

LiAnn took a business card from the counter and scribbled her cell phone number down on the back. She slid it across the counter. "When Carmella D'Nucci comes back, call me immediately. It will save me hours of sitting in a parked car in the heat outside, waiting. Wouldn't want to scare off any of your regulars, right?"

A twisted grin appeared on Carl's face as he picked up the card. "Oh, that bitch, huh? Double espresso with a shot of hazelnut. Orders it every time, then complains about how I make it. Always insists on a discount. Never leaves a tip. Can't say I'm shocked she's a suspect in cyber-stalking. Woman gives me the creeps, you know? No problem picturing her as a bully. Be glad to."

"Great. Thanks again for your willingness to help. We'll be in touch."

Carl's face crinkled as confusion spread across it. "Say, this number...it ain't our area code. What department you from?"

Karina shot LiAnn a look, and LiAnn responded with a slight nod.

In a flash, Karina leaned across the counter, her face inches from the pasty one of Carl. She growled, "You just lost your brownie points with me. I thought you were smarter than that. You really want to know, Coffee Boy? I'm afraid we'd need to go for a ride. A *long* one."

For a second, LiAnn wondered if the boy would faint, piss his pants, or scream. When angry, Karina was an imposing figure. She carried her 5'10" frame like she was 6'5" and three hundred pounds.

Carl shook his head no.

Karina gave Carl one, last harsh look before she moved. "Thought so."

They walked out in silence toward the car. Karina headed to the driver's side but LiAnn pushed her toward the passenger side. LiAnn didn't want her to drive. The girl was too upset. Once back inside the car, LiAnn fired up the engine, enjoying the rush of cold air.

Karina exploded. "What in the hell is going on? Why is that bitch scoping me out? I don't know her! She never knew I existed until today, and I introduced myself as Vivian Pickard!"

"Breathe, honey. We'll figure this out. Come on, let's head home and get on the computer.

BLOOD TIES

You still have access to all your investigative sites from We've Got Ya?"

"Unless Cal's changed all the passwords, yes. If he did, I'll just tell him I need access."

"Good. We need to do our own snooping into who this woman really is. Know thy enemy, right?"

"Yeah, then blow thy enemy to kingdom come. Oh, that bitch is lucky I didn't know all this earlier," Karina fumed.

Neither spoke for a few minutes, both of them lost in thought. Once on the freeway, Karina let out a gasp. "Oh, my God! Do you think it's a possibility this ties to Jubilee somehow? Maybe Carmella worked for them at some point, learned the tricks of the trade? Maybe she read online about the appeal, started researching, found my name in the news archives. Obviously, she's learned quite a bit about Cecil from snooping around his apartment. Knows who Gram and Grampa are, since they are the only ones to come see him. Probably searched about them, too. Wonder if she's scoped you out, too?"

Karina's words made LiAnn push the gas pedal harder. "Okay, that's freaky. I was just thinking the same thing. The woman has no idea she just screwed with the wrong family."

"No doubt. Drive faster."

"Not a word about this to Gram and Grampa until we figure out how all this ties together. Okay?"

Karina's answer was a nod of agreement. Neither of them spoke on the rest of the forty minute drive. LiAnn noticed the puffy white clouds to the east had changed to dingy gray. It looked like a storm was moving in, and fast.

25

FINAL CHOICES

"**N**ow that dinner's over, and I've made you all wait long enough, it's time to retire to the living room and have a drink."

Caesar watched his guests nod in solemn agreement as each rose from the dining room table. None of them said a word as they walked to the living room. Carmine reached the bar first and starting pouring drinks. Caesar ambled over to the locked safe behind his favorite portrait of an Italian winery at sunset, took it down from the wall, unlocked the safe, and extracted his notes. When he turned around, Franco, Carmella, Vincenzo and Carmine were all staring at him while they pretended to sip their drinks. Caesar could feel their combined tension from across the room. He motioned for them to sit. Once they were all seated, he moved to the center of the room.

"I have made some decisions, some of which I'm sure you all will like, and others you may not. However, they are my decisions to make, and each of you know when my mind is made up, I won't change it. Wanted to make that perfectly clear before I begin. No debating issues. What I'm about to say is the way things will be. Got it?"

Each nodded in agreement. Only Carmella, his tough baby sister, had the guts to speak.

"Caesar, we've never questioned or doubted you before, so we won't start now. What's on your mind?"

Caesar held her gaze for a full minute, searching for any traces of insincerity. Seeing none, he began. "I'm retiring and moving to the tropics in two weeks. Before I go, we will all participate in one last job. Our quarry is worth a substantial amount of money. Enough, in fact, that should any or all of you choose to do so, you could retire as well. However, if you all wish to continue the businesses without me, then here is how it will run. Ownership of The Magnolia will remain at status quo, only changing hands upon my death. At that time, as you all know, each of you will own twenty-five percent. However, my stake in Happy Days Retirement will transfer to Carmella four months after I leave. Carmine will dispatch Nick Shonnert in a tragic suicide, and Carmella will be appointed to his position. Nick has become more of a liability than an asset. So, congratulations baby sis, you just became a COO, of course, should you wish to continue."

Stunned, Carmella choked on her brandy. She recovered quickly and raised her glass in a mock toast. "To breaking the glass ceiling!"

Caesar turned his gaze to Franco, whose eyes were as big as saucers. "Franco, you will be the point man now, in charge of taking the orders and making sure they are filled in a timely manner." Franco blanched, the blood draining from his face. "Don't worry. I have all the codes and what they mean right here," Caesar said, holding up the papers in his hand. "Our contact overseas does not need to know there has been a change in the guard, right? All communication is done through email, so don't worry, you won't need to try and sound like me. If you follow these instructions, my departure will remain our little secret. When I leave, you will be in charge of maintaining my residence, and I will leave my computer here. Our contact might become suspicious if he detects the emails were sent from another location, and believe me, he would know. You know how the Asians are when it comes to technology."

Franco responded by gulping down the rest of his drink. He looked like he was about to throw it back up. Caesar wondered why Carmella decided to marry the idiot.

"Okay, so our first order of business is completed. Now, onto the last hurrah, for me at least. Though I hesitated in the beginning, I have changed my mind about Cecil Pickard. Our research into his holdings is just too much to walk away from. The next order needs to be filled within two weeks. The recipient of Mr. Pickard's organs is weakening, and our contact is getting antsy. Well, more than likely, *his* client is getting antsy. Now, I know this choice poses a few twists, since our donor has some close friends, but I don't believe this group will have any trouble taking out an old couple and two women, am I right?"

Carmine snorted, "Cakewalk."

Carmella added, "Before today, I would have questioned the ability to pull this off, but after what I found out earlier, I concur with Carmine. Cakewalk."

"Would you mind expounding on that, please?" Caesar asked, intrigued.

Excited, Carmella rose from her perch on the couch and went to the bar, refilling her drink. She took a hefty sip and replied, "Well, as you know, if we use Pickard as the next donor, we had the issue of his friends, a.k.a., the beneficiary and his family members. I had a very interesting conversation with Mr. Pickard and his *niece*, who is actually Karina Summers. Recognized her from my research. At first, I was worried because it seems old Pickard is suspicious about his bank accounts and called her in for help. They even went so far as to give her a cover name. However, none of that matters now. He mentioned in passing that next Saturday, he is going to Branson with the Tucks and their daughter. So that means..."

Carmine interrupted, "That taking them out just became quite simple."

"Exactly!" Carmella gushed. She slammed her drink down and smiled. "Four out of the five will be together, leaving the last straggler alone at home. I mean, it's like the Heavens are smiling down on us right now. The timing is perfect."

Caesar chewed on the newest piece of the puzzle, happy to see it fit in perfectly with the one he created in his head the night before. His excitement was short lived as a strange thought emerged. "Well, that is quite interesting news, although I am a bit distressed to hear your sleuthing activities were detected, Carmella. You must be more diligent in the future. That little conversation might have simply been a ruse, said in hopes of luring out the person who has been sniffing around Mr. Pickard's bank accounts. On the plus side, if they knew for sure it was you, I doubt they would have gone to such lengths. If they had enough evidence, surely they would have gone to the police."

Carmella's excitement waned as a look of anger, followed by worry, crossed her face.

Caesar continued. "Never mind that now. Either way, it works out in our favor. It is time to lay out the rest of my plan. Is everyone ready?"

Four heads nodded in agreement.

"Fantastic. Carmine, as I mentioned earlier, you are to help Nick the Prick craft his suicide note before he departs to the other side. Make sure the cops have no doubts he took his own life when his dead body is discovered in his home. This needs to be accomplished first, no later than Wednesday. Carmella and Franco, you are responsible for ensuring Mr. Pickard and his friends do not survive the return trip from Branson, if, in fact, they are going. Carmella, you are in charge of monitoring Mr. Pickard. We need to know if he truly is going on this trip, and if the rest of our marks will be with him. If not, we will have to alter our plans. If that is the case, we will reconvene and adjust accordingly. If it is the truth, then Vincenzo, you will accompany me to take care of the last straggler, the daughter. I won't be able to live with myself if I don't enjoy one last hit. Unfortunately, she will disappear and nothing will be left to find since she will be rendered down to a pile of smoldering ashes. Franco, you and Carmella will meet us at the funeral parlor on Saturday night. Make sure the oven's hot. Once we finish with the daughter, you two will head to Missouri to set up the tragic car accident."

Vincenzo's grin lit up the room. "Finally! Some excitement for me. I get to be on the front lines for once, rather than picking up the dead and cutting up their corpses."

"Don't let your eagerness override common sense, Vincenzo. Karina Summers has skills of her own. Former private investigator, and from my research, it looks like she has quite the temper. An affinity for guns, along with her mother, who is a retired cop. We must plot and plan for any and all scenarios, and be ready to adjust on the fly." Carmella added. "I've met her, remember? I promise you, she won't go down without a fight."

Caesar smiled, a real, genuine smile. The rush of adrenaline made his body tense. "Good. I like feisty prey. Makes the kill much more memorable. I'm sure it will give me many hours of satisfactory memories to relive while I'm on the beach. Now, the meeting is adjourned. Franco, follow me into the study, please. We have some documents to go over. The rest of you, enjoy the brandy."

Franco piped up, "Need to use the bathroom first. I'll meet you in the study."

Nodding his approval toward Franco, Caesar turned his attention to Carmine and Vincenzo. They clinked glasses and toasted, but Caesar could see the look of concern behind the eyes of his longtime friend. Carmine was savvy enough not to question orders in front of others, but

Caesar knew later, Carmine would come to him privately and ask why the decision to move was made so fast. Caesar was already prepared for that, and planned on telling him to mind his own business, and that their partnership was over. He didn't want Carmine coming with him to Tahiti. No way would Caesar let anyone he knew be around to watch as his mind slipped away before he put a bullet through his brain.

"Caesar, I need to tell you something before you meet with Franco. Okay?" Carmella worked to keep her face stoic.

"If I recall correctly, I said at the beginning of this meeting my mind was made up. Don't try to change it, sister."

Carmella shook her head. "No, no, I would never do that, Caesar. I just...need to ask you something, and I really want you to consider it before you give me an answer, okay?"

Intrigued, Caesar replied, "All right."

Carmella's warm hand touched Caesar's arm, which was something she rarely did. The Calvanio's were not the touchy-feely types. She lowered her voice so the others wouldn't overhear. "Please, I know you want to take part, to have one last thrill kill, but let Vincenzo or Carmine handle the Summers girl."

Caesar tried to keep his anger at bay, for his first thought was Carmella was questioning his abilities. A dig at his age. "What, Carmella, do you think I'm too old to handle a simple hit?"

"No, it's nothing like that. I'm well aware of your strength and capabilities, and have no doubts in that area. I, well, as I mentioned earlier, I've met her. I've shared with you almost all the information I found out about her and her family, but left out one minor detail. Well, actually, I think it is a major detail, since I came face to face with her. She looks a lot different in person than the images I found online."

Annoyed, Caesar asked, "Oh, and just what detail would that be?"

Carmella sighed and took another hefty drink. "She looks just like Romella. I mean, enough they could pass for twins. I, oh, I don't know. I just think it might be difficult for you since she looks so much like her. Might make you hesitate for a split second, and hesitation can get you killed."

Caesar searched his sister's face, noting the real worry behind her eyes. No trickery, no hidden agenda. "No need to be concerned about me. The Cat doesn't let anyone stop him once the hunt begins."

BLOOD TIES

26

STORMY WEATHER

Lightning skittered across the darkened sky, sending fingerlike tendrils through the menacing gun-metal gray clouds. Karina only made it to *three Mississippi* before booming thunder rang through the fields. The rain had stopped, but the light and sound show still played. Ranger whined at her feet, nudging her bare leg with his moist snout. Karina stood, walked to the back door, and pushed it open. Ranger bounded inside the dark house, his claws clicking on the hardwood.

"Whoa! He sure is scared," LiAnn remarked, moving out of Ranger's way. The two glasses of tea sloshed their contents out as she shifted her trajectory. She heard the liquid hit the linoleum. "Oh, crap."

Stepping inside the door, Karina felt around the counter for the dishtowel. She bent down and wiped up the mess. "Sorry, didn't know you were in his path. Poor thing. He doesn't know what to think about all the noise. Storms in Cali were never like this. He probably thinks we're in a war zone."

LiAnn nodded toward the screen door. "Come on, let's watch it roll out. I've always loved summer storms. Isn't much we can do right now anyway since the power's out."

Once settled on the porch, drinks in hand, Karina remarked, "Nature at its finest, displaying her raw power. Wish she would have waited until tomorrow, though. Puts a damper on my research."

"What, are you afraid to use your computer because of the storm?"

"No. Like an idiot, I forgot to charge it before we left earlier. Battery's dead. I could use my phone, but it doesn't have much juice. Don't want it to croak. Got to keep an eye on Cecil's place."

"I'd offer mine up, but it's dead too. You know, smartphones are great, when they work. With all they can do and cram into such a small space, why is it so hard to make a battery that actually lasts?"

Karina chuckled, "Geeks do enjoy their petty torments." Another burst of light danced across the sky. The concussion of the thunder made the entire house rattle. "Wow, that's close. Where's Gram and Grampa?"

"Both are sound asleep in the living room. It's so cute. Sitting side by side in their matching chairs, Grampa with the remote in his hand, and Gram with her knitting needles. I mean, it's a Norman Rockwell moment. How they are sleeping through all this noise is beyond me. Before they fell asleep, they were discussing the new neighbors. They are concerned about who bought the farm adjacent to theirs. I told them I'd work on finding out. Gram's biggest worry is they are meth heads."

Karina fidgeted in her seat. The storm made her nervous, and not just because she was eager to get online and start hunting for information. What she feared was the capability of wind so strong, it sucked her and Ranger up in a funnel cloud and plunked them down in Oz. Not exactly the way Karina desired her remaining moments on earth to be spent. "Okay, once the power comes back on, we'll see what we can find."

LiAnn noticed how nervous Karina was and remarked, "Honey, it's okay. It's just a pop-up thunderstorm. It will pass soon enough."

Unwilling to let Mother Nature win, Karina shook away her fears and changed the subject. "We haven't had much of a chance to really talk about your date with Jimmy. I really do want to hear all about it, since what you've alluded to sounds like it tanked. I was hoping we could shelve that for later because I wanted your opinion first."

"About?"

"Would Jimmy be a good source to ask about Carmella? Can you trust him, and if so, do you believe he'd open up?"

LiAnn thought about that for a few minutes before responding. "I don't know. We actually did discuss her briefly during dinner. He's known her for quite some time. Taught her son art in school years ago. Seemed genuinely sad about the boy's passing. After he retired, it was Carmella's idea for him to come and teach art at

The Magnolia, so my gut instinct would be no. I mentioned I felt guilty for thinking Carmella had been looking at me funny, then finding out her facial expressions were off due to the murder of her son. Jimmy said he thought that was part of it, but the other part could be jealousy."

Karina cocked her head in confusion. "Jealousy?"

LiAnn smiled. "You know, female competition. According to Jimmy, Carmella's used to being the one ogled around The Magnolia. I changed the subject after that, dismissing it all in my mind. Now, I'm not so sure my first perceptions weren't on target. The woman looked at me like I was public enemy number one."

"Ah, yes. That shoots the Barbie effect scenario down in flames."

LiAnn gave Karina a disgusted smirk. "Not every blonde with a rack is hated by every other female."

"Says the blonde..."

"Very funny. So, you didn't ask Cal for help? You know, give him a research project to work on?"

Karina groaned. "I'd rather gouge my eyes out, thank you. Besides, this is personal, not business. I'm perfectly capable of doing my own sleuthing."

"Uh-huh, never said you weren't. I just enjoy annoying you."

Lightning crackled again, and thankfully, it was further away. Karina made it to *seven Mississippi* before the thunder boomed. At the same time, the lights came back on and the house phone rang. Karina jumped, nearly dropping her glass.

"LiAnn?!"

Both of them were on their feet, heading inside. "Yes, Pop?"

"Your suitor's on the horn."

Karina burst out laughing, enjoying the looks of irritation and embarrassment spreading across her mother's face. "Hey, he's persistent. Obviously, he hasn't given up on conquering Mt. Barbie. Play nice, you might score us some good intel."

Three hours had passed since the storm ended, and Karina's eyes were tired from staring at the computer. She glanced over at her mom, who was busy studying the notes she'd compiled during their research. It was near midnight, and both of them were exhausted, but both were too stubborn to call it quits. Karina leaned back in the chair and stretched. "Well, at least none of my bank or credit card accounts have been jacked with. That must be the silver lining, right?"

LiAnn set the pen down and commented, "Since when are you the glass half full one?"

"Guess it's the heat. Does crazy things to the brain. Okay, I need a change of scenery and to take my contacts out. Let's hash out what we know while I put these babies nighty-nite. You know," Karina said, walking to the bathroom, "I would have been happy with smaller boobs or a few inches shorter, in exchange for better eyesight."

"Hey, blame your father. Apparently, his genes were stronger in the outward features department. Be happy you have my brains."

"Trust me, I am. So, what am I missing here, Mom? What's your thoughts on all this?"

"I think it's too early to start making judgment calls on what exactly we are dealing with or how it pertains to you. It sure would help if Cal would call or text with the passwords for the search sites. Oh well, let's stick with what we know for sure then build from there."

Contacts out, Karina let a small sigh of relief out as she applied eye drops. Glasses in place, she stepped back into the bedroom. Karina plopped down on the bed and stared at the ceiling. "Fair enough. One, we know someone tried to access Cecil's bank account. Two, we know the location where it happened. Three, we know Carmella D'Nucci was at The Coffee Mug on the same day. Four, Cecil caught Carmella leaving his apartment. All that adds up to is what both of us have seen so many times during the last three years. Elderly people are easy targets for criminals. Cecil has a lot of money, no one to really help him manage it, and an employee hired to help take care of him. Said employee decides to lift some cash. That part's clean. The rest is murky."

"I think your original musings might be on target. My guess is Carmella worked at some point for Jubilee," LiAnn stifled a yawn. "You know how much nationwide press coverage the trials received. I would imagine current and former employees gobbled up every news article or report the second one hit print or TV. Both of us had our pictures splashed across the screen a few times, so that might explain why Carmella gave us such odd looks. Even if she isn't a former employee, she does work in the senior housing field. I'm betting every senior living facility in the country kept up with the case. You know, running around like crazy, trying to plug up and fix the holes in their own companies before a suit could be brought against them."

"Interesting. Go on," Karina urged.

"Carmella is head of healthcare, which means she probably subscribes to trade organizations about the industry. Maybe her initial reaction was that we already *knew* about her activities pertaining to Cecil, and assumed we were investigating."

Karina sighed and rubbed her eyes. "You're probably right. Huh, guess my little act of Cecil's grand-niece was a waste of time. After seeing me leave his apartment, Morticia has to know we're on to her. Hope it doesn't scare her off. We need more evidence before we go to the police with all this."

"Morticia. Classic. In terms of evidence, actually, we don't. We have plenty for them to open a case against her for fraud and maybe even attempted identity theft. Now, in terms of how this all ties to you, oh yes, much more." LiAnn stood up and moved to the desk. "Do you mind if I drive for a bit while we wait on Cal? I want to look at something real quick."

Opening her eyes, Karina grinned. "Be my guest. Impossible to get a ticket for speeding on the internet."

"Always the comedian. That you get from Grampa."

Ranger grunted from his spot on the floor, stretched, then promptly stuck his wet nose on Karina's cheek. She grabbed her cell phone, groaning as she rose from the bed. "I'm going to take Ranger outside for a minute. Be right back."

Her mom was busy clicking keys, staring intently at the screen, and simply waved her response. Once outside, the humidity slapped Karina in the face with its wetness. Ranger was oblivious and bounded out toward the barn, his favorite new location to relieve himself. In seconds, she lost him in the dark, his black coat melding perfectly against the backdrop of the night. The smell of damp, wet hay assaulted her nose, making it tickle. Karina rubbed it twice, hoping she didn't start sneezing.

Staring up to the star-filled sky, Karina wished answers to all her questions would miraculously appear. What was she going to do about Bo? Continue seeing him, knowing full well the relationship would end? It wasn't fair to use him as a salve to soothe her broken heart. He stroked her ego, made her feel sexy and desirable. Pushed all the right ecstasy buttons with ease unlike anyone ever had before. Even Cal.

Karina cursed under her breath, wishing she hadn't thought about her ex. Hearing Cal's voice on the phone earlier complicated matters inside her head. She was walking the fine line between love and hate. When she was with Bo, her feelings for Cal, good and bad, were more of a creamy tan, rather than blaring black or raging red.

On top of all the soap-opera crap in her life, Morticia Adams gets thrown into the fray. The reasons the woman decided to check up on Karina didn't matter. What mattered was the bitch actually was trying to steal from not only a senior citizen, but a family friend. The woman had no idea she just stepped into a hot, steaming pile of cow manure.

For a few moments under the cover of darkness, Karina let the thrill of the hunt burn through her. It wiped away the confusion over the men in her life. Pushed aside her guilt for enjoying the fact she had something to sink her teeth into, even though it stemmed from someone she cared about.

Karina had a new adversary to defeat. A new player to outwit. Someone to take down who was screwing around on *her* turf. She let the terrified look on Carmella's face when she opened the door fill her mind. The way the fear exuded out of Carmella as they locked eyes for the first time. Karina remembered her first words, spoken with a twang of a New York accent.

Jerking her eyes open, Karina whistled for Ranger. "Come on boy, inside! Mommy's got an idea!"

"**F**ind anything?"

LiAnn was back on her spot on the edge of the bed, rummaging through her notepad. "A few things that make things even more confusi...Karina, what's wrong?"

Karina sat down in the chair and let her fingers fly across the keyboard. "Nothing. I just had an epiphany while outside with Ranger. The heat actually made my brain cells all fire at the same time. I'm going to do a bit more sleuthing from a different angle. I'm tired of waiting to hear back from Cal. So, what did you find?"

"Carmella's website said her company provides services to facilities all over the state, including two locations in Hot Springs. The Magnolia and another, bigger facility called Green Pastures. The second place isn't just an independent living facility. It also has a memory care section and a skilled nursing facility. I went to the secretary of state's website to see who owned Caring Hands, Loving Hearts, Inc. healthcare. No surprise, really. Carmella D'Nucci is listed as the President and Franco D'Nucci as Secretary and Treasurer. I pulled up the obituary for Ray-Ray D'Nucci, and sure enough, Franco is her husband."

"Uh-huh, and?" Karina mumbled as she typed.

"What I was hoping to find was she was also the registered agent, you know, so we would maybe get lucky and her home address would be on there. It would make finding out where she lives much easier since we aren't having much luck finding anything else. I mean, seriously, not one social media account! Not even for her company."

"Hey, let's not hate on those of us who aren't on social media."

"Honey, you and I both stay away because we know how dangerous it can be, plus we never wanted our identities compromised. The only other type of people in the digital age now, besides ones like us, who steer clear of it don't *want* to be found for a reason."

"True. Okay, so what else did you find?"

"I was a bit disappointed they used someone else as registered agent, but decided to follow my hunch. Guess where it led me?"

"To the end of this story?" Karina clicked on a link.

"Nice, daughter. You sure get cranky as the evening wears on. Did you want to hear what I found or not?"

"Sorry. Go on," Karina muttered.

"The registered agent for both companies is the same person, whose mailing address is in Hot Springs. Name is Vincenzo Molinero. On a hunch, I searched all companies in Arkansas with the same registered agent. Turns out, there are four of them, and all in Hot Springs. The Magnolia, Caring Hands, Loving Hearts, Lombardo's Ambulance Service and Slumber Land Funeral Parlor."

Karina stopped typing. She turned around and looked at her mom, who was doing her best to sit still on the edge of the bed. "Wow, that's odd. No, creepy. A senior living facility, a funeral parlor and an ambulance service?"

"I've saved the beefiest morsel for last. Vincenzo Molinero is not only the registered agent of Slumber Land, but the president. And Franco D'Nucci is the president of Lombardo's Ambulance Service."

"Well, this just zoomed past creepy to downright sinister in a hurry. What the hell is going on at The Magnolia?"

LiAnn tapped her notepad. "I'm not finished. I typed in Vincenzo Molinero's name into the search engine, and get this: I found an article from a newspaper in New York from over twenty years ago. A Dr. Vincenzo Molinero had his licensed revoked from the State of New York for ethical violations. What I don't know is if he is the same guy or not, but if he is, what is he doing here, running an ambulance service?"

Karina went back to the search bar. This time, she typed in *Franco D'Nucci Carmella D'Nucci birth death marriage New York*. Her fingers drummed on the desk as she waited for any results to pop up. "I don't know about you, but my gut is in a knot. Usually, that means I'm on to something."

"Oh, mine too. Where is that mind of yours taking you to?" LiAnn moved to the other side of the bed for a closer look at the computer screen.

"Hang on." Karina's heart pounded when she saw the first link was from the obituary archives of *The New York Post*. She felt her mother's warm breath inches from her face as she viewed the screen.

In silence, they both read the article. By the time Karina reached the end, she was shaking. She knew her mother got to the last part when LiAnn sucked in a huge gulp of air, followed by "Oh, my God."

"As I was saying, I remembered Carmella had a hint of a New York accent. No wonder she isn't on any social media sites. Now that I know exactly *what* family she belongs to...oh, damn. Carlos Calvanio was her father! Help me out here, Mom, because I'm kind of freaking out, but that name—he's who I think he is, right?"

LiAnn gave a curt nod. "Yes. Remember, we watched that show about the mafia on TV years ago, and part of the segment was about him and his son, Caesar the Cat Calvanio? The one who fell off the face of the earth years ago not long after the murder of his father, Carlos."

Karina hit print and saved the page as a pdf file on her hard drive. It took her several attempts because her shaking fingers kept hitting the wrong button.

"Honey, it's time to call Cheddy Singleton. Like, right now. He can put us in contact with the Feds, because somehow, I think they might be interested in what Carmella Calvanio D'Nucci is doing down here. Oh, Jesus, what have we stumbled upon?"

Karina didn't answer. Instead, she stood and went to the nightstand by her bed, opened the drawer, and retrieved the loaded Glock. "Remember my motto about blasting a hole big enough to kill them, then make up your own story? Well, it just went from motto to mantra."

27

INTO THE DEVIL'S LAIR

Sweat trickled down his neck, and his back itched like crazy from the barbs of the holly bushes, but Lucas remained still. He'd been in the same spot since four a.m., and his knees, back and shoulders ached. Under the cover of darkness, he slithered through the streets dressed in all black, his hair hidden by a black skullcap, until he reached the house across the street from 119 Sycamore Lane. The entire edges of the yard were surrounded by mounds of the holly bushes, all uniformly manicured to precisely five feet high and five feet wide. A perfect hiding spot to burrow into to spy on Caesar Calvanio's home.

Lucas had to pee like a sonofabitch, and he hoped his quarry would leave soon before he pissed himself. Finally, his patience was rewarded. A black car pulled up to the gate. Lucas adjusted the binoculars and watched Carmine poke his head out of the window while his stubby fingers tapped in the code. 9351*. The tall, wrought iron gate opened, and the vehicle disappeared up the curvy drive. The excitement, the adrenaline rush, quieted his bladder.

In the distance, Lucas heard the sounds of life from the other residents of Sycamore Lane. Doors slammed, cars started up, parents tugged their unwilling children to their vehicles so they wouldn't be late for school. A school bus never appeared to haul the little brats away. Apparently, the rich bastards on this side of town refused to let their precious offspring get carted around like cattle.

Lucas listened to the familiar noises around him while he waited for the car to leave. Nick had given him Caesar's address on Saturday, and it took him three days to work up the nerve to even look up the address on Google maps. He was so paranoid, afraid his every move was monitored, Lucas went to the Garland County Library to use their computer to do his recon. He spent hours looking at the aerial and street view. The house of his enemy was enormous, one of several in the neighborhood surrounded by a gate. By far, 119 Sycamore Lane was the biggest house in the area and sat on a small rise, overlooking the city. A twisted grin danced across his face as Lucas wondered what the neighbors would say if they knew exactly *who* lived in the big house on the hill.

The Wednesday morning school and work rush over, the street was quiet. Other than the occasional yap of a dog, Lucas heard nothing. He focused his attention on the gate. It was attached to a brick wall, about fifteen feet high, encasing the entire property line of Caesar's place. There were a few large trees around the perimeter, ones he could climb and jump into the yard from if careful. The biggest problem Lucas needed to work around was the security cameras. He noticed two by the gate and figured there were plenty more inside and on the house.

His skill set did not include breaking and entering. So, after countless hours staring at the dark ceiling of his cramped bedroom,

Lucas made a decision. Stick to the basics. He knew the address, and that a security gate surrounded the place, so the logical next step was to scope it out. Get a feel for Caesar's habits. When the old bastard left, came back home. His gut told him Carmine would be like his shadow, and sure enough, he was. Lucas picked the perfect time to hide in the bushes because his biggest obstacle just disappeared.

He had the gate code.

Seconds later, the gate creaked and whined. The black car waited until it could slip through the opening. Lucas watched, his heart pounding in his chest, as the vehicle passed less than twenty feet from him. The windows weren't tinted, and he could clearly see Caesar in the passenger seat. The sedan turned left and disappeared.

For the next ten minutes, Lucas watched the rest of the neighborhood from his hiding spot. The mosquitoes came out, buzzing around his exposed face and hands. He ignored them. Lucas shifted his body and continued searching the quiet street until he was satisfied no one was around. Stowing his binoculars in the backpack to his left, he sat up. He removed the skullcap and black sweater, shoving them deep inside the bag. It was a tight fit, considering it was crammed full of everything Lucas would need to start his life over with, once the job was done. It also held water, a few energy bars, and several changes of clothes.

Holding his breath, he stood and darted out from the holly bushes. In six quick strides, Lucas was across the street, standing next to the security box by the gate. His mind screamed at him to turn and run. It followed the command with a warning. Sweat poured down his forehead and back, and his body shook with terror. Ignoring the internal warnings, Lucas punched the code in and the gate cranked to life. When the opening was big enough for his slender torso to slide through, he stepped inside.

Lucas ran up the steep driveway. When he reached the top, he pushed all doubts about the decision from his mind. This was meant to be. It was his destiny. Or the powers above were smiling down on him. Fate intervened. Whatever it was, Lucas couldn't help but squeal like a little girl as his gaze settled on the garage.

It was open, and attached directly to the side of the house.

Can it really be this easy?

Once inside the garage, Lucas paused to listen.

With his luck, a pack of hungry, half-starved guard dogs would descend on him, feasting on his flesh until their master returned. Fear pulsed through his body. His heart thumped so hard, Lucas wondered if he was on the verge of a heart attack. Never, in his whole life, had he been so terrified. He stared at the door leading into the house, swallowing a mouthful of spit. There was a security pad next to the door, and it was blinking. Taking a deep breath, Lucas closed his eyes, promising himself if the passcode wasn't the same as the one to the gate, he would get the fuck out. Get on his bike and ride. Ride until he reached Mexico. Disappear and never be seen or heard from again.

But, if the code is the right one...

He wrapped the edge of his shirt around his hand. No sense in leaving any evidence, no matter which way the plan went. His fingers were trembling so much, Lucas had to hold his breath to steady them. He mentally counted.

One. Two. Three!

The code worked. The light turned from red to green. On instinct, Lucas reached down and tried the handle. The knob gave way and he opened the door, and Lucas Hill knew his life would never be the same. He'd just chewed his way out of the trap, and it was time to dispatch the hunter who set him up to begin with. His first order of business was to mark his new territory by pissing in the bastard's own bathroom. Then, he would tromp through the place until he found the master bedroom.

And the perfect hiding spot to wait until his prey arrived back home.

28

ON PINS AND NEEDLES

"I can't stand waiting around. Jesus, you would think someone would give us some kind of update by now!"

"Shhhh. Karina, keep your voice down. I don't want Gram or Grampa to hear." LiAnn watched Karina pace back and forth on the porch. The light from the ceiling fan reflected off of Karina's face at an odd angle, and it made the sneer on her lips look quite sinister.

Seeing her daughter so fired up wasn't helping her own mood. LiAnn was just as mystified about the lack of contact. They'd spent over an hour on the phone days ago with Cheddy Singleton, telling him every detail. Karina had even emailed him all the links to the information they'd uncovered. He listened, and told them he thought it was worth looking into, and even called back a few hours later with the name and contact number of the local FBI field office. He promised to contact the agent first, to give him sort of an overview of what was going on, and then they were to call the next day.

They tried.

Twice.

No one from the Little Rock office returned their calls until yesterday. When the agent did call, he was quite vague. Stated they were investigating, and should the FBI need any more information from either of them, they would call back. The wait was driving both of them nuts.

Karina stopped pacing and sat down on the swing. "Government, bureaucratic bullshit. Cal always said that's why private investigators never lacked for work. No offense, former cop, but the law has a tendency to wait until something *really* bad happens before they get involved. I mean, yeah, some dude calls and gives us the song-and-dance routine, but that's it. Ridiculous."

LiAnn nodded in agreement. "Believe me, I know. Look at how long it took most of the domestic violence laws to change? I remember a time when an order of protection was only issued if the victim was in the hospital on life support!"

Karina's gaze softened. "Sorry, Mom. I don't mean to take my anger out on you. I just...I don't understand. We handed them a hell of a lot, and one, two-minute phone call is all we get? Talk about frustrating."

LiAnn leaned forward and patted Karina's trembling shoulder. "Breathe, baby. Listen, you and I both know we aren't nuts. Or overreacting. Something is going on at The Magnolia. Both of our internal shit-storm-o-meter alarms went off—loudly. At least we are keeping an eye on Cecil. That bitch has only been back in his place once and she didn't find squat. Actually," LiAnn said, hoping her next words would make Karina smile, "Cecil seems to be enjoying the whole covert-ops thing. At lunch today, he was full of piss and vinegar, grinning from ear to ear. He even got into a verbal sparring match with another resident, Wylie Wilson, about baseball.

When we left, Cecil hugged my neck and whispered all was well. He followed it up with a big smile."

Karina rolled her eyes. "Mom, he doesn't *know* what we do. He thinks Carmella is just a random thief, out to score some quick cash from him. If Cecil knew who she really was, he would be freaking out."

"Well, he doesn't. And it's our job to keep him, and everyone else, calm until all this gets sorted out."

"I can't wait until she is put in cuffs and led away. I just want five minutes alone with her before she's hauled off. No, ten. She wouldn't look like Morticia Adams when I finished with her. More like a jacked-up zombie."

"Okay, let's change the subject before you explode. Did you get all the materials purchased for the barn? Bo's picking it all up tomorrow, right?"

Karina took a deep, long breath and exhaled it slowly before she responded. "Yes and yes. And before you ask, he plans on staying with me while you all are in Branson. Not that I need protection, since I have my Glock and an arsenal of weapons, thanks to Grampa's stash. Add Ranger and all the electronic equipment, I'm sealed tight. Remember the mantra—I will shoot first. Screw asking questions."

"What about the cameras? Are they all set and working?"

They both glanced up at the small camera perched above the back door. "Yep. Motion detectors are all working, too. It was a tad difficult getting everything in place, since I did it all in the dark after Gram and Grampa went to bed, but I managed."

LiAnn frowned. "I hate keeping this from them. Thank goodness neither of them noticed the equipment."

Karina stood and stretched. "Bo noticed yesterday. He asked me about them. Told him we were being cautious after learning about the meth activity down here. Pretty sure he bought it, but when I asked him not to mention it in front of Gram and Grampa, he gave me an odd look."

"You haven't told him what's really going on, right?"

"No, and I feel bad about that. After all, if something really sinister is going on that revolves around the freaking mob, hanging around with me sort of puts Bo in danger. I plan on telling him the basics when you all leave tomorrow. Give him a chance to make a decision on his own whether he wants to stick around or not. It's only fair."

LiAnn shuddered. "Well, that doesn't make me feel any better about your safety while we're gone. What if he decides he doesn't want to play around with the mob? Then you'll be left here alone. I'll be a jumbled mass of nerves with worry."

Karina lowered her voice. "Mom, stop. I'll be fine. I won't go anywhere without my gun. Besides, I have a feeling nothing I could say to Bo Barton would make him leave. I believe he has grown quite fond of me in the last few weeks."

"Good to hear," LiAnn replied, watching Karina's face. She stared at her daughter intently, noting the sparkle behind her eyes. "Seems to me, the feeling is mutual."

"Could be. Too soon to tell just yet. So," Karina said, a hint of mischief in her voice, "now that we have some time to talk, tell me, what's going on with Jimmy? Date details were lost in the mix the last week, and I would rather hear about him than talk anymore about this mess."

LiAnn fidgeted in the chair until she found a comfortable position. "Not much to tell, really.

The food was good, the wine fantastic, but the company? Hmmm, too needy. It was kind of weird. The charming man I made a date with didn't show up. Instead, the one who did was too eager and way too pushy. The vibe was all wrong, so friendship is all that's in the cards for us. And I didn't like that he called me so soon after. Again, the neediness factor is too high. Made noises about checking on me because of the storm. Wanted to know if I planned on coming to listen to him read the final chapters of the book he's reading on Saturday since it will be his last performance. I'll give him a plus point for tenacity, but it isn't enough to outweigh the minuses."

"Mom, are you sure it wasn't just first date jitters on both sides? Or maybe you're a bit set in your ways now, being single for so long?"

LiAnn shook her head. "At first, I thought so but the more he talked, the more my gut told me no. I cut the evening short. He took it well, up until the phone call last week. When I told him I wouldn't be able to attend his reading because I would be out of town, I don't think he believed me. He hasn't been the same toward me since. Painting class on Tuesday and today was interesting. Things are, I don't know, strained.

Don't get me wrong, he was kind. And polite, just distant."

Karina smiled. "Understandable. Poor guy was too busy licking the wounds to his ego. So, did you happen to ask him anything about the mob wench?"

"I almost did today, after everyone else left the room. At the last second, I changed my mind. Figured he would either be irritated I was pumping him for information on someone he knows and clam up, or think it was just a ploy to talk to him. You know, give him false hope a relationship was still possible through idle chit-chat."

Karina grinned. "Don't you think continuing to attend his painting class does that already?"

"Exactly. It can't be helped, though. What better way to keep an eye on Carmella? It would look rather suspicious if I just hung out at the place and watched people come and go."

Karina didn't answer. She was staring out into the dark night, her eyes glazed over in deep thought. Finally, she asked, "Your decision to keep Jimmy in the friend only category doesn't have anything to do with Crigger, does it?"

LiAnn blushed. "Andrew is thousands of miles away. Of course not."

"Andrew? You slipped, Mom. You never call him by his first name, well, not since you two were dating. The walls in this old house are thin. I've heard you on the phone with him the last few nights."

LiAnn let out a huff of air. "He's...been concerned about how Melissa's death affected me. And you, for that matter."

"Uh-huh. Okay, Mom. Whatever you say."

"It's late. I need to go finish packing before the trip tomorrow." Irritated, and unwilling to discuss the subject any more, LiAnn rose from the chair and walked over to the back door. "And you need to rest, too. You'll need all your energy the next few days. Building a barn isn't in your bag of tricks. Be careful with the hammer."

Karina snorted and stood. "I plan on letting Bo and his crew do all the pounding. I'll just supervise."

LiAnn shook her head, deciding to let the comment slide. "Good night, sweetheart."

29

BAM. OVER. DONE.

Nick was beyond exhausted. His body felt like he'd run a marathon. Or the Iron Man race. It was after midnight, officially Thursday morning, and he hadn't slept in over two days. Nervous energy kept his frazzled brain from shutting down. Every time Nick closed his eyes, he saw the terrified face of Ray-Ray right before he pulled the trigger.

He knew the vision would haunt him the rest of his life. It was all he could do to drag himself to work each day, putting on the mask of boss.

His nerves were beyond frayed. When the phone would ring, he'd jump. If someone poked their head inside his office, he cringed, fearing it would be Carmella with instructions for their newest victim. Or, even worse, she found out he'd killed Ray-Ray, and came to end his life.

The thought of facing Carmella made Nick's ulcer bleed double-time. Even the ding from an incoming email made his skin crawl. So, at home, he kept all the lights off, cocooning himself inside the silent walls. The only light in the house was from the TV, which was muted. He wanted the flickering images, not the noise.

The last several years of his life, Nick had been a ball of constant paranoia. Health failing from the perpetual stress, it only worsened after he'd been forced to commit murder. The heavy, overpowering guilt was like a vise around his chest. Every breath, each movement, made it constrict tighter. The day of the poor kid's funeral was the worst.

Not just because Nick went on a drinking binge. Or made the stupid, stupid mistake of talking to Caesar and Carmine at The Regency. Nor was it the decision made, in his drunken stupor, to sit on the back porch, enjoy the last beers in his fridge, and make final phone calls.

Drunken, apologetic mumbles spewed out to Sabrina and Shaun about how much he loved them, how proud he was of the people they'd become. They listened, but didn't say much in response. Sabrina muttered she loved him too but had to go study. Shaun simply hung up. After the last call was placed to Teri, Nick's plan would forever extinguish the fire of guilt in his chest with one shot.

Bam. Over. Done.

Take the punishment he knew awaited on the other side, if there was such a thing as continuing on after death. If the grave truly was the end, Nick's terrible memories would fade away and disappear with the final beat of his worn-out heart. If continuing on was true, the way Nick figured, it couldn't be any worse than the Hell he was already living in.

No, the worst thing that happened to him that day was meeting Lucas Hill. Because Lucas extended something to Nick. Something he craved more than anything in the world, and was so far out of reach, Nick had erased the word from his vocabulary.

Hope.

Hope to finally be free of the shackles keeping him chained to the sick, fucked-up world of

Caesar Calvanio. The chance to loosen the vice, breathe. Walk away from the nightmare. Sleep for more than two hours at a time. Stop puking up vibrant red blood. Maybe even get off some of the medications he couldn't live without. Leave Happy Days Retirement, and spend the rest of his life trying to atone to his family for the mountains of mistakes of his past. Lucas threw him a rope, and Nick grabbed on to it, but he wasn't sure which situation was worse. Being numb and deprived of hope, or feeling the warm sensation of escape grow inside him.

Because if the rope broke and his hopes were dashed, the pain would be unbearable.

After the long, late night conversation with Lucas, discussing the plan to obliterate their common foe and all his minions, Nick was initially excited. No, he'd been euphoric. Though the kid was a stranger, they bonded immediately. Like two kidnap victims who'd been held in isolation for so long, their first contact with each other exhilarating. Telling another soul about the horrors endured was liberating, but the high left not long after Lucas did. They agreed on the decision not to go to the police, and that their only hope for salvation was killing their captors.

Nick knew there was no turning back the

second he gave Lucas the home address of Caesar. They opted not to discuss the particulars of the plan with each other. Lucas said he would take care of Caesar, followed by Carmine, and then disappear. Nick was to wait until the news broke about their deaths, then swoop in and dispatch the remaining family members. The thought process was Caesar's kin would be reeling from his death, and drop their guard. After all, they already lost their child. Another death would hopefully leave their soft underbellies exposed.

So, for the past three nights, Nick had mentally mapped out his own exit strategy. Nick knew he was too intimidated by Carmella to actually confront her face to face, and her monster of a spouse, Franco, was even worse. Besides, Nick wasn't the violent type. He lacked the physical ability. Instead of trying to overpower them, he figured the best plan was to outsmart them.

Nick glanced over at the vials of medicine and syringes on the table next to him. Potassium chloride and morphine, stolen from the drug stash at Green Pastures. Nick was a good cook, and everyone at Green Pastures knew it, since each year during the holidays, he would bring in a dessert of some sort for the staff. Every year, Nick would try a new recipe, but always made gooey brownies as well. Carmella insisted on it, for she loved them. Once Nick let his mind actually consider a scenario where Caesar and Carmine were dead, his plan formed easily. Bake a batch of brownies laced with enough morphine to take down an elephant, deliver them in person to Carmella and Franco, and once they ate them and the drug took effect, slam a needle in each of their necks full of potassium chloride.

Their deaths would be on his hands, but Nick could live with it. He had to. After all, how many innocents had they killed and dismembered over the years? Plus, it was a fitting end to their lives. They would die the same way they killed their prey.

Nick knew from the cryptic note left in his mailbox earlier the time was near. Though unsigned and only a few words, the game had begun. *Let the good times roll* was all it said, and all the information needed. He leaned over to the table and grabbed his reading glasses and flicked on the lamp. Before he was too drunk to keep his hands steady, Nick picked up a syringe and a vial of potassium chloride. The needle slid in and he watched in silence as the clear liquid filled the syringe. Nick repeated the process until he had four syringes full. Once finished, he lined them up on the silver tray on the table, smiled, and turned the light off.

A chuckle left his lips. Freedom was only a few days away. His family would finally be safe, and Nick could begin the long process of recovering from the nightmare. Maybe he would visit a shrink. They couldn't break confidentiality. No, he wouldn't do that. Too risky. He would just learn to live with it all, and maybe, eventually, the terrible memories would fade away. All he had to do was watch the news, and strike at the appropriate time.

"Something funny?"

Nick froze at the sound of Carmine's voice. He could tell it came from the kitchen. Panic barreled through his chest. Nick's mind gridlocked as a million thoughts raced through it. If Carmine was in his house, it could only mean one thing: his time was up.

Too terrified to respond, Nick listened. Heard the sound of footsteps thudding his way. Nick set his drink down on the table next to him. On instinct, he palmed a syringe. *Please, God. Help me. For my family.*

Still staring straight ahead at the TV, he saw

from the corner of his eye Carmine emerge from the kitchen. In seconds, the monster stood beside him, less than a foot away. Nick's tongue finally unlocked. "Laughing at the danger of hope, that's all."

Carmine let out a loud chuckle. "Hope? Nicky Boy, you always were a strange goose, that's for sure. So, I guess you've probably figured out why I'm here. Time's up. However, before you go, you have some writing to do–things to get off your chest."

Nick pulled his gaze away from the TV and looked at Carmine. His eyes were glinting with the anticipation of the kill. The silver barrel of the gun in Carmine's right hand shimmered under the light from the TV. Attached to the end was a silencer. In his other hand, Carmine held a piece of paper and a pen. Time slowed for Nick as everything clicked in his mind. Carmine would have him write a suicide note then end his life. Images of Teri and the kids flashed by. Nick wondered if his body parts would live on in others. The panic inside him waned as the rush of adrenaline, the will to survive, took over.

"No."

Carmine threw his head back and laughed. "Well Nicky Boy, you *did* find your lost balls, didn't you?" He tossed the paper and pen into Nick's lap. "Too bad it happened so close to your expiration date. Get up. Go to the kitchen and sit down, and let's work on crafting a heartfelt goodbye to your loved ones. Oh, wait, you don't have any of those left, do you? Now, move or I'll shoot you up where you sit, and write your final words myself. I promise you, they won't be near as poetic as your own."

Jaw clenched, Nick rose from the chair. Carmine stepped away, brandishing the gun like a pointer. Nick moved across the hardwood in his bare feet, Carmine right behind him. Once Nick crossed the threshold into the kitchen, he coughed. Hard. At first it was a fake cough, but soon, it wasn't. Droplets of blood spewed out of his mouth, all over the kitchen floor. Nick doubled over, reaching out with the hand that held the syringe to the counter for support.

"Cough sounds bad, Nicky Boy. Summer cold, eh? Don't worry. I've got a permanent cure for you right here."

The second Carmine leaned over his shoulder, the gun near his face, Nick went into action. He jerked his head and the base of his skull connected with Carmine's nose. Nick heard the sickening crack and the anguished yelp of pain, followed by the clatter of the gun as it skittered across the floor. He swung his arm up and buried the needle in Carmine's neck, pushing the plunger. Blood and snot ran down Carmine's face, his eyes backlit with fury. Nick tried to back away, but stepped on the gun. He stumbled just as Carmine's arm shot out, his meaty fist connecting with Nick's jawbone.

The blow sent Nick flying backwards, his body crashing into the cabinetry. Bright, white light exploded in front of Nick's eyes. When it disappeared he saw Carmine jerk the needle from his bleeding neck, then crumple to the ground. Spasms rocked his body. Nick noticed Carmine glance toward the gun to his left. In two swift strides, Nick crossed the kitchen floor and kicked it away from Carmine's reach.

The man was gasping for air, a strange, gurgling sound in his throat. Nick's adrenaline pumped through his system as he realized Carmine was on his last legs. A sensation of triumph at offing the goon made him grin. *You're a killer for sure. Two in less than one month! This is so wrong. So...not happening.*

The sense of accomplishment was short-lived. With a final grunt, Carmine rolled on his side, one hand clenched around the needle hole on his neck, the other in his jacket pocket. In that split second, Nick realized he wasn't in the clear. He turned and made it to the doorway before the muffled *pop* reached his ears. Red-hot, searing pain tore through his back, thrusting him forward, and Nick fell face-first onto the floor. He tried to scramble to his feet, but his legs wouldn't cooperate. With his cheek firmly stuck to the floor, his mind and body stunned from the impact of the bullet, Nick realized he couldn't feel his legs.

His arms still worked, so he dug his fingers into the floor and tried to pull himself forward. Terrified another bullet would rip through him any second, he had to get away. His cell phone was less than ten feet from him, on the floor next to the chair. If he could just reach it in time, he could call 9-1-1. He didn't care at this point about involving the police. What they would find upon their arrival, or what they would uncover during an investigation. Nick just wanted it all over. Once and for all.

The house was quiet, no movement from behind him. The gurgles had stopped and Nick prayed the bastard was dead. The room seemed darker, the distance to the phone, longer. With one final burst of energy, Nick's fingers clamped around the phone. He tried to punch the buttons but couldn't see the screen. Everything went black.

In the darkness, Nick cried out, "Forgive me, Teri."

30

THE TRUTH UNFOLDS

"Be safe, honey. Don't let your guard down for even a second while we're gone. That means curtailing horizontal activities with Bo. I mean it."

Karina forced a smile and hugged her mom. "I think we already had a discussion about your constant worrying. I'll be fine, Mom. Promise. Now, scoot, before you wind up in rush hour traffic. Cecil is probably wondering why you haven't arrived yet."

LiAnn gave Karina a disapproving look as she

climbed behind the wheel of *Dragula.* "Love you."

Junior stuck his head out the window and yelled, "Don't forget to feed the chickens. Oh, and if the power goes off again, remember there are plenty of candles in the junk room."

Karina watched as her mom put the car in gear and everyone waved goodbye. About fifty yards down the driveway, they passed Bo as his truck lumbered up the drive. She saw her mom motion for him to stop, and a quick conversation between them ensued. Karina rolled her eyes, wondering just what in the heck her mom was saying to him. With her luck, she probably told him Karina was on her period, or some other trumped-up tale to ensure sex was off the table. Thankfully, the discussion didn't last long.

Bo pulled up and climbed out, a huge grin on his face. "Mornin', sunshine. My, but your ma was in a mood. She told me I best keep an eye on you while they're gone, or she'd kick my rear from here to New Orleans. Guess you weren't kiddin' about her bein' overprotective."

Any other time, Karina would have been annoyed at her mother's meddling, but given their current situation, she understood. Though Karina never expressed her thoughts out loud, she was worried about not only her mother, but Gram, Grampa, and Cecil. Karina returned Bo's smile. "Momma hens always worry about their chicks, especially if they only have one. Sorry about that. So, are you ready to go get the material? I have some things I need to discuss with you on the way."

"First things first, doll," Bo cooed as he wrapped his arms around Karina and kissed her.

For a few blessed moments, Karina melted into his sensual embrace. Lost herself inside Bo's lips, his talented mouth. The feel of his strong hands down her back. Forgot all about the craziness in her world as Bo's kiss washed it all away.

Bo pulled back and looked at Karina, his smile even brighter than before. "As I was sayin', first things first. Got to have my mornin' fix of catnip."

Despite the constant worry swimming around in her mind, Karina laughed. "Oh, so I'm just a drug fix, huh? Didn't picture you as the type to get addicted."

Bo swatted Karina's rump. "Darlin', I'm a full blown junkie. You cast some kinda spell on me, that's for sure. Now, come on. I'm takin' you out for breakfast at my favorite place before we go get the material. Hope you like biscuits and gravy."

"Okay. Let me go get my purse and lock up. Be right back."

Karina turned and went inside. She grabbed her gun and shoved it in her purse, took the phone off the charger, and double-checked the camera on the back porch. Ranger followed her every move. When Karina reached the front door, she gave him the command to stay and guard. He whined but complied, his big, brown eyes reflected his sadness at being left alone. Once outside, Karina checked the lock on the door, stood on her tip-toes and re-positioned the camera. Satisfied things were locked up tight, she bounded down the front steps.

Bo was inside his truck, waiting for her. Just as she made it to the passenger door, she heard a vehicle approaching. Karina turned to look, and grimaced. *Perfect timing. Not.*

Karina opened the door and set her purse inside. Bo was busy looking out the rearview mirror and didn't notice Karina extract the gun and slide it in her back waistband. "Babe, hang on. Unexpected company just arrived. Listen," she said, a heavy sense of dread hanging in her throat, "I wasn't planning on bringing this up until later, after breakfast, but plans change. You'll need to hear this, too. Come on."

Bo looked at Karina, his head cocked in curiosity. "Karina, what are you talkin' about? And, why are the cops here?"

The black car with its tinted windows and unmistakable look pulled up and stopped behind Bo's truck. Karina let out a long huff of air. "Just, come on. Once they leave, I'll fill you in with all the other details, as soon as I make sure they are the real deal."

Two men exited the car, stuffed inside their suits. Matching black sunglasses and shoes topped off their look. Karina wondered why all federal agents insisted on dressing alike. Maybe they were all forced to take the same fashion classes at Quantico. It was probably taught by the same fool who told them the unmarked cars would blend in.

Idiots.

The one who'd been driving spoke first. "Ms. Summers?"

She shut the door and walked toward him. Karina stopped at the tailgate and leaned against it. "Yes. And you are?"

"Special Agent Winslow. This is my partner,

Agent Phillips. I assume you know why we are here."

Karina could see Bo had exited the truck, but he didn't come closer. Instead, he held open the driver's door and watched. "I take nothing at face value, gentlemen. Need to see some I.D. please."

In a well-practiced move, both men pulled their badges from their pockets. They held them out so she could see. They looked authentic enough, but as Karina well knew, documents were easy to forge. "Excuse me for being cautious, but if you really are who you claim to be, you'll completely understand my concern. So, which one of you spoke with Melissa Doster?"

Special Agent Winslow removed his sunglasses and replied, "Ah, you are on edge, Ms. Summers. Neither of us did, because it was Cheddy Singleton who contacted our office about you and your mother, Detective Tuck. By the way, is she here as well? We'd like to speak with you both at the same time."

Karina's heartbeat slowed down a fraction. She glanced over at Bo and motioned for him to come over. She waited until he was by her side before responding. "Yes, I am on edge. Still am, actually. Again, I'm sure you understand why."

Both agents eyed Bo with mild interest. He returned their gazes, his face projecting a sea of calm, but Karina could feel the tension in his muscles. His hand rested on the small of her back, and she felt him stiffen when he touched the gun.

"We do. We only have a few questions, then we'll be on our way and let you get back to your day. Would you please have your mother come out and join us?"

"She's not here. Won't be for the next several days. Whatever questions you have, I will be able to answer. She knows nothing more than what I do."

"Perhaps this conversation needs to be done in private, Ms. Summers?" Agent Phillips said, his focus never leaving Bo.

Bo tensed, so Karina squeezed his hand. "Gentlemen, I would like to introduce you to my boyfriend, Bo Barton. Whatever you need to ask me, or say, feel free to do so in front of him."

"As you wish. Have you had any contact with the subject since we spoke last?"

"No. Not in person. I do have video of her

entering the apartment of Mr. Pickard from a few days ago, but nothing else."

"We'll need to get a copy of that. Email will be fine. What about your mother? Did she speak with her on Tuesday or Thursday while at The Magnolia?" Special Agent Winslow asked.

Ah, so they truly have been investigating. "She did not. We are pretty sure the woman is steering clear of us, ever since she saw me leaving Mr. Pickard's room. Now, I have a few questions of my own. Since you are here, the case is active, which means you took our concerns to heart. What have you discovered?"

Agent Phillips shifted his weight but remained silent. Special Agent Winslow answered. "We are still gathering evidence at this stage, Ms. Summers. We have confirmed, however, that the suspect is one and the same as you assumed."

"Tell me something I don't know, please. Like, have you figured out yet if her brother is here, too? And, is there more going on at The Magnolia besides stealing money from its residents? What about Vincenzo Molinero? Same guy as the doctor in New York?"

"We aren't at liberty to say more about an on-going investigation, Ms. Summers. We only came as a courtesy today, to let you and your mother know we are working the case, see if you had any new information for us, and to assure you not to worry. We'll take care of things from here, so please don't attempt any other undercover investigating. We have things under control. Oh, and one final thing. Please advise your mother to discontinue her attendance to Jimmy Calhoun's painting class, as well as her visits to the property, until we finish our investigation. For her safety, of course."

"What? Why?" Karina barked, but neither responded to her question. Both men turned and went back to their vehicle. Karina was furious, and had Bo not been next to her, would have given them a hefty piece of her pissed off mind. Instead, she bit her lip and kept her words inside. In seconds, the car backed out and disappeared down the driveway.

"What the hell was that all about? They were talkin' about that retirement home in Hot Springs, right? The Magnolia? Why did you feel the need to grab your gun? What's goin' on, Karina?" Bo asked, his voice full of worry.

"Bo, let me fix you breakfast here. It would be best for others not to hear what I have to say. Come on. I have a lot to tell you."

Karina saw the reluctance behind his eyes, but

he never said a word. He followed her inside in silence. Ranger didn't growl at Bo but never took his eyes off him, either. Her loyal dog had learned to deal with Bo's presence but still remained on guard. Once in the kitchen, Karina motioned for Bo to sit while she opened the fridge. "Coffee?"

"From the sound of things, I may need more than caffeine."

Two hours later, Karina sat at the opposite end of the table and watched Bo. Rather than drumming her fingers on the table, she rubbed Ranger's head. She told Bo everything, from beginning to end, and to her surprise, he never spoke during her entire monologue. Karina left no details out, and her last sentence was the question she didn't want to ask: Did he want to call it quits and part ways?

During the long tale, Bo's face displayed a myriad of emotions. Shock, confusion, worry, disbelief, and finally settled on anger. He sat rock solid, staring out the picture window in the kitchen, his eyes glazed over. The afternoon sun streaked across his hair, and a lump formed in Karina's throat. If he decided to end their budding relationship, she would miss him. More than she originally considered.

Karina had grown quite fond of Bo during the last several weeks. Besides their physical connection, she enjoyed his company. Bo was funny, a smile always on his face, a joke never far behind. He loved to tease, and was devoted to his family. A good heart and solid spirit. Karina wanted to prod him for an answer, but knew it was best to let him digest everything before he responded. Her stomach was in knots, waiting for him to speak. A wave of sadness and regret washed over her, for Karina couldn't help but feel he was about to get up and walk away.

When he turned to look at her, Bo's beautiful blue eyes bored a hole into her heart. He looked pissed as hell. Karina couldn't blame him. The implications of everything, how staying involved with her might even put his family in danger, anger for not telling him sooner, would infuriate anyone. Karina held her breath, steadying herself for an ass-chewing, followed by his departure.

"I'm not sure what pisses me off the most.

You thinkin' so little of me, or the fact some lowlife criminal has you and your family in her crosshairs."

Stunned, Karina stuttered, "Bo, I didn't tell you until now because..."

Bo interrupted, dismissing Karina's words with a flick of his hand. "No, I meant assumin' I would just walk away. Like a scared hound, runnin' home at the first sign of a predator in the woods. You seem to be under the impression I only think of you as a piece of ass, or a fun way to pass time until somethin' else catches my eye. I thought I made it pretty clear how I feel about you, Karina. You think I've been hangin' out here, workin' in this heat, just for my health?"

Heat flushed Karina's cheeks. Bo's reaction surprised her. "No, no, of course not. I...this situation could get dangerous. Not really sure what we are dealing with, and I thought I would give you the chance to steer clear. You know, in case things do take a turn to the ugly side. It's not every day someone with ties to the mob comes sniffing around. This has kind of thrown me for a loop, so..."

Bo stood and walked over to where Karina sat. Though still angry, his gaze softened as he extended his hand. Karina took it and rose from the chair. "My joke about bein' addicted to you wasn't all said in jest. It ain't been long, but in the last few weeks, I've kinda fallin' for you, Karina Summers. I like havin' you around, so if someone is tryin' to mess with that, they just became my enemy. And there ain't nothin' worse in this world than a pissed-off redneck. This Carmella chick may have ties to the mob, but she's still flesh and bone. If she tries to harm you, or anyone you love, I'll introduce her to my version of the Southern Mafia."

Bo kissed her, his lips warm and tender. His right hand stroked her hair with gentle caresses. The emotion conveyed through his mouth and body was subtle yet powerful, and it left Karina a bit unsteady. When he pulled his lips away, his hand moved from her hair to her chin.

Bo lifted her face toward him. "I ain't goin' anywhere. I made a promise to your ma to watch out for you, and I am a man of my word. Just one request."

Karina swallowed the lump in her throat and whispered, "What's that?"

"If I'm gonna be your man, which I assume I am since you introduced me as such, please don't keep secrets from me. A relationship will never last if it's built on deception. Deal?"

Warmth spread through Karina's chest, and despite her attempts to stop them, the sting of tears burned her eyes. Unable to find her voice, Karina simply nodded.

"Good! Now, before we go to the lumberyard, and my latest class on how to be a southerner starts, I want to learn a bit on how to be a P.I. Will you show me how this recordin' thing works on your phone? We've been havin' trouble at our farm with people stealin' equipment. Might just need you to install some at our place."

Karina grinned through her tears. "You bet."

31

GOODBYE, SWEET ROMELLA

Caesar said his goodbyes to Carmella and Franco on their front porch. He climbed behind the wheel of the car, anxious to get the day started. The last two had been spent at their home, going over every detail, all the nuances of the business, with Franco. The man wasn't the scholarly type, and training him turned out to be a bigger problem than what Caesar initially thought.

He pulled out onto the highway, enjoying the sensation of driving. Normally, Carmine drove him everywhere, so Caesar could use the time to mentally prepare for whatever they had planned. However, after the night he laid out the plans for his retirement, things became strained between the two of them. Carmine waited, just like Caesar knew he would, until everyone else left, and asked what was really going on. Caesar replied with the bare minimum and was surprised when Carmine continued to press him for the truth. Caesar exploded, informing Carmine to mind his own damned business and to get busy plotting out the death of Nick the Prick. Carmine stormed out in a fit of anger, and the two hadn't spoken since. Caesar knew once Carmine vented his frustrations on the unsuspecting Nick, he'd come around. If he didn't, Caesar would visit him one last time before he left for Tahiti to say his final goodbyes. He owed Carmine that much.

It had been years since Caesar had taken someone out, and he was excited. Giddy, actually. The hit was all plotted out. All he had to do was wait for the cover of darkness to execute it. While at the red light, Caesar glanced over to the duffel bag in the passenger seat. It was crammed full of all the necessary items to take out the girl, plus a change of clothes. Before Caesar left his sister's house, he'd checked the contents four times, making sure he hadn't forgotten anything. In the past, he wouldn't have because his mind had been like a steel trap, but things had changed. He'd changed. Gotten old. Forgetful. Sentimental. When the light turned green, Caesar forced his foot to remain steady on the gas pedal, even though he wanted to burn rubber. He would wait to satiate his need for endorphins to flood his brain until later.

There were only two things Caesar had left to do before departing the states for good. Once his final kill was completed later, he'd head home and burn every piece of paper, any shred of his former life, including his disguises. He wished he could live out the remainder of his time on earth under his real name, rather than continuing to hide under the alias of the man's whose identity he stole nearly thirty years ago. Only a handful of people, including The Prick, his delivery boy Lucas, and Caesar's family knew his real name. It was a necessary part of living out in the open, under the radar of the Feds. Unfortunately, it just wasn't in the cards. To remain untouched and hidden, Caesar couldn't risk it.

The other item he needed to address was a more pleasant task. He pulled into the parking lot of Carmella's favorite flower shop, went in, and purchased a dozen white roses and a candle. Caesar paid with cash and never said a word to the young girl behind the counter. Once back in his car, he drove out past Lake Hamilton for ten miles. Admiring the view, a sense of melancholy hit his gut. He would miss the beautiful state's scenery, but certainly not the weather. The humidity wreaked havoc on his joints. Tahiti was a tropical climate, and he knew it would be humid there as well, but he hoped the brisk trade winds would buffer the moist air.

Caesar arrived at his destination. Several months had passed since the last time he walked through the rolling acreage, and just seeing the endless green grass and rows upon rows of headstones made his heart pound. Gathering up the flowers and the candle, Caesar exited the cool interior of the car and walked the path that would take him to Romella's grave.

Though still early in the morning, the heat bore down on him as he trudged uphill. Each time he visited, the path seemed to elongate. Caesar was out of breath and sweat dripped into his eyes by the time he stopped in front of

Romella's headstone. His knees popped as he crouched down to place the roses at the edge of her grave. Retrieving the lighter from his pocket, Caesar lit the candle and smiled as he set it in the holder he had specially designed.

After glancing around to ensure he was alone, Caesar closed his eyes and whispered, "I miss you. Going to leave next week, and I'm afraid I won't be able to come back to visit anymore. I hope you understand. It's time. Time for me to move on, to put my past to rest."

"*Liar.*"

Caesar jerked at the sound of Romella's voice, his blood pressure soaring. It wasn't from inside his mind. She was behind him. Her presence was strong. Opening his eyes, he turned around, praying she wouldn't be in the form of the ruined corpse from Ray-Ray's funeral. To his relief, she wasn't. Romella's long, raven hair flowed behind her in the gentle breeze, blue eyes shimmered with life, and her white dress floated around her, a small smile on her lips. Her feet hovered several inches above the grass.

Swallowing hard, Caesar returned her smile. "No, I'm not, my love. I'm doing exactly as you've begged me to do in the last few months. I'm retiring and moving. To Tahiti. You wanted me to, remember? Said you wanted to spend eternity in paradise."

Romella's features hardened, and anger danced behind her eyes. "You lie, Caesar. You want to leave me for that blonde whore. I saw you two together. How you looked at her. The way she looked at you." Her face shifted. Silent tears fell from her eyes as sadness replaced the anger. "You fell for her, didn't you? You're finally leaving me for another. A cop, no less. My, how you've changed since my death."

Pain at hurting her thrummed in his chest. Caesar reached out to touch Romella's hand, but it went right through the ethereal form. He craved to touch her, to gather her into his arms, reassuring her of his undying love. Since he couldn't, Caesar responded, "Ro, you're wrong. I was just...using her to gather information. For business. Nothing more, nothing less. She was simply a means to an end, that's all. In fact, she won't be alive after Sunday. Carmella and Franco are taking her out, along with her family. I promise. Look, see?" Caesar pulled out his plane ticket to Tahiti from his pocket, holding it up. "I was just researching the last job. Doing my portion tonight, and by this time next week, it will be just the two of us. Forever."

Romella floated closer, her ghostly figure less than a foot away. "Oh, Caesar, you really mean it?"

Caesar's heart skipped several beats as he looked into her eyes. "Yes, my love. I do. No woman, not even LiAnn Tuck, means a thing to me. Only you. It's always been you."

He closed his eyes, imagining his arms around her, kissing her full lips. Embracing her with such force, his darling Romella would never be able to leave again. Cold spread through his body, and Caesar wondered if her ghost just passed through him. When he opened his eyes, Romella was gone, the candle extinguished. Tears raced down his cheeks as Caesar knelt in front of the polished marble. His fingers trembled as he ran his hand over the engraved headstone, his heart heavy, and the stone ice-cold. The words tore at his soul. *In Loving Memory of Romella Calhoun. Beloved wife. Always loved, never forgotten.*

Rising to his feet, Caesar took one last look and left. Romella wasn't in the ground, at least not her soul. She was alive, waiting for him to join her on the warm, sunny beaches of Tahiti. One final job to complete and he would be able to be with his beloved Romella. Caesar walked away with a purpose, ignoring the heat and the throbbing in his knuckles, excited to start the final chapter of his life.

It was time to go get Vincenzo and start prepping.

32

THE WORLD EXPLODES

Exhausted from hours of back-breaking work, Karina sat down in the grass next to the barn. She heard Ranger barking near the edge of the tree line and smiled. His new favorite hobby was annoying the squirrels. From the corner of her eye, Karina watched Bo walk over to his truck and shut the tailgate.

The last seven hours had been grueling. It took two trips to the lumberyard to load Bo's truck with supplies. They stacked piles and piles of wood in neat rows about twenty feet from the old barn, along with fifteen buckets of white enamel paint. Once they finished, they tackled the interior. Grampa told her to only save the tools and tack, the rest she could toss. It took three hours to go through all the items, decide what to keep and what to junk, and separate into piles. Karina had three blisters on her palms, numerous splinters, and sweat covered every inch of her body.

Other than water breaks, they'd only stopped twice. Once to eat lunch, which had been hours ago, and when her mom called to say they arrived in Branson. The sun was almost gone, and the mosquitoes were out in droves. Karina couldn't wait to take a shower and scrub the grime and itchy patches away.

"Feel like a southerner yet?" Bo teased, joining her.

"Almost. Just one more bug bite, and a beer, and I'm sure *y'all* will be a permanent part of my vocabulary."

Ranger's bark grew louder and Bo remarked, "Your dog is ahead of you. Sounds like a regular ol' huntin' dog. He'd make a great duck dog. Ever taken him huntin'?"

"Does stalking Frisbees in the park count?" Thunder rumbled and drowned out Bo's response. Karina groaned. *Not another storm. Why can't it just rain without the light and sound show?* "What did you say?"

Bo jumped to his feet and pulled Karina up as well. "I said it's about to rain. Pour, actually. Gonna need to cover this stuff up. Don't suppose you've got a tarp or visqueen hidden in the house, huh?"

Karina looked over at the exposed items, jumping when another loud clap of thunder boomed. "Uh, no. I haven't finished all my southerner classes yet, so there may be hope for finding something like that later. Ranger! Come on, boy. Let the squirrels hide in their nests in peace!"

Bo swiped a quick kiss across Karina's sticky forehead. "Love that mouth of yours for so many reasons. Now, I'm gonna dash to the farm and pick some up. I best hurry, before the bottom drops out. Damn, the weather report this mornin' said only ten percent chance of rain. Good thing they don't get paid for accuracy. They'd starve."

"No kidding. Listen, thanks, Bo. For everything, including sticking around. I'm going to take Ranger inside and start dinner. I'll wait to take the world's longest shower until you get back. I'm sure I'll need plenty of help washing all the sweat off my back."

Bo winked and climbed into his truck, gunned it, and spun dirt and gravel behind the massive tires. Ranger bounded across the yard at full speed, terrified of the coming storm. Karina knew exactly how he felt. The clouds were dark and ugly, the setting sun nothing but a memory.

Karina went inside the barn and gave it a final once over. It was strange to see the building empty. It was no wonder Grampa didn't want to watch it come down. Tomorrow would be hard for her as well, and the barn hadn't been a part of Karina's life nearly as long as it had Grampa's. Satisfied there was nothing left to salvage, other than one section of the front door, Karina walked out. She ran her hand across the section carved by her great-great-grandfather. Though Karina couldn't see it in the dark, she knew it read *Tuck Manor, Est. 1839*.

There was no way she'd destroy it. Bo had promised to cut the piece out and put it aside, restore the decrepit wood, and then attached it to the inside of the new door. He didn't laugh at her, or judge the sentimentality of the gesture to save the piece of her family's history. For some reason, Karina found his understanding sexy as hell.

Evening had settled in, which made her jittery. The storm rumbled in the distance, and Karina hoped it wouldn't take much longer for Bo to return. Not only did she want to get the materials covered before the rain arrived, but she didn't relish the idea of being alone in the house when the storm roared in.

Ranger bounded around her feet like he was herding her toward the house, anxious to get inside. Together, they crossed the pasture and front yard in the darkness. The clouds covered the moon, so Karina used her cellphone as a flashlight. The sound of a vehicle made her pause on the steps. She hoped it was Bo, so she waited to see if it kept going down the main road, or turned onto the driveway. When it continued on, she sighed and went inside, locking the door behind her.

"Come on, boy. Dinner time. Yes, who's Mommy's good boy?" Karina cooed to Ranger as they walked to the kitchen. "You like Bo, huh? You must since he still has his ass left. Guess what? Mommy does too. Likes him *and* his ass."

Ranger grunted and made cooing noises of his own at her while he waited for the nuggets. She filled the bowl and he dug in. After refilling his other dish with fresh water, she went to the fridge and grabbed a handful of ice cubes and a beer. Dropping the chunks in his dish, Karina opened the beer and took a long swig.

"I was cut out all along to be a southerner," she quipped, patting Ranger on the head. "Mommy does love her beer."

He ignored her and continued to inhale his food. Karina left the kitchen and went straight to the bathroom, eager to remove her contacts. All the dust and dirt from the barn had irritated her eyes. The second she pulled them out, the itching ceased. Turning the faucet on, Karina let out a squeal of delight when she tossed the first handful of cold water onto her face. She rummaged around for the facial cleanser on the counter, and after finding it, washed the grit away.

Satisfied her face was clean, Karina slid off her filthy clothes and tossed them into the hamper. For a second, she stared at the inviting shower and almost caved. No, she told Bo she'd wait, and a shower with him would certainly be more enjoyable than alone, so she slid her glasses on then flung her tattered robe over her shoulders. Karina grimaced at the reflection. *Terrycloth is sexy as hell. Not. Oh, and my hair is a masterpiece. Mom will be proud because this ensemble will not ignite any passionate thoughts in Bo.*

She opened her purse and took out the Glock, and pocketed it in the robe. It would stay there until Bo returned. With everything going on, having the weapon nearby made her feel better. Her cellphone beeped from the bathroom, and Karina grunted, realizing she left it in the pocket of her jeans. It was a good thing she hadn't chunked them straight into the washer. Once she reached it, her heart skipped a beat.

The video program was on, and streaming live was the interior of Cecil's living room. It was hard to see much at first since the only light came from a lamp on the table, but Karina could see and hear movement. A flashlight appeared then, sending a bright beam across the couch.

"Come on, come on, bitch. I know it's you. Turn the lights on. Let me see your face."

Less than five seconds later, her request was answered. The overhead light in the living room came on, and sure enough, Carmella D'Nucci stood in the center of the room, dressed in black from head to toe.

Karina scooted over to the computer chair, fumbling for her charger. No way she'd let this latest piece of evidence slip from her grasp because the battery croaked. Her fingers shook from anger while she watched the bitch pilfer through Cecil's apartment. Something about the entire situation was different than the last time she'd watched Carmella skulk around. It dawned on Karina that Carmella wasn't even trying to hide her presence, and she was moving methodically from one location to the next. Before, Carmella had perused the place in a hurry, making sure she left the room exactly how she found it.

Not this time.

Carmella was trashing the place. Flinging open drawers, rifling through the papers, letting pages fall to the floor. For a few seconds, Karina was dumbstruck, watching the frenzied woman ransack the living room. Ranger was barking downstairs, the crackles of thunder slammed outside, but she pushed it all away.

Karina's sole focus was on Carmella D'Nucci.

Unwilling to interrupt the video feed, Karina set the phone on the desk and powered up her laptop. Fury barreled through Karina the longer she watched. Cecil hadn't even been out of his apartment for a full twenty-four hours.

Karina pulled up her email. She had to get in

contact with Special Agent Winslow, send him the video once it finished. Thank goodness Cecil heeded their advice and removed all his banking information from their hiding spots. They were safe and sound in a safety deposit box at First Southern State Bank.

The bitch could search for hours and would find only one. Her mom's idea was to leave information on one account in the apartment for Carmella to find. Cecil had already transferred all the cash out into another, so if Carmella, or anyone else, tried to access it, all it would do was seal the person's fate.

Karina tried to concentrate and type out an email to the FBI. Between the booms of thunder, and Ranger's barking, and the rush of adrenaline in her system, it was difficult. Her words would be a jumbled mass of misspelled nonsense if she didn't calm down. Lifting her hands from the keyboard, Karina took a deep breath and focused her attention out the window on the barn.

For Cecil. Breathe. For Cecil.

The second her fingers touched the keys again, the hairs on her neck stood erect. Lightning crackled across the sky, illuminating a shadowy figure dart behind the barn.

Her skin turned clammy as goose bumps

popped out all over. Karina went on alert. Ducking down, she scrambled across the floor and reached up to turn off the light. Before she could touch the switch, the room went black. Keeping low, she moved to the window. The front porch light was out, too. Karina peered out across the yard, praying she was overreacting, that the loss of power was from the storm and Bo's truck was in the yard.

It wasn't.

Two sounds hit her at once: Ranger's incessant barking morphed into a throaty growl, and the unmistakable sound of the screech of the door to the back porch. She'd only heard the ominous snarls during Ranger's training. It was the final warning to a target before he attacked. Whoever just entered the house was about to have his limbs ripped off.

Extracting the gun from her robe, Karina reached for her cell. The video of Carmella would stop the second she touched the screen, but it didn't matter at this point. She dialed 9-1-1 while crouching by the door.

"9-1-1. What's your emergency?"

Cupping her hand over the receiver to amplify her voice, she whispered, "Karina Summers. 817

Highway 35. Junior Tuck's place. Intruder inside the house..."

The sound of Ranger's yelp of pain interrupted her words. She fought the urge to rush down the stairs to his aid. Instead, she disconnected the call and flicked it to mute. She shoved it into her pocket, opened the door to the hallway, and stepped out. The house was dark and silent. Fury mixed with fear for Ranger pushed every other emotion away. Her bare feet made no sound as she moved, gun at the ready.

Then, it hit her. The stench of rotten eggs made her gag. Tears formed but she ignored them. Karina could hear the hiss of the gas coming from the kitchen, probably from the oven or water heater. Terror thundered in her chest when the next smell hit: smoke

Shit!

Steadying her back against the wall, Karina peeked around the doorway into the kitchen. It was too dark to see Ranger or the intruder, but she heard the scratch of Ranger's claws on the floor, along with his low whimpers. Thankfully, nothing else. No heavy breathing. No footsteps. Tears poured from her eyes, so Karina dropped to the floor and crawled toward the sound of her dog. In seconds, she felt Ranger's furry coat.

Ranger was over one hundred pounds. Karina stuck the gun in her pocket and heaved with all her might. Once in her arms, she braced her back against the countertop and scooted in the direction of the door. Lightning sparkled across the sky, illuminating for a brief second, the door, and the silver handle of the enormous blade sticking out of her beloved dog's neck.

Coughing, sputtering for air as spit and tears ran down her cheeks, Karina threw her body weight against the screen, stumbling out into the yard. She made it halfway to the barn before the world erupted. The concussion knocked her several feet into the air. Ranger's body flew out of her arms, Karina's screams of anguish were drowned out by the explosion.

The entire pasture looked like it was bathed in daylight. Burning heat rushed over her as shards of debris peppered her exposed legs and arms. Karina landed hard, face-down, in the grass. The impact nearly knocked her out, but she fought to remain conscious.

This. Isn't. Happening.

Disoriented, she opened her eyes and searched for Ranger. She tried to whistle, but her mouth was full of blood. Though the fire from the burning embers of what was once Gram and

Grampa's home provided plenty of light, Karina couldn't make much out. When it finally sunk in it was because her glasses were gone, panic welled up inside her chest.

I've got to get out of here and I can't see!

Ears ringing from the blast, she tried to listen for sounds of the intruder, but it was no use. Just as she wiggled her left arm out from under her body, blurry movement to the left made her stiffen.

Karina knew she only had one chance. Holding still, she waited for the attacker to close in. Her right hand eased inside her pocket and clamped around the gun. Thankfully, her hair covered most of her face, so she watched through the strands as the figure moved closer. When less than five feet away, she jerked.

Rolling to her right, Karina pulled the gun from her pocket and fired four quick shots. The first missed the target, but the remaining bullets didn't. Two slammed into the torso and one into the head. The body crumpled to the ground.

"Screw you!" Karina stood on wobbly legs and walked over, gun aimed at the still body. She squinted, and realized it was a man. One she didn't recognize, and he was obviously dead.

Half his head was gone, and blood poured from the wounds to his upper chest.

"You bastard! Why did you...oh, my God. Everything is gone. You killed my dog, you sick freak. Destroyed our house, tried to kill me. *Fuck you!*"

The dead bastard wouldn't feel a thing, but Karina didn't care. She raised her bare foot and brought it down with all the strength she had left on his crotch. "That Carmella bitch sent you, didn't she? Or some other fucking mobster, like Caesar Calvanio." Karina continued to stomp on his balls, accentuating each word with her heel. "Don't. Screw. With. My. Family."

Out of breath, she backed away and stared at the flames. Tears rolled down her face, and she was actually thankful for the moment her vision was blurry. Anguished sobs burst out, and she mumbled her thanks to the Heavens above none of her family had been home. Her body started to tremble as cooling rain fell from the sky. Karina knew the adrenaline crash was imminent, along with a hefty dose of shock.

Karina sank to the ground and crawled toward Ranger, ignoring the pain from her injuries. "Oh, Ranger. I'm so sorry. You tried to warn me, I didn't pay enough attention. Oh, God, I'm sorry.

Hang on, buddy. Help is coming. We'll get you to the vet, I promise." She choked out, a whimper of sorrow left her mouth when his still body came into focus. In the distance, she heard the faint whine of sirens. "Help is coming."

"Not in time to save you, bitch."

On instinct, Karina went for her gun. Searing hot pain exploded inside her head, filling her visions with bursts of white and yellow. She felt her body fall forward, the gun fly from her fingers, and the scratchy fur of Ranger's body on her cheek. Moaning, Karina felt around for the knife embedded in his body. As her fingers found the cold steel, the last thing Karina saw was a boot inches from her face.

33

THE THUNDER ROLLS

Caesar had Vincenzo drive by the large farmhouse and park several hundred yards away on an unused dirt road. They retrieved their weapons and headed toward their destination in silence. Less than one hundred yards away from the driveway, they stopped and watched a pickup truck leave. Caesar extracted his night vision binoculars and zeroed in on the property. He saw someone walk into the barn, heard the yapping of a dog in between booms of thunder.

Crouched low in the scrub of trees, ignoring

the pain in his hands and knees, Caesar smiled. "She's alone. Remember, no shots. The sound will carry, and we don't need the cops to roll up on us. Only use the gun as incentive to force her to go outside. Chase her toward the barn, which is where I'll be. With this." He flashed the hunting knife in front of Vincenzo's face. "Understand?"

"Yes, boss." Vincenzo followed his response with a nod.

Caesar could see the disappointment in Vincenzo's eyes, even in the dark. "Ah, don't worry. I'll make sure the first slice only immobilizes her. You can finish her off with your own blade. Deal?"

Vincenzo's smile was big and bright. "Deal!"

"Oh, and one more thing."

"What's that, boss?" Vincenzo whispered.

"Take out the dog first. Quietly. Neither of us need to be missing chunks of flesh."

Just as they'd discussed on the drive over, they split up. Vincenzo at a light trot, Caesar at a brisk walk. Once he reached the edge of the tree line, Caesar stopped. He scanned the yard, barn, and house with the binoculars. Watched their target exit the barn and jog across the yard, the dog right next to her. In seconds, they were inside the house. Adrenaline pulsed through Caesar's body, making him feel more alive than he had in thirty years. His hands trembled slightly as he envisioned the first moment the sharp, thin blade pierced the delicate flesh. The high he would feel as warm blood spilled out, the terror in the eyes of the kill when she realized death was but mere seconds away. For Caesar, it was better than sex or any drug.

Satisfied it was safe to move, Caesar exited the cover of trees and jogged across the field until he reached the barn. Thunder boomed, followed by several bolts of lightning. The last burst of light kept him from crashing into a pile of wood to his right. His heart rate elevated when he noticed an old pickup to his left, thinking it was the truck from before. When Caesar realized it wasn't, he shook his head at the silly paranoia and continued forward. With his back against the wall, Caesar peered around the corner. It took him several seconds to focus the binoculars, but finally, he caught movement by the back door.

Unfortunately, so did the dog.

Its bark was loud, and the sound carried across the yard all the way to Caesar's hiding position. He cringed, wondering if the decision to let Vincenzo be a part of the hit was the right one.

Their quarry, this former private investigator, was probably in tune with her four-legged beast and would recognize the warning bark.

"Come on, come on dickhead. Shut that dog up!" Caesar whispered.

"This isn't going to end well, Caesar. Leave. Let it go. Come, be with me. I need you. Want you by my side. The sun is warm. Hurry."

The sweet, inviting voice of Romella drifted in Caesar's mind. He pushed it aside, unwilling to answer her back. Too much was at stake. Rather than respond, he peered through the lens of the binoculars and saw Vincenzo's body appear on the porch. Knife in hand, Vincenzo entered the back door. Less than three seconds later, the barking ceased.

"Thatta boy!"

Removing his backpack, Caesar stuffed the binoculars inside, took out the knife, and set the pack against the wall. He waited for the scream, the sound of panicked feet thudding his way. Any second, Karina Summers would run across the yard, away from her pursuer, straight into his path.

As seconds ticked by into minutes, sweat formed on his brow. The storm intensified, and the first droplets of rain fell. *What the hell is taking so long?* Irritated, his stomach in knots, Caesar moved from his position behind the barn. Within seconds, he saw Vincenzo sprint across the yard toward him. Caesar froze in mid-stride, a heavy sense of dread slammed into his chest. *What's the fool doing? Where's the girl?*

It happened so fast, Caesar didn't have time to process it all. The back door burst open, and the woman ran from the house, carrying the limp body of the dog. She struggled to stay on her feet and was heading straight for Caesar, though she seemed unaware of his presence. Knife clenched in his fist, he steadied himself for her arrival. Caesar sensed Vincenzo to his right, closing in on her.

He took a deep breath and scowled. The wet night air was heavy with the scent of natural gas. The second his brain registered the odor, the house exploded. The blast knocked Caesar backward, his head slammed into the damp ground. The impact knocked the air from his lungs and left him slightly dazed as everything went black. When images appeared again, Caesar saw the faces of the members of El Rhukn leering and laughing while they beat the shit out of him.

"Caesar? Why didn't you listen to me? I told you. Leave. Now."

He fought and clawed his way back up through the murky dark inside his mind. *No. Not until it's finished.* Caesar managed to sit up, scanning the area around him for the knife. It was about ten feet to his left, so he crawled over to it. Once back in his hand, Caesar heard the screams from the girl, and before he could force his body to comply with his instructions to stand, four quick gunshots rang out.

Vincenzo's body jerked as the bullets ripped through his flesh. Guilt slammed into Caesar's chest as the fleeting discussions about wearing vests whizzed by. Fury replaced his sadness when the last bullet entered Vincenzo's forehead. Nothing they could have donned would have saved him from having half his face blown off. Caesar knew his friend, his last remaining cousin, was dead before his body hit the ground. In horror, Caesar watched her slam her foot into Vincenzo's poor, dead crotch. Over and over, while screaming vile, disgusting words.

Unbridled, raw anger pushed all other thoughts out of Caesar's head. He stood and strode toward the girl, who finally stopped stomping on Vincenzo. She was crying, crawling toward her dead mutt. Caesar heard the faint wail of sirens in the distance, and knew he had to hurry. He pulled his gun from his holster, holding it like a club. In seconds, he was right behind her. Heard every word she muttered to the corpse of her dog, promising through her tears help was on the way. After announcing his presence, Caesar summoned every ounce of strength he could muster, and slammed the butt of the gun against the back of her skull. She collapsed and crawled away, but not far enough to save her from the impact of his boot. Blood shot from her nose and mouth, and the bitch was out cold.

"It's too late, Caesar. Can't you hear the sirens? The cops will arrive any moment."

Panic clenched in his chest. There was no way he had time to get the car, come back, scoop up the bodies. Caesar spun in a circle, his eyes taking in the entire spread. The red and orange flames from the fire illuminated the area. The house was gone, along with the garage, and he could see through the flames a car burned inside. No good. Then, he remembered the old truck he'd passed on his way to the barn. It was his last hope for escape.

His body seemed to forget his age as Caesar

sprinted across the pasture. The driver's door was unlocked, and he jerked it open. He fumbled around for the keys and came up empty-handed. The squall of the sirens grew, along with his fear. Yanking the small flashlight from his back pocket, Caesar maneuvered his torso until he was on his back. Though it had been fifty-five plus years since he hot-wired a vehicle, his muscle memory kicked in. Within seconds, the truck rumbled to life.

Caesar climbed behind the wheel and took off. The light from the raging inferno was enough he didn't need to turn the headlights on. The little bitch hadn't moved. He slammed on the brakes and stopped, inches from Vincenzo's body. It took all his strength to haul Vincenzo from the ground and into the bed of the truck. By the time Caesar latched on to the legs of the girl, he feared he didn't have any gas left in his limbs. He was panting and sweating like a fat woman during sex. The first time Caesar tried to lift her limp body into the passenger's seat of the truck, he lost his grip. She moaned softly as her head landed on a chunk of smoldering wood from the house.

"Focus, darling. Warrior mind and body. Remember what Master Yamashita taught you.

Warrior mind and body. Hurry, husband. The wait for you has been too long. I'm afraid much longer alone, and my soul will fade away. You are what tethers me here, but time is running short."

Romella's voice, her worry and fear, ignited Caesar's muscles. Terror at losing her forever almost brought him to tears. Focusing all his angst to his limbs, Caesar looped his arms around the girl and pulled her up, stuffing her body inside the truck. Ignoring the searing pain in his back and shoulders, he finished securing her in the seat. He yanked the tape from his pocket, ripped of a large piece, and smashed it across her lips. Grabbing her arms, he wrapped the tape around them twice. Slamming the door, Caesar ran to the other side, hopped in, and gunned the engine.

In the distance, he saw the blue lights flashing. Caesar didn't have time to pause, or turn around to retrieve his backpack. He hit the blacktop and tromped on the gas, pushing the old rattletrap to the limit. In seconds, he passed the road where Vincenzo's car was parked. Speeding through the curvy, two-lane road in the dark was dangerous, but not nearly close to the danger of leaving evidence behind. Caesar brushed the worry aside, glanced in the rear view mirror, and seeing nothing but darkness, turned on the headlights.

By the time the cops picked through the debris and pieced together what happened at the Tuck residence, and who was involved, Caesar would be long gone. He did a mental rundown of the contents of his pack, satisfied nothing inside of it would link back to his identity. Vincenzo's car was another matter. Considering he was dead, and nothing would be left of him after the trip to Slumber Land, the cops would find themselves at a dead end.

As the adrenaline rush wore off, Caesar had to grip the steering wheel harder to maintain control as he pulled onto the freeway and headed to the outskirts of Hot Springs. He slowed down to the speed limit, praying the taillights were in working order so he didn't attract attention from the law. Every few minutes, he glanced over at the girl to make sure she hadn't woke up. She was still out cold. Her hair was matted on her face with blood and dirt, body slumped in the seat, head against the window at an odd angle. Laughter hung in the back of Caesar's throat as he pulled around to the back of the building. Carmella was going to have a field day with her, once she found out the little bitch killed Vincenzo.

34

PREY BECOMES PREDATOR

Lucas paced back and forth inside Caesar's bedroom. He'd been hiding inside the lair of the Devil for two days, jumping at every sound, waiting for the old geezer and his companion to return.

They never did.

After the first night, huddled inside the closet, back crammed against the wall, Lucas had eaten all of the rations from his pack. He tried to stay awake, but his body betrayed him and, sometime after three a.m., he'd crashed. When he awoke inside the dark space, panic raced through his chest, his mind playing tricks on him. For a second, Lucas thought he was locked inside a coffin and he bolted. When he burst through the doors and recognized the location, he nearly pissed his pants.

He'd spent the remainder of the day roaming around the house, barefooted, gun in hand, checking every nook and cranny. At first, Lucas was hopeful the old fart returned while he was asleep, had a heart attack or stroke, his stiff body waiting to be found. After a thorough search of the massive place, Lucas went back to the closet, retrieved his bag, and prepared to leave. He couldn't stand the thought of staying, pressing his luck any further. Fate may have intervened and allowed him easy access to the house, but it turned on him when Caesar and Carmine didn't return. Maybe the bastard took a vacation with his goon. Or they had a car accident and were in the hospital. Got lucky with some broads in some high-priced hotel room, took too much Viagra, and their hearts exploded, leaving them with permanent stiffies. Lucas didn't know, and honestly didn't care.

However, the second his fingers wrapped around the door knob, something inside his mind told him no. To stay. If he left, Lucas would spend the rest of his life on the run. Always looking over his shoulder, see their faces in crowds. He couldn't, *wouldn't,* live that way. He'd retraced his steps and went back to the master bedroom, set the bag down, and waited. Went downstairs twice to the kitchen and fixed something to eat. Rummaged and rifled through every unlocked cabinet and desk drawer, not really sure what he was searching for, but enjoying the satisfaction of snooping. When Lucas found the old man's laptop, he couldn't stop himself. Lucas threw it on the hardwood floor with all his might, laughing uncontrollably as it shattered. It took ten minutes to pick up all the pieces and toss them into the fireplace. While the plastic and metal sputtered and popped, a sense of relief hit him. Though he'd never been contacted via email, there was a possibility that somewhere on the hard drive, his name might be mentioned. Best to dispose of any evidence tying his name to Caesar's.

He'd lost count of the times he went to the window and peeked out. All for nothing. The day crept by, and by the time ten p.m. arrived the night before, Lucas was mentally wiped out. Too much thinking. Too much worrying. He stunk, so he left the bathroom door open and filled the enormous tub up with water, and slid inside, giddy from yet another intrusion into the private world of his enemy.

It was almost eleven p.m., and his nerves were shot to hell. His nails were chewed down to their nubs, his stomach in knots. Lucas couldn't make it another twenty-four hours. If his enemy didn't arrive by midnight, like it or not, he would leave. Nick Shonnert would be on his own to deal with the nightmare. Lucas might be forced to spend the remainder of his days in a state of paranoia, but at least there would be distance between him and Caesar.

The wad of cash in his pack was enough to take him across the country. Fuel for his hog was cheap, and once Lucas made it to Alaska he'd have enough left over to buy a truck of some sort. He'd have a head start and could go anywhere he wanted. Mexico was his original choice, but that would be an obvious place to look, since most criminals ran to the border. No, if Lucas was forced to leave without completing the mission, he'd head to Alaska. He'd watched hours and hours of TV shows about the vast state, and there were plenty of places for him to go, live off the grid. Find a nice, native girl to teach him how to survive and keep him warm at night. It would be hard to get used to the change in weather, but it would certainly be better than being dead.

A bright light caught his attention, and Lucas jumped. He moved away from the window, slamming his back against the wall. His heart pounded in his chest as he eased his way toward the glass. With shaking fingers, Lucas pushed the curtain aside and watched a vehicle trudge up the drive. As it entered the garage, he noticed it was an old truck. It looked like the one he made deliveries with. His stomach flip-flopped and he nearly threw up. Lucas couldn't see inside the cab, but it had to be either Caesar or Carmine.

Then, it hit him. If they were driving the truck, it meant it was time for a delivery. No one had called him. The chill of fear made him shiver. What if they knew he was in the house?

Crouching low, Lucas scrambled across the floor, grabbed his pack, yanked out the gun, and dove into the closet, which was bigger than his kitchen. Pushing his way through the suits and shoes, Lucas wedged his body in the corner and waited for whomever drove up to come inside.

Though terrified, Lucas couldn't help but smile. He checked the gun, made sure the safety was off. A final showdown was about to take place, and no matter which way it went, Lucas knew it would be the end of his body-parts delivering days.

Forever.

35

VACATION - OVER

LiAnn sipped her drink and watched the twinkling lights of Branson from her perch on the patio. Her parents were settled into their room, and Cecil in his, all sawing logs after a long day. Karina had picked out a beautiful location for them. Rather than staying at a hotel, she'd found condos, and reserved three, right next to each other. They were fully stocked with everything necessary to enjoy a carefree vacation, plus each sported fabulous views of the city.

Once they arrived, they drove around and checked out the local tourist haunts, went by a tackle shop to buy bait, followed by a trip to the grocery store for supplies. It was late in the afternoon by the time they arrived at the condos. Insisting her mom relax, LiAnn had cooked dinner for all of them, and before nine o'clock rolled around, Mom, Pop and Cecil were out.

She glanced down at the phone. A brief conversation with Karina when they arrived was the only action it had seen. Not a peep from Crigger in over thirty hours and Karina hadn't called back. Crigger's lack of contact didn't really shock her, for he had been acting very strange the last few days. Though he mentioned he was on vacation, Crigger had yet to tell her where he was. Their relationship, or lack thereof, hadn't been a topic of conversation either. They simply talked about mundane things.

Conversations were always surface level, and LiAnn had yet to mention what was going on at The Magnolia. She almost told Crigger the day before about the trip to Branson but decided against it. They were in contact with each other, even though certain topics were left alone. They were *talking,* which was a big step. She kept with her original idea to let Crigger be the one who broached feelings.

Though tired, LiAnn couldn't sleep. Her mind figured her daughter was enjoying the free run of the place, probably tangled up in the sheets with Bo, or simply exhausted from working. Her heart had a difference of opinion. Worry pressed against her chest for Karina's safety. LiAnn was second guessing the decision to leave.

Oh, stop! She's fine. In lust and frolicking around. Give her a call. It will ease the worry and annoy the heck out of her.

Before she changed her mind, LiAnn punched redial. It went straight to voicemail, and her chest tightened. The worry bug was back, making its way up her spine. She tried again and got the same results. Duel emotions battled for control. The practical side said Karina's phone had died, which was a plausible reason it went to voicemail. Maybe Karina forgot to plug it in while working and playing with Bo. Or Karina was trying to call her at the exact same moment.

The emotional, motherly instincts called bullshit. *Something is wrong.*

LiAnn tried one more time. Her worry turned to fear when her daughter's voicemail greeting played again. Rising from the chair, she went back inside to turn on the TV. Maybe another storm hit and knocked out the power. Just as LiAnn picked up the remote, her phone rang. *Oh, thank God! You're such a worry wart!*

But it wasn't Karina. It was Crigger.

Damn!

Annoyed, LiAnn answered. "Hey, Andrew. May I call you back? I'm trying..."

Crigger cut her off. "LiAnn, where are you?"

Shivers ran up her spine at the tone in Crigger's voice. He was out of breath, and she heard the unmistakable sounds of radio chatter and sirens in the background. *Why is he calling me when on scene? Makes no sense! He's on vacation!* "I'm in Branson with my parents. I really need to call you back, Andrew. I'm trying to get in touch with Karina."

"Oh, thank God. LiAnn? Please, listen to me. Text me your location, and sit tight until the state boys arrive. Do not answer your door, or take any phone calls from anyone. Period. You and your family are in danger."

"Andrew, what are you talking about? What is going on, and where *are* you?"

"I don't know how to say this any other way but to spit it out. I'm...at your parent's farm."

LiAnn's legs wobbled and she collapsed onto

the bed. A wave of dizziness made the room spin. "Come again?"

"No time to explain the particulars. The farm, oh, God, the house...it's gone, LiAnn."

Tears raced down LiAnn's face, her heart in her throat. The blood in her veins felt like ice. Her next question she didn't want to ask, but had no choice. "My daughter? Is she..."

"The crews just finished searching. She wasn't in the house. From the looks of things, she made it out with Ranger before the explosion. A cell phone and gun were found in the yard. Gun's been fired, four shots to be exact. A guy named Bo Barton was here, and he said your dad's truck is missing. Cops have swarmed the place. The lead wants to talk to you."

Explosion. Oh, Jesus. Karina! My baby.

Fury burned through her senses. She knew who was behind this, and why. It was time to tell Crigger, and protect her parents and Cecil.

Pushing her emotions into a dark corner, LiAnn stood and walked over to the table, yanking her gun from inside her purse. Voice tight and low, she growled, "Andrew, put me on speaker. I'm going to tell you what's going on, and then you go find my daughter."

36

INTO THE HEAT OF THE NIGHT

Carmella stood like a statue, her face frozen in fury. Franco tried to wrap his arm around her shoulder, but she brushed it off. Without a word, she walked over to the controls on the oven and fiddled with them.

Caesar watched the temperature gauge zoom past 1800 degrees. He was exhausted, his muscles screaming. They needed to hurry and get things rolling before his body gave out. His mind was already slipping. Romella's voice inside his throbbing head grew insistent. He needed to take control of the situation. "Franco, let's bring them in."

Carmella turned and shook her head. "No, you sit and rest, brother. Better yet, wash and tend to your wounds. I'll finish cleaning what you miss when we're done. We'll go get them."

Caesar reached up and winced as he touched the goose egg on the back of his head. When he pulled his hand back, it was covered in blood. Rather than argue, he turned and walked to the small bathroom. He could hear their footsteps as Carmella and Franco exited the cremation room.

Once inside the bathroom, Caesar shut the door and flicked on the light. His skin was a sickly gray pallor, and dark, cranberry-colored blood covered the base of his neck and shirt. A few cuts from the debris were on his cheeks, forehead and nose. His arm was even worse. There was a large gash above his right elbow, deep enough he could see the bone. Carmella would have to stitch it up before he left, or it would never stop bleeding.

It took him over ten minutes to wash up. The water was cold and refreshing, but it didn't help his mindset. Romella's words were non-stop, begging him to listen.

"Caesar, please. You're hurt and need to leave. Please, get me to Tahiti. Now. Things are growing fuzzy, and I can barely see you."

Caesar tossed another handful of water onto his face. Romella was right, and he knew it. The entire evening had been one giant cluster-fuck. All his careful plans shot to hell. He should have let Carmine take out the girl. Never should have involved Vincenzo. Caesar let his pride get in the way, the urge to prove his stamina and manhood, by partaking in one more hit. Leave the life with one more notch on his belt. Stupid, stupid mistake.

The sound of Carmella's voice brought Caesar out of his disturbing thoughts. She was yelling at Franco, ordering him around like she usually did. Just as he assumed, Caesar heard her tell Franco to put Vincenzo in first since he was larger and would require more time to incinerate. Carmella needed to calm down before she made a mistake. Her emotions were running high, and Caesar knew it. Saw the anger in her face when he retold the story of how Vincenzo died. Caesar was the only person who could bring Carmella down when she was wound tight, so he left the bathroom.

Determined to help, Caesar made his way across the floor. Carmella and Franco had both bodies on separate gurneys, side by side. They were busy removing Vincenzo's clothes, Carmella cussing a blue streak. She kept glancing over at the still body of the girl, muttering what she was going to do to her once it was her turn. Screaming about how she was going to enjoy killing the rest of her family.

Caesar followed his sister's gaze over to the girl. Her body twitched, and he realized she was awake. Carmella noticed, too.

"Franco, you finish with Vincenzo. I'm going to play. Little Vivian is awake."

Caesar moved across the floor and helped Franco load Vincenzo's body into the oven. The heat was intense and made Caesar feel woozy, but he pushed on, despite the sickening feeling in his stomach. For a second, his vision blurred, so he closed his eyes and waited for it to pass.

Carmella hissed, "You little bitch. Thought you were so smart, didn't you? You and your mom. Ha, joke's on you! They'll all be dead in less than forty-eight hours. It will be such a tragic end to the Tuck clan. Family killed in a car accident, and the daughter missing after the house blew up. Who knows? Maybe you'll be a suspect. It won't matter to you, because, in less than two hours, all that will be left of you will barely fill a lunch sack. Now, keep those pretty eyes open while I cut you up. I want to see your pain."

Carmella pushed the mound of matted hair from the girl's face. When Carmella realized her victim was out cold again, she slapped her. Caesar stared at the spectacle, determined to enjoy watching his sister carve up the bitch. He moved away from his spot by the gurney so he could get a better view.

When he did, time seemed to stand still. Caesar heard nothing but the beat of his heart. Under the bright lights of the fluorescent bulbs, he gasped as crushing grief and utter confusion consumed him. Romella stared at him from the table, her beautiful blue eyes wide with fright. Her slender body trembled as she tried to wriggle away from the scalpel. The joy of seeing his beloved wife in the flesh again was overshadowed by worry for her safety. Caesar blinked, unsure if he was dreaming or not. The minute he heard Romella's voice, clear as a bell, he knew he wasn't.

"Help me, Caesar! She's going to kill me! Don't let her cut me again. Oh, God, the pain! Stop her, please! We can't be together if she burns me alive!"

His body on autopilot, unsure of anything other than saving his wife, Caesar lunged. With his head down, he used it as a battering ram, right into the torso of the woman trying to kill his bride. From the right, he heard the voice of a man yell, along with the *oomph* as air left the lungs of the woman with the weapon when she crashed to the floor. Romella's face was contorted in pain, tears streaming from her eyes. With a gentle caress, Caesar touched her forehead and whispered, "It's okay, Romella. I'll take care of them. Rest now."

Rage fueled his muscles. Caesar pulled the knife from his back pocket and spun around, the blade slicing with ease through the soft neck of the man. The woman screamed as the man crumpled to the floor, blood pouring from his wound.

"Caesar! What are you doing? Stop! She's not Romella! I told you!"

He spun and faced the woman as Romella screamed from the table. *"She's lying, my love! Don't listen to her! Save me! She's just some stranger, trying to trick you!"*

The woman scrambled toward the scalpel, but Caesar was faster. He grabbed a handful of hair, yanked her head back, and slit her from ear to ear, nearly decapitating her.

Breathing heavily, Caesar let go and moved back toward the man, his gaze never leaving Romella's still body. "See, my love? It's okay. Don't cry. They can't hurt you anymore. Let me dispose of them and then I'll take you home. We've got to pack for our trip."

While humming softly, Caesar picked up the corpses of the strangers who tried to kill his wife. One by one, he tossed them into the oven, smiling as the flames engulfed them. Once finished, he scooped up his unconscious wife and carried her outside. "That's it, my love. Rest while I take you home. You can't imagine how excited I am to sleep by your side tonight. I've missed you."

Caesar ignored the confusion in his mind. Unsure where he was, or even how to get home, he couldn't let Romella know about his fears. There was an old truck close to the door. He reached it, but no keys were inside. Glancing around, he saw another parked about fifty yards away. Back screaming, arms aching, Caesar walked with gentle steps across the blacktop until he reached the truck. He eased Romella onto the ground, mindful of her back as he leaned her against the tire. She moaned but didn't open her eyes. "Hang on, my love. Just another minute."

The driver's door was unlocked, so he opened it. No key. Something in the back of Caesar's mind urged him to look under the floor mat. Sure enough, a small, silver key rested underneath it. It slid in the ignition switch with ease, and after two tries, the engine started.

"Okay, baby. We're going home."

37

FIGHTING BACK

Karina tried to open her eyes, but the lids were impossibly heavy. The throbbing in her head was intense. Her mind was flooded with strange sounds, visions. She heard a female's voice, followed by a man's. No, *men*. The tones were distinctly separate, but she couldn't quite make out their words. The sensation of moving was next. She was on something cold, hard, but her arms tingled from the rush of warm air.

Open your eyes! Figure out where you are!

For a split second, Karina could see, but it

made no sense. Carmella? In a flash, as searing pain from her cheek stunned her, the woman disappeared, and Karina succumbed to the inviting darkness.

Moving. She was moving. Someone was carrying her. She could feel her body in his arms. Softness. A pillow? Warm water on her head as gentle fingers cleansed her face. *Hospital! Oh, thank God, I'm at the hospital. Got to get up. Call Mom. Warn her. Oh, Jesus. Tell her it's all gone. Destroyed. Gram and Grampa will be devastated! And Ranger, my poor Ranger.*

"Shhh, don't cry, my love. You're safe now. Relax and let me take care of you. You've got to heal before we head to Tahiti. Don't want people thinking I did this to my bride. Oh, Romella, my beautiful Romella. It's okay. Those monsters can't hurt you anymore. Did them up right, I tell you. They are burnt to a crisp right now, though I still don't understand how we wound up in a funeral home, or why they wanted to kill you. No matter," the voice cooed, resuming the gentle strokes on Karina's cheek, "we're here together, right now. Forever, my darling bride."

Fear pulsed through Karina, allowing her thoughts to clear. *Not in the hospital. Where am I? Who the hell is talking to me? Why is he calling me Romella? No, don't panic. Breathe. Keep your eyes closed and listen. Reach out with your senses. Get a feel of the surroundings. You're in a bed somewhere. Oh, Jesus, my hands. Can't move them. I'm tied up? Okay, think. The gas at the farm. The explosion. The figure by the barn. But, I killed him! There's no way he's still alive. Another partner? Yes, I remember what he said before I passed out. Wait, did he just say funeral home? Could it be...?*

Full clarity washed over Karina, and though she tried to stay calm, her breathing became labored. She knew exactly who was sitting on the edge of the bed, wiping her brow, and the knowledge petrified her. Karina kept her eyes closed as she decided to test the theory and moaned, then whispered, "Caesar?"

"Oh, my love, are you awake now? Don't try to move, you have quite a few injuries."

I'm right! Fuck, I'm in the bedroom of a mobster, but one who seems off in the head, thinking I'm...Jesus H. Christ! Carmella said I looked like someone she knew who had died. Romella must have been Caesar's wife! No doubts now. I'm in deep shit. Think of something to ask for that will make him leave the room. Got to free my hands.

Karina let her eyes flutter open and croaked, "Water?"

"Of course, my love. Have some right here. Let me help you sit up."

Without her glasses or contacts, the room was blurry, but the man in front of her was close enough Karina could make out his features. He was elderly, his hair a mixture of silver and black. Numerous cuts were on his face, and dried blood was all over his shirt.

Was it hers or his?

Karina struggled to pull up the memories from earlier. She had killed one man, but someone else knocked her out. Had it been him? Was the old man capable of such violence? She dug deeper and remembered some of the patients from the nursing homes. People with dementia or other mind-altering issues sometimes turned violent during an episode when their minds went on the fritz. Karina focused on the man's dark brown eyes, noticing they were full of worry and love, along with a strange, vacant look. She recognized it. The man was in the middle of a full-blown attack.

The pain in Karina's head made her stomach lurch as he helped her sit up. He let go and reached past her. In seconds, a glass was at her lips. As she took a drink, Karina could feel how swollen her lips were. Images of a foot coming at her roared back. She winced while trying to twitch her nose. Her throat burned as the cold water trickled down it. "Thank you, Caesar."

Caesar smiled and patted her shoulder. "Anything for you, my love." He stood and walked across the room.

Karina squinted while trying to watch him. The only light was from the lamp next to the bed, which didn't help. A rush of relief swept over her when she was able to move her feet. Only her hands were tied.

The man might be in the midst of a mind-break, but he didn't seem to trust her completely since her wrists were still bound. Karina needed to figure out a way to rectify that problem. *Bathroom. Tell him you need to pee.*

"I'm sorry about the decorations, my love. I couldn't stand looking at things that reminded me you were gone. I still have them. They are just in storage. Don't worry. We'll simply buy new ones once we settle in Tahiti. Oh, wait until you see the bungalow I bought. It's beautiful. I don't have any clean clothes for you, so this will have to do until I can go shopping."

Karina could tell he was rummaging around in a dresser drawer of some sort across the room. Soon, he was back, holding up a man's undershirt and a large pair of khaki shorts. It dawned on her she was wearing her robe, with nothing on underneath. She could feel the cool air on her thighs and chest.

Keep him talking. "Tahiti. That sounds lovely. Can't wait."

"Me either, my love. And here you were worried we wouldn't make it in time." Caesar cooed, setting the clothes next to her. "Now, let's get you into the bathtub and cleaned up first. That robe is filthy. By the way, why are you wearing it? What happened to the dress I bought you?"

His voice shifted and Karina sensed the accusatory tone. She had no idea what he was talking about, and no time to think. "Things are still sort of hazy, Caesar. I don't remember."

Caesar stepped away from her, his face full of confusion. "Why were you so...different at the funeral, Romella? You said some awful, wretched things to me. They upset me deeply."

Oh, shit. What does that mean? "I'm...sorry,

Caesar. Transitioning back into this realm is rather difficult. If I hurt you, I didn't mean to. Forgive me?" A hint of relief spread across his face, but he didn't move. Her brain spun, trying to think of what to say that would sway him to untie her. She saw the sorrow behind his eyes, the look of grief and distrust. Karina had to hurry. "Caesar, I love you. I've waited so long to be with you again. To feel your arms around me, hold you tight. Please, come here and let me hold you. I need to be near you. It gives me strength."

A lone tear trickled down his face. He hesitated for a split second before he shuffled forward and sat down next to her. Karina held up her bound arms, forcing a look of sadness to show on her face. Controlling her fear as he pulled a long switchblade from his pocket, she prayed he planned on using it to free her. Sure enough, with one quick slice, her arms were unbound. Before Karina could even blink, the knife was directly above her heart.

"Tell me how much you love me. How you will never leave me again. Make me believe you."

Steady. Inflict maximum emotional impact, then strike. "Oh, Caesar. You have no idea how awful it's been. I could see you, but not touch you. I was alone in the dark for so long. So very, very long. My love for you is what allowed me to return. Kept me going when I thought I couldn't withstand another minute away from you. I loved you before, but the time away from you made it deeper, stronger. You are my world, Caesar Calvanio."

Karina saw a flicker of pain in his eyes. When he leaned forward to kiss her, she head-butted him, while simultaneously knocking the arm with the knife away. Karina heard the metal tinkle across the floor, and his roar of anger. She bolted from the bed and scrambled to retrieve the knife.

"You lying bitch! You're here to torment more, aren't you? Dead, alive, whatever you are, *leave me alone!*" Caesar screamed. He lunged across the bed, and his hand caught her right ankle.

Karina kicked him in the face with her other foot, sending him flying off the bed. Her knees slammed hard when she hit the floor, but she ignored the pain. Spotting the knife, Karina grabbed it and struggled to her feet.

She hated the fact things were blurry, and she would have to wait until he was closer than she wanted to stab him, but it couldn't be helped. Her best plan of action was to whip him into an emotional frenzy, causing him to attack her like a wild man. "I'm not your wife, you stupid old fool. I'm Karina Summers, the woman you tried to kill earlier. Remember? You and your friend blew my family's house apart. But I killed him, just like I will you. Bring it on, you old bag of bones. It's time to pay for what you did to my family, to me. To my dog. *Bring. It. On.*"

Caesar was faster than Karina gave him credit for. In a flash, he was in front of her, his arms swinging in circles, ready to pummel her to the ground. Karina's training took over, and she easily outmaneuvered him.

Jerking her body in the opposite direction, Karina spun and drove the knife deep into the spot between Caesar's shoulder blades. When he fell forward, on his knees, she noticed the gun tucked behind his back. Her own balance failed on the slick floor.

Karina wobbled to the left but remained on her feet. She saw his hand reach around for the gun. With her ability to look around for a weapon compromised, there was no choice left except to tackle him.

When their bodies collided, they both fell to the floor, her body pinning his. Caesar didn't let go of the gun, and Karina struggled to yank it from his hand. Her face was pressed against his back, right next to the knife. Caesar screamed and writhed underneath Karina, surprising her with his strength.

Karina held on tight to the gun, but the impact of his elbow with her temple knocked her off his back. She recovered quickly. Unfortunately, Caesar did too. Karina froze when she realized she was staring down the barrel.

"Die again, bitch!" Caesar shouted, his voice full of anger and terror.

In a brief blip of time, Karina saw her salvation arrive from the corner of her eye. Shards of glass from a large, crystal vase peppered her face and arms, along with blood splatter from Caesar's head. The kid standing above Caesar screamed, "No more death! No more!"

Stunned from the impact, Caesar lost his focus on the gun. Karina moved fast, grabbed it, then rolled left. Once far enough away, but still close enough to see, she stood, motioned for the shocked kid to move, and fired.

Karina emptied the clip into Caesar Calvanio's body, enjoying every jerk, each burst of blood. Tears raced down her face from the joy of being alive, the satisfaction of killing him, and the horrendous nightmare being over.

Once the smoke cleared, Karina trained the gun on the freaked out looking kid. She figured he had no clue she was out of ammo, and she was right. Both of his hands shot into the air. "Thanks. Now, take your gun out of your belt and slide it toward me. So, who the hell are you?"

"Oh, just a guy who wanted the Devil off his ass." Lucas said as he bent down and set the gun on the floor in front of him.

"Well, *just a guy*, got a cell phone?"

"Yeah, but it's dead."

Karina growled, "Death seems to be contagious in this house. If you don't want to catch it, I suggest you find me a phone. Like right now. No tricks, or you'll join your friend." Karina matched his steps, making sure to keep the distance between them steady so she didn't lose sight of him. He walked over to the edge of the bed and picked up the phone. "Put it on speaker, dial 9-1-1, and tell them to send help. Gunshots fired, then hang up."

Lucas did as told, and in seconds, the dispatcher answered. "9-1-1, what's your emergency?"

"Need an ambulance and police to this address. Gunshots fired, and got a dead man here. Hurry."

Karina motioned for the kid to hang up. "Good job. Now, have a seat in that chair, and if you move..."

"Trust me, I won't. I've seen you in action. Besides, the Devil is already dead."

"Smart boy. The Devil? Hmmm, how appropriate. Say, you had a gun. Why didn't you just shoot him?"

"I've...never shot anyone before, and I was afraid I might miss and hit you instead. I figured if I rang his bell, you'd finish him off. I was right."

Chuckling softly, Karina moved to pick up both his gun and the phone. She punched in a number, and waited. On the second ring, her heart skipped a beat when a strange, male voice answered with: "Hello? Who's this?"

Another round of fear slammed into Karina's chest, making her head spin. "Where the hell is my mother, you asshole? If you've harmed one hair on her head, I swear to God..."

The sound of her mother's voice in the background made tears of relief roll down Karina's cheeks. She heard her mother yell, "Who is it?"

Karina screamed out at the top of her lungs. "Mom! It's me. Are you okay?"

"Give me that phone!" Karina heard her mother yell. A bit of static followed, but then the voice Karina wanted to hear more than anything in the world said, "Baby, are you okay?"

Relief caused Karina to collapse on the edge of the bed. "Yes. Are you?" Her mother's wails of joy were so loud, Karina had to hold the phone away from her ear. "Hey, not so loud. I have a raging headache. Oh, and guess what?"

Through her tears, LiAnn choked out, "What, baby?"

"I shot first, and didn't ask any questions because I already knew the answers. Pretty sure I'm going to be famous. I just killed a mobster. Two, actually."

38

INTERNAL RADAR

LiAnn walked out onto the porch and sat down in the swing next to her father. She rubbed her eyes and stretched. "Well, Mom's out like a light. Karina finally crashed, too. She wouldn't quit doting on Ranger until he fell asleep next to her."

Junior smiled. "She does love that dog. Knowin' he made it sure did put some pep in her step. Our little gal brightened right up when Bo delivered him in one piece from the vet."

LiAnn's anger rose at the mention of Bo. She

was still pissed as hell at him for not protecting her daughter. She would never forgive him. Ever. When Bo drove up with Ranger a few days ago, LiAnn had to leave and go outside, afraid she would make good on her promise to kick his butt all the way to New Orleans. Her father's voice broke through her angry thoughts.

"Say, Crigger?"

"Yes, sir?"

Junior cleared his throat twice before continuing. "I...don't rightly know the words to thank you with. For everythin'. I take back all the nasty things I've thought about you over the years. We owe you a lot. You've given us a place to rest our heads and saved my granddaughter's dog. Kept the press away and allowed us to stay in your home, this quiet space, to regroup. Ruth and I are grateful."

Crigger produced a small smile, glancing over at LiAnn. "You're more than welcome, sir. I just wish..."

Junior interrupted as he stood. "Wishin' for the past to change ain't never helped anybody, 'cause it don't work. Now, I'm off to join my wife, after I thank the Lord, once again, in my prayers. We have our family, so really, what have we lost? Not a damn thing that matters." Junior bent down and kissed the top of his daughter's head. His gnarled finger brushed away the tears on her cheek. "Goodnight, sweetheart. Don't stay up too much longer. You look like you need some rest, too. After all, you've been awful busy takin' good care of everyone else. Night, Crigger. Keep them shoulders strong for my little girl."

"I certainly will, sir."

"Goodnight, Pop. Love you."

Junior paused at the door. "Love you too, sugar. Oh, and Crigger? It's high time you call me Junior. Sir is reserved for strangers and friends. Family calls me by my given name."

"Thank you, si...Junior."

The porch fell silent. Crigger stood and came over, sitting down next to LiAnn, draping his arm over her shoulder, pulling her close.

LiAnn felt safe inside Andrew's arms. Tears fell as she listened to the steady beat of his heart. Pent-up emotions from the last three days ran free in her overstimulated mind.

The first two days were a blur. The drive back from Branson, keeping a smile on her face as she lied to everyone, telling them they had to return to Arkansas because Karina had been in an accident, had been difficult. Seeing Karina in the hospital bed, her face swollen, discolored from her multitude of injuries, made LiAnn physically ill.

When the doctor told her Karina had a concussion, broken nose, and several spots of embedded shards of glass in her back, LiAnn went numb. So did her parents and Cecil after LiAnn pulled herself together, sat them down in the hospital waiting room, and told them the truth. When she got to the part about the house, her parents were stoic, their faces devoid of emotion, but Cecil fell apart. Poor Cecil. He was overcome with grief, thinking it was all his fault.

Fortunately, Crigger intervened and filled in some of the gaps of the story LiAnn was unaware of, trying to make all those present understand *none* of them were at fault. They were all victims of a vile, despicable group of people. Even after Crigger spoke, there were still numerous unanswered questions.

When they all trudged back into Karina's room, they sat in stunned awe as she retold the story to the two FBI agents and the lead investigators from the Grant County Sheriff's Department, who had snuck into Karina's room while they were gathered in the waiting area.

What LiAnn heard made her blood boil. The bastards had gotten away with their evil schemes for so long. Her daughter, and her entire family, had been targeted by the freaking mob. When Karina recounted how she woke up in the bedroom, bound and the ensuing fight, LiAnn's vision blurred. She nearly passed out from the abject horrors her child endured, and at the same time, was overcome with relief and pride Karina had survived.

At first, the agents had doubts on several aspects of the story, especially the morbid details of black market body parts, derived from some kid named Lucas Hill. Karina let out some steam and lit into the agents. Told them if they had done their jobs properly, they wouldn't be talking to her in a hospital bed, her family wouldn't be minus a place to live and all their possessions wouldn't be a pile of smoldering ashes. Karina ended her tirade by insisting whatever laws Lucas Hill had broken, he had saved her life, not them, and if they didn't take that into account when charging him, she wouldn't hesitate to go public with some very unflattering words about the shoddy investigative tactics of FBI.

LiAnn wanted to stay by her daughter's side the first night but didn't. Karina was a tough girl, and her parents needed her. After all, they had

565

no home, no clothes, nothing. LiAnn tried to rely on her training, to push aside her mental pain, focus on the proper next steps, but her mind was gridlocked. Too much stimulation, too many things in her lap to deal with.

Crigger noticed and convinced her to follow him to the cafeteria to get some coffee for everyone. On their way, he finally explained why he was in the state.

Not very many times in LiAnn's life had she been shocked into silence, but after Crigger told her he had retired, driven to Arkansas, purchased the farm next to her parents to be near her, there were no words.

They clung to each other in the cafeteria and Crigger told her the thought of spending the rest of his life without her was too much to bear. Crigger arrived at his new home a few hours before the explosion, his plan to surprise her shot to hell when he saw the fireball in the sky. He pulled up right behind the cops and Bo.

Crigger said he almost shot Bo, thinking he was the responsible party, until he noticed Bo was tending to Ranger while tears streamed down his face, muttering his apologies to the night sky for failing to save Karina.

Andrew's presence was a Godsend for LiAnn.

He took Cecil back to The Magnolia after Cecil finished giving his statement to the detectives and federal agents. Upon Crigger's return, he loaded up the rest of the family, insisting they stay with him. By nine o'clock the first night, they were all settled inside Andrew's big farmhouse, the press unaware of their location.

The second day was spent out shopping for clothes and necessities for everyone since they had zilch. LiAnn had finished only minutes before Karina called, threatening to punch someone if her mother didn't spring her from the hospital.

News cameras greeted LiAnn when she arrived at the hospital. Neither she nor Karina said a word to the news teams when they left moments later. Afraid they might follow, LiAnn had zigzagged through the streets of Hot Springs until she was confident she'd lost anyone on her tail.

LiAnn had to change her phone number since somehow, it had been leaked to the press. Before she did, LiAnn called Calvin and told him Karina was fine. Caught him just as he arrived at the airport, ready to board a flight bound for Little Rock. LiAnn could tell he was beside himself with worry after watching the news. Karina called Calvin after LiAnn picked her up. It took almost the entire drive back to Sheridan for Karina to convince Calvin she truly was okay, and he didn't need to make a trip to Arkansas.

The local news reporters were bad, but the network anchors were relentless. The more information uncovered, the worse it became. Crigger rented LiAnn a car under his own name, had it delivered to his house, allowing her to drive into town without being detected. Of course, once LiAnn picked up Karina at the hospital, her cover car was blown, but not one reporter had sniffed out their location so far.

She made the mistake of turning on the news on the second night. The story was headlining every channel. The reporters were practically tripping over their drooling tongues, eager to spit out the juicy details. LiAnn couldn't blame them, really. After all, how often did such a sick, twisted, morally reprehensible story emerge?

Once the family was back together in one place, a little bit of the load seemed to lift from each of their shoulders. Karina was thrilled and not too surprised Crigger had retired and moved. At the dinner table later, while discussing when they should go look at what was left of the farm and see if there was anything left to salvage,

Karina leaned over and whispered in LiAnn's ear, "See? It's the blonde hair and those boobs!"

At that moment, LiAnn knew her child would be just fine.

The two FBI agents working the case had stopped by before dinner earlier with updates. In stunned silence, all of them sat in the living room and listened as they recounted even more disturbing news. Franco and Carmella D'Nucci, along with their cousin/partner, former doctor Vincenzo Molinero, were dead. The cops caught a lucky break identifying them, because someone drove by and noticed the lights were on and the front door wide open at the funeral home less than a half-hour after Caesar left with Karina. The poor cop who responded to the call was shocked at what he found upon arrival. Blood was everywhere, and he had the presence of mind to turn off the oven. Although not much was left, there was enough to identify the charred remains.

Another strange twist, courtesy of hours of grilling Lucas Hill, was the deaths of two other men. Nick Shonnert and Carmine Del Vecchio were found dead inside Nick's home. The agent stated the coroner listed their deaths occurred early Thursday morning, and according to Lucas,

Carmine was Caesar Calvanio's right-hand man. Nick Shonnert had been another poor soul roped into service by the mobster, forced to use his position at Happy Days Retirement Living as hunting ground for new victims. Nick had been shot and Carmine had been pumped full of potassium chloride.

Special Agent Winslow said numerous arrests of doctors in on the scheme in the surrounding states were forthcoming, after they had investigated the dates and locations where Lucas made deliveries.

So far, the Feds had determined forty-three seniors died suddenly within twenty-four hours of Lucas' deliveries, and every single one had been cared for by Carmella D'Nucci's company, plus taken by Lombardo's Ambulance Service to Slumber Land Funeral Parlor. The agents assured the entire family they wouldn't stop until all players were brought to justice.

Questions were minimal as each of them tried to absorb the nightmare. Special Agent Winslow also mentioned the ownership of The Magnolia was up in the air, since all the parties who owned it were deceased. Happy Days Retirement Living's status was up in the air as well, because the remaining owner, Nick Shonnert's ex-wife, had a stroke when the news broke and was in a coma.

LiAnn's mother spoke for the first time then, inquiring in a soft voice about what would happen to the residents who lived at The Magnolia, as well as the other facilities. The answer was a shrug of Agent Winslow's shoulders.

The last piece of information was about Caesar Calvanio. Their investigation uncovered he had been living under the name of Jimmy Calhoun, ever since disappearing from New York years ago. Their research concluded that Jimmy Calhoun had been an elderly resident at Green Pastures at one time.

Jimmy Calhoun's driver's license, social security card, ownership papers of various companies, including The Magnolia, were discovered inside Caesar's house. A one-way ticket to Tahiti was found in Caesar's pocket, under the name of Jimmy Calhoun. However, after running his fingerprints, they confirmed the truth about his identity, which matched up with Karina's story.

When LiAnn heard the news, she had to excuse herself and go to the bathroom. She threw up so violently, she almost passed out. Her precious child was waiting outside the door after LiAnn freshened up. Karina had grabbed her and gave her a bear hug.

In her usual fashion of trying to make light of things, Karina whispered, "You were wrong, Mom. Your man radar is just fucking fine. Just fucking fine."

The memory made LiAnn chuckle, and Andrew said, "That's what I've been waiting for. Your sweet laughter. I knew you'd be okay once I heard it. Willing to share what made you laugh?"

LiAnn turned her head and gazed up at Andrew, her heart full of love, even in the midst of all the turmoil. "Oh, just the irony of internal radar."

Andrew leaned down and kissed her, and LiAnn knew her daughter was right: her man radar was on point.

39

ONE AND DONE

"**M**om, I want him there with me today, so please, be civil. For me, okay?" Karina watched her mother force a smile.

"Only because I love you."

"Thank you. Look, I know you still blame him, but you shouldn't. Things might have turned out worse than they did, if he'd been at the house with me. You think I would be able to live with myself if Bo had been injured, or killed? Trust me, I wouldn't. As I've said before, I've grown fond of him."

LiAnn held her hands up in mock surrender. "Okay, okay. The horse is dead. Stop beating it."

"Good. Now, let me finish getting ready. Bo will be here any minute to pick me up. We'll follow you."

Karina sensed her mother was about to protest, but didn't. Alone, Karina stared at her reflection in the mirror. The bruises were an ugly shade of yellow and green, in stark contrast to the white bandage across her swollen nose. There wasn't enough concealer in the world to make Karina look presentable, so she concentrated on her hair.

In less than an hour, she would be blinded by the lights of the news cameras at The Magnolia. Karina's rationale for agreeing to an interview was simple–one and done. Give the media ghouls some juicy tidbits and let them feast. Like throwing a bloody stump at a horde of zombies. Karina made sure all outlets knew this was the only time she would speak publicly about what happened, and her family wasn't to be bothered, harassed or questioned.

Ever.

After the news conference was over, a celebration lunch for her and her mother would follow. Cecil Pickard insisted on it. He, along with all the other residents, wanted to thank them both for not only uncovering the nightmare at The Magnolia, but for potentially saving numerous lives in the process.

Finally finished and dressed, Karina sat on the edge of the bed and ran her hands across the warm fur of Ranger's back. A lump of tears caught in her throat as Karina stared at the bare spot around Ranger's neck and the stitches.

A spark of fury replaced her sadness, followed by satisfaction. She made the two bastards pay the ultimate payment for the damage they caused. Their disgusting, worthless lives were over, and they would never be able to harm anyone again.

Sometimes, late at night while Ranger slept quietly next to her, Karina wished she could have witnessed the death of Carmella. Watching her get tossed into an oven would have been priceless. That image would be one she'd actually enjoy reliving in her dreams. Karina bent down and kissed the top of Ranger's head, glad he was still a part of her life.

A soft tap on the door made Karina jump. Ranger swung his head toward the sound but didn't bark or growl.

"Hey, babe, ya decent?"

"Come on in, Bo."

Karina blinked twice, startled by his attire. Bo was wearing a white dress shirt with a crimson red tie, black slacks and shoes buffed to perfection. A massive bouquet of red and white roses was in his left hand, and a small, ornately decorated gift box in the right. The man looked and smelled amazing. Even Ranger whined and thumped his tail.

"Thought ya might like some flowers, seein' as it's a big day for ya and all."

"Wow, look at you! The ladies at The Magnolia will have heart palpitations when you walk in. These are lovely. Thank you." Taking the flowers, Karina leaned in and gave Bo a gentle kiss. She couldn't wait for her lips to get back to normal so she could really enjoy the act of kissing. Eyeballing the gift box, Karina asked, "And this is?"

Bo blushed and handed Karina the box. "Just a little somethin' I thought ya might need."

She fumbled with the bow and opened the gift. Inside was a brand new cell phone. "Oh, no doubt! Been jonesing for one for days now. Funny, I was going to ask you to take me after lunch to get a new one."

"I hope it's okay, but I got ya an Arkansas

number. Figured you'd be stayin' a while. It's...on my plan, but that don't mean we're engaged or nothin'. The lady at the cell store said ya can transfer it to another plan anytime."

Staring into Bo's vibrant blue eyes, Karina's heart melted. She could see the emotions swimming behind them. The look of lust had been replaced with concern, compassion and, dared she think it?–love.

She remembered the day when Bo brought Ranger home. He almost broke down while apologizing for leaving her alone. Remorse and grief beamed across his face. He held her close and she could feel the tension in his muscles. Karina finally made him laugh when she said, "Hey, stop. Recall, I took out not one, but two, former mobsters. My injuries look ugly, but really, I'm no worse for the wear. So, did I pass the country girl test?"

Bo had laughed. "A plus."

She had pulled him close and whispered, "I'm thankful you weren't injured because I'm addicted to you, too."

Shaking the memory away, Karina took a step back from Bo and set her new phone on the table. "Thanks, Bo. Let's worry about all the particulars later. Come on. We'll be late for the press conference. I want to hurry up and get it over with, so I can spend some time with Cecil. He's been a basket case, according to Mom and Grampa, ever since all this mess happened."

"Sure thing, darlin'." Bo reached out and took Karina's hand.

Karina grabbed on to it like it was a lifeline.

"**B**oy, howdy! I ain't never seen so many bright lights and fake smiles in all my days! Honey, did ya feel like you was talkin' to a wax statue?"

Karina laughed at her new friend, Wylie Wilson. He sat across the round dining table from her, sandwiched between Cecil and Grampa. The remaining chairs were filled with Gram, Mom, Bo, Crigger and gram's friend Betty Dravis, and another new face, Seth Thomas.

"They certainly had the personalities of wax, that's for sure. So glad it's over. Hopefully, they'll leave us all alone. They got the gory details and plenty of images of my banged-up face, which is what they wanted."

"Ya gonna watch the news tonight? I know I am. Save all the news clippin's too. You two are heroes, and the first ones I've ever met in person." Wylie gushed.

Junior chimed in. "Ain't no two people in this world ever been prouder of their family than us. That's for sure. Ain't that right, Ruth?"

"Proud and relieved. My two precious girls are alive and that's all that matters. Period." Ruth added.

Wylie looked over at LiAnn and winked. "I always knew there was somethin' not right about that black-haired minx. And it weren't just the fact she was jealous about how beautiful you are. Felt it in my bones, ya know?"

Seth interjected. "That is the biggest load of...hogwash I've ever heard you say, Wylie! You drooled every time Carmella walked..."

Cecil interrupted Seth's outburst. "Ms. LiAnn, Ms. Karina? We all have somethin' we'd like to give you, as a thank ya for what ya done for all of us."

Karina noticed tears filled Cecil's eyes. Bo tapped her shoulder and she glanced around. All the residents had gathered behind the table, smiling. "There's no need to..." Karina said.

Cecil interjected. "Never ya mind that kind of

talk. I was the next in line, and y'all came to my aid. After me, it could have been any of the others here," he said, sweeping his arms around toward the group. "We all owe both of you our lives."

Betty added. "Cecil's right, ladies. Though it's not much, since all of us are on edge worrying about where we'll be living soon, us gals made one for each of you. Stayed up for almost two days straight! It was like old college days for us again. Hope you like the colors."

Wylie and Betty each produced a large box from under their chairs. Wylie handed his package to LiAnn, and Betty set hers in front of Karina.

Karina exchanged an embarrassed glance with her mom before tearing into the box. Inside was a handmade quilt. The background was white, and the squares red, each boasting a beautiful magnolia bud. In the very center square, the words *Thank you* were embroidered. Karina looked over at her mom's gift, which was an exact replica. Tears formed in her eyes at the thought of the countless hours spent by women who were total strangers, to create something so beautiful. "These are...absolutely breathtaking, ladies. Thank you so much."

"Oh, yes, thank you!" LiAnn choked back her own tears.

"We just wanted you both to have something from our hearts. A little thing to remind you every time you snuggle up underneath one, how much we admire and appreciate you both." Betty said.

Cecil stood up and addressed everyone. "The events of the last week have been hard on us all. Almost lost people I love, and at my age, I ain't got many of those left. No matter what any of ya say, it's my fault this here wonderful family don't have no home anymore and almost died. Now, I know all of us have been rubbin' our worry stones, wonderin' what will happen to this old place, now that the monsters who owned it are gone, so I wanted to let y'all know not to fret no more."

"Them's the most words I've ever heard ya say, Cecil, even though I don't understand what ya meant. Why shouldn't we fret no more? Tomorrow we might be livin' on the streets!" Wylie moaned.

Cecil took a deep breath and walked over to where Karina and LiAnn sat. He put a hand on each of their shoulders and announced, "Because I put in an offer to buy this old place and it's been approved." The room erupted in applause and murmurs as all the elderly residents piped up at once. Cecil yelled over the noise. "I ain't done with my news, so hang on."

Cecil squatted down in between Karina and LiAnn. Tears ran down his face and he implored "Ms. LiAnn, Ms. Karina, ain't none of us ever gonna feel safe here again unless the two of you run it. I know ya can. You've got the knowhow. And we trust y'all. Completely. All of ya can even stay here for free while Junior and Ruthie's place is bein' rebuilt. Please, please say yes. We need ya. And, when I go, I'll leave the place to ya both."

The room fell silent as tears streamed down the faces of everyone, including Karina and her entire family. Thirty pairs of cloudy eyes bored into her heart. After all that happened, how in the world could Karina say no? She certainly knew what *not* to do in regards to the day-to-day running of a senior living facility, so it wouldn't be too difficult to figure out the correct ways.

Karina looked at her mom. The second their eyes locked, she knew they were on the same wavelength. She glanced at Bo, who was grinning from ear to ear with pride. Crigger had the same beaming smile. "Gram? Grampa? What do you two think?"

Ruth cleared her throat as she wiped her tears away with a napkin. "I think that's the best job offer I've ever heard."

"I agree. Mr. Wilson, we accept!" LiAnn answered. The words were followed by an outburst from the entire group. Tears flowed, hugs ensued, handshakes all around.

Wylie Wilson surprised them all when he jumped up on the table, glass in hand, and yelled, "Well, today certainly is my day, 'cause now I've got *two* gun-totin' muses to drool over every day! Amen!"

A few minutes later, while everyone else was talking about the crazy twist of events, LiAnn leaned over and whispered, "You're sure about this, right?"

Karina nodded in response. It took her a few seconds to swallow the lump of tears in her throat. The irony of the entire situation was almost comical. She'd left Cali for a variety of reasons, including a chance to steer clear of anything to do with the senior housing industry. Now, she would be running one. The rulers of the cosmos sometimes had a sadistic sense of humor.

"Yes, Mom. I'm sure. We wanted a new life, and boy, did we ever get one. So," Karina lowered her voice and winked, "which one of us is the boss?"

LiAnn laughed. "As stubborn as we both are, it would be best to be equals."

Karina didn't respond. She threw her arms around LiAnn's neck and hugged tight. Their embrace said more than words ever could.

About the authors

Ashley Fontainne

Award-winning and International bestselling author Ashley Fontainne is an avid reader of mostly the classics. Ashley became a fan of the written word in her youth, starting with the Nancy Drew mystery series. Stories that immerse the reader deep into the human psyche and the monsters that lurk within us are her favorite reads.

Her short thriller entitled *Number Seventy-Five*, touches upon the sometimes dangerous world of online dating. *Number Seventy-Five* took home the BRONZE medal in fiction/suspense at the 2013 Readers' Favorite International Book Awards contest and is currently in production for a feature film (www.number75thmovie.com).

Ashley's paranormal thriller entitled *The Lie*, won the GOLD medal in the 2013 Illumination Book Awards for fiction/suspense and is also in production for a feature film entitled *Foreseen* (www.foreseenmovie.com).

The paranormal/southern gothic horror/suspense novel, *Growl*, released in January of 2015. The suspenseful mystery *Empty Shell*, released in September of 2014. To learn more about Ashley, visit her website at www.ashleyfontainne.com

Lillian Hansen

Lillian Hansen is the proud mother of Ashley Fontainne. A grateful daughter of parents who raised her to love and respect the principles upon which America was founded. Lillian is the granddaughter of a brave young woman who immigrated to the United States from Denmark at the age of 18 without speaking any English, who built a career, a family, and became a proud U.S. citizen.

Lillian values the diverse, life-enriching experiences squirreled away in her memory banks and is fond of all four-legged critters, especially cats. Lillian resides in Oregon, and *Blood Ties* is her first novel.

Coming soon

Coming soon

Blood Loss, Book Two of The Magnolia Series

Author's Note

A special thank you to Jeff LaFerney and Elaine Raco Chase for countless hours of hard work and effort in helping me create this book!

Other Books by Author

Novels by Ashley Fontainne
Growl
Empty Shell
The Lie – soon to be the feature film FORESEEN
www.foreseenmovie.com
Number Seventy-Five – soon to be a feature film
www.number75themovie.com
Eviscerating the Snake Trilogy:
Accountable to None
Zero Balance
Adjusting Journal Entries
Poetry and Short Story Collection
Ramblings of a Mad Southern Woman
Coming soon
The Magnolia Series – co-authored with
Lillian Hansen
Blood Loss

www.ingramcontent.com/pod-product-compliance
Lightning Source LLC
Chambersburg PA
CBHW020454020726
47493CB00001B/26